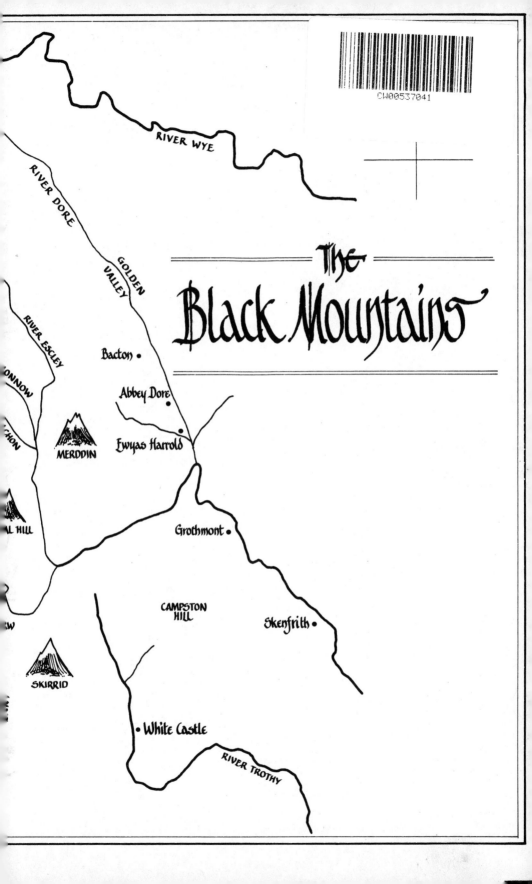

The
Black Mountains

RIVER WYE

RIVER DORE

RIVER ESCLEY

GOLDEN VALLEY

Bacton •

Abbey Dore •

MERDDIN

Ewyas Harrold •

Grothmont •

CAMPSTON HILL

Skenfrith •

SKIRRID

• White Castle

RIVER TROTHY

PEOPLE OF THE BLACK MOUNTAINS

I   *The Beginning . . .*

People of the Black Mountains

I *The Beginning . . .*

RAYMOND WILLIAMS

Chatto & Windus
LONDON

Published in 1989 by
Chatto & Windus Ltd
30 Bedford Square
London WC1B 3SG

A CIP catalogue record for this book
is available from
the British Library.

ISBN 0 7011 2845 3

Jacket illustration: *A View in North Wales* by
Walter Williams, reproduced by permission of Sotheby's

Photoset by Rowland Phototypesetting Ltd
Bury St Edmunds, Suffolk

Printed in Great Britain by
Mackays of Chatham PLC, Chatham, Kent

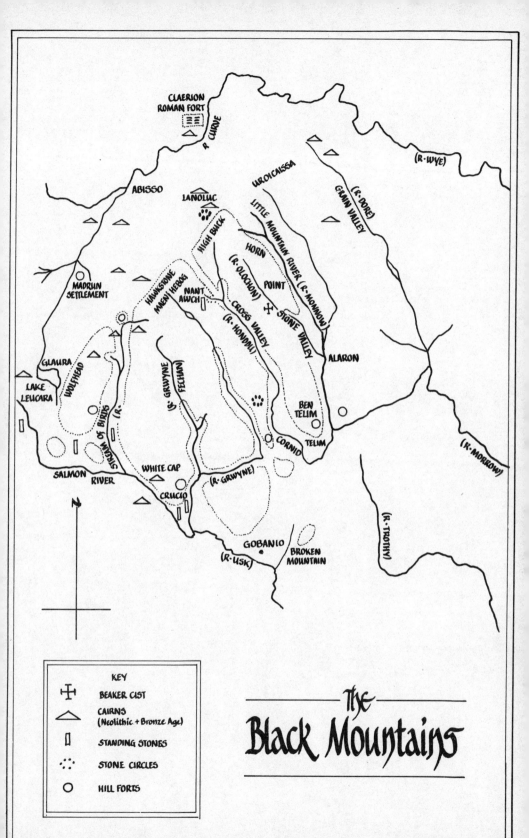

CLAERION
ROMAN FORT

R. CLURÜE

(R. WYE)

ABISSO

LANOLUC

URDICASSA

(R. DORE)

GRÄIN VALLEY

HIGH BUCK

LITTLE MOUNTAIN RIVER (R. MONNOW)

HORN

MADRUN
SETTLEMENT

HAWKSTONE
MAEN HEBOG

NANT
AWCH

(R. OLOCHON)

POINT

STONE VALLEY

GLAURA

WOLFHEAD

(R. GRWYNE)

(R. FECHAN)

CROSS VALLEY

(R. HONDDU)

ALARON

LAKE
LEUCARA

STREAM OF BIRDS

(R. ——)

BEN
TELIM

(R. MORROW)

CORNID

TELIM

SALMON
RIVER

WHITE CAP

(R. GRWYNE)

CRUCIO

(R. TROTHY)

N

GOBANIO

BROKEN
MOUNTAIN

(R. USK)

KEY

BEAKER CIST

CAIRNS
(Neolithic + Bronze Age)

STANDING STONES

STONE CIRCLES

HILL FORTS

The
Black Mountains

First

———◆———

See this layered sandstone in the short mountain grass. Place your right hand on it, palm downward. See where the summer sun rises and where it stands at noon. Direct your index finger midway between them. Spread your fingers, not widely. You now hold this place in your hand.

The six rivers rise in the plateau towards your wrist. The first river, now called Mynwy, flows at the outside edge of your thumb. The second river, now called Olchon, flows between your thumb and the first finger, to join the Mynwy at the top of your thumb. The third river, now called Honddu, flows between your first and second fingers and then curves to join the Mynwy. The fourth river, now called Grwyne Fawr, flows between your second and third fingers and then curves the other way, south, to join the fifth river, now called Grwyne Fechan, that has been flowing between your third and your outside finger. The sixth river, now called Rhiangoll, flows at the edge of your outside finger.

This is the hand of the Black Mountains, the shape first learned. Your thumb is Crib y Gath. Your first finger is Curum and Hateral. Your second finger is Ffawyddog, with Tal y Cefn and Bal Mawr at its knuckles. Your third finger is Gadair Fawr. Your outside finger is Allt Mawr, from Llysiau to Cerrig Calch, and its nail is Crug Hywel. On the high plateau of the back of your hand are Twyn y Llech and Twmpa, Rhos Dirion, Waun Fach and Y Das. You hold their shapes and their names.

Yet the fingers are long and skeletal, curving on themselves, and at their edges and in the plateau there are glaciated cwms and cross valleys, red rockfalls and steeply gouged watercourses. Beyond the hand are other heights: Troed and Llangynidr to the west, between Rhiangoll and Lake Syfaddon; Brynarw and Sugar Loaf to the south, and then the isolated Skirrid, the Holy Mountain; east, each ridge running lower, Cefn and Arthur's Seat and Merbach, before the dip to the meadows of Wye.

Beyond these outliers are two rivers to the sea. Mynwy carrying Olchon and Honddu flows to the circling Wye. Grwyne and Rhiangoll flow into the Usk. Wye and Usk, divided by Wentwood, the old Forest of Gwent, flow to the ancient seariver, the Severn Sea, where Wales now looks towards England.

The hand of the Black Mountains. From a distance, in good light, the long whaleback ridges are blue. Under cloud they are grey cloudbanks. But from within they are many colours: olive green under sunlight; darker green with the patches of summer bracken; green with a pink tinge when there are young leaves on the whinberries; dark with the heather out of flower, purple briefly in late summer; russet with autumn bracken, when at dawn after rain the eastern slopes can be red; pale gold in dead winter bracken, against the white of snow. Yet black, a cellular black, under storm cloud: a pitted honeycomb of darkness within darkness.

The valleys are always green, for the grass is bright there. Yet from the ridges they seem woodlands, with farms and fields in clearings. At midsummer, on the closely trimmed hedges, there are stands of honeysuckle and of pink and white wild roses, and on the banks beneath innumerable foxgloves. It is close looking up from the flowers to the steep bare ridges, but the contrast is sharp: above the bleak open tops, with their heather and sedge and cottongrass and peat pools, their paths which dissolve into endless sheeptracks, their sudden danger with few landmarks in low cloud and mist; and below the settled green valleys, with their network of banked lanes, their patchwork of fields, the few ploughlands above the sandstone a wet dark red or dried pink; their scattered stone houses, rough layered or ashlar, from brown or grey towards pink and green under rain. This settled and that open wild country are still within the shape of the hand.

Press your fingers close on this lichened sandstone. With this stone and this grass, with this red earth, this place was received and made and remade. Its generations are distinct but all suddenly present.

GLYN TO ELIS: I

◆

Glyn was driving faster now. In the dark the road was safer. The lights of anything coming would show much earlier than any sign by day, when every corner was blind and the high hedges muffled sound. The banked road was too narrow for passing except at a few hardened gateways. Yet although unsigned it had its marks: the tightness of a corner; the open red earth of a newly dug drain; a rebuilt culvert; a stretch of broken drystone wall; twin yews that arched over the second long pitch.

The headlights shone on the hedges. Roughstalked bracken, on the banks, stood proud to the elbows of hazel. Tangled holly and hawthorn, field maple and blackthorn, spread under rising rowan and ash. Trailing greenberried brambles, fruiting honeysuckle, late briars and columns of seeding foxglove, stood out from the body of the hedges. There were hartstongue ferns and the glossy leaves of ramson, under webs of fruiting vetch.

Glyn and Megan were late. There had been a delay at the hospital, where Megan had to wait for a letter to her doctor and Glyn had been impatient and then cajoling in the office. Then between Builth and Llyswen, along the fast road by the Wye, they had a sudden engine failure, finally traced to a fuel airlock. In the fading light, with Megan holding a torch, Glyn traced the fault and at last sucked petrol through the pipe. He could still taste the raw sourness in his mouth. It was long dark when at last they turned into the mountains.

Glyn had set out early that morning, to bring his mother back after the operation. She was now to stay with her father Elis until her husband Edwin Sayce came back from Strasbourg. Glyn would stay on with his grandfather until term began in Cardiff.

It was not far now to Llwyn Derw. They were turning and

climbing to the watershed, and were suddenly clear on the open mountain road. Towards Rhos Dirion the headlights of a distant car, going away, swung in an arc in the dark sky. The lights of the valley were spread below them: bright yardlights of farms, at scattered distances. At night the pattern of the settlement could be seen most clearly. The oldest farms were on the flanks of the mountains, where the old springs rose. The new farms and houses of the last two hundred years were nearer the valley road but only a few directly on it; most of them turned aside, making the small customary distances.

Across the whole valley there were more than forty lights, irregularly scattered. But the darkness between them was so deep that the eyes soon lost the known features and saw only these isolated points. Their ordinary relations were sunk in the night, in the wide darkness under the black ridges. Glyn had often, from the car, tried to pick out the outside light of his grandfather's house. But as often as he thought he was certain he would again lose his bearing.

Then, as he got nearer, the road dipped again, the high hedges were back, and most of the lights had gone.

They were rounding the bend by the church. There was a winter sand-and-salt heap by the lychgate. The church was isolated on its spur, at its traditional distance from the world of the farms.

'They've lopped the beeches,' Megan said.

'The wind was breaking them.'

'The wind harrows this whole valley,' Megan said, touching her face.

Glyn looked across at her. As she saw his movement she willed a smile. But she was drawn and pale, in the machine-green glow from the panel. The delay on the road had been hard, for her.

Tanhouse, Perth y Pia, Tir Mynach, Old Fforest, Felindre. Glyn rehearsed the succession of entrances as he stared at the twisting road. At the corner below Pentwyn the line of the road led straight to the shallow ford of the Mynwy, but the metalled road swung right, up a long pitch. His mind was now partly ahead, running to each expected place, and partly where he was, within the enclosing headlights amid the rushing darkness. Yet the place would come for certain, after the swing round the corner by the long stretch of holly and the sharp turn under the oak tree to the lane. He would see the big covered light on the outside wall above the mounting block, and at last the softer brown-curtained lights in the windows.

'Has he been well?' Megan asked, forcing her voice.

'Yes, as usual. He's got so much more energy than the rest of us.'

'Seems to have more energy.'

'Yes, because he lives in one piece.'

'He's sixty-eight, Glyn.'

'In one piece, in one place. It makes all the difference.'

'Perhaps it does. But I've known him longer than you.'

They were passing Felindre. Beyond the big outside light there were truck headlights in the yard, where two boys were unloading hurdles. A shape moved suddenly from the open gate: a young black sheepdog was running fast at the car.

'Keep going,' Megan said urgently.

'Yes, though I'll never get used to it.'

'If you slow he'll think you're more risk.'

The dog seemed to go under the car but he was only snapping at the tyres. As Glyn accelerated the dog dropped back and lost place. Then it stopped suddenly, its protection of a boundary completed. Glyn laughed and tapped the wheel. He took the corner jauntily. He touched the horn twice.

There was no outside light on the wall. As he stopped at the gate he could see that the windows were dark. He unlatched the gate and opened the back door, unlocked as usual. The whole house was dark and silent.

'Taid?' he called. 'Taid, are you there?'

There was no reply. He switched on the passage light, then went out to help Megan. As she came under the light he saw how pale and tired she now was. She was looking anxiously around for her father.

'He's probably just out for a while,' Glyn said, across the absence. Megan didn't answer. She went through to the living room. As she switched on the light she saw a note on the table. She looked for her glasses to read it, but Glyn was close behind her.

The note read:

Dear Megan and Glyn – I am almost certain to be back before you see this, but I am leaving it in case you are early. Tom Davies called with a load of ash blocks and we've stacked them in the shelter. It is such a lovely day, so still and bright, that I'm taking a lift back with him so that I can go once again along the best of all walks through these mountains: what you've heard me call its heart line. I shall go up by Twyn y Gaer and along its old pastures to the Stone of Vengeance, then to the old circle at Garn Wen and the Ewyas tower, along the ridge above the reservoir and Terren yr Esgob, past the Blacksmith's Anvil and the Bird House under Twyn Tal-y-Cefn, over Rhos Dirion and the mouth of Rhiw y Fan to Twmpath, across the road at the Gospel Pass and along the ridge to Penybeacon, then as always above Blaen Mynwy and past Llech y Ladron to our spot height above Blaen Olchon and so along the Cat's Back to the Rhew and the lane to the house. I know the distance of this walk within yards but say for safety fourteen miles; in the old days in this weather just over the five hours but say now just over the six. That makes it back home by five at the latest, and I'll see you then or soon after. – Love, Elis.

'What time is it now?' Megan asked. As she spoke she took the note, written on the back sheet of an old calendar, and looked down at the writing: the large, angular, official hand.

'Twenty past nine.'

Megan turned the note over.

'He's always so careful, when anyone goes up, making them give an exact route.'

Her hand was trembling. Glyn put his arm across her shoulders.

'He'll be all right, Mam. He knows every yard of the way.'

'It's still a very long walk at his age.'

'I'll go up and meet him if you like.'

'Not in the dark, Glyn. You'd get lost yourself.'

'He won't be lost, Mam.'

'Then what could have happened, to be as late as this?'

Glyn looked away.

'The moon will be up in an hour, Mam. And it's full.'

'It's still dangerous at night.'

'Not if you know it.'

She stared into his face, on the edge of tears.

'Look, mam, I'll make some tea and get a fire going. Then if he isn't back I'll get my things and go and find him.'

Megan nodded. He settled her in the front room and lit a wood fire in the old grate. He made tea and brought biscuits and cheese. She was shivering in her chair. He put a rug over her knees.

'Don't fuss me Glyn. Go for him.'

'I'll get my things.'

He changed his shoes for climbing boots, took off his jacket and put on two jerseys and his orange cape. He put a torch and compass, cheese and whisky in his rucksack, and took the old blackthorn stick which Elis had cut for him on his twelfth birthday.

'There's plenty of wood for the fire,' he said, going back to his mother.

'It's all right, I am fine.'

He looked round the room, filled with Elis's records of his lifetime in these mountains. On the stone walls were three large aerial photographs, several maps in picture frames, enlarged photographs of dolmens and hillcamps.

On a specially-made table below the window was a large relief model which Elis had built by contours in sliced layers of polystyrene. Behind Megan's chair was a tall glass cabinet, filled with specimens of the different-coloured sandstones and with his various finds: rows of flint arrowheads, a roughly finished stone axe, an incised bone, a blackened coin, broken sherds of pots. The room seemed so inhabited by Elis's interests that it was difficult not to look round for him, to find him at your shoulder explaining. After his parents' divorce Glyn had grown up in this house: at first with his mother and then, when she had gone back to London to work, with his grandparents Elis and Gwen. When he was sixteen Megan set up house with Edwin Sayce, in Berkshire, but he had chosen to stay in Croes Hywel. Then Gwen had died and for three years he lived alone with Elis, until he went away to university. It was here, always, that he chose to come back.

'Should you be waiting?' Megan asked.

'I'm just giving the moon a chance.'

He walked across to the relief model. The surface of the polystyrene was lightly pitted but there was still a smoothness of shape and a crowded, inhabiting detail of features and names. All these were accurate on the model but they were very unlike those desolate tops, of heather and sedge and bog cotton and peat pools, of rutted tracks which narrowed suddenly into sheepwalks and unexpected hollows, of long featureless ridges and false ridges as you climbed.

It seemed at times, walking there, an entirely empty world. But this was the paradox of the place and the history. The features, the periods, were all there, to be marked and to be visited. The shapes of the land and the shapes of the history could be carried in your mind, slowly learned and verified. Yet often, alone on a dark ridge, with a storm coming in from the west, you could feel entirely cut off not only from the present but from any real sense of the past. Then there was only, and intensely, an immediate and indifferent physical world.

'I'll go now then, Mam.'

She reached for his hand.

'Be careful.'

'Of course.'

He switched on the outside light, and walked to the darkness of the lane, where he stood, waiting to adjust to the deep country dark. Slowly, beyond it, he became aware of another dimension of light. The sky was very clear, with thousands of stars. The surface of the lane was reliable so he walked looking up. The familiar shapes of constellations were like the shapes of landscape and history traced in another kind of darkness. Names which had been given could still be identified, and in so deep a common memory, which had been learned until it seemed natural, recall seemed easy. But it proved superficial until, beyond the details, a fuller process flooded through: a long looking, a naming, a finding of memorable ways.

The rough skyline of Crib y Gath was now above him. If Elis was coming by the lane he would easily see and hear him. There was no counting how often they had walked down this lane together. It was not Elis's native valley; he had been born by the Honddu, across two ridges southwest. But he had come to Llwyn Derw in Croes Hywel when he married, and had worked from apprenticeship to retirement as a telephone engineer in these mountains; retired where he had worked. In a different generation he would have been a recognised scholar, for with his work, which had taken him all over the area, he had always combined a sustained study of its geography and history, laying hands on anything and everything he could read. Yet as 'just a telephone engineer', he claimed only an amateur and a native knowledge. Glyn, he had said, would become the professional: 'If you want to, that is. If it means enough to you.'

The lane was very steep past the big wild cherry. After the tarred surface ended it became a rutted track, under a dark canopy of holly. Glyn climbed over the chained gate to the open track at the top of the fields, the beginning of the unfenced mountain. It was suddenly much lighter. At this higher level he could see the beginning of moonrise, southeast over Mynydd Merddin (the old 'Ferdun' he had recently been tracing in the Book of Llandaff). It was turf now under his feet, the close-bitten turf of the sheepwalks. Ewes lay under the bank of a crumbling stonewall, though he could only see them when they moved, hearing his footfall, and tended away. Strange stubborn and docile beasts, endlessly suspicious and endlessly vulnerable. In their varying kinds they had been grazing this mountain for more than five thousand years.

As the climb became steeper he made a conscious effort to regulate his breathing, and when he was walking more easily he began to call.

'Taid! Taid!'

The old Welsh name for his grandfather had become warm and singular, going back to early childhood. It was now so much a part of him that in some sense it defined his life. He could remember his father only as a distant and static figure: a dark shape lifting him and staring narrow-eyed into his face. He was now, as it happened, most often encountered in footnotes: J. W. L. Parry, historian: the brilliant young man who had gone, trailing his first book, to Pittsburgh; who had found another job there, another woman; who had never, except for business, come back. He died in an air crash when Glyn was ten: a distantly reported death, felt only in Megan's then surprising grief. His real fatherly relationship was with Elis, 'Taid'. Edwin Sayce, when he visited with Megan, was polite and professionally interested: a politician set on his dealings in a powerful contemporary world. As he got older Glyn noticed that though Sayce was kind and loving to Megan he was almost openly embarrassed by Elis, taking his enthusiasms as obsessions, his excited talk for garrulity, his intense local interests for simple nostalgia, another name for backwardness. Glyn himself, with his well-certificated education, would, it was implied, soon do very much better than that.

The high call was not answered. The mountain was empty and quiet.

Amateur and professional! But it could never reduce to that. In so many details professional scrutiny mattered: textual, comparative, theoretical. Certain books which Elis had valued turned out to be unreliable; others were wholly misleading. As the evidence was tested, by a number of disciplines, it was both extensive and uncertain, richly suggestive but open to sharply different interpretations. All that must be accepted, as the work of inquiry. Yet the kinds of scrutiny that were built into these disciplines had their own weaknesses. Pushing away, often coldly, the enthusiasms of the amateur, they would reduce what they were studying to an internal procedure; in the worst cases to material for an enclosed career. If lives and places were being seriously sought, a powerful attachment to lives and to places was entirely demanded. The polystyrene model and its textual and theoretical equivalents remained different from the substance which they reconstructed and simulated. Only the breath of the place, its winds and its mouths, stirred the models into life.

'Taid! Taid, this is Glyn! Taid!'

The long rhiw was empty as far as he could see. But there were many dark patches: boulders at the edge of the track; gorse patches; last surviving thorns and rowans, dwarfed and bent from the wind. You could not be certain of any of them until you came very close.

To know traces and to learn to interpret them could be only the beginning of memory. A long forgetting, it had been argued, was the first condition of history; a discarding of enough for the essentials to be remembered. In these mountains there had indeed been a long forgetting, but of a different kind. What mattered, day by day, was a living memory. To speak of the history was to shift a dimension. It was twenty-five thousand years, a thousand generations, since the hunters had come from their caves on the Wye, before the last ice age, following the herds of horses that moved to this grazing in summer. When the last great ice had retreated, twelve thousand years ago, other hunters had come, for elk and giant Irish deer and, when the forest had spread again, for aurochs and boar. But in the shapes of these same mountains, that was another country.

The moon was now full and clear above Merddin. Glyn stared along the slopes at its strange light. The whole shape of the country was visible, yet not as in daylight, though the familiar features recurred. The pale light had a greenish tinge, though the suggestion of colour made too strong an emphasis. Shadows now marked the difference: solid and sharply distinct, without the diffusion of light, the dissolving of hard lines, that come with the soft northern sunlight. In fact the blocks of shadow, from a tree or a boulder or the ridge of a watercourse, were the clearest and most certain objects in this night world.

Solid traces of memory! The mountains were too open, too emphatic, to be reduced to personal recollection: the madeleine, the shout in the street. What moved, if at all, in the moonlit expanse was a common memory, over a common forgetting. In what could be seen as its barrenness, under this pale light, there might be the sense of *tabula rasa*: an empty ground on which new shapes could move. Yet that ideal of a dissident and dislocated mind, that illusion of clearing a space for wholly novel purposes, concealed, as did these mountains, old and deep traces along which lives still moved. An empty and marginal land, in which the buried history was still full and general, was waiting to be touched and to move.

Through millennia, in different ways, this massif was a frontier. The great iceflow along the Wye, four hundred metres deep, grasped and ground at the mountains but could not overrun them. The waves of many invasions had beaten against them, submerging the lower ground. Hunters and shepherds and warrior horsemen claimed the plateau and then the ridges. But Roman, Saxon, Viking, Norman had been content with strongpoints at their edges. The forts and castles of that long social control were now crumbling. But still they defined and imposed the effective political shapes.

Fifteen hundred years of almost continuous fighting, on this frontier which the land had defined. The high names and the legends appeared to record it: Caradoc and Ostorius; Ithael and Offa; Gruffydd and Harold; Iorwerth and Clare; Glyndwr and Henry. Here, in the courts of the Norman lordships, when four languages were being spoken within a day's march, the tales of a legendary Arthur had been translated, interpreted, recomposed. The plumes of that kind of history had been detached and taken for quite other display. Yet in the massif, another life had persisted in deeper and customary memories.

Below the track, from a dark hollow, there were sheep moving again. He looked across and could see, on the far side of the gully, the low mound of a stone-age grave. He turned away from it, suddenly chilled. All the known graves were so embedded in these mountains that by daylight they were no more than ordinary features, marking the direction of a walk. There was a different feeling now, under moonlight. All the places and their relationships had in some way changed. There was still no answer to his repeated calls, yet he found that he kept swinging round, as if somebody was close to him.

Below the grave, on the slope of the gully, was the hollow where the sheep had been disturbed. He could see into it clearly. It was the eroded dugout of an ancient hut, of a kind which was found all over these mountains. The turf and drystone walls from which the roof boughs had been arched were now crumbled and grassed, but the open, long-trodden entrance was still clear.

He had often walked into one of these hollows and closed his eyes, trying to feel its generations of life. Sometimes what he knew and what he sensed came briefly together. But more often there was only the indistinct awareness of some long presence. It was more than a sequence of particular moments – the specific times, the changing ways, of the extended history. It was a more settled, permanent sense, of men and women on these mountains, handling earth, stone, trees, grass, animals: people deep and gone into this place but still seeming to shape it.

Perhaps the different kinds of memory were different regions of the mind. At his books and maps in the library, or in the house in the valley, there was a common history which reconstituted memory, a cast of mind which could be translated anywhere, in a community of evidence and rational inquiry. Yet he had only to move on the mountains for a different mind to assert itself: stubbornly native and local, yet reaching beyond to a wider common flow, where touch and breath replaced record and analysis: not history as narrative but stories as lives.

He was climbing hard now, on the steepest part of the track, stamping with shorter steps against the pitch. A dark shape moved suddenly on the skyline. He stopped and pointed at it, but could not make it out.

'Taid, is that you?'

The shape moved again, and he saw that it was a pony: one of the local mountain breed, white or charcoal grey or bay roan, with fine manes and tails; partly descended from the herds which the early hunters had followed; in modern times the pit ponies of the South

Wales coalfield. Beside it, on the ridge, there were others, three or four turning and moving. He drew breath and climbed past them.

When he reached the ridge he felt the beginning of the mountain wind, a special quality of air that belonged only to the tops. The odour of bracken was sharp and then gone. Under the force of the wind, cold and tightening on his face, was the sour smell of peat but above it, in the air, an extraordinary sweetness.

'Taid! Taid!'

Except for the rush of the wind there was now a deep silence. He realised, with a shock, that he had been certain of meeting Elis long before this. Now only the far open ridges lay ahead.

He swung round suddenly. The sense of a close presence had come again and alarmed him. But there was nothing to be seen, under the spreading moonlight or within the blocks of shadow. The ponies had moved away down the ridge track.

'Marod . . .'

Where had that strange word come from, that distant word? It seemed not to have been uttered but to materialise, breathe, in his mind. A sound suddenly distinct but not his own word.

He looked up at the moon. It was full and very beautiful, its smudges of features clear on the shining globe. There was some strange pulse now in his body, some rhythm that seemed to be shaping him.

'Taid!'

His call was sharp, reaching out into the silence of the empty mountain. He pushed his body forward, against the strange rhythm beginning to alter him. His boots brushed heather that encroached on the narrow track. He set his steps with care but found, as he walked, that he was following the rhythm which had come into his mind. There were no words to the pulse but then suddenly again:

'Marod . . .'

Then came an easier stretch of track, where no heather grew but only the softer clumps of whinberry. He looked all around, in the empty expanse of pale light and deep shadows. The pulse was faster now. The rhythm was echoing his own sharper breathing.

'Marod at once . . .'

He stopped and looked back at the horn point of Crib y Gath, above the valley of Olchon. He closed his eyes.

'Marod at once woke . . .'

Marod, Gan and the Horse Hunt

◆

Marod at once woke when the Aldi child cried. He sat up, short-breathing. He felt across, straight-armed, to where the child was lying, away from the step, between Aldi and the sister. But the sister was moving in her sleep, drawing the child across her breast. The cry faded to rough breath.

Marod rubbed his arms and got up. The four others were still sleeping, in the heavy warmth. He pulled on tunic, breeches and boots. He pushed aside the leather curtain over the inner cave.

It was just getting light. The morning air was fresh but not cold. The sharp smell of juniper smoke hung in the outer cave, where the rest of the family were sleeping. He made careful way over their sleeping hide-rugged bodies. He was almost at the mouth before he saw that one other was awake. The crippled boy, Gan, rested on his elbow by the hearth. He was watching Marod with sharp eyes.

'Good?'

'Marod yes, good.'

The boy's voice still piped, a child's voice, though the shoulders and arms were heavily muscled. Marod had known for many years the weight of carrying him. He could remember the rock where Lerod had put the little boy while he was entering a strange cave beyond the seariver. Marod, guarding above, had seen the cave bear rush from another entrance and Gan cry and fall. Lerod and Marod had driven off the bear but the boy's legs were crippled. Lerod had been drowned that winter in a storm during fishing, and Marod had taken Gan. The boy's legs were useless but wherever he was set he worked at flint and bone, and as his arms strengthened he could, while still sitting, throw far and straight.

Marod felt the hearth. The grey embers of juniper were warm and unbroken. They would hold the fire till the day was known. He moved out over the terrace of the cala. Piran had not finished his chipping of the black chert. There were loose, coarse fragments around the red-veined quartz anvil which Marod had carried from the river. He felt an edge on his thumb. It might make for a flickstone.

He walked back to the entrance of the cave, and crouched at the small bed of clay in a sheltered fissure of the rock. He extended his fingers, carefully, to the rows of carved counter bones which were embedded in the clay. He touched the longer bones which marked the full moons of winter; each was the size of his broad thumbnail. He counted them to five on his extended hand. Gan was watching each of the movements.

'Marod, it is the herd moon.'

'You have watched well,' Marod answered.

He straightened and walked across the terrace to its edge above the river. The morning light was shining on the long straight flow, as he crouched to look at the lowest peg, three manlengths below the terrace. The current was lapping it. The level was falling. And at Trout Rock, yes, the current was slowing. The white and green of the central current was slowing to grey and then brown at the banks. What were left of the fish would be in the browning bank pools. Pink thrift was flowering over the stones of the banks, and the creeping buttercup was coming into flower. Marod stood, looking deep into the river, as it ran slow and slowing to the far bend by the place of the firestone. Now that the river was falling he must watch the herd.

He ran down from the platform and through the splash of the brook bog. The sphagnum was greener among the sedge. Scrub willow and juniper were shooting again, after the heavy cutting of winter. He loped the lower track to the lookhill but then had to stamp and shorten his steps. His hard stamp slithered in the scree to the ridge. There was knotweed and tussock grass and sorrel beyond the last of the juniper. A lost flint edge caught the light. He stooped and retrieved it. His pace shortened again to the ridge.

The horse herd was not in sight. He felt the flint edge hard inside his fist. Before sundown yesterday he had come to look and they had been on the second rise, grazing up. He raised his left hand, palm inward, and looked beyond it along the ridgeway. The low hills

curved above the Little Mountain River. He looked to the third and
to the fourth, where he might still just see them. On the fifth, too far,
he would not see them. But between the fingers of hills? There was
no sign.

The mountains rose in the distance, beyond his hand. On the long
line of black mountains there were patches of snow, now catching
the light. The ridges were straight, like the lower edges of storm
clouds. It was the summer place for the herd and for the people. A
long summerday's distance, with children. A man's winterday
distance. But the herd would move slowly, grazing as they went.
What days now between the herd and the people? For an ambush at
Little Riverjoin it might already be too late. Yet with another day's
delay the herd could be through towards the plateau. It would be
good to find them before the narrow foothill valleys. That must
mean moving today.

Grey geese rose, sharply, in the wet lands beyond Little Mountain
River. Their wings were white over the dark marshes and brackish
pools and small islands. In what disturbance? For now others were
rising, beyond counting, like the snowcloud of angry birds when
people went for the eggs.

Still nothing of the herd. No sign at all, along the open ridgeway.
Marod looked back down at the cave and the river. There were
women now on the terrace, Almar and Alpir, and Algan coming out
to them. The Alva child was playing by the anvil. Thin smoke was
beginning to rise from the hearth, willow smoke, thinner than
juniper. The sun was just clearing from the morning cloudbank.
There was a sharp flash of light along the river. Sun spearing the
water.

Marod looked again at the empty ridgeway and then walked
slowly down. In the next cave they were also moving. He saw
Maran looking up at him. He spread his arms, slowly, three times,
and watched Maran repeat it and then turn to the others. The day
was beginning.

He felt a rising excitement as he ran to the terrace. He went at
once to Almar and touched her forehead. He told her of the horse
herd and of the geese. She looked closely up at him and pressed her
fingers, heavily, on his shoulders. He smiled and went into the cave.
Piran, dark-skinned as after a summer's hunting, was standing there
with the sister. They were playing with the Aldi child. The sister was

not looking at Piran. They were touching, though holding back, through the child.

Their wish to touch would be seen by Almar. She would watch and arrange it, after the summer with the herd. Through the winter and especially during Aldi's fever the sister had been changing. Marod remembered White Gorge beyond the seariver, where he had gone for Aldi, and the sister so thin, so large-eyed, light-eyed, light-haired, the tall family of the White Hills – pleading to come with Aldi, and the family agreeing, for they had too many girls. The only argument had been with his own family, to have brought two mouths across the seariver. That had smouldered, and from Piran flamed, until the Aldi child was born a boy.

It would be good living now, on the foals from the herd. Marod spoke to Piran and they walked together to talk with Maran. The brothers were soon agreed but Piran wanted the men to set out at once, to catch the herd before the riverjoin. At last it was decided. Five men would go now, to find the herd but not to move on it. Three men would be needed to carry the cripple boy Gan. They would walk with the family, eight women and six children; two of the children to be carried. They were not to go past the riverjoin but would all hope to reach it by nightfall.

Piran went at once, with the youngest men. They left, running, holding their bonetip spears high, as in the games of boys. Marod waited and ate with the others. The women were packing willow baskets and leather bags, and the men were bundling the hides. He put the firestone in his pouch and then stamped the hearth. When they were ready to leave he crouched and lifted Gan, for he would take first turn and see if what he feared was true. On the first rise past the brook bog through the heavy smell of flowering mint, he already knew. After the winter the boy was much heavier. He sat very still on Marod's shoulders, afraid to move or speak and make extra trouble. But the weight bore hard. Marod breathed heavily.

The family were all in good spirits. It was always a good time, this move into summer from the staleness of the cave. The women were talking happily and the sun was warm. Once they caught sight of Piran and the leaders, crossing a ridge ahead, walking. Marod stared through the crippled legs at the distant mountains. The long ridges were still black but there was now a lighter colour on the hump beyond the first ridges; the hump before the plateau. Gan's rough hands, lightly touching, brought sweat on Marod's forehead. It ran down into his eyes. He saw a boulder ahead, just below first ridge. The purple saxifrage was flowering, a wide pool of colour. He would get to that and change. And even as he thought this Maran came up beside him, ready for the next carry.

There was still no sign of the herd, or of the group with Piran. Walking easily now, Marod searched every fold of the low hills. There were occasional movements, too small to be sure of. The geese had settled again on the wet lands below. But now the flies were following the sweat of the family. The children, impatient, kept flicking and hitting. The Alva girl-child was scratching her face. And there were more flies ahead, rising in clouds from the droppings of the herd, where he had seen them grazing yesterday. He could see from the droppings, now drying among the scatter of white avens, that they had moved before dark. But how far and where? They must keep moving on.

The family rested by a brook in the second fold. The Alva child's face was swelling. One eye was almost closed. Almar splashed her face and gave her wet sphagnum to hold on her eye. Marod looked at Gan but the boy at once turned away; he did not want look or word. Maran also had been staring at him, and the brothers' looks met. Maran looked away at Algan, who was cupping water to drink from the brook. Marod shrugged and shook his head.

They were moving again, and it was Marod's carry. He tramped steadily, with short steps. On the south slope which they were following there was a stand of dwarf birch and they kept just above this, below the wide stretches of crowberry and silverweed. There were more flowers now: wide spreads of creeping yellow buttercup. The bright colour danced in the eyes. The sun was higher and very warm. Gan's weight bore so heavily that it no longer seemed separate but part of himself. He could feel in its sweat and strain the actual burden of being crippled. When it had happened to Gan, in the cry of fear to Lerod, Marik, then living, had wanted to abandon the child. How could hunters live with a cripple to burden them? It was not his mother Algan who saved him, but Marod, still young and strong, impatient with his doubting and weakening father. Yet the burden is different in talk at the hearth from the crushing weight on the back.

They made two more stops at brooks in the folds. The sun was lowering now. The children were tiring and the whole pace slowed. There was still no sign of the herd or of Piran. They moved up the last rounded hill, through a wide brightness of flowering thrift to the open view to the west. The main line of mountains, with the sun beyond them, was now black indeed. Marod felt the chill of first seeing them. Yet from this point, where the river turned far below, one peak, Broken Mountain, stood out from the rest. It was catching the late sun and was green and golden. But still the lateness was everywhere. The yellow buttercups among the grass, on the downward slope, were beginning to close.

Marod ran the last distance, to look down at the riverjoin. Two young men were sitting with their feet in the river. There was no sign of the other hunters or of the herd. Marod shouted in anger and ran down towards them.

It was less than he had feared but it was bad enough. They had come in sight of the herd on the fourth rise. There were three foals. Piran ordered his lads to run between the foals and the river, but the whole herd had rushed into flight. They expected Piran to stop, to wait on the hill. But he stalked across open tussock and sedge, and before he was in spearthrow the herd sprang and galloped towards the mountains. Piran and the others had gone in chase, though there was no chance.

'If we see them again before the high plateau,' Marod said, angrily, 'it will be more than we deserve.'

The lads agreed.

'And before we can kill on the plateau,' Marod said, 'the family will be hungry.'

'It is Piran,' the older lad said.

Marod spoke formally, raising his hand.

'It is we-all who must hunt. Piran is making it we-some.'

'It must be we-all,' the other lad replied.

Marod pulled off his boots and bathed his feet in the water. It was like the water of winter, stinging his skin. The family were straggling down from the hill. Maran, carrying Gan, was at the back. All threw down their bundles and rested, except the children, who went to the water, drinking and then picking watermint and buttercup. It would be a cold night, by the riverbank, in the huddled rug hides.

It was almost dark before Piran and his followers came back. Piran, smiling and dark skinned, began boasting of how near he had come. Neither Marod nor Maran would listen to him, or say anything themselves. But when the family settled to sleep they talked quietly together. There was now, they agreed, only the one good chance. All the men and lads must leave together, before first light. They must try to split the herd and drive some, a few even, into one of the narrow closed valleys below the high ridges. The best of the valleys would be the Little Stone, below Horn Point.

This manoeuvre would be difficult, but the rest of the plan was much harder. If they failed to split the herd, and it was making for the plateau, the women and children must be not too far behind. But if the men and lads were to move at first light, making their best pace, the crippled Gan must be left at the river. No man could be spared for carrying him, and no woman could manage it. Given an early kill they could quickly get back to him. Even with a late kill, two could come back, with meat enough for the boy. That would be better than coming back for the whole family. But if Gan was to be left, he must have most of the food. Then with his spear and by the water he must manage until they returned.

They talked it through again, looking up at the stars. It was not what either wanted, but it was now all they could do. To lose the herd for some days would be to risk the whole family.

'Though if a storm,' Maran said.

'If a storm we lose the herd.'

'If a storm on the boy.'

'I hear you,' Marod said.

Marod woke Almar. He told her of their next day. He then lay awake a long time, making shapes in the stars. He seemed to see the shape of a bear, but as he stared his eyes watered. At last his tiredness took him.

It was Maran who woke him. There was low cold mist from the river. They went quietly around, waking the men. Soon the eight were crossing through the water. Marod made Piran lead. As it became lighter they began a slow run. They were climbing steadily now. Every man went quiet.

Then suddenly there was the herd. They dropped to the ground. The herd was spread widely over the long flat spur. But not only their own herd. At least one other, making for the summer pastures, had joined them. It was very large. There were a number of young. They were all quietly grazing.

Marod stood and looked at the herd and the land. The flat spur stretched back, in a wide curve, beyond Horn Point and the ridge towards the high plateau. There was a dip slope south to the river and then a stand of willow below Horn Point, where the valley again divided. Little Stone was the narrow valley to the south. The other was more open, rising gently to the spur.

It might just be possible to divide the herd, for a group of seven was grazing towards the dip slope, away from the rest. There were no young with them, so they would be easier to separate. But to drive them down would gain nothing, with the dividing valley beyond. Three men must go round now, following the river to the stand of willow. Then if the other hunters could split off the seven, those three could block the open valley and try to drive into Little Stone.

It could easily go wrong. There were not enough men. But it had to be tried, and it had to be Maran to go to the willow stand. Marod lay and talked quietly. He told Piran that he should lead an assault on the herd, a diversion, while the others were getting the seven away. Piran was eager and happy.

Maran and two companions left at once, dropping quickly away from the herd. The rest lay and watched. It would be a long wait. The sun was clearing the morning cloudbank. The high sky was a pale blue. Marod looked back along the ridgeway, trying to find the lookhill above the cave, but it could be one of two. There was no sight or sound of Maran and the others. They could only watch for them at the willow stand. The sun was warm before they at last saw them, tiny dark figures, and though Maran would be raising his arms there were no limbs at this distance, only dark lines. The sun was striking the high crag of Horn Point. There was greenstone under it, softer than the brown.

The gap had narrowed while they were waiting, but there was still just a chance. Now! Marod led quietly through the pale tussock grass. They halved the distance before the herd was aware of them, and stopped grazing. But the seven ponies, although they looked up, were not moving closer to the others. Piran and his two stood up and raced at the herd, not shouting. As they ran the herd was preparing. The stallions came through and stood facing the men. The mares and the young collected behind them. A fine yellow stallion stood at the point of the defence.

It was now that Piran shouted. Marod and Seran were racing for the seven. Two were already moving, to break back to the herd. Marod threw his spear, at a useless distance, to try to turn them back. A little red-brown mare, with a white patch under her eyes, reared and turned back as the spear landed. Marod and Seran ran in. The seven turned and moved down the dip slope.

Everyone was shouting now. Piran should have broken off but he was walking, slowly, towards the big yellow stallion, who was standing his ground. The other stallions were just holding. The mares and the young were already moving away. The yellow stallion, the height of Piran's shoulder, reared in threat. Piran shouted and threw his spear. Then suddenly, along the spur, the whole herd was galloping away. They were so fast and young that they were beyond pursuit. Piran retrieved his spear and went down to the others. He had so nearly, he said, solved all their problems at once.

But they were already running, spreading widely, to keep the seven ponies down the slope. The lives of the family now depended on this. As Marod waved, the men moved into an arc around the frightened seven. They must wait until the animals were quieter, and then drive them slowly and cautiously.

While they were waiting the sun clouded over. Marod looked up anxiously. It was thin grey cloud from the west. He looked down at the seven, now grazing along the river. He felt a sudden chill. Was it only the sweat drying on him, or the loss of direct sun? He looked again at the cloud. He waved the men up.

They moved steadily, widening their arc. The little red-brown mare was the first to notice them. She moved away, but slowly, as if only looking for better grass. The other ponies looked up. All but one also moved, but again slowly: drifting away. Marod accepted the pace. Moving slowly and then stopping, and then slowly again, they kept up the slight pressure. Marod watched Piran anxiously, but he was moving well, in the rhythm of the others.

The cloud was now thickening. Marod stared west, where they were now losing sky behind the black ridge. The storms in these mountains could be very sudden. But the ground air was still, and there could be only the slow walk, the stop, the slow walk again, along the valley towards the willows.

Marod did not doubt Maran. He would be watching every move

and would know exactly when to come out. He had imagined this so often, in the slow drive, that when he saw them break from the willows and spread to block the wider valley, it was already sharp in his mind. But now the ponies were alarmed, seeing men both ways. They might break at any moment. Marod stood ready to run.

But they drifted again, into the mouth of Little Stone. Marod, watching them, felt a weight lift from his back. The kill was coming nearer, but that would be different. The real pressure, always, was anxiety for the family, and inside that anxiety the weight of holding back. They were beautiful now, the seven fine horses. Their lovely bristled manes, the yellow-white of dried grass, moved softly behind the pricked-ear heads. The long tails were flicking against the flies. In these seven, more than in the general herd, the skins were a warm reddish brown. For so early in the season, they were shining with health.

The arcs closed. Marod saw Maran lift his arm and sent his own signal back. As the seven moved on slowly, into the closed valley, Maran and his two were climbing, fast, beyond Horn Point to the uneven rocky ridge, to reach the stone-littered pass at the farther end.

It was all now coming together. They would kill and eat. He felt the firestone in the bag at his waist. He thought back to the women and the children. He relaxed.

He was looking up at the steep dark ridge to the south, watching a hawk circling, when everything suddenly changed. The seven horses were still moving quietly ahead. But now there rose, as if straight into the air from behind the ridge, at an extraordinary speed, a bank of thick cloud, white at first but then with swirls of dark colour as it streamed upward. Marod pointed it to the others but they were already watching it. He looked up at the near ridge, beyond Horn Point. Maran and the others were well along it, within reach of the pass. So stand places, hold.

The storm came down fast, as if it had seen them and was dipping towards them, its cloud and mist streaming directly at them. Marod had only just pulled up his hood when the ice wind struck him. There was winter, suddenly, all around him: slicing ice rain and bitter mist. None of the others could be seen as the storm swirled around them, though he heard one, perhaps Seran, shout. Marod turned his back to the wind and rolled for cover behind a small bank

covered with sedge. But the wind searched him out, hunting for
wherever he was hidden, moving to strike and pierce through every
turn of his body. In his mind he could see the herd along the spur,
grazing quietly in summer, only that morning. But now in Little
Stone Valley, in the open, it was winter and hunger again. The
hunger had come as the ice wind struck him. The taste of meat kept
coming and going, empty and sour in his mouth. His bowels were
aching. Still trying to hide from the bitter wind, he tightened his
hands on his spear.

The storm raged beyond counting. There was no more sun. Once
he heard a whinny from one of the seven, lost in the icy mist that
filled the valley. It was not near. Perhaps they were still where they
had been when the bank of cloud had risen.

For all that world must still be there. The hawk would be down,
in the shelter of a rock. All the creatures would be sheltering,
enduring and silent. Yet now the valley itself was becoming silent.
The wind was dropping as quickly as it had risen. The icy rain
stopped, but the low cloud and mist, in the freezing air, was
thickening in the absence of wind.

Marod stood up. He cupped his hands to the bird cry. It was
immediately answered, from several directions, through the cold
mist. He walked towards what sounded the nearest, but stumbled
and lost his way. He repeated the bird cry. It was answered from
very close and he found Seran. They spoke in whispers, and then
Piran found them. He whispered that they should try moving up
valley through the mist, hoping to come close on the seven and make
a kill. But Marod was against this. The danger of losing them, back
out of Little Stone Valley, could not be risked, for the family also
would have been exposed to the storm.

They spread out and waited. Marod crouched, locking his hands,
to contain himself. It was very long. At times the mist seemed to be
lifting but then it swirled and thickened again, rolling downhill like
white water. There was silence everywhere. Crouching over his
hands, he tried to remember, in his body, all the ground from the
riverjoin, thinking of the different paces of the hunters and of the
women and children. He must find the moment and the place where
the storm would have reached them. It would have been on the wide
spur, where the main herd was grazing. Without shelter of any kind,
unless there had been time to get to the dip slope, they would be

huddled together, the women bending their heads and the children wrapped in the centre.

There was danger in staying still. He could feel the first numbness in his feet, inside the wet skin boots. He stood and stamped vigorously. His whole body surged with the movement, but the mist was not thinning and he had again to settle, hard-breathing, to wait.

At different times, through the long wait, one or other came to exchange a few whispered words and then to go back to his place. Marod stared at the mist in the direction of Maran and his companions, on the near ridge. Was it lifting at last? There were two bird cries. The others had noticed it. Yet it was acting very strangely.

The high ridge to the south, where the storm cloud had risen so suddenly, was now beginning to show again, while below it the mist was still holding. Marod took up his spear. He heard the sound of a slipped stone, ahead up the narrowing valley. They would all be standing now, eyes straining through the mist. There, again, stones slipping.

The mist was certainly lifting. Marod could see Seran away to his left. He waved him forward. The south ridge was now clear along its whole length, but the sun was down behind it and all that side of the valley was darkening. As he quickened his pace there was a whinny of alarm, not far ahead, and again the sound of stones. He stopped, breathed deep, and sent out three high alert-cries. There were answers from each side of him but he was listening for answers from above. The seven were moving away now. As the mist lifted he caught a glimpse of one of the mares.

Then it came, faint and distant, the high alert-cry from the end of the Horn Point ridge, where Little Stone Valley narrowed, in shale, to the pass to the plateau. Marod lifted his head, laughing. They had them now. They could kill before dark.

Lifting his spear for throwing, he pushed forward. As the ground rose every shape was becoming clearer. He could see five horses now. He looked for the shale, beyond the last grass hillocks, where the valley narrowed under the cliff of red rock. There were no figures at the pass but Maran would know his moment. The valley was darkening all the time, a line of black shadow moving up the northern slope.

The five horses had stopped at the edge of the shale. The first had ventured in, then slipped and retreated. The men closed steadily. A red mare, facing them, turned suddenly and went in, slithering, on the shale. The others stood uncertainly, but as the men still advanced they turned and followed her, heaving and scrambling for a footing. The men ran to the edge of the shale, and suddenly Maran and his two were standing in the notch of the pass. They had loose stones for their slings and aimed them down at the legs of the horses, which were scrambling, terrified, in the deep shale. There were several hits on the legs. Maran and the others lifted their spears.

But now the men also were scrambling. A young stallion, bleeding from a leg, broke back and ran through the line. Seran threw and missed. Then the red mare was down. Marod and Piran ran close and speared her. The big eyes rolled as she threshed her bleeding legs. Then Maran was above her, driving a last, deliberate thrust to the heart. She was dying but the others had broken, two back down the valley, one through and over the pass to the plateau. Piran began a chase but came back. Maran finished the mare with a stone.

The valley was now clear but the line of dark shadow was approaching the northern ridge. There would only just be time. Marod asked Seran to go back for the women and children. The men took the mare's legs and heaved and slid the body down to a flattened area of shale. Then the butchering began: first the sharp cut of disembowelling. The smell was heavy in their noses and throats. As Maran stooped with his flint axe, to begin to sever the head, Marod went down to the little river.

By a small white waterfall beside thin flat grass and stones he laid down his spear and gathered dried grass and sedge. He stacked it carefully beside the firestone. While Piran helped Maran with the cutting of the meat, Marod and the others went back to the willow stand under Horn Point, to cut and carry armfuls of firewood. It was getting dark as they put down their loads. Standing at the waterfall, listening without attention to its steady flow, Marod took out the firestone. He struck with a flint at its roughened end. As he began to get sparks, he made a nest of dry grass. He had to blow and blow to get a thin acrid smoke, but there was at last a little flame. He built edgestones round it. He stayed crouched, adding stalk by stalk, twig by twig, until the heat began to centre. His eyes were streaming from the smoke, and he was coughing from his dry throat.

He had just left the fire when he heard sounds down the valley. A child was crying. He remembered the moment of waking that morning. The women and children came up, and were soon moving all around him. There was hardly any talk. There was too much tiredness and cold. But now the skin tents were going up, and Almar was at the hearth, arranging her stones. Piran, laughing, came down with the first cuts of meat.

He licked his hands as he put them down for Almar to scorch.

Marod stood, heavy-eyed. Some part of his mind was still back in the storm. But now the children crowded near the fire, and Almar gave them meat. The others stood in a circle and waited. As the meat came ready it was handed round and eaten. Soon there was talking, a rising strength of talk. When fat suddenly flared on the fire they could see each other properly, and there was a laugh from one of the girls. The women began singing. Maran came slowly across and stood close to Marod. They looked at each other. They said nothing.

The children were put in the tents to sleep. Several of the women followed them. The men walked up and down, between the camp and the shale, carrying the cut meat back to the pool above the waterfall, where they islanded it with stones. Down the valley the sky was lightening. The shape of Horn Point stood against the night sky. There were stars to the west and the south, but none north and east. They heard bird cries, not their own. But now the heavy sleep was coming.

Marod and Maran were up and away at first light. Piran saw them going and ran and overtook them. They walked fast, in silence. It was a bright morning, like the morning of leaving the cave. It was hard to believe that there had been so fierce a storm, in this bright warming air. The sun would be high before they were back at the riverjoin. They walked very fast, without rests. Across the wide grassy spur their bodies were running with sweat. A heavy scent of honey rose from the flowers. The main herd had gone, but two mares and a young stallion were at a distance, grazing.

'Ours,' Piran said.

The others did not answer.

They crossed the spur and followed yesterday's track. Marod's face was hard set. They could now at last see the river below them. They walked steadily down. Then Piran broke and ran ahead. They saw him reach the crossing, where the two rivers joined. They saw the splash as he ran through. Gan was lying where they had left him, on the far bank. Piran was shaking his shoulders.

Marod and Maran crossed slowly.

'Dead,' Piran shouted. 'Dead. Dead.'

Maran squatted and felt the boy's throat. Piran, shouting, pushed Maran's arm aside and hit the boy's chest hard, with repeated blows.

'Wrong,' Piran shouted. 'Wrong. Wrong.'

Marod felt sharp tears in his eyes. The crippled boy was lying with his back to the mountains. When the storm had come, that had been the only movement he could make. Some time in the night he had died of cold.

Marod looked down at him. The soft doeskin breeches were wrinkled along the useless legs. The muscles of the shoulders were hard under the stained tunic. The spear was tight in the clenched fingers.

Marod crouched and looked into the eyes. 'Marod yes, good.' The thin voice of a child. He closed the wrinkled eyelids. He pushed his hands below the stiff body and lifted. He took the heavy weight in his arms. He turned and walked through the river.

Maran and Piran walked beside him. There would be very short carries, taking turns, but there was enough of the day. For Gan must be brought to the mountains to be again with his family. There could not be full burial and the colouring with red ochre, but there could be flowers gathered: the dark blood of saxifrage. There could be a cairn, cara for cala, by the summer hearth. Laid with his flintspear and his knife, he would sleep beside them.

Varan at the Edge of the Great Ice

◆

Metan left the embered hearth and walked slowly through the brookswamp. He climbed the heath and scree to join Varan on the lookhill. He smiled when he saw Varan's face: the light grey eyes staring, the wide mouth gaping.

'Yes, but see,' Varan said.

For the bright morning sun had escaped the cloud and across the plain, beyond the first ridges, rose shining cliffs of ice. Metan stared at the wonder of it: the edge of the iceworld.

Now Varan was turning. He lifted his arms, the wrists and hands curving inward but still apart, and looked back over his shoulder, in trial, straightening his elbows and curving his hands. And now Metan could see the shape. There were two great arms of ice, and within the arms, but the hands not joined, were ridges of black mountains.

The southern arm, with its icecliffs, was nearly as high as the mountains. It stretched towards them, in lower cliffs and crevasses, until it ended in knuckled hummocks and meltlakes, beyond the line of a little river. The northern arm was not so high, and from the elbow it was flatter, but at its shoulder the icefield was vast and into the far distance the sky was pale above it.

The mountains folded within the arms had patches of snow on their heights. Beyond the line of the little river, which slanted across the tundra between the lookhill and the mountains, were two dark outliers. The ice pushed against the flanks of the one to the south. Varan moved his hands to its shape. It was a bison lying, seen sideways, from the shanks near the ice, along the hard spine, to the massive shoulders and head. Varan lifted his hands. It was as if the beast could rise, shake free, and stand clear of the ice. Yet as they continued to watch it was massively still.

Between the two outliers the long ridges were different: flat spinal bones rising to the west. The ridges ran back to a dark mass, and at its centre, at the highest, they could see a snow-covered hump, shining white now under the sun.

'The edge of the world,' Metan said.

Varan shook his head.

'The beginning of the iceworld,' Metan said.

Varan squatted and picked a grey pebble. He rolled it in his hands. He gazed again at the ice arms holding the mountains.

He was silent, remembering the story he had heard as a boy in the valley of caves in the Southland: in the heavy warmth of winter, by smoking fires and in the shadows of lamps, with double hides hung at the entrance, the men bright with feathers and ochre, and the women with ivory amulets and skirts of shells, and the men and women dancing, the music of horns and drums, the ochred beasts on the walls, and the teller Da Salin, who had seen more than forty summers: his voice between the dances, this of many tales, told and told again through the days of dancing. At some tales, this among them, the young men had shouted and laughed.

'For it is told for a truth that the hunters Laran and Ragod, in the days of our fathers, went beyond the north edge of the world. They were journeying in search of the herd of the ice horse, white creatures much larger, much fiercer than our own, for they live not on grass but on the ice itself, and the herd eat the ice. And it is so great a herd that when it stampedes in the spring the rattle of its hooves is a long roll of thunder and the rush of its running is the great ice wind of the north. And this wind is more than air, for it is a blow of dust and of fragments of ice, so strong and so piercing that at three mandays from the plain where the ice herd is running the drumming is so loud and the knives of the wind so sharp that even the bravest hunters turn back to the Southland.

'Against this white ice wind, towards the edge of the world, Laran and Ragod journeyed, and they crossed, the first men, the second seariver, which flows round the cliffs and the icepeaks at the edge of the world. And by the sun setting in summer their line from the crossing of the first to the second seariver was seven mandays. And the iceworld is one manday beyond the second seariver, which is deep and fierce. Yet Laran and Ragod found a crossing, at a place where the seariver makes a curve and there is a red cliff and the riverbed is hard.

'And Laran and Ragod went beyond it, the white wind often blinding them, but still they followed the sun as it sets in summer, now sinking red and swollen into the peaks of ice. They came then to an unknown river, flowing fast and greenwhite from the ice, and this also they crossed, under a grey cliff, where the river turns twice. And at the northern turn there is a small cave, that no man before them had entered. There Laran and Ragod made fire and slept.

'And on the next day they walked, against the knives of the wind, to the very feet of the icecliffs, and they climbed the cliffs, a long climb, until they stood above them and could see the whole ice-world, as vast and as endless as the western sea. And across the icefield, grazing with their young, stretched the herd of ice horses, the huge and marvellous white beasts, and Laran and Ragod killed a mare and they ate . . .'

Varan opened his fist and looked at the grey pebble. He began tossing it, jerkily, from hand to hand. For it had been exactly seven mandays from the crossing of the first to the second seariver, by the line of sunset in summer. At the wide curve of the second seariver, under a red cliff, there had been a crossing, an easy one, where the pebbled riverbed was hard. Half a manday beyond it, by the line of sunset in summer, a small greenwhite river turned twice, by a grey cliff. Above the river were two caves, one with two galleries and larger than the other, but both small. Neither was cala. In neither was there hearthsign or smokestain, nor at the entrance the marking mancairn. The ice could not be seen from the caves, but from the lookhill it was clear, at a winter manday. There was no herd or any sign of the passing of a herd. The great ice land was silent and empty, a blue-white glitter under the sun.

Varan tossed the pebble and then strained and threw it, far out, towards the black ridges of the mountains. He looked down behind him, to the caves and the river. The lads were coming up from fishing. There were shouts as they made their way. In the larger cave, beyond the terrace, Almet was waiting and coming with child.

Almet lay, sweating, on the bed of sphagnum, wet and cold along her legs. Sister Alina was turned away, bent over and working. There was a noise on the step and suddenly Varan was standing there. He looked big against the light. He was carrying the bond-horn that she had given him at the season. At the rounded end of the horn was the old worn carving of the bullhead.

Memories came back, between the pains. This was the horn she had given to Ladar, for her first child. A sickness came suddenly in her throat and tears on her cheeks. That little girl baby, the thick dark down on her head, but she had held her for only a few breaths before Ladar had taken her to be drowned.

The pains were starting again. Sister Alina looked round at her but did not come across. Other memories crowded from the shadows of the cave. Ladar had died that same year of his wounds from the young bull in the southern grassland beyond the great marsh. In the next season she had given the bondhorn to Munor, at the end of her seventeenth summer. Then came the joy of a boy-child from Munor, the dancing and the necklace of brown and white shells. The boy had lived three summers: broad-shouldered, bright-eyed, with Munor's drygrass hair. He had walked in his second winter and talked in that spring.

The pains came again, crushing down. She saw again the screaming of her run along the seariver, as the little boy, playing for fish with a stick, was down and gone so suddenly, in the racing current. Almet cried and Valin came to her. Almet felt her large wet hands on her forehead. Varan was gone from the entrance. The pains tightened, forcing down.

Her lips were dry now and her eyes were heavy. For now again and who would it be? In the new season the horn to Varan: dark, quiet Varan, his hands holding and tossing pebbles, his grey eyes distant, as if living beyond them, but his slow words always kind. It had been talked through on their journey. The women had said that she must keep even a girl-child, for she had given one girl and had had her boy taken, and the numbers of the family allowed it. But there was then the bad spring and the herd had not come. Varan had urged, suddenly, that they should strike north, to trap a herd towards the edge of the ice.

It had been a heavy journey for Almet, pregnant. In each long day she had heard the men saying that without a herd the numbers were wrong, so that to be let live it must be a boy-child. Yet Varan had still been certain that they would find a herd, in the land before the icecliffs. He remembered, he said, a story, and in part believed it.

The pains were quicker now and Alina was holding her. But there was not only Alina's voice, soothing. There was another, strange voice, hoarse and shouting, as if from the roof of the cave. There was a long white streak, with brown edges, where the hoarse voice was shouting, and it was pressing down and down at her. Then the streak faded to a loose mist. Alina was lifting and slapping. There was a loud cry.

Almet licked her dry lips. She could not find her voice.

She tried again, forcing the sound from her throat.

'Who?'

Alina seemed not to hear her.

'Who?' she asked again, trying to lift on her elbows.

Alina looked round at her.

'Of us,' she said quietly.

'Girl?'

'Of us.'

Tears burst from Almet's eyes. The lamp was guttering and the cave seemed suddenly darker.

'Alina, let me hold.'

'Wait.'

'She must live.'

'Wait.'

'Live!' Almet screamed.

Varan had heard the cries. He was standing looking down at the river, which was twenty manlengths below the terrace in front of the caves. The greenish white of the water was from the ice. There were eyes of that colour. The eyes of Almet.

The other men were talking behind him. He did not listen. He had heard. He turned from the river and squatted to look again at the strange stone which the lads had carried up. It was shiny and very hard, with pale red veins. It was roughly squared. It had been flaked many times at its edges. In the southland he would know that it had been used by men. But could it be so here, at the edge of the iceworld? Could its edges have been flaked in the tumbling stones of a spate? The main shape still held his eyes: the shape and the strange, alien veins. He moved his fingers over it, gently. As he closed his eyes it was the shape of an anvil and he could see a stranger crouched over it, hammering.

'You will look at Almet's child.'

Varan opened his eyes. He looked down at his fingers on the stone. Metan was standing above him. Varan could not answer. His mind was too far.

'You will look at Almet's child,' the steady voice repeated.

'There is time.'

'You know it is a girl-child.'

'I know it is a girl-child.'

He put both hands around the stone. He straightened and lifted it. Metan watched him, frowning.

'In the southland I would know that this is a man's stone.'

Metan said nothing.

'Yet here can it be a man's stone? These caves are not cala. There is no smokestain in them, no mancairn marking them. And since we crossed the second seariver we have seen no manlife.'

'Varan, leave the stone. See the child.'

'There is still the story of Laran and Ragod.'

'You do not believe the stories of Da Salin?'

Varan put down the stone.

'I hear them. I wait. And I now hear the story of the journey of Laran and Ragod, and the marks of that journey are true.'

'The marks are not the story. The story is of the ice horse.'

Varan smiled and looked across towards the caves. The other men and women were gathered, watching them, waiting to give their voices on the girl-child. Varan touched the ivory pendant that hung by a thong from his neck.

'I will see Almet's child.'

'She is perfect,' Metan said.

Varan walked to the big cave. Alina was waiting by the step. She stared into his face. He looked past her, waiting for his eyes to change to the cavelight. He stepped in to where Almet was lying. She was holding the child close.

'You are well,' Varan said, taking the bondhorn from his belt and laying it beside her.

She did not answer.

'It is a girl,' Varan said.

She closed her arms tightly, covering the small head.

'She is perfect,' Varan said.

Almet looked up at him.

'You cannot take her, Varan.'

He put out his hand and touched her wet hair. Her eyes, staring at him, were reddened with crying.

'We are at the edge of the ice,' Varan said. 'There are now three summer moons.'

'I will be strong, Varan. I will fish and follow the hunt.'

'There is fish here, and pica, and there are birds on the wetlands. But there is no herd to dry for the winter.'

'You will find a herd in these moons.'

'I cannot tell. Unless it is the ice horse.'

She pulled away from him.

'I do not believe in the ice horse,' he said. 'But there are the marks of the journey of Laran and Ragod, and those marks were brought back, for the story to be told. Laran and Ragod killed and ate, at the edge of the ice.'

She reached for his hand.

'Then we will keep her, Varan.'

'I cannot tell. There is also the story of the great cave, of Mamcala, where the sacred fire always burns. For the fire to burn men must kill and eat.'

'We will keep her, Varan.'

Varan released his hand and touched her lightly on the forehead. He went out of the cave and took Metan up to the lookhill. Between the shining arms of the ice there were the black mountains.

'We see ice, Metan, but we see also mountains. It is not the edge of the world.'

'Yet can a herd live, so close to the ice?'

'We do not know all that lives.'

They looked out together. They saw the dark outliers, very clear now against the glittering icecliffs. The one to the south was still a bison lying. Beyond it, between the ice arms, were the dark spinal ridges.

'For one moon,' Varan said. 'If we do not kill, we go back at once to the south.'

'The women will stay?'

'The women will stay. There are fish in the river.'

'We shall keep the child?'

'If we kill we can keep her.'

They looked out again at the icefield. In the pale sky above it there were movements of air and now suddenly many colours were shining there: shifting colours, as in the feathers of birds when a breeze stirred them. They watched the colours moving. Neither dared to speak.

At last they went down. Varan spoke and the voices were given. The men and lads ran for their spears. Alina came from the cave, carrying an armful of bloodied moss and on it the birth cord. Varan took the armful from her and went to stand above the river. He held it above his head. The others, men and women, gathered round him. He closed his eyes, thinking he could be holding the infant girl. Then he opened his eyes and shouted. He cast the moss and cord far down to the river.

The river! Glyn looked around, dazed, on the open mountain.
The oldest traces are not memories. Marks on a stone trace a
hand. Ochre on bones traces an attended life. But these are few and
far between. Until the traces of human life are extended, the history
is only a history of earth.

Yet this, he knew, could indeed be traced. The heart of the Black
Mountains had been formed by an ancient river, flowing for many
millions of years from an old red continent. From the edges of
volcanoes, from scree-strewn uplands, across plains of mud, the
great river had meandered across a coastal plain to the sea, bringing
down mud, silt and sand, coloured red by hematite. It had laid these
in shoal and floodbank, bed upon bed.

In the first era the deepening layers were moulded, across a wide
delta, by currents and the surges of waves. River channels, blocked
by coarser sediments, overflowed into floodplains. In places the sea
broke in, across the wide flats. The bones and armour of fish and sea
creatures, deposited over millions of years, became the substance of
siltstones, mudstones, red sandstones, to a depth of seven hundred
metres in what is now the heart of the mountains.

In the second era there were changes in the levels of land and sea.
The sea covered the plain, leaving a layer of cornstone – conglomer-
ate pebbles of lime and sand – over the old red sediments. When it
pulled back shallow freshwater lakes, wide alluvial mudflats, and
brackish lagoons remained. The great river and its tributaries
brought down more red sand and silt, laying sandbanks and shoals
in the shifting channels, across the delta fan and the floodplain. In
strong and shifting currents the sandbanks flooded and dried and
flooded again. As the shoals dried they were pitted and crevassed
and eroded. New river channels broke through, flooding new

sediments. The sandstone of this era was layered to a further depth of five hundred metres.

The levels changed again. The sea pushed in, leaving limestone. The river still laid down sand, but green or brown and micaceous, eventually pressed to shales and flags, two hundred metres thick. Above these, as the river flowed on, came more reddish-brown sand: the final layer, three hundred metres deep.

The substance of the Black Mountains had been set in place, but their shapes were still to come. The long ridges and upland valleys – mountains that would seem unchanging – were deep yet still unformed.

The earth heaved and uplifted. The great sandstone layers dried and eroded. Then the earth once more subsided and on the southern flank fast-flowing rivers left grey river grits and pebbles of quartz. Later again, the sea moved relentlessly north, over the coastal plain and the freshwater deltas of the old continent. In this vast change, the deep layers became islands, in a warm shallow sea. Reefs formed at their edges. Their position on the earth was now near the equator.

South of the islands – where there is now a visible change across the valley of the Usk – the shallow sea built cliffs of limestone. Again the earth moved; there were avalanches under the sea. The warm shallows became muddy deltas and swamps, with vast, damp equatorial forests, whose vegetation decayed and turned to peat. In time the old forest layers to the south compacted to coal seams: what would be the Black Mountains looked across to what would become the coalfield of south Wales. The sea was still tropically warm. The islands were now baking deserts.

There were again vast movements of the earth, folding the old rocks east and west. Faults and fractures ran northwest and southeast across them. Red dust storms blew from the old lands. Seas flooded and retreated. The great reptiles lived in the sea shallows and in the swamps at their edges. And now the levels of the oceans themselves moved. On what had been the red desert uplands were volcanoes and lakes and tropical forests. The great reptiles disappeared and in their place were flightless birds and small mammals. To the south there were again vast movements of the earth, new landforms shifting their places on the planet.

On one of the red sandstone islands, on the shoals of the river of the ancient continent, the range of the Black Mountains was at last formed. Thrust and folded, it took the shape of a hand, with wide rivers flowing around it: a shape awaiting its history.

Then came, through millions of years, the great movements of ice. In its earliest advances it covered all this land. In its last advance it surrounded but did not cover the hand of the mountains. It reared and ground at its edges, in a slow frozen tide lapping and breaking on land, throwing up shining cliffs and glittering peaks. On the north, along the scarp, the ice sheet had a depth of four hundred metres. Glaciers pushed to east and west, covering the foothills and invading the transverse valleys. In the high valleys, including Olchon, were smaller glaciers and deep snow beds. Above them, on the long ridges, the ground was bared by freezing and thawing. Gradually the ridges were smoothed, through thousands of years, into the now familiar whalebacks, with terraces of debris in the valleys below.

Glyn settled and looked around. This was a history of earth, but now, at last, came widespread human traces. Before the last of the ice men and women had hunted this land. Between the advances of the ice there were long warm millennia, in which the highlands were forested, and before the final advance there were wide grasslands where herds of reindeer and bison and horse grazed and were hunted. The traces of Gan, of Marod and his kin following the herds, almost thirty thousand years ago, were left in Little Stone Valley: Blaen Olchon, now in darkness below him.

But then the great ice returned. Twenty thousand years ago the hunters had moved south, where the herds were more plentiful. But from time to time, as if into unknown land, small groups returned: the kin of Varan and of Almet carrying her threatened girl-child. At a double turn of the curving river – the later Guuy or Wye – they found the two caves where the family of Marod, seven thousand years earlier, had wintered. All signs of that earlier occupation had been buried in debris and silt; only the anvil, displaced, had survived. The river itself had cut a deeper gorge below them. Uncertain yet persistent, they had hunted the very edge of the ice, which in its vast shining cliffs, enclosing the Black Mountains, set limits to their world.

The deep ice lasted here for five thousand years. When at last it began to break up and retreat it left a scraped and devastated land. Sea levels and river depths had changed and were still changing.

Over the deep frozen earth the bitterly cold land was only slowly repopulated, on the moraine gravels and in the alluvial clays. From the moss and lichen through grass and sedge there came again a wide treeless heath and a rough grassland. Slowly a fertile earth was recovered. Juniper, dwarf willow and dwarf birch came back to the valleys. True birches came to grow in scattered stands. Under the northern scarp of the mountains, after the great icemelt, there was a large, pear-shaped glacial lake: what became Llyn Syfaddon and then Llangorse lake.

Much later the lake shrank and the forests returned. But already, thirteen thousand years ago, among the thinly scattered birches and pines, the generations of hunters were back, moving out from their winter caves along the mountain ridges to the summer of Leucara, the icewater lake.

The Summer Lake and the New Blood

◆

It was the time of yellowing leaves and of red skies. At the last flake of this moon they must recross the mountains and return to Mamcala, to be settled before the deep snows. The hide bag of pebbles, which the oldest woman, Telo, had gathered and counted in the spring, was now almost empty; only two hands remained.

It had been so good a summer, at the icelake of Leucara. The seventeen of Pirin and his fierce blood had rushed to the seariver. Only the weak, Pirin said, could live on the icewater fish. But for the close families of Mirin and Sarn there had been all the good fish they could eat, and there had been eggs and herbs and buds and groundberries. Through the moon of the shining leaves there had been a horse herd on the plateau and they had killed until it moved off behind its stallions to the endless hills of the west.

Yet, though happy at this distance from the restless anger of Pirin, they would be too few, without his group, for the hard hunting of winter. A run of hard seasons and of many accidents had diminished them. Mirin, the strongest, had been crippled for two winters and could now only talk of the hunt. It was saddening to see his lean body, with the heavy shoulder muscles and the livid scars of old wounds on his forearms, as he hobbled, dragging his useless right leg, to fish alone by the lake. Telo, to whom he had come tall and strong from the Fire People of the seariver, at first smiled but now cried when she saw him scraping the hair from his face, as if he were still a young man. The bristles were grey and the thin hair of the head was grey. When he stood, proud of some fish, and came to show it to her, he dragged and rolled like a wounded beast that an arm was already lifted to go in and finish. Under their shelter at night he was shy like a boy, trembling and clenching his body if she came near or touched him.

The lead had passed to Sarn, but he felt its weight. For he was older than Mirin, his thick hair and beard already white for eight winters and now his stocky body plump through the eating of summer. Sarn and Telo were mountain blood, of the same mother. It was Telo who had to reckon the blood of the family. But she could talk easily with Rano, the dark-skinned quiet woman who had been exchanged, carrying her infant son Gan, by a people hunting north whom they had never met again. She had borne Sarn two sons and two daughters. Mirin and Telo had two strong hunting sons. The mothers sat long days by the lake, reckoning the blood for the return to Mamcala. They agreed that Pani, Rano's daughter, should go to Varan, elder son of Telo. The younger daughter Liri must wait. The other young men, their sons, must go through the seasons to women of Pirin's blood: Tamid son of Rano first. There must be now at least one other child, hard as it would be when they had lost so many men for the winter hunting. The child would come to Pani and Varan.

It was easy to explain the foreseeing to Pani. Dark-skinned as her mother, she laughed for the return and the blessing in Mamcala. Varan took little notice, for the young men kept to themselves, and there was always running and wrestling and throwing spears by the lake. Through the long warm summer, with its abundance of food, the aches of winter and of reckoning were eased and almost forgotten.

The whole family sang in the evenings, under the clear skies. Crippled Mirin watched, shading his eyes, as the young ones jumped in one of the fast seariver dances which he had brought when he had come to Telo. There were also the old, slower, mountain dances, in which Sarn and Telo joined. As the nights got colder, and the mornings began creeping with mist, the days became busy, making ready for the return, but in the evenings they still sang and danced. And there was now a new excitement, for at last, just in time, elk had come to the far side of the lake. Varan and Adran, following a trail, had seen stripped bark on a stand of pines. It was too far for the crippled Mirin but Sarn saw and confirmed it, by its height, as a sign of elk.

The young men began standing in watches. On the second morning Varan and Adran, inseparable brothers and hunters, saw three elk cows move down to the lake, wading in at the shallow edges to feed on water plants. At the first smell of Varan and Adran approaching them they splashed to the bank and ran away. Mirin, blaming the impatience of his eager sons, gathered all the men and talked of how they must hunt.

That evening was especially happy. Gan found an elk dance. He came while the others were eating. He moved his dark body heavily, in a stiff-legged shuffling step. His head was bent forward and his lower jaw was drooping and hanging. The others laughed until the tears came as he continued the slow dance. Then the children jumped up and shuffled behind him, all making pendulous faces. Soon the men and women, watching, were making the faces at each other, laughing helplessly. And then Varan brightened the fire. He had done what Mirin had advised and gone to strip birch bark. Mirin had shown him how to make a horn from it and now Varan was blowing it, redfaced, and from the bark horn came the loud grunting cry of an elk cow. Suddenly, with a roar, Adran was dancing in front of it, bulling it, and the boys began miming the bulling as Varan went on blowing the grunt from the horn.

For it would not only be the cows. This was what the horn and the dance were saying. With the yellowing leaves the bull would be looking for the cows, after the summer away on his own. There was a small stand of pines, and below it hummocky ground, to the west of the lake. By the moves which Mirin had talked the hunters would be in the pines, before first light, and would wait for the cows to come down to the water. They would let them wade in as deep as they wanted, sucking their feed. Then they would move into the hummocks and Varan would blow the horn. The bull might come, unwary. Gan mimed his coming, in a heavier shuffling. They would shoot arrows at his legs, to lame him. Gan mimed him lame. There was a touch of miming Mirin in the dragging leg. The children laughed.

By the fire the men looked over their tools for the hunt. They had flickbones, just shorter than a hand, barbed and pointed from antler and bone. The older men had kept to barbing on one edge only, for a roundarm throw with the barbed edge forward. But the young men had worked to notch and barb on both edges, to make the whole tool lighter. They threw these straight-armed, holding the pointed end between the fingers and making the tool spin in flight. But still their main tools were bows, strung with tendons, the barbed arrowheads bound and stuck with blood to birch and juniper shafts. Working older juniper down to an arrow's thickness was long and pleasant, in the fragrance of red-brown shavings. They had also throwing spears, pointed with flint, and stone axes and clubs.

They were glad to be handling the hunting tools again. These were the real weight of their lives. It was easier to catch fish in the lake, wading and spearing or carrying stones to make small weirs on the inlets where the levels dropped through the summer. But these slower and quieter ways could not be danced. The fish were always more distant, even when wriggling in the hand and with those staring eyes. They did so few things. It was only a simple passing between spear and fin. But the animals did so much. They looked around. They watched and hesitated. They stood ground or ran. They flared from contentment to fear or anger. They called, in their different cries. They explored and mated and suckled. All these shifts of their lives could be seen and danced.

Before dawn next morning all the hunters except Mirin were in the stand of pines. Two boys were on the ridge above them, looking out for the elk cows. It was important, Mirin had emphasised, to let them through without alarm and then move to the hummocks where Varan would call the bull. They must then shoot for the nearest, preferably the bull, but above all pick only one animal, for their combined attack, letting the others go. By their numbers, Mirin said, this was required like law.

It was cold as they waited. The young men were in their light deerskin summer tunics but white-haired Sarn had pulled on his winter fur, leaving his legs bare. There was now no joking, and only a little talking. Even Varan sat with his elbows on his knees and his head between his hands, as if in sadness. As the pale light spread downward from sky to lake they looked out at the thinning banks of mist. At their edges the mists were moving like water creatures. Crows were feeding on the rough ground towards the lake. In the pine stand where they hid a pipit was moving along the branches, searching for insects. Brin mimed to throw a flickbone at it, but Sarn angrily raised his hand. The pipit caught the movement and rose circling into the air. The sky was pale and cold where they all watched him flying.

It was full light and the mist was lifting before the elk cows came. They had been feeding further up the slope, on pine bark. There

were again three. The men saw them as soon as the boys on the
ridge, who were playing with pebbles. The cows moved without
hurry, in their awkward walk. Brin laughed silently and then hastily
covered his mouth. Gan looked across and made the pendulous elk
face. Brin had to press both hands to stop laughing. When the cows
at last reached the water, two leading and a lighter one behind, they
waded in slowly. The waterfowl moved a little distance away. Sarn
lifted his hand for the move. They circled, upwind, round the pines
and crawled through to the hummocks. There was now wide open
ground behind them, and they could not know which way the bull
would come, if he came at all. But to where the cows were wading
there was one likely track. Varan raised the birch horn.

'Yes,' Sarn said, and Varan put the horn to his mouth. He took
deep breaths, preparing himself, but his first blow was a failure and
his face was bright red. He rearranged his fingers and blew again.
The familiar grunting call came but it was not very loud. He stood to
ease the pressure in his chest. He blew again and it sounded loudly
and then very loud. Brin rolled on the ground, trying to hold his
laughter. Sarn and Gan watched the cows in the lake. They did not
move or even look up.

Varan had to rest. The sun climbed higher and the last feathers of
mist disappeared. There was a wide brightness along the lake. The
water was shining from the sun in the greys and whites of geese. In
places it dazzled, the small movements across it, like a breeze in
feathers, too bright for the eyes. Along the damp banks, herbs and
sedges were wintering from dark green to brown and black. When
they had come down from the mountains the yellow caltha had
been flowering. They had eaten the young shoots and chewed the
flowerbuds with fish. Little willows were spread on the nearest
bank, their egg leaves now yellow against the greys of the water.
Towards the camp, where the women and children were waiting,
wide leafy patches of saxifrage and thrift crept through the brown
scree and the breaks of red earth. These had been lifesigns, heart-
signs, of intense purple and pink when the horse herd was still on the
plateau. Beyond them the soil thinned but in the deeper hollows
dwarf birches grew, their jagged leaves now a bright yellow. Behind
the camp, on the long slope to the mountain, were groves of tall
birches, their white trunks skinning and peeling, their leaves a paler
yellow. Growing more thickly, beside the deep water gullies, were

low green junipers, with the blue and black berries that were sharp
and fragrant to chew and then spit out. Higher again spread
crowberry, with its black fruit to pick and eat before the birds. It
had been a summer of birds: waterfowl and singing birds: eggs and
nestlings to eat and still so many flying and singing. Beyond the
birch and the crowberry the bare scarp was steep, pink-runneled
with snowmelts. Many springs now shone in the sun where they
flowed over rockfaces. Above them, always, was the sharp hard line
of the ridge: the black ridge.

Varan had recovered his breath and was ready to blow again. But
still, as the grunting calls came, nothing happened. The young men
were getting tired of lying cramped in cover. Left alone they would
run for the cows. Sarn spoke to hold them, praising Mirin and his
words for the hunt, but he knew he could not hold them for long. As
he was speaking, soft-voiced, Adran, who was facing him, rose
slowly and pointed.

A bull elk, the largest any of them had seen, had come out from
the pines and was looking down towards the lake. Its size froze
them. The cows were the height of the larger horses, at the hump on
the shoulder. This bull, his dark-brown pelt grizzled around his
head, stood taller than the tallest man. His palmate horn was
massive. His pendulous head, and his large dewlap, were the
features which Gan had danced. But they looked different now, in
his formidable presence.

Sarn felt thumping in his heart and sharp breath in his nostrils. He
slapped his palm on the earth. He repeated the plan. He folded his
hand to his mouth, Varan blowing the horn. He stretched his arm
and folded it back, the bull coming. With his right arm he showed
the draw of the bows. Then he swept in a wide curve, pointing down
to the lake. He moved his feet to show the chase. He opened his
hands. They were agreed and ready. He held up a single finger: the
reminder to close on one. He then looked back at the bull and
signalled to Varan to blow.

Every face was drawn, as the birch call sounded. The bull turned,
uncertain. Then he moved, suddenly, directly towards them. He
came very fast, his long legs eating the distance. If he came straight
he would be over them. Sarn shouted the alarm. The bowmen were
crouched, arrows tight, along the hummocks. The bull stopped. He
was now five man lengths away. He bellowed and the sound seemed

to shake them. Signing the bowmen to keep down Sarn pointed to Varan to blow again. Then everything happened very fast.

The bull trotted quickly towards them but as the bowmen stood and shot he veered and was away. The others threw for his legs, jumping from the hummocks and racing to get close. Two flick-bones hit, in the near back leg: one high in the haunch, one below the knee. He bellowed again and swung round but now the hunters were spreading and shouting behind him and he galloped towards the lake. It was full chase now. The hits in the leg were not slowing him. At the lake's edge the cows were disturbed. Two splashed back to the bank. As they reached drier ground they moved away south, down the shore. The bull swung, following them. The third cow, the smallest, was only just coming out of the water. Brin and Tamid veered from the bull and raced towards her. Sarn and Gan hesitated and then followed them. Varan and Adran still chased the bull. The cow tried to splash back but Brin and Tamid were on her. She was hit with spears and went down. Blood spread in the grey water. She struggled up and went in deeper. Sarn, following, shouted for space. He threw his spear for behind the eye. It hit and went home.

Sarn looked down the lake. Shading his eyes from the dazzle of the water he could see Adran and Varan still running: inseparable brothers, the tall sons of Mirin. But the elk were far beyond them. The bull was already up with the cows, running fast. Sern cupped his hands and called the return. He waited and repeated it. Adran and Varan were still running. He was called from the lake to help with the cow. She was almost down, her legs thrashing the water, but Tamid and Brin were deep to their chests, slipping as they tried to get close. Gan, still on the bank, was smiling and watching. Sarn took his axe from his belt. He waded in and chopped down on the neck. The legs kicked, convulsively, but her strength was almost gone. He hit again, through the water, and she slumped and fell.

Gan now waded in and they got behind the body and began pushing and dragging her through the water. The great head lolled in the spreading bloodstain. At last they got her to the bank and pushed her clear of the sedge. Tamid shouted the high call of the kill. Brin had squatted and was stroking the cow's long upper lip. Sarn smiled. The lip would be the best of the eating. It must be saved to share with the women and children. Already in his mouth he could taste the dry meat of the carcase and then sharp in his nostrils the strong-tasting fat. Brin stood and made the shape of the elk, the stiff legs and the pendulous head, as in Gan's dance. Gan was looking away. The others grinned but Brin did not dance. There was a gash in his leg where a kick had caught him. He would need sphagnum for that.

Sarn, exhausted, lay back on his hands. When he had at last got his breath he looked south along the shore, to where Adran and Varan had been running. There was no sign of them.

'What happened?'

'The bull turned and they stopped,' Gan said.

'Then?'

'The bull followed the cows again. Adran and Varan went after them'.

'Running?'

'Walking.'

'This shows that they have thought. They will track the wounded bull.'

'You call that thought?' Gan said, looking down at him.

He was short, thinfaced and weakeyed, much darker-skinned than the others. His questions often crossed what the others had agreed, though they were not angry like those of Pirin; only straight and quiet, as in his mother Rano's voice.

'I mean,' Sarn said, 'that they are not chasing and wasting their breath.'

'You mean that,' Gan answered, 'but you mean also that they are right in tracking the bull.'

'He was hit in the hind leg.'

'But Mirin's words were clear. Only the one animal.'

'If he is hit he may be crippled. They may come up on him.'

'And then two can take him?'

'It will be difficult. But one can return for us.'

'Neither may return. They may think they can take him and then they will try. Adran and Varan will try.'

'But we can't go after them now. We must cut and carry.'

'It would be better thought if they came back and helped us. What they are doing is very dangerous.'

'You know Adran and Varan. They want that bull.'

'Yes, Sarn, that is the danger.'

Sarn looked across the lake to the camp. The women were already walking round to them, with the children trailing behind. There was a shout and the boys from the ridge were running down towards the kill.

'Can we go for the bull, with Adran and Varan?' one of the boys asked.

'No,' Sarn said, 'you must stay to carry.'

He pushed himself up. His back and legs were aching, but he knew that he must cut. He looked again down the empty shore and then squatted to slice the lip with his flint blade. He gave it to Brin to wash in the lake. Then he set to work gutting and skinning the carcase. When Telo and Rano arrived they sat close beside him. They took the pieces he cut and washed them. The young men and women were loaded for the carry. Sarn went on cutting, his hands bloodied. Whenever he rested he looked south, to see Adran and Varan returning. There was only the open ground and the long dazzle of the lake. Telo had not spoken to him but she had followed his looks. On the far shore, below the camp, they both saw the dark figure of Mirin, watching.

It took all day to complete the cutting and carrying. When they were back at the camp a meal was prepared. Parts of the liver were sliced and set on hot stones at the edge of the fire. The lip was incised, through the skin and fat, and thyme was rubbed into it before it was hung to roast. After eating they made up the fire and sat close around it.

Mirin had asked for every detail of the hunt. He had then become silent. While the others were still eating he hobbled to the lake and looked out, against the setting sun. When he came back he said nothing. At last Sarn spoke to him directly.

'They should not have gone?'

'They went.'

'They are your sons, Mirin.'

'They are my sons.'

'Are two men enough for a wounded bull? Two as young and strong as Adran and Varan?'

'For this wounded bull? Hit only in one leg?'

'There were two wounds, Mirin.'

'It is not enough.'

'Then they may lose him?'

Mirin twisted his face.

'That would be best, Sarn.'

He limped away.

By noon next day Adran and Varan had still not come back. Tamid and Brin went looking for them, carrying double spears and running. It was dark before they returned. They had found no sign of them, and seen no elk.

'They are strong,' Sarn said, 'they will follow till he drops.'

Mirin turned away and spoke quietly to Telo. The others moved closer, to listen and to speak. For now Telo showed her distress.

'We will stay,' she was saying, 'for as long as we must, until Adran and Varan come back.'

'To the last flake of this moon,' Mirin said, quietly.

'Until our sons come,' she cried.

Mirin looked away.

'It is five nights,' he said, 'to the last flake.'

'They will come, Mirin. They will come because they know that we need them.'

'If they do not come, Telo, we must leave for Mamcala.'

'We will not leave our sons,' Telo cried.

Mirin waited. Rano and the girls gave their voices to support her. He limped away to the edge of the lake.

On the two following days Tamid and Brin searched again, south of the lake. They went as far as the river which flowed east under the high peaks but again found no trace. Mirin was out each day, watching for their return, but as soon as they had reported he turned away alone. In the evening of this second day Gan followed him.

'You do not expect your sons, Mirin,' he said directly.

'They may come.'

'Mirin, you do not expect them.'

'Tamid and Brin have searched south. But they may have turned west.'

'You want us to search west?'

'It is wide. There is little time.'

They woke the following morning to find that Gan had already gone. They were anxious and angry that he had gone alone. Rano was especially distressed, for her first son was weaker than the other young men. He returned, exhausted, after dark. He had seen elk, he reported, moving west, but he could not identify them and there had been no sign of Adran and Varan. There was now only one more night to the last flake of moon.

Next morning, early, Gan spoke again to Mirin.

'You do not now expect your sons?'

Mirin turned away. His scraped face was drawn and discoloured.

'Will you say,' Gan asked, 'that they may find their own way to Mamcala?'

Mirin stared at him: at the thin face and weak eyes, at the darker skin.

'You ask hard questions, son of Rano.'

'I ask a hard man.'

'In what I cannot help I will not speak.'

'Mirin, you help when you speak.'

'And hinder when I walk.'

Gan nodded. He had known that Mirin was thinking of how he would delay the family, on the return across the mountains to the caves. But now the return could no longer be delayed. There was an unwillingness to talk about it, among the others, but Gan took Sarn aside and spoke quietly. At last Sarn gathered the family and spoke. Adran and Varan had gone far for the bull but each night they would be watching the moon. When they were ready they would make their own way to Mamcala, but now the family must leave.

'I will not leave my sons,' Telo cried.

'They are not here, my sister. They will not return here. They will return to Mamcala.'

'You cannot know that.'

'For the safety of all we must leave for Mamcala,' Sarn said, stubbornly.

Telo cried and Rano comforted her. The others gave their voices with Sarn, except Mirin, who did not speak.

'Mirin,' Telo cried, 'these are our only sons, our only blood.'

'I know it, Telo.'

Early next morning, while the lake was still covered in mist, they set out to climb to Birch Pass. Mirin had left even earlier, while it was still dark. They caught and passed him on the track. He waved them on. He would come late to the first camp, by the stony river Karona. Each morning the pattern was repeated. It took them three days at the pace of the children and of Mirin. From noon on the third day Tamid and Brin ran ahead, to clear the caves of any animals that had lodged through the summer. Gan walked with Telo, often talking to her, though she barely replied. It was now very cold, with a piercing wind from the north. The sky was grey and heavy. When they turned, as always, for their last look back at the mountains, they saw only a black wall against the dark sky and there were snow clouds gathering. The bright lake and the long days of summer were now a world away.

There was soon deep snow around the caves but they were warm inside and had good food from the elk. The river below the caves was not frozen and there were fish to catch. The men, except Mirin, went out each evening to set traps and cover them with handfuls of snow. Each day they expected the return of Pirin and his company, but the new moon came and there was no sign of them. Nor was there any sign of Adran and Varan.

Telo now hardly spoke. She had shrunk into grief and seemed to have aged many years. Rano stayed close to her, talking and comforting. Each day they watched Mirin on the terrace, busily making traps and new tools. At night they were often awake when he got up and moved around, to ease the pain in his leg. Once Telo followed him and saw him standing at the mouth of the cala, wrapped in his long furs. He reached out his left hand as if to grasp the waxing moon, its rough edge on that side. Soon he would be reaching his right hand, as the moon waned. With the deeper snows there would now be no return. Pirin and his company would have found a cave above the seariver. Adran and Varan, far from winter shelter, were now almost certainly lost.

As the moon ended, Rano spoke with Telo. While the men were out trapping and the girls and children down at the river they went together to Mirin.

'Mirin,' Rano said, 'your blood is now lost.'

He stared but did not answer.

'In the family now,' Rano said, 'there is only your blood.'

He looked away from her to Telo.

'It is true,' Telo said. 'There are the children of Sarn and Rano, but no others for new blood.'

'There is Gan,' Mirin said.

'Gan is half blood to Liri and Pani.'

'Then there can be no new blood. Until Pirin and his company return.'

'And if they do not return?'

Mirin looked away.

'You brought strong blood,' Rano said, 'when you came to Telo from the seariver.'

'But that is finished,' Mirin said.

'It is finished with me,' Telo said quietly.

Mirin looked into her face. He put down his half-finished trap and walked away.

On the next day Rano and Telo approached him again.

'We have spoken,' Telo said. 'We have agreed.'

'What have you agreed?'

'That Pani should bear the new blood.'

'There can be no new blood. Did you not explain it to me? To keep the flow of blood there must be the blood of others. And there are now no others.'

'There is one other, Mirin.'

'What other?'

'It is yourself.'

Mirin looked from Telo to Rano. Rano smiled.

'I am old, I am a cripple,' he said.

'Your blood is strong and other.'

'But Pani is a child.'

'She is ready for new blood.'

'I could never do it. She would run into the snow before lying with me.'

'She would not run into the snow.'

'She would not want it.'

'No. She wants Varan. But Varan is lost.'

'Then we must wait. She must wait. Until another year.'

Telo looked into his face. She was crying. She moved and put her arm across his shoulders. He looked away.

'I bore you strong sons, Mirin, but now they are lost. You are too strong, my husband, to be without sons.'

He did not answer. Rano waited and then spoke.

'We need your blood, Mirin. You were always the strongest.'

He did not answer her but turned to Telo.

'The new blood would not be yours, my Telo.'

'It is so. I would wish it. But I would look on your new son.'

He got up and limped away. Below him, along the river, the

young women and the children were crouching at the edge of the water, looking down into its bright flow. Tasa, tasa, the flow of the winter river. He put his hand to his eyes. His heart was beating fast, as at the climax of a hunt. He again turned away.

On the next day, when the men had gone to their traps, Telo and Rano kept Pani with them, while Liri and the children went for water and firewood. Mirin, working on a spearhead on the terrace, saw them together and at once moved away. Dragging his leg, he forced himself upwind along the ridge from the caves. He barely knew what he was doing. His thinking was frozen and he could not breathe easily. All he knew was the need for distance from the women talking at the mouth of the cave.

The mothers sat with Pani at the fire. Rano had brightened the flames with cuts of pine.

'You are pretty from the summer,' Telo said, looking at Pani. Pani smiled. She had carefully braided her long dark hair, as she did every morning. Her eyes were bright and her cheeks glowed red in the cold air.

'You are ready to have a child,' Rano said.

'You said that I would. When Varan comes.'

'Varan will not come now.'

'He will come. I know Varan. He is strong.'

'Pani, you do not know those mountains in winter. No man can live in them. No man can even pass through them when the deep snows have come.'

Pani looked between them.

'Then I must wait. Perhaps they went south to the seariver. They will be with Pirin.'

'I do not expect it, Pani. And we are now so few, we must have the new blood.'

Pani stared at her mother.

'Before Varan comes?'

'Yes.'

'But the blood does not allow it.'

'There is blood that allows it.'

Pani jumped up. Her eyes were wide and staring.

'There is no blood. You have told me.'

Rano got up and put her arm around her daughter's waist.

'If Varan comes back, my dear, there can be another child.'

'No. I am waiting for Varan.'

Telo got up from the fire. She rubbed her aching back with her hand.

'We live as a family, Pani. The men hunt and trap, but they do not eat where they kill. They bring the meat back to us, as we women bring shoots and berries. We live as a family, we share within the blood. If it were not so we should die, for we can none of us live on our own, looking only to ourselves.'

'I know this, Telo. But I will wait for Varan. He too is of the family.'

'Yet while he is not here the men must still trap, the women and children still gather. We cannot wait until he may come. We can hope but we cannot wait. We must live as we are and as the family needs.'

Pani looked round the terrace, as if trapped. Then she shouted at Rano.

'But it just isn't possible. There is no man.'

'Yes,' Telo said, 'there is a man.'

'It is Mirin, my child,' Rano said, and tightened her arm round Pani's waist.

Pani said nothing. She was pale with shock. She widened her large eyes and stared not at her mother but at Telo.

'He has lost his only sons,' Telo said.

Pani still stared at her.

'If you had seen him, Pani, when he came from the seariver. He was the tallest and strongest man I had seen, taller and stronger than I had imagined a man could be. And though he was fierce and fast in the hunt, he was shy and gentle when he came to me.'

Pani could still not speak.

'You see him now,' Telo said, 'old and grey and crippled. I see him like that and the tears sting me. But when I am near him I know the spirit is still there. He is still the strong Mirin, the brave one.'

Pani licked her dry lips.

'You cannot want this, Telo.'

'But I am too old to bear his children, yet we need his blood.'

'You cannot want it.'

Telo smiled.

'He does not want it,' she said.

Pani stared.

'*He* does not want it?'

'No, for he has turned from his life, like a wounded beast. He would crawl away, not to be seen.'

Pani looked away. She was silent for some time. Then she pulled away from her mother and walked round the fire.

'When Varan comes back . . .' she said, looking across at the older women.

'Yes,' Rano said. 'When he comes back, yes.'

Pani looked down at the fire. With the edge of her boot she pushed a half-burned pine cut into the firebed. It flared at once. Telo looked away up the ridge. She could see the dark figure of Mirin by a rock under the pines. It was beginning to snow again, in soft heavy flakes. She glanced at Rano and then set off up the ridge. Rano walked with her daughter into the big cave.

Mirin heard Telo coming. He swung round and straightened himself. Telo looked into his face, then went close and put her arm around him.

'Come with me.'

He shifted, impatiently. He would never allow anyone to help him to walk.

'Come close. You can lean on me.'

He did not move. As she looked up she saw tears on his scraped cheeks.

'Come,' she said again, and suddenly he was moving and letting her help to take his weight. The wind gusted and the snow blew into their faces. Across the dip towards the lookhill the snow was falling into rising thick mist, and all the country beyond them was now hidden. Telo smiled as she felt Mirin moving beside her. She took the weight but felt it only as closeness.

When they reached the terrace the pine cut was still burning. Its flame darted and coloured in the snow of the gusting wind. Telo held Mirin close as they entered the cave. There was a guttering light in the outer chamber but the inner cave was dark. Rano came from the darkness and reached her hand to Mirin. He had to sit and swing his leg to get over the low wall under the hides. Telo was close behind him.

Rano moved away as Telo held Mirin's shoulder and eased him down to the wide bed. She bent over him and kissed his lips. She went on kissing until at last he responded. She reached out to Pani, who was lying beyond them. She lifted Pani's arm and put it over Mirin's shoulder.

'My love,' she said, kissing Mirin again. Then in the darkness she was gone. Mirin felt the warm arm around him. His eyes closed and his body moved.

Telo and Rano were at the fire when Pani came out. She crouched beside them. Nothing was said. Through the thickening snow they could hear the shouts of Liri and the children coming up from the river.

Cara Daughter of Cara

◆

All the families came to the lake that midsummer. The time of Mirin and of Telo, and of the child of Pani, was far back and forgotten. Over three thousand years, in a country becoming kinder, the hunting had continued but the small families living at the very edge of survival had grown and extended until they were large and prosperous, each with its own hunting district. In the cycle of their years the families met, in succession, for the midsummer feast at Locara on the lake, at Carsab on the beach below the cave on the seariver, and at Arcala by the riverjoin south of the old inland caves. The families from the seariver were much the most numerous: the Pirans and the Fishers and the Old Fire people: more than two hundred in all. There was also the family from the western hills, the big-boned people whom the others called the Bears. In their own place, this year, were the two families who hunted the Black Mountains and their valleys.

The Bears, as always, were the first to arrive. It was a joke that the Bears never knew exactly when it was midsummer and so had to come in time for the others to tell them. It was also said that their life was so rough, in the bleak western hills, that they became sour and longed for the honey of the richer lands. Yet they were strong, powerful people. Whenever there was throwing and wrestling it was always a Bear who won. Their gifts of bear and beaver skins were abundant and generous. The Black Mountain families looked askance as these skins were exchanged for shell necklaces and amulets from the seariver families, in their pretty but slight forms. The Black Mountain gifts, customarily, were of deerskin, of which their cutting and sewing were very fine.

It was exciting as they assembled and the first news was passed.

The weather was warm and sunny, and the days before the feast melted into each other, in easy and unhurried sitting and talking, over the wide grassy slopes. It was a time of such happiness, without pressures, that it would be an effort to move to the different rhythm of the feast-day itself, though they all knew that this was why they had met. As the Bears and the Black Mountain families sat above the glittering lake, with the flowers around them abundant – golden buttercups, stiff-stalked blue centaurea, wide spreads of pink thrift, pure and delicate white avens, brilliant sprays of blue valerian – they looked up from talking and saw one of the seariver families arriving, filing through the pass, the sun glinting on their shells. It was a time of certainty and acceptance, a resting time, in a life which only the pressures of hunting had made possible. It could not stay like this. They must part again, scatter to their lands, hunt their own territories, live in their own ways so that winter and spring could be survived. But for the moment it was enough that they had all come together, that there were gifts and plenty, and that their ways were confirmed. The work of the feast-day was of a different kind, for the years still to come.

Great fires were lit on the evening before the feast, at hearths on the eastern edge of the lake, facing the setting sun and with the mountains behind them. It was now that the girls must begin their long dance, in rings of each family moving from fire to fire. The young men squatted in their ranks in the outer rings, looking in at the dancers. In the long, gentle midsummer dusk, and in the shifting lights and shadows from the slow-burning fires, the rhythms of the dancers were relaxed and softening. Many of the older men and women sitting beyond the young men, talking quietly or chewing and listening, felt their eyelids heavy at the edge of the firesmoke, and the slowly moving figures beyond them were blurred. When full darkness came there were many who slept, but still the girls, in their short doeskin tunics, must sustain the slow rings of the dance, and the young men must squat in their bands, with the tools of the hunt at their sides.

It was an early dawn, in a pale clear sky. Now the horns were sounded, at each fire, and the girls ended their dancing and moved away to the birch groves beyond the older men. The young men stood, stamping and running on the spot, flexing their arms. There were shouts for silence and then the second horns sounded. Fifteen at once raced away, and the midsummer hunt, on which so much depended, had begun.

Cara daughter of Cara watched the boys lope away. She was tired and must try to sleep but she was still too excited. She was one of fifteen girls, from the six families, who had been named for wedding this midsummer. Through the long dance she had watched the fifteen boys who had been named, as they squatted in front of the ranks. By noon, when the boys must return, each with his catch to qualify for the wedding, she must be washed in the lake and have her hair dressed with flowers.

Cara knew that by custom she had no real choice among the boys, though she could refuse once, and with enough determination, against heavy disapproval, even twice. It was always the boys who chose first, in the order of success of their hunting.

Yet still in the pale dawn Cara daughter of Cara could imagine the best of days. Her mother and sister had pointed to a yellow-haired boy from the Pirans, called Marus. He was already bearded and muscled, jumping and running beyond the others, laughing in his successes. And indeed he had stared at her, followed her with his eyes, in each ring at the second fire. All the other girls were saying that he was certain to win in the hunt, though nothing was ever certain in that: a boy might find a big red stag in his first wood and be lucky.

But Cara daughter of Cara was not thinking of Marus. Though she had given no sign, the boy she had watched was the only young Bear in the naming, very tall and still thin, as if he had outgrown himself. His name was Ral. He was like all the Bears, shy, slow, quiet. When she had tried to catch his eye from the ring at the third fire he was always looking down, and his fist was clenched on his spearhandle, as if at any time he must be ready to leap and attack. None of the other girls spoke of him, so that if it had been the girls choosing there would have been no difficulty. Yet perhaps, clenching his spear, he would do well in the hunt. And if he did not win there was still a chance, for there would be several girls, she was certain, chosen before her: the three girls of the Old Fire people, who were agreed by everyone to be the prettiest, with their braided and shining black hair and red cheeks, and then the tall, lovely, dark-red-haired girl from the Bears, who by the law could not be chosen by the Bear Ral.

Cara daughter of Cara was the only girl named this midsummer from the Saran family who hunted west and north from the Black Mountains. The family had wished there could be others, for they needed young men. The hunting was still fair in their district but there had been a run of bad winters, around the time when Cara daughter of Cara was born, and again in the last four years, when seven of the older men, five still in their mid-twenties, had died. In these colder winters, with the long months of snow reducing the game, all the inland families had declined while the seariver families, with their shellfish and sea creatures, were getting more numerous all the time.

It was sometimes said among the inland families, following stories handed down from the old ones, that the trees were eating the hunting. Indeed in every generation there were more trees: the birch stands spreading widely; clumps of high pine, oak and hazel becoming common on the midslopes of the mountains; alder and willow thickening around the lake and along the rivers. It was still an open running world, with the summer flowers everywhere, but the Black Mountain families were not sure that it could last. They looked to Cara daughter of Cara to bring them, at this wedding, the best and strongest of the young men. Yet that was always how they thought and it was not how she thought, though she could never say so.

For there would always, she knew, be hunting, there would always be enough. It was as they got old, in their thirties and the few sour old ones past forty, that they started looking backward and forward, foretelling and grumbling, because the only life worth having was slipping away from them. They would then of course try to make the young ones think in their old ways. But every one of them, after all, had had their own real day: the women when they had been girls dancing, in the long slow rings at the fires; when they had been washed and flowered and had waited for the hunting boys to come back, with the blood on their shoulders, carrying or dragging their game; and the men who had been boys, in the freshness of the hunt, loping so easily in the midsummer dawn, in the thrill of that day when they could hunt against the others and come back to choose among the waiting girls.

For that was the high peak of life, and everyone knew it. It was only as they went slowly down from that peak that they learned the other kind of talking: about the dead; about old stories of spirits; about the weather and the winters; about the changing game; about the trees; about the faults and strange ways of the outer peoples. As they lost their teeth they could not bite into life any more. They could only chew and roll and pick at it, old gristle words where they had once shouted and laughed.

This talk was going on now, among the women who were guarding and preparing the girls. She heard the name of Marus mentioned several times, but more often the names were of the old ones. There was a long story of a burying: the grey head of the oldest of the Pirans, Navar, which had to be struck and struck again to be severed from the body, and then the difficulty of flexing the stiff old legs.

Cara daughter of Cara let this talk drift past her. If this was life she would sleep until it was time to wake for a new life: not the red ochre of the burying but the fresh blood on the shoulders of the young men bringing their game. They would dive into the lake and wash the sweat and blood from their bodies. Then they would come naked up to the birch grove and the girls would stand in line. The boys would approach one by one, in their order, and each would offer his hand to a girl. It would be very quiet suddenly. Ral would offer his hand, stretching the long thin arm. There would be blue valerian and pink thrift in her hair.

'Cara! Cara!'

It was her mother's voice, and the hand on her shoulder was shaking her roughly. She opened her eyes, slowly. The sun was high in the sky, but not yet at noon.

'There is time,' she said, sleepily.

'No. The first are already back.'

Cara sat up quickly. It was true. There were already several boys down by the lake with their catches. The men were gathered around them, pointing and talking.

'Who?' she asked.

'It is certain to be Marus,' her mother said excitedly. 'He was the first back and with so fine a stag that it had to be cut to be carried.'

'Yes, Marus, of course,' Cara said.

She got up and walked with her mother to the part of the lake where the girls must be washed. Most of the other girls were already there, laughing and splashing in the clear water. Cara stared at the girl from the Bears, whose name was Lasa. The skin of her body, which the tunic had covered, was the whitest she had seen. It looked very strange among the warm brown skins of the others, and the dark-red hair stood out sharply against it. Lasa was very thin, with small breasts. Cara went on staring at her, thinking of Ral, until her mother roused her and she was ducked and washed quickly. She did not want to splash and talk with the others, and she especially kept away from the Old Fire girls, who were already too easy and sure of themselves. The others were teasing Lasa, who looked so different from them. Lasa stood very still, with a fixed shy smile. Cara did not approach her. Her mother, impatiently, washed her again, and they walked back to the birch grove.

There was shouting down by the lake. Other boys had come back. They were now nearly all in but Cara was almost sure that Ral was not among them. It did not matter, there was still time. And perhaps he was only behind because his catch was so big. Then she forgot Ral, forgot them all, when she saw the flowers that her mother had prepared for her. They were not just the thrift and sprays of blue valerian that Cara had imagined, but perfect white avens and fine red rock-roses, the rare ones that must have been picked high up, in the scree under Waterfall Rock that morning while she was sleeping. And she could not have conceived the arrangement that her mother had made of the flowers, in a high open chaplet. As it was tried on it fitted exactly. It felt so beautiful that Cara wanted to take it off and look at it again. But her mother held her hands and smiled at her and told her to leave it in place. Cara smiled and rested. With such beautiful flowers nothing could now go wrong. It would be good whatever might happen. Let the others reckon and wonder.

The girls were all around her now, washed and with flowers in their hair, the warm sun drying their bodies. There was a lot of talking and laughing, and Cara began laughing with the others. It was getting near time. In the talking and pointing by the lake the order was nearly settled. Perhaps Ral was there, perhaps not; there were too many now to see. And they were looking up at the sun, and the hornmen were standing ready. An old woman, who had been at the lake, came hurrying back. The boys were there, she said, and Marus and then one of the Old Fire people had won, with stags. Only one boy had not come back. It was the young Bear, and it had been decided not to wait for him.

Cara daughter of Cara heard the old woman's words. None of the others seemed to take any notice of the last thing she had said. There was only the excitement that the boys were ready and would now be coming forward.

Cara clenched her fists. She scarcely understood what was happening to her. There was a sharp pain in her chest and her head was throbbing with some strange noise. She looked desperately around to find some look, some feeling, that she could share. But there was only the excited smiling and whispering of the readiness for the procession of boys.

Hardly knowing what she was doing, but driven as if by a sudden danger, Cara put up her hands to the chaplet in her hair and began tearing with her fingers at the flowers. There was a scream from her mother, who rushed and held her arms, pinching hard at the flesh. Cara struggled but then others were holding her and her mother was shouting over and over: 'Will you shame me, daughter? Will you shame me?' Cara did not understand what the words meant, only that there was shouting all around her and angry fingers pinching her arms and still this noise, this strange noise, in her head. As she struggled, uselessly, to get loose and tear at the flowers, there was a sudden darkness in her eyes and she went limp in their arms. The other women stood back and her mother bent over her as she fell to the grass under the high white birch.

In the moments after Cara daughter of Cara had fainted, the horns were blown at the lakeside. The procession of young hunters, each followed by men of his family, formed up and began moving, slowly, towards the birch grove. The women who had crowded round Cara rushed back to their places, and the girls stood forward in line, each beside the gifts from her people that went with the choice. Cara's mother and her two younger sisters were left alone, attending to her. She was very pale, lying on her back with her eyes closed, the avens and red rock-roses disordered in her thick brown hair. As the chanting began from the procession, she moved and cleared her throat. She opened her eyes and looked up. For some moments the eyes were dead and then life came into them and the blood rushed into her face. Her fists clenched and she rolled over on the grass and cried, her whole body shaking. When her mother put a hand on her shoulder, she shook it off roughly, sobbing out of control.

The men of the families halted, and there was a deep silence. The boys stood forward, and then Marus, carrying the head of his stag, stepped towards the line of girls. He was smiling broadly. As he came near the girl he moved his head from side to side, looking playfully along the line as if he would take them all. But then he walked confidently to Sila, the tallest of the Old Fire girls. He put down the stag's head and extended his hand. She was already smiling, as if it had been agreed between them. She took his hand, and the people clapped.

Then the Old Fire boy came forward and chose the dark-red-haired Bear girl, who took his hand without smiling. The other boys came forward in turn. There was one refusal, when a Fisher girl turned away from a Black Mountains boy. He flushed angrily but quickly chose a Piran. Among the last boys the game was less. The last of them all, a Fisher boy, carried only a duck, and there were laughs among the men.

Then the wedding was complete, and groups were formed around each couple, and there was general talking and laughing.

Cara daughter of Cara had cried herself out, but she still lay face down, refusing to face the others. Her mother's brother and his brothers had come through to stand above her, and there was angry talk between them and the women. Although the midsummer sun was warm, Cara felt cold as ice. She shivered as she lay, biting into the grass.

'That Bear!' one of the men said, contemptuously.

'If he even comes!'

'Perhaps he met a bear,' her mother's brother said, laughing.

'That would stretch him a bit more, the great lanky good-for-nothing.'

There was a shout from beyond the couples, and then there was pointing. Several people stood up to look.

'It's the Bear all right,' Cara heard a man saying.

'And with nothing,' another said.

There was a general movement to look. Cara, left alone, sat up. She put her hands to her hair and pulled out the broken flowers. She wiped the back of her hands under her eyes.

There was much talk and laughing now. As the people looked along the lake they saw the tall thin figure, moving very slowly.

There was nothing on his shoulders. But now they saw him stop and bend down to the water.

'He is hurt,' a man said.

'But he must still return alone,' said a deep, stern voice, one of the Bear men.

Cara got up quietly. She moved across the birch grove, away from the crowded people. Standing behind a tree at the edge of the grove she looked along the lakeside. The tall thin figure was moving again, but very slowly. Wiping her eyes and staring, Cara saw that he was holding both hands at his right shoulder. She stared again. There was something moving in the water beside him, something big and dark.

It was a very slow coming. As his walk could be seen, he was limping badly. But it seemed also that he was hauling the dark shape in the water, his hands at his shoulder. He stopped several times and bent over it, as if to free it from the bank.

Cara watched breathlessly. She wanted to run and help him with what he was dragging, but she knew that she must stay and she was in any case ashamed. Very slowly and painfully he made his way round to the place at the lakeside where the men had been assembled. They streamed down towards him. There was loud talking and pointing. Cara, left alone, went back to where she had been standing with the other girls. She picked up a few unbroken flowers, and arranged them in her hair. He had come back, with his game, and she would stand and wait.

There was a long delay. Then she saw her mother and her sisters and her mother's brother and his brothers, walking in a group towards her. Behind them, as they came nearer, she saw the tall thin figure of Ral, with two Bear men behind him. He was carrying what looked like boar tusks. He was limping badly. As they came nearer she could see that his left leg, from above the knee, was running with fresh blood.

The men stopped. Cara's mother and sisters came forward. Her mother looked at her, sternly.

'He is hurt?' Cara asked.

'By his second boar,' her mother said, unsmiling.

'He is badly hurt?'

'It is a wound. It will heal.'

'But he had come to choose?'

'He is too late to choose but he has come.'

Cara smiled. She stroked her hair over her shoulders.

'What was he dragging in the water?'

'He is strange,' her mother said. 'He killed a gilt early. Any sensible boy would have come back, but not him. He pushed on and was stalking a sow when a boar went for him. He slipped and the boar gashed his leg but he killed it. All he could think about then was to bring back the boar and the gilt. He wanted to show he was good enough, he said. But since the two couldn't be carried he had to cut poles for a raft and then load them and drag the raft down the lake. It took him much longer than he reckoned. He was certain that his choice would have gone.'

Cara stared past her mother at the group of men and the tall boy among them.

'Then he won't want to see the only one who is left.'

'He can still hardly believe it. It was you, Cara, he would have chosen if he had come in time.'

Cara looked away, feeling the blood in her face.

'Then he will come now and choose?'

'The men are against it because he did not come in time. And they say he might go lame and be no use to the family.'

'Then what is to be done?'

'I have said that I will tell you. And I have looked at his wound. It is only a tear in the flesh. With care it will heal. But I have also to tell you, Cara, that you are free to refuse.'

'Refuse him!' Cara cried.

Her mother looked into her face and then smiled.

'When you heard that he was missing?' she asked, putting her fingers up to the untidy flowers in her daughter's hair.

'Yes. Of course.'

'Then it must be, daughter.'

Cara smiled.

Her mother turned and beckoned. The men stood aside and Ral came slowly forward, trying not to limp but with the blood running freely down his leg. He put the boar tusks on the grass in front of Cara, and held out his hand. She took his hand firmly.

'But now you must sit,' she said quickly. 'Your wound must be dressed.'

Ral said nothing. There was a dead pain in his eyes and the sweat was standing out in beads on his pale forehead. There were red weals of the dragging thong over his right shoulder.

'Sit with me,' Cara said, and moved him slowly down to the grass beside her. He kept tight hold of her hand.

The women moved around them and began washing the wound. Then they laid fresh damp moss on it, trying to staunch the bleeding. Cara took a handful of damp moss and wiped his face. He drew back slightly but kept looking into her eyes.

It was not the day she had imagined; the choice from the procession; the gifts and the talking; the preparing of meat for the feast; the wild dancing of that night. It would happen for all the others but she had only this tall, wounded boy, whose midsummer dance must wait. She still held his hand tightly, looking down at the lake where the preparations were starting. It was not what she had imagined but she felt its rightness, looking into his pale serious face.

'Ral.'

'Cara daughter of Cara,' he said, and tightened his grip on her hand.

Incar's Fire and Aron's Pig

◆

Incar sat leaning back on his hands, on the layered sandstone which overlooked the northern valleys. It was the day of the third night of the moon of the leaf, but the woods which filled the steep valleys below him were brown and bare, in a thin and hungry light. On his way to the ridge he had seen, close, the beginnings of growth in the birches. He had yellowed his fingers on the early hazel catkins. But it would be the end of this moon before there was any real growth. There was no movement at all in the grove of durmast oaks, where old and shrivelled brown leaves still clung to their twigs. The light of these days was extending but the trees moved much slower than the people.

Incar remembered the words of Imar brother of his mother, many suns ago when Incar was a boy. 'The trees,' old Imar said, 'are eating the people.' Incar had not understood, but Imar had explained. In the days of the old mothers there had been fewer trees in these valleys. The animals had grazed over open grass. On the wide grassland below the plateau, from Curve River to the Ice Lake, there had been as many flowers as there were stars in the night sky. It had been easy hunting as the herds grazed.

Then from mother to mother the trees had closed in. The hunters of the old days would not know these valleys. Even to see their true shapes meant climbing to the ridges. For the valleys were filled now with trees, like leafmoon lakes. Incar remembered and repeated the words of Imar, for in his own life he had seen it. Every year there were more trees, birch and hazel springing fast into every clearing, and the oak groves extending. In winter men could move through these woods, but in summer the close growth made every movement difficult and the animals of the hunt were hard to see and take aim at.

Incar smiled, covering his eyes. He was remembering the day of Imar and the boar and the fish.

For it was a law of the hunting of pig that the hunter must not eat what he had himself killed. The law was known as the law of Maro, who had not made the law but had shown why it was good and must be obeyed. Greedy and boastful, hunting at leafmoon when the pangs are sharp, Maro had separated from the others and had killed a young sow. Overcome by hunger he had taken his knife and slit its belly and begun to eat the raw flesh. There would be plenty to carry back to the others, for roasting and sharing.

He ate his fill and then carried the rest of the carcase. He was pleased and only laughed when the others tried to shame him. For did he not bring back more meat than anyone else in the family? Had he not now brought more on his own back than any other single man? The law that they were mumbling was an old woman's story. It was not a law for hunters. Let them use their jaws on something better, like this good pigmeat he had brought them. But the others did not eat the meat of the sow on which Maro had broken the law. Maro laughed and ate more of it himself.

Then within a moon he was a changed man. He ate as greedily as ever but every day his body got thinner. The others watched and knew that the breaking of the law was eating his body. It made no difference now that he was being given lawful food, in the family sharing. What satisfied the others was never enough for him, and still his body was wasting away.

Maro did not die for some years but his body hungered into weakness. In his last nights his spirit was changed. He confessed that he was wrong to have broken the law. He had learned from his sickness that it was a good law. For there was no other reason, that anyone could think of, why so strong a hunter should waste away from the time of breaking the law of the sharing of food.

Thus the law of Maro was settled among the hunters. But now Incar remembered also the day when Imar the strong had cried while keeping the law. There had been bad hunting in the thick woods above the lake. Only Imar had killed: a young boar. He then waited for the others to kill, but they failed. All they could do was carry Imar's boar to the camp. Imar followed them, miserably. The women and children, young Incar among them, watched their return. Imar, proud and upright went away from the hearth. The best parts of the boar were cooked and shared by the others.

It was a day already close to young Incar, for he had begged Imar to allow him to go with the men on the hunt, and Imar had refused. Angry with everyone, Incar had left the camp and gone down to Curve River. By luck he had caught a kelt salmon: brown – mottled but weak after spawning. His mother Carina had wrapped it in leaves, waiting to see what the men brought from hunting. Seeing Imar leave the hearth she took the salmon from the leaves and cut it open and gutted it. Incar smiled, seeing every movement of her long fingers holding the tiny flint blade. On the leaves she made a paste with two small bird's eggs and the last of the stored hazel nuts. She then crushed and mixed in herbs. Incar remembered the sharp scent of thyme. She filled the gutted salmon with the paste, and laid it on a hot stone by the fire. She had a small wooden bowl of water and with a wooden ladle she sprinkled the fish to keep it moist, and several times turned it. The strong smell of the boar, roasting on a spit above the fire, was heavy in the air. But she leaned, holding back her hair, to smell the fish, and at last smiled that it was ready. She wanted to send Incar but when he would not go she went herself to fetch Imar. She drew him back, holding his hand. She squatted and cut a piece of the salmon. She held it in front of his face. He smiled and ate it, rolling it in his mouth. It was the next day before he came to Incar and thanked him for catching it. But Incar was happy, since from that day he was allowed to hunt with the men.

'The trees are eating the people,' strong Imar had then said. His words had been right. There was an abundance of wood for fires and tools and stakes and shelters. There was wood to carve and shape. But in the vast and spreading growth it was hard to use the old spears and flickstones and increasingly difficult even to get in arrowshots, through the dense bushes and trees. Birch, pine and oak; hazel and elm; buckthorn and dogwood; bramble: all were like traps to catch hunters.

Incar looked far out, watching the wind. It was blowing from winterset, below summer west. He was trying to fit the wind to the shapes of the valleys, and to the spurs and low ridges which crossed and briefly turned it. He was looking also for places where it ran out beyond the trees to the slopes above the treeline. He was searching for a place where he could set and start a fire.

For there must now be a fire, to blaze through the dry winter woods, to burn fiercely and make clearings, where the grass would thicken and the animals gather. Yet he must align it, by the wind, where it would run into open grass, so that it would at last blow out.

He thought he could see it. He moved his hand at arm's length to follow the line. But still he hesitated. Fire was dangerous and once set would go its own way, like a beast running. There was this one best place, not far from the big oak grove, on the other side from where the family had settled. If this wind held it could be done.

Everyone was up at first light. Incar climbed the low ridge. He wet his forehead from his tongue and turned to make sure of the wind. It was still blowing, not strongly, from winterset. The older women and the smallest children were to stay at the shelters. But all the others except Incar and the frail boy Aron, the child of Incar's own body with the river girl Aril, must climb the main ridge and walk along it in sight on the skyline. From Horn Point they must go down to the second low ridge. They must be there, standing and watching, before Incar set the fire. He would not go down to the fireset until he had seen them move from the skyline.

The wind freshened while Incar and Aron stood watching, but its line was still good. The others looked small now, thin dark figures along the ridge. Aron was watching the figures intently. Incar saw that his lips were moving.

'Are you saying the words, boy?'

'No, Incar, I am counting.'

'Yet we know their number.'

'We know the number who left.'

Incar looked down at him. He was a strange boy, always with a frown on his face, as if in pain from his frail body though he said it was not that. He spoke very little in the ordinary way, but it was as if he stored his words. For at times, when the others were busy or inattentive, a great flow of words would come out of him, about something he had noticed and was trying to explain. He spoke often in ways that made the others laugh. It was of course hard for him that, too weak for hunting, he could not lead a proper life. Yet he showed no signs of envying the other boys when they were wrestling and running and chasing. Even his eyes did not follow them, for he worked long days at shaping the tiniest flints for arrowheads and on other days would be somewhere staring at the ground or drawing in the earth with a stick. At times he spread pebbles where he was drawing in the earth and arranged and rearranged them into childish groups of his own. Rana mother of Incar had shown him the counting of pebbles for the moon and the season and he had followed this eagerly, but still also he arranged his own shapes.

'Those who left are together,' Incar said.

Aron looked up, frowning.

'Incar, there were four hands and three.'

'As I said. Together.'

'There are still four hands and three.'

Incar turned away, impatiently. He looked up at the far ridge. The leading figures had halted, at the rocks of Horn Point. They would now gather to go down. Incar moved to the fireset. He had brought from the hearth a small branch which had been left to smoulder at the edge of the fire. It was still warm to the touch but had no colour or smoke. He took the hardened and pointed birch firestick and placed it between his open palms. He began rolling it rapidly, with its point in a hole in the old branch. He had dry grass ready as the smoke slowly rose, in a thin thread. Aron, frowning as he watched, laid the grass loosely around the hole. It curled and then blackened. A small flame ran out at the end of a stalk. Aron put on more grass, so that it lay loose. As it briefly flamed, he added curls of white birch bark which took the flame, and then stubs of pine bark. Incar withdrew the stick. The fire now burned brightly, in its set among the stones.

Incar looked again at the ridge. It was now bare of figures, and he could see movement down towards the trees. He breathed deeply, walking back to the fire. It was always a terrible moment, to set a fire beyond a hearth. Only a few could be found who would take it into their hands. He stared at the small fire of bark. It was like watching a harmless animal – a big-tailed squirrel – and enjoying its movements. Laid in a row beyond it were the resinous pine torches, to be set in the line he had chosen. It would be easy to pick up each torch and light it and carry it to the clumps of dried bracken and bramble that were ready along the line. But then at once the world would change. It would be like walking, unarmed, into a pack of wolves, who would rise and snap in so fast a movement that it would be beyond any man to control or keep level with it. Once the first torch was set, the fire would be beyond him. It would burn fast in the bracken and bramble but then, with a roar, and with an angry cracking of branches, it would lift and run into the dry winter wood. There would be smoke and burning fragments rising against the sky, and the great pack of beasts would be loose.

Incar breathed deeply again. He was saying, silently, the old words of the fire:

> 'Leap, but leap away
> Burn, but burn from us
> Rise, but not against us
> Eat, but eat only your own.'

Aron, frowning, had licked his fingers and was turning his hand for the wind. Incar looked down at him.

'Yes?'

'Incar yes, good.'

'The words are said.'

'The line of the wind is good.'

Incar took the first torch and lit it. He carried it, slowly, to the farthest clump of bracken and bramble. He breathed deeply again and then plunged the torch in the clump. It caught at once but he did not stay to watch. He must run and set all the torches to the clumps. Each time he ran back, Aron held a torch ready but unlighted. He was too young to be allowed to handle fire.

Incar ran till he was breathless. All the clumps were now burning. It was still only a line of small fires, like a line of hearths, but slowly, as he watched, these were spreading, and then one seemed to leap into a thicket of thorn, and there was the first growl of the change. A brief gust of wind swirled the smoke and then the flames were running and rising and a heavier black smoke was thickening to a cloud. The growls became roars and the running was everywhere. Flames leaped high through the rising smoke and then suddenly fell back to it, before leaping again. There were sharp cracks of small branches burning, and then, at last, a deeper single roar.

Incar breathed out deeply. Aron, close beside him, began coughing on drifting smoke. They moved back, watching. Incar took his bow and fitted an arrow for any creature that might run out. Aron, too weak to draw a bow, had an old throwing-stick that he had been given to play with.

There was a sudden squealing down by the river, just beyond the edge of the fire.

'Pig,' Aron shouted.

Incar ran down, his bow drawn. Aron panted behind him. The fire was licking at the edges of the river. Most of the animals would cross the water and get to safety, but some would run, frightened, this way or that along the bank. Straining to see through the smoke, Incar pointed the direction of the squealing. Then, through a clearing gust, he saw a young boar, at the very edge of the river. He aimed and loosed his arrow but as it flew the boar was slipping away downriver. He could hear other movements beyond it, and he knew that it was gone. But there was still a loud squealing. Aron, stumbling, went down to the river, just short of the blackened line of the fire. He dropped to his knees there. Incar, coming behind him, saw a very small, striped young pig which was struggling and squealing in a branch-and-thong snare. Aron looked up over his shoulder.

'Aron, did you set the snare?'

'Incar, I set it. And two others beyond, you can see, but they are empty.'

'Good boy,' Incar said. 'Here, let me finish it.'

He picked up a stone to kill the young pig.

'No,' Aron said, laying his body across it.

'Come on, move. We need it to eat.'

Aron squirmed, still covering the pig. He was frowning and very pale.

'Don't be stupid, boy. Move.'

'Incar, you must listen. There will be plenty to eat, when the others kill. There will be more than we can eat, as in all our good times.'

'Do you want to loose this little pig?'

'Incar, I do not want to loose her. For there are good times when we all catch and eat, but there are also bad times, when the hunting is hard and the animals few.'

'It is life, boy. Do you not know?'

'Incar, I know it. But I have watched and considered. We can take this young pig to our place. We can make a fence around it or we can tie it to a tree with a thong. Then through all the leafmoons it can be given food from the woods. It will grow until acorn-moon and then again be given food. Then when our bad times come there will be this large pig for us to kill and eat.'

Incar laughed.

'You're a strange one, boy. This is a game you're playing. Why should we feed a pig? The pig is to feed us.'

'Incar, it is not only this pig. If we could snare a young boar we could fence them together and they would couple and bear more pigs. There would then always be meat for us.'

Incar smiled.

'Aron,' he said, kindly, 'it is not your fault that you are sickly, and that your weakness keeps you from hunting. It is to comfort yourself that you would keep this pig.'

Aron bowed his head. The pig squealed and struggled but the snare held.

'Whether I am weak or not,' Aron said, 'there are times when the strongest and the fastest, the best men of any of you, hunt and do not find, shoot and do not kill. Then our stomachs cramp and we must crawl for voles. We must wait for eggs or nestlings, or we must stand all day in the cold rivers for fish. This is so with me weak, it would also be so with me strong.'

'It is so, Aron. It has to be so.'

'Incar, it does not have to be so. Yes, there will be hunting, for most of our food. But if we take young pigs alive there can be eating without hunting, in our bad times. And our food will be fenced and tethered beside us.'

Incar laughed. He leaned down and ruffled Aron's hair.

'Play your game, boy, if you like. I will not kill her.'

Aron smiled and rubbed his teeth.

Incar ran back up the slope. The fire was now racing through the wood, leaving blackened ground and some larger trees burning or smouldering. A huge cloud of smoke hung over the valley, along the line of the river. The smoke was whiter as it rose above the level of the trees, and then blue like a summer sky as it moved further and higher. Incar smiled. The line had held. The wind had not changed though it had dropped a little. All the work was now for the others, waiting with bows and clubs at the far edge of the wood. There would be a feast of fresh meat after the long winter. When the ashes had cooled they would go in and do some clearing. They would find places near the river where new grass would come and they would wait for animals to come to graze it. From the fear of the fire there would be fresh food to eat. And the devouring trees would for some seasons be kept away.

There was squealing again, by the river. Aron had loosed the little pig from the snare and was holding it tightly in his arms. He looked awkward and even helpless, struggling with the creature. Incar felt a strange love for the pitiable boy. It would be good to help and soothe him in his game.

'Where will you take her?' he asked.

'I shall carry her to the camp.'

'Are you sure you can manage her?'

'Incar, I will try.'

'Go on then, boy. I must walk the ridge to the others.'

Aron started back. He was holding the little pig clumsily but very close. He would be lucky, Incar thought, to get it back, and if he did it would soon get away again. But it would keep him occupied, while the others worked.

It had not been so good a kill, at the far edge of the fire, as they had expected. When Incar arrived at Cross Ridge the main fire had almost burned out, though tongues were running beyond the treeline into the smaller bushes. Two red fawns had been killed and carried to higher ground. There were also squirrels and several birds. But most of the animals that had run from the fire had veered away, seeing the men, and had splashed through the river to the unburned woods beyond. A brown bear had come through, along the riverbank, but they had left it alone.

After a rest and talk they got together for the carry. There was still a strong smell of woodsmoke, all over the valley. It followed them as they climbed to the ridge. Seen from above, the burned wood was black and smoking. Incar, coughing in the lingering smoke kept looking down at the ugly blackness. He was remembering his hesitation, his holding of his breath, before setting the fire. It had burned as he had foreseen it, looking from the ridge at the ground and the wind. But there was still a sadness and a fear in the black smoking ruin. And it would still be long to wait before the springing of new grass and the animals gathering there.

Aron was not in sight when they got back to the settlement. Remembering, much later, that he should see what had happened to him, Incar searched and at last found him behind the shelter where he lived with his mother Aril. Aron, helped by Aril, had dug a pit there, to his knee, with an antler-pick. He had driven in stakes around its edge. He had woven hazel through the stakes, as for a shelter. From the ground of the pit to the top of the hazel was the boy's own height. Down in the pit, its body caked in mud, was the small striped pig.

'When did you make this pit?' Incar asked, surprised.

'Incar, I began it when we came from the winter caves.'

'You were hoping to catch such a pig?'

'I wanted a pig, but it could have been some other.'

'You like the taste of pig?'

'I think a pig will be easy to keep.'

'It will not be easy. But why do you wish to keep it?'

'Incar, I told you. When it is leaf-fall this pig will be large, and there will be many acorns. We can keep it until our bad times.'

Incar smiled.

'Yet it is always easier to hunt, boy. Although you cannot hunt.'

'Incar, it is not always easy. You have told me this yourself.'

'When we move for the winter we must kill it.'

'Incar, yes. But if I could get a young boar, there would be new young. If we tried, we could keep our food near us. We would not need to move for the winter.'

Incar laughed and stroked the boy's hair. He was strange and pitiable, but there was no badness in him.

'Not move,' he said and again laughed. 'But it is life, Aron, to move with the seasons. It is life to move and to hunt, to go to the places that are best for us, and to walk and enjoy them. There is the warmth of the caves in winter, above the rush of the river. There is the glitter of the lake in the summer, and then the great green of the forests, the sweet air of the plateau and of the high ridges. Always, as we move, we have our mountains and our valleys, and as we move we belong to them and we feel our own life moving. It will not come for you as it came for me, when my hair was first tied and the old ones walked us to learn these shapes in our bodies. But you must hear me, Aron, for this is becoming a man. We learn these movings and these shapes to know our own lives through them.'

Aron was hanging his head.

'I know, boy,' Incar said. 'It is hard for you when we move. You are slower than our pace.'

Aron said nothing.

'But try to keep your little pig,' Incar said kindly. 'I will tell the family not to kill it.'

It was more than a moon before Incar saw Aron again. Aril said that the boy now spent most of his days fetching food for his pig, mostly roots from the edges of the woods. When he was not at this he was setting snares, trying to catch a young boar, but he had failed. Incar and Aril laughed, but there was also a sadness between them. Since Aron had grown sickly they had kept a distance from each other. They liked each other well, but the sign of weakness between them was clear.

Towards the end of the second leaf-moon Aril went to visit the river family in which she had been born. When she returned she had news. A new family had come from the seariver: strangers of another tongue. There were many of them, though the number was not certain. Their skins were very brown, their hair black. They were good hunters but also they set woven traps for fish, and in places they laid stones in eddies of the river and dammed it into pools. They were not passing through. They had come to stay, perhaps through the seasons. The old river people were worried, because there was not really the hunting to support so many more.

Incar also was worried. With the woods pressing on them, they were at their own limit, between the mountains and the caves. If new people were coming – not only these but perhaps others to follow – it would get very much harder to live. It was said that in the days of the old mothers there had been many more people, and hunting at will. The families had met regularly and had exchanged gifts. But now from all sides there was the pressure of the forests, and new people were a threat.

Yet nothing could be done about it. They must simply hunt harder. And the women must see again to the reckoning of births, to keep the family to its numbers. Incar explained this to the women, but they laughed. They had already made the new controls, instructing the girls.

Walking back from his talk with the women, Incar heard a loud shouting behind Aril's shelter. When he got there he saw several lads taunting Aron about his pig.

'It's the only female he can get,' one shouted, and one of the bigger lads was threatening to leap the fence into the pit and kill the pig for roasting.

Incar shouted them down, but they did not move away. Aron sat with his back to his fence, frowning.

'Incar, Aron can't hunt,' young Ralan said. 'So he keep this shitty little pig, all fat it is down in his pit.'

'He can keep it if he wants to,' Incar said.

'But he's mad,' Ralan shouted. 'He said we should all dig pits and make fences and catch young pigs and put them in there. He just wants to watch them at it.'

'You don't have to do what he says,' Incar said. But it was hard, trying to answer them, when they were only saying what he thought himself.

'He says he has watched them in the wood,' Ralan laughed. 'He says it lasts a long time, the old boar won't get off.'

'It's true,' Aron cried.

'That's all he can manage,' Ralan said. 'Watching pigs at it.'

'And he says the old sow has four or five young at a time,' another lad put in.

'She does,' Aron shouted. 'I have watched.'

'It's quite true,' Incar said. 'The old boar is on a long time, and there are four or five young.'

'All he's got is the one shitty pig,' Ralan shouted. 'What good does that do him?'

'It does you no harm,' Incar said.

At last the lads drifted away. Incar went to speak to Aron, but the boy avoided him and hurried into his mother's shelter. Incar could hear him there, sobbing.

Two mornings later Aron's pig had gone. Three of the stakes had been pushed over and the fence had fallen into the pit. Aron, hardly able to speak, said that he was sure it was Ralan and the others who had pushed the fence down. They denied it. They said there were wolf tracks between the oak grove and the pit, and Incar looked and saw that this was true.

'He should be hit,' Ralan said. 'Keeping that shitty pig and drawing the wolves in close to us.'

Aron was crying too much to speak again. Aril took him away. But later she said to Incar that he had taken her out and shown her. There were tracks of wolves but there was no blood, in the pit or along the track to the trees. Incar looked and found that the boy was right.

Yet there was nothing to be done. Aron had been lucky, really, to keep the pig that long. And in any case, except to amuse a sickly boy, it had been a waste of time.

'We must find him something else to do,' Incar said to Aril. 'Because, whatever happens, he'll never be much real use.'

G lyn put his hands on the layered sandstone: the rock now
known as Llech y Ladron, the Stone of the Robbers: the rock
on which Incar could have sat, tracing the wind for the fire. Below
him, in the moonlight, stretched the wide plateau of Parc y Meirch,
the Field of the Horses. It was a place of watershed, with Mynwy
flowing south and the old streams of the blocked icefield flowing
east and north. All across this plateau, and on Cefn beyond Cwm y
Cadno, where the squares of forestry were a hardlined black, the old
arrows of the hunters were common. On a morning of autumn
ploughing in the foothills, the low sun, shining on the ridges of red
earth, strikes sudden gleams of tiny arrowheads, briefly seen from
the tractor. They will last infinitely longer than the red or yellow
cartridge cases now scattered under the hedgebanks. The hunting
has never stopped but the generations of hunters are another order
of life.

They were no single order, Glyn knew, though their living by
hunting and gathering seemed to bring them together. From the
hunting of Marod or Varan on the tundra to the hunting of Incar in
the thickly wooded valleys, there had been a common purpose, but
a greater variety of means.

The earlier scattered groups, in the more open country, moved
easily in ceremony and exchange, until the rising fertility of both
land and people occupied more ground and set more barriers
between them. Traces remained of change and variation in all the
tools of hunting and butchering. If the traces were memories the
differences of life and of feeling would be equally marked. In one
kind of history the generations are seen as epochs: single herds
which move through the country, acknowledged as innumerable
but seen as common. Little else can be felt as the generations appear

to rush past. Yet the true pace, always, was local and day by day. What had happened, and failed, in the case of Aron and his pig, must have happened, failing or briefly and intermittently succeeding, many hundreds of times. Two thousand years were to pass, eighty generations, before another hunter, the young Gord, saw the decisive change from hunting to herding and cultivation happening, on a slope of the northern plateau.

Through the long line of hunters the mountains and their valleys continued to change. When the elk was hunted by Mirin and his family the soil was thinly bedded over the stony litter left behind by the ice. Melting on the slopes of the mountains caused oozes and drifts of head which smoothed the higher surfaces and formed flat terraces below. Tumbling streams from heavy winter snows cut deep gullies and rockstrewn watercourses across the steep slopes. Slowly the soil deepened. The icewater lake became smaller: herbs, shrubs and willow and alder trees began to thicken along the valleys. From about nine thousand years ago the climate became settled, in warm summers and cold winters. Slowly the treeline moved high up the slopes, mainly birch on the heights, but oak and elm below, with clumps of juniper, raspberry, guelder rose and cherry, ivy and mistletoe. By the river grew willows and alder and on the still mainly open land flowers spread widely among the stones: rock roses, cornflowers, mountain avens, thrift.

In the days of Cara, the hunting was especially good. The people lived in small mobile groups, each with its hunting area, but came together, over a wider land, for the meets of midsummer. Where they settled to hunt they made shelters from branches covered with bracken or heather, or in winter with hides. They made their fires outside the entrances and worked nearby on wood, flint and chert. They beheaded their dead, flexed their corpses and smeared them with red ochre. A physical mix of people, intermarrying between groups, most were tall and long-headed, with fair or brown hair, speaking variant forms of an old common language of the northern hunting peoples.

More than a thousand years later came a time of great change. The climate grew wetter as the prevailing winds blew from the great ocean to the west. From the distant era of Marod and still in the days of Cara and Ral, there was a long landway north and south with only rivers to cross. Yet by the time of Incar and Aron, with the melting of the icesheet, the sea had pushed over this landway and the peoples now lived on an island. The old seariver widened and became tidal, its strong currents pushing up towards the ancient caves. The oak and elm woods spread with heavy undergrowth of hazel and cherry, hawthorn and holly, while mistletoe and ivy became common. Ways of hunting had to change from the old skills of the open ground. With the heavier rainfall the old upper hunting grounds became covered with blanket bog as the treeline fell back. In the close woodlands the bow and arrow became more vital, for stalking smaller groups and solitary animals: red deer, pig and aurochs. The gathering of shoots, nuts and berries had always supplemented the open-ground hunting, and as it now became more important the women had greater say in the families. Most families still moved seasonally, but by the lake and the bigger rivers new, semi-permanent summer settlements were beginning. Then as this lower ground became sodden and swampy, the settlements moved higher again.

The outlook of the people also changed. They were more cautious and more local. Yet while Gord grew from boy to man, new people were coming in small boats, across the open sea and up the seariver, and what they were bringing was very different: discontinuous and strange.

Gord and Namila See the New People

◆

There is a small red landslip, on the western slope of Wolf Head, where the heather grows so thickly around the edges that it is possible to lie unobserved, even from close by. Below this landslip, in the warm sun, Gord and Namila lay looking down at Glaura, their summer settlement by the lake.

Under the blue sky the whole world was silent. The short mountain grass was soft and springy. Gord pulled a mauve thyme flower between his fingers and dropped the tiny petals, slowly, over Namila's light brown hair. They were now both fifteen. Namila, daughter of a mother from the Bear Hills, was taller and fairer than any of the other girls of the family. She was taller than Gord, who was himself one of the taller young men and had thick, curling, dark-brown hair.

They had often walked together to the landslip. Their mothers and their mothers' brothers had accepted this. With Namila's mother Gord was a favourite. Even as a boy he did not come only for food but always brought something, a fish or berries or a handful of mushrooms. They were still young but already an accepted couple. In the summer they would build their own sleeping shelter, near Namila's mother's hut, in the copse of holly and hawthorn at the northern edge of the lake.

Gord kissed Namila, feeling the sun warm on her face. Namila, unexpectedly, pulled away. She tried to push him up. Thinking only that she was playing, he pressed down more heavily, but she whispered:

'No, listen.'

Still thinking she was playing, he pressed harder. Namila hit him hard, with her open palm, on his bare back.

'Listen,' she said again.

He sat up and looked around. There was nothing in sight. There was only the green open mountain, running down to the oak forest, and beyond it, very bright and still, Ara, the wide lake.

Namila scrambled up and caught Gord's hand. She pulled him quickly back to the cover of the landslip.

'There, again,' she said, and pointed.

Just south of the landslip there was a hard rocky jut, the jaw of Wolf Head, which stopped their view to the south. Gord, now serious, heard the next sound clearly: a strange animal sound, but unlike that of any animal he had heard. As they listened intently there were two more cries, lighter and weaker. They stared at each other.

'That was like the cry of a baby,' Gord whispered.

'But the first was not.'

They lay with their heads camouflaged by the thick dark branches of heather. They lay as if before stalking. They did not speak. They heard more of the strange cries.

Namila gripped Gord's wrist, and spoke closely to his ear.

'There are these small cries, but the first that I heard was of a wolf.'

'Not up here,' Gord whispered back, but he touched the flint hunting knife at his waist. Namila was carrying a smaller knife: for wood and plants, not flesh.

They stared past the rocky jut, now a hard black line against the sun. Beyond it open mountain grass spread to the first oaks.

'There,' Gord said, but they had both seen it, in the same instant. It was a small, reddish brown animal. At its highest point it would stand just above a man's knees. It had black horns, curving in a circle back over the neck. Its legs and tail were short.

'A new deer?' Namila whispered.

Gord shook his head. He did not know. But now, moving slowly and grazing along the lower slope, more of the strange animals were following. There were six of the same size and colour, and among them four young, much smaller. It was from the young that the baby cries came. They were grazing but also running to get milk from their mothers.

Gord smiled and rubbed his hands.

'How easy.' He said.

Then came a larger animal, with much darker hair, but there were patches of white on its sides, behind a dark line at the shoulder. Its horns were larger, and spread more widely, but with the same circular shape. There was a hairy brown ruff below its lower jaw.

'The buck,' Namila whispered.

Gord was watching excitedly. He was getting ready to stalk under Wolf Jaw, on the wind away from the animals. He was sure that he could get within running distance of the young. He was about to get up when Namila again grabbed his wrist. Walking slowly behind the animals, taking no apparent notice of them, were three people. Gord and Namila drew down in the heather, watching in startled silence.

The people were very strange to them. They could see from one bearded man that they were fully grown, but if this had not been so they would have thought them boys and girls. The tallest was less than the shoulder height of a man. Their hair was black and long; the bearded man had black body hair on his chest and shoulders. They were hung around, on back and waist, with bows, axes, nets and bags.

The animals were still grazing ahead. More had come into view: Gord counted three fives, including six crying young. But the people were not making any move towards them. Indeed the men they had first seen now sat on the grass, easing the burdens from their backs. Slowly, as Gord and Namila watched, others, including women, came into view and joined them. They all sat together, resting, except for one man who walked on, with a huge wolfdog following him. He walked away from the animals, down towards the oak-woods. There were now, altogether, a score of people, of whom three were children. They looked much alike: all very short, with long black hair. It was not easy, at this distance, to be sure between women and men. All wore light skin tunics, but there were more axes and bags than bows.

The animals had spread out, over the wide grassland. Yet what people could these be, to be so close to game yet making no effort to hunt? It was disturbing to Gord and Namila to see these people behaving so strangely, as if they did not belong in the same world. Yet there was no cause to fear them. They were small and lightly armed, and they were either not hunters or very bad and careless hunters. Yet if they were not good hunters, how could they eat and live? There was not, in this season, enough gathering to keep even so few alive.

Gord looked at Namila. Each found the same look of strangeness and wonder. Namila was first to laugh. Gord was slow to follow, still watching the animals and thinking of their meat. Yet her laugh at last came through to him. She touched her forehead and twirled her finger. She held her other hand out straight, then lowered it, jerkily, until it was nearly on the ground. She then again laughed, helplessly. The new people were very mad and very small. He had only to look.

The man with the huge wolfdog was now walking back to the others. Gord touched his knife. If he had brought his bow he would go down beyond the grazing animals and then up through the trees to get one or two. But it might be better to wait and watch these strange people. There would be such a story to tell when they went down to the lake.

They watched, in silence, though Namila still often laughed, while the sun moved lower in the sky and the people and the animals below them continued as before. But then, suddenly, the people were getting up. They moved down the slope towards a streampool. As they straggled along, Gord touched Namila's wrist. They moved very quickly along the scarp and into a deep watercourse. They moved fast down it, until they were into the cover of the trees. Gord wanted to move round and come closer to the animals, but Namila insisted that they should go down at once and tell the others. Since he had no bow, he agreed.

They ran the forest trail to their settlement by the lake. They were out of breath and excited, but they began telling their story to everyone they met. The older people seemed not to believe them. There could be no new deer; all the deer of the land were known. These would be in some seasonal coat which they did not recognise. As for the people, there had been many stories of these little dark ones, but they were always from a distance. Nobody you knew had actually seen them; they had always been seen by someone else.

'You have only to go now to the streampool under Wolf Head,' Gord insisted.

'There will be time tomorrow,' Ordan, his mother's brother replied.

'That is too slow.'

'It is not too slow. It is you too young and impatient.'

'But shall we not go now with our bows for the animals?'

'We have meat enough. We can go tomorrow.'

Gord had to agree. Yet he went on talking until tomorrow was settled: that they would leave at first light. Ordan at last consented.

Ordan, Gord and Ordan's brother Aradon were up and moving at first light. They took bows and spears. They moved quietly up the familiar forest trail and then through the thinner oaks to the edge of the mountain grass. Gord brought them out where he had seen the animals grazing. They were still there, still quietly grazing, though none very near to the trees. Yet two or three, as they watched, began slowly moving towards them.

The people were further off and could not be clearly seen. They were moving around the streampool. There was an echoing sound of hammering.

Gord then caught Ordan's wrist. The small man with the big wolfdog had come away from the others. He was pointing to where they were standing, with their bows and spears ready, under the thin oaks.

The Voyage of Idrisil and Dubanak

◆

The brothers-by-blood Idrisil and Dubanak had prepared all winter for the sailing. On the low hills above the Bay of the Islands the people and their sheep had come to live so well that there were now too many of them. Many years earlier, Gizon, the mother's brother of Idrisil and Dubanak, had gone as a boy to the White Land beyond the sea, where many of the people had settled, though he and others had returned. Listening to Gizon's stories of the White Land, which he praised so much that even as children they wondered why he had decided to come back, Idrisil and Dubanak had it always in their minds that when they were grown, and could claim a tithe of the sheep, they would build boats and gather friends and sail together for the White Land. A bad summer of parched, overcrowded grazing had decided them, and now, in the spring and after the lambing, they were ready for their adventure.

They had assembled between them eight boats, covered with treated hides. Each had gathered brothers and cousins to work on the boats and prepare for the voyage. Idrisil had three boats, to carry himself and eight other young men, with seven young women, three of their children, and the youth Tarac, now fifteen, whose mother and mother's brother had died. Between them they had their tithe: a good ram, ten ewes and six of the new lambs. They had also Idrisil's dog and the big dog which Tarac had raised from a puppy, the largest dog in their place, which was Tarac's constant companion. Dubanak had five boats, through the wider kin of his children's mother Saril. In his boats there would be twelve men, twelve women and seven children, and their tithe was two rams, fourteen ewes and eighteen lambs.

All the boats were stocked with fresh water in hide bags, with dried fish and nuts, and with some last precious hay. Before they could sail they had to turn the ewes to what pasture they could find, to assure the milk. They had then to wait for the wind to come from the line of winter sunset. For four days, Gizon had told them, they must follow the rocky coasts of their own land, far to the south, sailing two days towards sunset and then two days towards sunrise. They could then put in on an open coast, and renew their water and pasture. They must then wait until the wind was settled from winter sunset. In that wind they could sail to the White Land in five or six days.

It went at first as they had been told. They reached the open coast and went ashore. Rested and fed, they sailed northward, slowly, waiting for good wind. They came to a big island where they again went ashore and found water and pasture. Some of the women wanted to stay on the island, which had only a few people. But Dubanak wanted only the White Land and Idrisil supported him. It was agreed to wait until the good wind came. Meanwhile they were strong and rested from the sea.

The wind turned with the new moon, and they loaded their boats. Dubanak, wearing his white skin cloak, stood in the leading boat and shouted for the White Land. The others shouted with him, and all their spirits were high.

For two days and nights, in a now rougher and heavier sea, they held their course, with a following wind. They were tired and sick, but the course could be held. Then on the third morning the wind slackened and dropped, and before evening a new wind came, from winter sunrise. By the stars that night they saw how much their course had been changed.

Dubanak's boat was still leading. He shouted across the waves that all the boats must stay close together. The men tied lines between them. The same wind blew heavily all the next day, and they were afraid that they would be driven into the endless western ocean. Yet they had no choice but to go on.

On the fourth day, after noon, they saw land ahead of them, and began cheering for the White Land. But when they came nearer it was not as they had been told. There were red cliffs and grey and green rocks. It must be some other land. There were many sick now, and the ewes and lambs were weak. But they could see nowhere to land safely. They had to sail on through the night. During the darkness the wind shifted and they were driven further away from the strange coast. By morning they were again in open sea, out of sight of any land. Sick and weakened, they sank into sad and heavy silence. The children slept uneasily. Two of the lambs died and the women prepared and shared them to be eaten.

The wind dropped again. They were drifting in open heavy seas. Then they saw dark cloud starting to build from the western ocean and by noon the cloud was over them and a strong wind was blowing from spring sunset. Out of sight of land, knowing nothing of where they might now be driven, they huddled from the wind and from the heavy rain. It was their twelfth day from the Bay of the Islands. The White Land seemed a lost dream.

Yet before sunset they again saw land, and soon there was land on either side of them, as if they were in the mouth of a great estuary. There were openings on the coast to their north and they tried to steer towards them, to the safety and rest of land. They were making some headway but at dusk the wind and rain grew stronger, and as the light faded they were hit by a violent storm. Several of the lines between the boats broke. Others were cut away, because in the turbulent waters each boat was endangering the other. The last Idrisil saw, before the light went, was his two other boats, not too distant, and Dubanak still in his white skin cloak, with some of the other boats, dropping away astern.

The storm blew for most of the night, and towards morning they had a strong tide behind them and were being driven up the seariver. At first light they saw land quite close on each side, but as Idrisil looked back he could see only his own two companion boats. There was no sign of Dubanak and the others. The storm had now blown itself out, and they must try to make land. But they were almost at the end of their strength, and for several hours they could only drift. Then in the early afternoon Idrisil at last saw Dubanak's sail, and the others beyond it. He made ready to go into land. Either shore would do, whichever proved easier.

They were making good progress towards the southern shore, which had a flat coast and low green hills beyond. On the northern shore they could see the smoke of fires and a settlement, but all they needed was the nearest land. Idrisil was choosing a landing beach when there was a shout from Tarac. Looking round they saw a great wave, beyond anything they had encountered even in the rough open seas. It was moving up the seariver towards them. It was already lifting and driving the boats of Dubanak.

Idrisil shouted and they doubled their efforts to get in to the shore. But the currents had shifted and they were steadily pushed back towards the middle of the seariver. They passed a small island, but could not reach it. They were being driven helplessly, and the great wave was coming nearer all the time.

Tarac shouted and pointed ahead. As they were now being driven, the smoke of the fires which they had seen earlier was directly ahead of them, on the northern bank. They could see small figures of people running down to the shore. In the narrowing estuary the current was now racing and hurrying them onward. They held tightly to the sides of their boats, looking ahead at the settlement, where there was a flat beach under a bluff of high grey rocks. The people of the settlement were gathered and pointing. Idrisil shouted and waved his arms for all to be ready, and then slewed his boat to get in towards the settlement. The other boats followed, though it was hard to get out of the driving current. The great wave was now very close behind them.

Suddenly they were in calmer and much shallower water. Idrisil jumped out, and the other men followed him. They began dragging the boats to the shore. Men like themselves were wading towards them. Then again Tarac shouted. The great wave had caught Dubanak and his boats and was driving them fast up the centre of the river, away from their landing. The wave was like a wall of water, as tall as a man, and the boats were rocking helplessly in its thrust. As they watched, forgetting themselves, two of Dubanak's boats were overturned, and they could see the heads of people and of sheep tossing in the turbulent water. One of the women raised a great cry. The others watched in silence, for there was nothing they could do.

The great wave still rushed up the narrowing estuary. Briefly Idrisil saw his brother-by-blood Dubanak, standing in his boat and throwing his white skin cloak at the wall of water that was carrying them. There was then a turn in the estuary and the wave and the surviving boats were driving beyond it. The turbulence of the wave lapped into their own shallows. With help from the land people they finished towing their boats ashore. The animals were unlashed and scrambled away to higher ground. The children were lifted and carried safely in. All sank on the beach, under shock. It was some time before the land people could lead them up to their huts, and give them food and drink.

The land people spoke their own language. They could easily understand each other, past a certain local strangeness. Idrisil, recovering a little, asked how this could be, since this was not the White Land to which their own people had journeyed.

'In what you call the White Land, my son,' an old man, Siluyak, told him, 'many of our people are indeed settled. It is on this same great island of Albion, washed by the same seas, but it is beyond us, to the east.'

Idrisil thanked Siluyak and said:

'The boats that you saw, that were caught and driven by the wave, were of my brother-by-blood Dubanak and his companions.'

Siluyak bowed his head, gravely.

'We saw two lost in the water,' Idrisil said, 'but may the others be safe?'

'It cannot be known,' Siluyak replied, 'but I fear for their safety. What you call the wave is well known on the seariver. We have learned to reckon it, and to fear it, as the hunting of the sea. When we know that it is coming we keep away from the water.'

'We had no knowledge and no choice. We were driven by storms.'

'It is understood.'

'But now we must search for them.'

'Some of our own young men have already left. Others are ready to search on the southern bank when it is possible to cross the currents.'

'It is a great kindness, my father.'

'It is the law, my son.'

The exhausted survivors were cared for by the land people. Their animals were fed and fenced. But there was soon bad news. The young men who had followed the great wave, from their bank of the seariver, had seen two more boats upturned and floating empty. They had seen no signs of any survivors. On the two following days the river was crossed, and the southern bank was searched. But only corpses were found, except for a ram, which was brought back. It was the big dark-brown ram of Dubanak, with the grey-white patches on either side of its back. The ram was tethered with Idrisil's ram.

The sadness of their loss slowly settled. Fifty-one people had left the Bay of the Islands. There were now, alive, twenty. Of fifty-one sheep, sixteen were left to them and the ewes and the lambs were weak.

The settlement by the seariver was very well established, with more than a hundred people, a healthy flock of sheep, fenced pigs and two oxen for grain ploughing. There seemed to be no shortage of food, but it was soon clear to Idrisil that they could not stay, beyond the terms of the law, in this crowded settlement. At half-moon he talked with his own people and then went to Siluyak.

'Your people have been kind, my father, within and beyond the law. But we must now be ready to move to our own place.'

'Yet you are few, my son.'

'We are few for when our children are grown and will marry, but we are enough to find our own living and raise them.'

'You have only sheep, my son. You have no grain.'

'We can hunt, my father. And the herbs are growing.'

'Yet you will need good grazing. We can perhaps direct you, but it is for you to decide.'

On the following morning, which was clear and warm, Siluyak led Idrisil away from the settlement, along a track through the oak forest which lay just inland. When they had walked for some time they turned along a narrow side track and climbed to the ridge of a low hill, covered with oaks. Idrisil looked out. For almost as far as he could see there was only the same dense forest. There was occasional grass, under the thinner trees, but the rest was useless for grazing.

'It is not possible, my father. We shall have to go on up the bank of the seariver.'

'But do you not see the mountains, my son?'

Idrisil could see a blue wall of mountains, to the north. But he knew nothing of such country. It looked only alien.

'We hunt in the near forest ' Siluyak said. 'But for two summers our young men have made their way through to those mountains. What they tell us, for a certainty, is that where the forest ends, on the side of those mountains, there are open woods of slender durmast, and among them good grass that is fit for many sheep. The only people who now live there are hunters.'

'Do many hunters live there?'

'They saw only very few.'

'It would be two or three days through the forest.'

'For a hunter, less. The mountains are not so far as they look. But for you, with children and with animals to drive, it would be several days.'

'Would we follow the river?'

'There are two rivers, Salmon and Sab. You would follow Salmon River to the west. Its upper valley is within those mountains.'

Idrisil was silent, watching. He practised closing his eyes and remembering the shapes of the land ahead of him. On the wall of mountains he found three shapes to remember: two that came to points, like a broad arrowhead, and one which was round and very high. As he walked back with Siluyak he was tense and apprehensive. This was not the White Land, the great plains of cleared open grass, of which Gizon had boasted. It was a strange, difficult, unknown country, though he did not doubt that Siluyak had told him the truth.

The rest of the company were taken to look at the mountains. They gave their voices to go. Tarac was most eager. They went back and prepared for their journey. They left their boats to the people who had sheltered them. For the journey they were given good food, more than could easily be spared. They were also given a precious bag of the seed of emmer wheat.

They were seen on their way by Siluyak until they could look down into the valley of the west river. Then they pushed on alone. Tarac and his great dog walked in front. The other men spread to keep the sheep together. All had to move at the pace of the children, though there were some spells of carrying. They camped that night by the river, and then followed it as near as they could, keeping to higher ground for the grazing, for two days.

The mountains were nearer now and had changed in colour. They were green and dark brown, though suddenly black towards sunset. On the fourth day they were among the mountains. After camping overnight by a fast white stream, where there was a little grazing, they pushed up to the edge of the forest. Where the oaks thinned it was as they had been told. A good grass was springing everywhere.

As the trees thinned it was now the sheep that were leading. They could be trusted to find their way to the best grass. The weather was fine and warm, and it was all going easily. Having camped again by an upland stream, under a great boulder of reddish-brown stone of these mountains, they moved on next day, following their sheep. They were moving always west, to the far side of the mountains, where the grass was still better. Towards evening they rounded a high squared bluff of the mountain, and in the distance, below them, there was a lake, shining in the sun. The sheep spread out ahead of them, grazing. They rested and watched them until just before sunset, then found and tethered them, beside a pool in one of the small mountain streams.

There was no need to go further. They had reached a good place, with more grass and water than they would ever need. They loosed the sheep early next morning, and began to prepare to make a settlement. It was then Tarac who saw, at the edge of the oaks where the sheep were grazing, three strangers with bows and spears.

The Meeting of Hunters and Shepherds

◆

O rdan the hunter shook Gord's hand from his wrist. While
Gord and Aradon were watching the strangers, Ordan had
seen one of the animals moving away from the herd towards the
trees where they were standing. It was now within bowshot. He
lifted his bow and waited, following the animal along. As it stopped
and lowered its head to graze, he shot. The flint-tipped arrow went
hard in behind the shoulder. The animal fell. Ordan drew his chert
knife and walked across to it. Gord and Aradon followed, uneasily.

Ordan crouched by the dead animal, running his hands through
its strange hair. He was looking closely at its head and the curving
horns when Gord shouted in alarm.

The wolfdog was hurtling towards them, its fangs bared. They
stood together, lifting their spears. The strange man was running
behind it but now he stopped and whistled. The wolfdog checked,
still snarling. It was just beyond spearthrow.

The strange man – he was not old, he was about Gord's age –
turned now and called back to his people. Slowly, from the pool,
other men came out: first three, then two more. As they looked
down and saw what was happening, they hurried forward. They
stood together in a group. Gord could hear their excited voices, but
all the words were strange; he could understand nothing.

The young man whistled again. The wolfdog, reluctantly, went
back and lay at his feet. Then an older man, the bearded one whom
Gord had first seen, stepped forward. He lifted his arms. He was
holding a polished stone axe and a big knife. He let them drop to the
grass. He showed and moved his empty hands.

Ordan looked again at the dead animal. It was no deer; it was
something unknown. He looked at the men facing them. They were
what Gord had said: very short; black-haired. But they were strong

and heavily muscled. The axe and the knife that the bearded man had shown were very large, and shone in the light, but they were recognisable. He had to make an instant decision. He took up his bow and his spear, held them high and then dropped them. Telling Gord and Aradon to wait, he walked five paces towards the strangers.

Idrisil saw the hunter show his spear and bow and drop them. The hunter was tall and brown-haired. He wore short deerskin trousers and sandals. Across his chest and down his left arm were two long, pale, healed scars. His movements were quiet and controlled, but there was an angry anxious flush in his face and his hands were not still but were jerking under a compulsive control. The two others with him, a man and a youth, were physically similar: tall, restless, flushed. Idrisil spoke to Tarac, telling him to hold the dog. He then walked slowly to meet the hunter. He stopped, facing him, three paces away.

Each man spoke, the shepherd Idrisil first, then the hunter Ordan, in his own language. Neither understood any word of what the other was saying. Each tried again, and again failed. Idrisil said his own name, pointing to himself. Ordan repeated the name and then gave his own, which Idrisil gravely repeated. Idrisil smiled and held out his right hand. Ordan hesitated but then came forward and grasped it roughly. They looked deeply into each other's faces.

Idrisil saw pale, reddened, flushed skin; roughly-cut brown hair, short on the top of the head, straggling on the upper lip and in the curve of the neck, thin and loose on the chest, crossed by the long pale scar; loose lips, high gums, several upper front teeth missing; the whole body sweating heavily, beads of sweat on the forehead and upper arms. He had to look up. The hunter was a head and shoulders taller.

Ordan saw brown, deeply weathered skin; long glossy black hair, to the shoulder and over the lips and chin; startling blue eyes, against the brown skin and the black hair; matted black hair on the chest and shoulders and curling on the back; very regular white teeth, in a fixed smile. The body smelled of some grease but there was no sweat. The small, heavily muscled man wore an open shoulder tunic and a skirt to his knees. The skin of the clothes was reddish brown, with white patches. It was from the strange animals, worn with the hair still on it, facing outwards.

Idrisil withdrew his hand. Very slowly he lifted his arm and pointed to the ewe that the hunter had killed. The hunter was agitated. Idrisil saw his fists clench. Idrisil opened his hands, palms upward. The hunter, now excited, pointed at the dead ewe and then at Idrisil's tunic and skirt. Idrisil nodded, smiling. The hunter lifted his arm and pointed in turn, each time with a short stabbing movement, at the other sheep which were grazing around them. Idrisil shook his head. The hunter's eyes clouded, and his skin reddened again.

Ordan stared at the strange dark man. What was most strange was that these people and these animals were so close together, and yet neither seemed to notice or care about the other. The animals had moved a little away, but several were still within easy bowshot. And yet these dark people hunted them: there were the skins on their bodies. But now they were not hunting, though they had so many heavy weapons – axes and big bows with leaf-shaped flint points to the arrows. Even stranger, the unknown animals seemed not to fear the men.

Idrisil pointed again at the dead ewe. Moving first carefully back several paces, he walked round towards the ewe, keeping his distance from the hunter. Halfway down he gestured for the hunter to follow him.

Ordan walked down, keeping his distance. He glanced back at his brother and Gord, who were standing where he had left them, their spears raised. The dark men also stayed still, though the big wolfdog got up and moved a few paces before the young man pulled on the thong around its neck.

The bearded Idrisil crouched by the dead animal, and then turned and looked up. Ordan watched intently. Idrisil touched the animal's heavy teats. Ordan nodded. Idrisil touched them again and said some word. Ordan turned and pointed at one of the young animals, which was grazing nearby. Idrisil nodded but then touched the teats again and then touched his mouth. Ordan stared. Idrisil repeated the movements, and when he had again touched his lips he made movements with his mouth as if he were eating. Ordan pulled the knife from his belt, and made a cutting movement, as if to slice and eat the udder. Idrisil shook his head. Ordan moved from standing to squatting. He lowered his head, tapping his fingers against his forehead.

Idrisil the shepherd could not think what to do next. These were obviously hunters with no knowledge of herding. Unless he could explain, it would not be long before the whole flock was killed. Or else they would have to go back, not only across the mountains but down again to the seariver, away from these people. The hunter was watching him closely. He still had his knife in his hand. It was a very fine small knife, with a tiny blade.

Idrisil rose from crouching. He called to his sister's man, Suyak. Suyak made to come forward and the hunter swung quickly round, alarmed.

'No, stay, Suyak. Do not come down or there will be fighting. But run now to the camp. Bring cheese.'

'Cheese?'

'Yes, quickly.'

Suyak ran back. The women and children were watching from the pool. He shouted for cheese and some soft fresh cheese-curd was brought in a small pottery bowl.

'Are they dangerous?' the women were asking.

'They've killed a ewe. They look wild. We do not know.'

He hurried back down the slope, holding the bowl carefully. He was beginning to walk down to give the cheese to Idrisil when there was a shout from one of the hunters, who stepped forward, waving his spear.

'Put it down. I will fetch it,' Idrisil shouted.

Moving very slowly, he walked up and fetched the bowl of cheese. He took it down to the dead ewe. Pointing again for the hunter to watch, he touched the teats and rubbed them, as if milking. He then put the bowl of cheese up close to the udder. He lifted it slowly away and then, very deliberately, put his fingers in the bowl and took out the damp cheese and ate it. The hunter stared, following every movement. Idrisil got up slowly. He placed the bowl between them on the grass. He pointed to it and then to the hunter. He put his hands to his mouth as if eating.

Ordan hesitated. It was very clear but very strange. The bearded stranger wanted him to eat from this mess in the strange grey bowl. It was like the gesture of friendship between hunters but this did not look like flesh. The bearded one was showing that the mess had come from the udder, so it was not really food. Yet to refuse the offer would be to break the law and be an enemy.

Ordan touched his chest, pointed at the bowl and put his fingers to his mouth. The bearded one nodded and said several strange words. Ordan stepped forward and bent on his knee by the bowl. He put his fingers into the mess and lifted them to his mouth. The unpleasant smell came before the unpleasant taste. He felt like spitting it out but knew that he must not. The settling taste was very strange. It was more like a fungus than either flesh or plant, but the smell was very different. He chewed and swallowed the damp mess, with an effort.

Idrisil smiled. The distaste on the face of this big rough hunter, and at the same time his obvious effort not to show it, were very funny to watch. But he could still not be certain that the importance of the sheep was understood. He called to Suyak and Tarac to catch a ewe and to fetch a larger pot. The hunter watched every move suspiciously, but when Idrisil caught his eye he managed a broken-toothed smile and even, with a little bow, put his fingers in the cheese again and managed another mouthful, his nose again wrinkling. When the ewe was held, Idrisil squatted behind it and settled a black round-bottomed pot between its hind legs. He then reached through the legs and began to milk. It came well. This was in fact the best ewe, which had lost its lamb while they were on the sea.

The quick memory of the sea brought a rush of feelings. There were the changing fierce winds, the storm, the great wave. Within that rush of danger, there was the aching loss of Dubanak and his boats. It seemed already a long way back, but the pain was tender as soon as it was touched. While the memories raced, his hands continued to milk. He looked up at the hunter, who was standing open-mouthed.

When the milking was finished the ewe was released and ran off to join the flock, grazing down into the grass under the scattered oaks. Idrisil stood and showed the pot to the hunter. Ordan leaned forward, smelling the milk in the pot. He laughed, and Idrisil laughed with him. But it was then clear that the milk was interesting the hunter much less than the pot. Cautiously, gesturing for approval, Ordan reached out his large hand and ran his fingers over the outside of the pot, then made a loose fist and tapped it with his knuckles. He was now smiling with delight.

Idrisil made a quick decision. Taking the pot and holding it at arms' length, he offered it to the hunter as a gift.

Ordan could not really believe what he was seeing. There had been distant stories of these little dark men, but they were not really to be believed. Now here, in front of him, there were these strange new animals and the little men took milk and mess from them and drank and ate it. That was a low kind of life, beside the life of hunting. But they could not be just stupid, since they had this strange hard bag, which felt like stone but was not any stone he had seen. And now the bearded one was offering him the bag with the creature's milk inside it. These strange people could have no bad intentions. And living as they did, in a poor way, following the strange animals for milk and mess, they would be no trouble to the family and to the hunting. He did not want the milk, which smelled as bad as the mess. But the hard bag was different. Who would ever believe that there could be a thing like that?

Ordan made his decision. He walked down to the dead animal and lifted it easily on to his shoulder. He carried it up and placed it at the bearded man's feet. Idrisil smiled, and again held out the pot. Ordan did not take it at once. He went to fetch his bow and one arrow. He saw how the dark men put their hands on their axes but he kept the bow flat by his knees. Then, standing over the dead animal, he drew his bow as if shooting at it and then dropped the bow, at the same time holding up both hands and vigorously shaking his head. He touched his own chest. He pointed to his brother and Gord. He pointed down to the settlement by the lake. Then he again held up his hands and shook his head.

Idrisil smiled. This rough hunter was not stupid. If his people still lived more like animals than men, always chasing and gathering and knowing nothing of herding and planting, still they were men and could understand. He knew what the hunter was indicating, that his people would not attack the sheep. With that agreed, the pot was a small thing to offer. He again held it out and now the hunter took it, grinning. He even bent over it and smelled the milk, this time making no effort to hide his reaction to its smell. They laughed and again shook hands. Then the hunter went back to his friends and the shepherds watched them walking away through the trees until they were lost to sight.

Tarac and Lirisa

◆

For two moons after the meeting of Ordan and Idrisil, there were no more contacts between the peoples, though each at times saw the others and went their own ways. Idrisil and the other shepherds were busy preparing a settlement. The grass that the sheep preferred was among the scattered oaks at the edge of the forest. They moved some distance along the mountain to find an even better place, with oak-shaded natural clearings, where the grass grew strongly. There was then much to do. They did not know this country and could not be sure of its winters. And they were still so few, and the sheep so few, that the next few winters were certain to be hard.

It was good to know that hunting people could live off this country. Indeed there would be more than enough, for deer and pig were common in the oak woods. But none of them wanted to change to a mainly hunting life, or to live like the hunters by the lake. They must survive the winters, of course, but above all they must build up their flock.

From midsummer they worked very hard, over a wide area, cutting grass for winter hay and storing it. Only then did they begin building huts. In the continuing fine weather they had lived mainly in the open, but they began digging out round pits and lining and laying the entrances with stone. They also dug storage pits but apart from a heavy crop of hazelnuts they would have little of that kind to store. They had found a patch of lighter earth and scratched cross-furrows with their axes and planted the emmer that the seariver people had given them. But it was soon clear that they would get very little from it. The springing was late and thin, the growth in the cool mountain air very slow. It would bear little before sunstand, and the colder weather must then be expected.

After making the hay their first work, they began cutting branches for roofing the huts. Tarac had the idea of cutting coarse heather and packing it between the branches. Their settlement was beginning to shape up – they were now calling it Dereu – but still nobody wanted to imagine the winter. Some were already saying that it would be too hard to survive, and that at sunstand they should make ready to go back to the seariver. But really they did not know, and after the long disturbance and the terrible losses of the sea journey most of the family wanted only a settled place, taking a chance on what might come.

One morning Tarac was walking back to Dereu, carrying another load of heather with his big dog Rac running excitedly round him. He suddenly saw, at the edge of the forest, two young women standing. He knew from their deerskin tunics that they were from the hunters at the lake. One was extraordinarily tall, with long fair hair. The other was very tall for a girl, about Tarac's own height. Her hair was dark brown.

Tarac stopped and looked across at them. They had obviously meant him to see them but of course he must be careful. They would certainly have their own men watching them, and he must not approach them rashly. But then the tall girl held up her arms, and she was holding a great leaf with something shining inside it. The other girl held up a small willow basket. When they knew that he had seen what they were holding they placed the leaf and basket on the grass, and ran back into the forest laughing.

. Tarac picked at his teeth. Ordering Rac close beside him, he walked slowly down to where they had been. He was watching closely among the trees. He could see no men. But then he saw the girls, watching him at a distance from behind a great oak. Rac was sniffing at the things on the ground, and Tarac ordered him away. On the large leaf was a fine silver fish, with a bunch of some herb placed carefully on its gills. In the little willow basket there were fine fresh raspberries, filling the basket to the top.

Tarac squatted and took a few of the raspberries and ate them. The girls laughed and then hid their mouths. Tarac wondered what to do but then called Rac to him and made him do his trick. The big wolfdog would rear up and put his paws on Tarac's shoulders, growling as if attacking. As Rac reared there was a scream from the girls and one of them started to run forward, drawing a knife. Tarac

spoke to Rac and the big dog pulled down his paws and completed
the trick, rolling over at Rac's feet and showing his white belly. The
girls stood and laughed.

'Tarac,' Tarac shouted, pointing several times to his chest.

'Rac,' he shouted, pointing down at the dog.

The girls laughed.

'Tarac,' he called again, touching his head and his chest.

'Tarc,' the tall girl called.

A hunter, a young man, with curling dark brown hair, came out
from behind a tree. He was carrying a bow and a long spear. He
spoke strange angry words to the girls. Tarac saw it was the one
who had been with the hunters when the ewe was killed. He had
now stepped in front of the girls. He had put his bow down but he
kept hold of his raised spear.

'Gord,' the young man called, touching his head and chest as
Tarac had done.

'Gord,' Tarac called.

Gord moved a few paces and pointed at the girls.

'Namila,' he called, pointing at the tall one.

'Namla,' Tarac called back.

The girls were laughing but Gord was still stern.

'Lirisa,' Gord called, pointing to the other girl.

'Liris,' Tarac called.

He saw the blood come up in her face. The tall girl was still
laughing, but this one was now uneasy.

. 'Liris,' he called again, but now instead of answering she turned
and ran back several paces. Tarac stared after her, bewildered. But
now Gord and Namila, holding hands, were walking slowly towards him. Gord was still carrying his spear and watching Rac
carefully. Tarac spoke to the dog. It moved towards them and
submitted, its head down on the grass between its outstretched front
legs. The girl Namila was quite without fear. She spoke to the dog,
using strange words. Then she said 'Rac,' very clearly, and again
'Rac.' The big dog slithered towards her. She looked down at it,
smiling.

Tarac was getting ready to try to talk, and to thank them for the
fish and the raspberries. Gord and Namila, also, were ready to talk.
Gord called to Lirisa, but she stayed where she was. Namila shouted
something to her but she shook her head. Then she turned and ran.

Namila spoke to Gord and began running after her. Gord, now alone and uneasy, looked away from Tarac. But Tarac held out his hand, and with his other hand pointed at the fish and the berries. Gord touched the outstretched hand but then went quickly back into the trees.

Tarac went on staring, long after they had gone. He knew, suddenly, that he wanted them to come back. He wanted to know these people, to be with them and learn to talk to them. He could still not understand why Liris had run away. He wanted to see Liris and the others again.

But they were gone and that was that. There was work to do and he must get back to his own people. He carried the gifts carefully, leaving the bundle of heather. The family were pleased and surprised. They ate the raspberries at once, and the fish that evening. Its pink flesh was very fine.

During the next moon, which was the last before sunstand, Tarac often wanted to take Rac and go down through the forest to the lake, to find Liris and Namila and Gord. But somehow he never went. There was always too much work, and he was in any case uncertain. Then just after sunstand, with the nights now colder and the days cooling, he at last went. It was very dark in the forest and he was glad that he had Rac. He had reminded himself to approach the hunter camp cautiously. He was carrying a sheepskin which he would offer as soon as he was seen.

He could see the lake now, and the rough shelters this side of it. There was no sign of any movement: no people, no smoke of fires, no human sounds. He went on looking around, until he was close to the first shelter. It was very much rougher than the huts his own people had been building. It was just a stack of leaning branches, without pit or wall. There was still no one in sight. All the debris of the settlement was scattered on the ground between the shelters and the lake. There were old hearths, broken firewood and many bones. Near the edge of the lake there was a rotting and stinking pile of fish cleanings: some heads, many tails. There were broken and discarded arrows, without their tips, and, sticking up into the air, an old black and rotted willow basket.

The settlement was deserted. The hunting people had gone. Tarac had guessed that they might move with the seasons, but he was surprised that they could have gone so quietly and so quickly. It would be a long time, if ever, before he saw Liris and Namila and Gord again.

He looked out across the lake. He was feeling the sadness of a long run of separations: from the crowded settlements of the Bay of the Islands; from Dubanak and the others who had been lost in the seariver; and now from these new people of his own age. There were so few of his own people in the mountain with their sheep, and Tarac was isolated among them: the eight couples and three children. He wished that he had come down earlier, to show Liris and the others that he wanted their friendship. It was bad standing alone in this strange country: not the fertile White Land of Gizon's stories but only these black, wild mountains and the cold grey lake.

Dark clouds were gathering in the western sky, above yet another range of mountains. Before Tarac got back to the settlement it was raining heavily, and a strong wind was driving through the forest. He was glad to see that they had lit a big fire among the huts.

The heavy rain and wind after sunstand was the beginning of their winter. Day after day, through the leaf-fall moons, there was rain and wind. In the first moon after leaf-fall there was no wind but the air was full of low cloud and drizzling mist: a cold damp that made its way into everything. The sheep managed reasonably well, though the grass now stopped growing and they were put to the stored hay. It was the only time of year when the sheep were easy to control; they came now like dogs for their feed. In the well-made heather-lined huts the people were dry against the rain, and kept reasonably warm, with plenty of firing on the hearths outside each door. Idrisil marked each night and then each moon with sharp incisions on his hearthstone.

But now moving about was increasingly difficult. The red earth turned quickly to a heavy mud, and every track was slippery. On the steep slopes of the mountains every gulley became a small stream, and down the deeper watercourses there were torrents of muddy light-brown water. Getting clean water was difficult, though they soon learned to dig and dam to make small waterfalls, with fishnets lodged in the piled stones above them.

The whole look of the mountains had changed. If there was brief sun the steep slopes glinted with rushing streams and flashing wet stones. From halfway up the earth was waterlogged. Even down by the oaks the grass squelched wherever they walked, except in one place, beyond the clearing and the huts, where the water seemed to drain through a different, greyer and stonier soil and the grass was relatively dry. Otherwise the whole mountain seemed to be oozing water, and they soon had problems in the huts. The damp began to sweat through the earthwalls of the foundation pits.

First Idrisil and then others went for stone. They found that the surface sandstone, in some formations, was layered and could be split. Soon they were dragging these layered stones and flagging the hut entrances. On the uphill side of the pits they built stone revetments, with piled smaller flat stones laid together in a wall. They also upended and packed medium flags. They knew this kind of building from the long houses of the old settlements in the Bay of the Islands. But the abundant stone of this mountain, soft and layered as if shaped by strange hands, was much easier to work with. Yet the cold damp of the deepening winter was still hard to endure.

In the second and third moons after leaf-fall there was frequent snow. On most days the mountain tops above them were white. As they watched the snow falling and lying they learned that Dereu was just below the persistent winter snowline, which was an arrowshot up from the last thin oaks. Snow often fell around the huts but did not lie for more than a few days. Further up the mountain one fall merged with the next, in lying snow, and on the tops and in the dark gulleys it was getting deep. 'We've arrived in the White Land,' Tarac joked bitterly, but nobody laughed. They had all seen occasional snow, but never this much.

It was now a hard time for hunting. With so few sheep they had to live through the winter as hunters, and they soon discovered why the hunting people had moved away. There were still animals in the forest, though most of the deer had gone. Their most common catches were hare and birds, with some pig. But in among the bare trees and over the waterlogged ground the stalking was very difficult. There were many days when they went hungry, but they were determined to hold on to their flock as long as they could. With a good flock, Idrisil said, this would be much better country for sheep than for hunting. There would be no real limit to the number of sheep they could graze. His words were brave but sounded slight when they looked at the small flock – two rams, nine ewes, five grown lambs of which two were tups – which they now actually had, on their strange cold mountain.

At the end of the snowfalls there was a half-moon of clear, still bright weather. The mountain tops shone and sparkled white in the sun. It was a strange, beautiful sight. Then there were warmer winds from the west, and it was less than a moon to the spring sunstand. Everyone felt happier but it was also the beginning of the hardest time. The stocks of hay were low, and it might be two moons before there was any good new grass. They continued to hunt, and there were soon eggs and young birds to eat. They also went now more often to fish in the lake. After sunstand they killed the first tup, but they did not feast on it; they used it slowly and sparingly. Then there were willowbuds down by the lake, and the first signs of life in the lower oaks. The first flowers came and the children picked them. But the hay was now very low and the men went long distances each day, cutting the old dried and windblown grass from new slopes, under neighbouring mountains, and carrying it back. They would manage to get through but eating would be thin for another moon. They killed the second tup. All the ewes were pregnant and were given the best of the hay. Idrisil said that they had put the rams in too early. In the next leaf-fall they must wait a further moon, so that the lambs would be born later, nearer the new grass.

There were six new lambs, of which one died on the first day. The stored hay had all been used and the men were only just getting enough fodder with long journeys to find dead grass. It was poor stuff. The ewes did badly on it. But now it was found that in the place with the greyer soil, which had been so much drier in the winter, a good new grass was springing, earlier than on the heavier slopes. They tethered the rams and the yearlings and kept this place for the ewes and the new lambs.

Through all the days of work spring at last came. There were long days of sun and some of lighter showers. Every day before sunset, when the work had been cleared, Tarac called Rac and walked up the mountain until he could look down at the lake. He was watching for the smoke of fires, to show that the hunting people had come again. But day after day he saw nothing. He did not know when they might come. He did not even know that they would come again to that place. They might hunt in different places in different years. But if they did come, Tarac wanted to know.

It was at the end of the middle moon, between spring sunstand and midsummer, that Tarac saw the first smoke by the edge of the lake. He shouted with delight and Rac, not understanding, barked furiously. Now that the smoke was there, Tarac could admit that he had not really expected it. It had been necessary to watch, but without real hope. Suddenly, with the smoke from that hunters' fire, he was again unsure of himself. The first impulse, to race down there, to run up and greet his friends, came strongly and then faded. He was assuming that they were friends, but they might already have forgotten him. And could he even be sure that they were the same hunters? He walked back down the mountain, ignoring Rac. He was amazed at the tangled feelings in his body.

He waited three days. There were now many more fires by the lake. The grass was springing strongly and the sheep were grazing among the trees. On the fourth morning he set out early, with Rac. He ran excitedly through the forest, and fell several times, for under the heavier oaks the ground was still wet. But Rac enjoyed the game. When the lake and the rough shelters were again in sight Tarac turned aside and hid in a thick grove of holly. He settled to watch.

The first people he saw, two men coming back from hunting with a small deer slung on a pole, he had never seen before. But they looked the same people; big, rough, brown-haired. Some of the shelters had been rebuilt, with new branches, and there was a new hut, not far from him, under a stand of white-flowering hawthorn. As he watched he saw a young woman come out of it. She was at some distance, but from her exceptional tallness and the bright fair hair he was sure that it was Namila. He watched as she went back into the hut and almost at once came out again. She was carrying a baby. She sat in the sun and put the baby to her breast.

Tarac's heart was thumping and he was fighting for his breath. Ordering Rac to lie and wait, he stepped out from the holly and stood in the open. Nobody noticed him. He walked forward ten paces and stood; then twenty paces and stood again. He could now see and recognise Namila's face. He was walking forward again when she jumped up suddenly, holding the baby tightly to her. She moved quickly back to the hut and laid the baby inside it. When she came out again she was holding a spear.

Tarac stood very still. He lifted his arms, to show that his hands were empty. But she had lifted the spear and shouted back to the other huts. Tarac felt cold. He did not know what to do next. Then he called Rac, who came bounding up to him. He spoke quietly and ordered the trick. The big dog put his paws on Tarac's shoulders and growled. Tarac waited, not daring to look at Namila. Then he heard her laugh and when he looked there were others around her and they were all laughing and pointing. He did not see Gord or Liris, but these who had come were friendly. He ordered Rac down and the big dog turned over and showed his belly. There was more laughing. Tarac squatted beside the dog and waited for them to come to him.

Two men came first, with Namila behind them. The men were laughing and pointing at the dog and Tarac. Then one of them made a sheep noise, and they both laughed. The others came closer, and there was a sudden chorus of sheep cries. Every time the baaing was initiated the hunting people laughed as if they would never stop laughing. Tarac looked at them uneasily.

Then in a moment of silence he looked up and pointed and said clearly: 'Namila.' The name was almost lost as the men went on baaing and laughing but he could see that Namila had heard him.

'Tarac,' he said loudly, against the noise, and stood and pointed to his head and chest. 'Tarac.'

He was so much smaller than any of the men that he became self-conscious, but he stood his ground, repeating his name. Namila was smiling towards him.

'Tarc,' she said.

He ordered Rac to stand. The men were suddenly still, watching the huge dog.

'Tarc,' Namila said again.

'Namila,' Tarac said.

She smiled and upended her spear, driving the point into the soft grass. She spoke rapidly, in strange words, to the others. It was not only the words but the voice that was strange: very high pitched and with strange sounds. The men who spoke back to her also pitched their voices very high.

More of the hunting people had now come across to watch. Suddenly he saw Liris, at the edge of the group. She was staring at him. He stared openly back. She was of his own age but she was not so tall as the other women. She was of Tarac's own height. He went on staring at her while the strange high voices sounded around him.

Namila and one of the men came closer. The man pointed to Rac and to his own spear, and then gestured back towards the forest. Namila repeated his movements. Tarac thought he understood but the hunter did not, for he repeated the movements and added the movement of lifting his spear and running a few steps, which was unmistakeable. Tarac at once agreed. He spoke to Rac and ordered him to run to the holly copse where they had been standing. The hunters smiled and one clapped his hands.

It was soon arranged. Three of the hunters took Tarac and Rac on a long slow run until they were at the edge of the forest above the western bank of the lake. They went in, spread out at calling distance. They had not gone far when a sow and four piglets broke from cover and raced away through the trees. The sow was outpacing them but they were almost on two of the piglets when there was a warning shout and they saw a young boar charging. Tarac ordered Rac against him. Rac would not chase. That was his training, to stay with the sheep. But against anything coming towards him he was fierce. The young boar swerved, seeing the size of the dog, but Rac leaped on him and turned him over and there was an angry swirling and snarling fight. The hunters stood close with their spears. Tarac watched, knowing the outcome. Rac was bloodied but he killed the boar.

It was a happy carry back to the lake, and along to the shelters. Tarac stopped at the water and bathed Rac's wounds. They were bleeding freely but they were not deep. The hunters waited for him and when they reached the first shelters made him go in front with Rac. All the people came out and greeted them. The boar was set down by one of the bigger hearths, and an old man began cutting it. He cut off an ear and handed it to Tarac. Tarac smiled and pointed to the offal and to Rac. The old man threw the dog a piece. Rac gulped it. Tarac looked for Liris. When he saw her, he walked over and offered her the boar's ear. There was an immediate silence all round them. Tarac looked and saw that everybody was staring.

Liris kept her face down. She was very still. Then she looked up slowly. She reached out and took the ear.

Tarac bowed, in the custom of his own people, and walked back to his place by Rac. Now the two men he had seen when they had first arrived, Gord and the big man to whom Idrisil had given the cheese, came forward. Their bare legs were stained with mud. They

were carrying bows and two hares. Gord spoke to Namila, and she
led Liris away. Tarac watched them go. He did not know if he had
done right or wrong. He waited for some time, while the boar was
being cut and shared, and then decided to go. Seeing him going, the
old man ran up with a haunch and pressed it on him. He took it,
embarrassed.

It was half a moon before Tarac went again to the camp by the
lake. He had talked to Idrisil and the journey had been agreed.
Three of the women walked with Tarac, with three men following.
They carried a pot of milk and a basket of cheese. At the edge of the
huts they stood together and waited. It was again Namila who came
out first, carrying her baby. The three women went forward to greet
her and to lay down the gifts. Then they came back for Tarac, and
brought him forward among them.

'Tarc,' Namila said.

She turned and went to her own people. Two men came back with
her, Gord and the big scarred hunter, Ordan. The shepherd women
stood close around Tarac.

'Lirisa,' Namila said.

Tarac did not answer.

'Lirisa,' she said again, but now to the women.

The women smiled and nodded.

But now the big hunter stepped forward.

'Ordan,' he said, pointing to himself.

The shepherd women bowed. Ordan stepped forward and put his
hand on Tarac's shoulder. He then pointed to the ground and to the
huts. The women waited. Ordan spoke in his high voice to Namila
and she went back among the huts. She came back with Lirisa, who
stood behind Ordan.

Ordan put his hand on Tarac's shoulder. Then he turned and
touched Lirisa. He again pointed to the ground and to the huts.

'Glaura,' he said repeatedly. 'Glaura, cala, glaura.' The shepherd
men and women spoke quickly among themselves. They could not
understand the strangers. But Tarac believed he understood. It was
what Idrisil had agreed: that if Tarac went to Lirisa he must stay
with her people. He pointed to himself and to Lirisa, to the ground
and then to the huts. 'Glaura,' he said clearly. 'Glaura, cala, glaura.'
Ordan laughed and shook his hand.

Tarac spoke to the women of his kin. They stood closely around

him, pressing against his body. Then they moved forward together
and each of the women reached out and touched Lirisa. She looked
at Tarac and smiled. The shepherd women moved a little away and
Tarac held out his hand. Lirisa took his hand by the fingers.

'Liris,' Tarac said.

'Tarc,' Lirisa answered.

The women called in the high song of the ceremonies of the
shepherds. Ordan waited and then went to the shepherd men, and
brought them to the hearth to share food.

Tarac and Lirisa lived together from that day. In the fall when the
hunters moved, through the mountain valleys to Cala, the winter
cave, he and Rac went with them, and hunted with them all winter.
When they came back to the lake in the late spring he could speak
and understand their language, and he went back with Rac to the
seariver settlement of their own people. He traded furs for a bag of
seed emmer. Near the lake he found an area of deep earth and sowed
the emmer. By the next fall he had a small harvest. His own people,
on the mountain, had now a sheep flock of twenty-six. When in that
fall the hunting people left for the caves, he and Lirisa stayed. Their
first child was born in one of the walled shepherd huts. Through the
following years, from the shepherds' huts on the mountain and
from the hunters' shelters by the lake, the two peoples grew ever
closer, sharing their lives.

G lyn stood on the ridge from Pen y Beacon to Gospel Pass. He shone his torch on his watch. It was a quarter to eleven. He made the effort to calculate the times and distances of his immediate journey: a difficult recall after that other dimension which had seemed to enclose him while he was searching along the first ridge. The moon was now higher to the south, beyond the mass of the mountains. He was looking out north over the wide valley of the Wye, where the fields and woods were dark but where there was a gleam of light from the curve of the river.

The track along the ridge was empty. Even the sheep and ponies had moved away from it. But far below, in the valley, the lights of Hay were clear, and beyond them, across the river, the lights of Clyro and Llowes. It was not even particularly late there, in those streets and houses, but Elis, by the broadest reckoning, was now six hours beyond his time.

'Taid! Taid!'

The shout was necessary, but he knew there would be no answer. The track was clear and empty in the moonlight. Glyn stared down at the broad valley, so full of life but with only the scattered lights for signs. He could see the close foothills, above the short steep valley of the Digedi. There were isolated yard lights at the farms, spaced at irregular intervals along the closest high pastures. Spaced in much the same way, along this northern scarp, were the places of the neolithic shepherds. On the broad flat grassland of Twyn y Beddau, towards Dan y Capel, there were scores of hollows of their circular huts. Immediately below, overlapped by the car park on the mountain road, was a marked watchstone within what had survived of a later stone circle. Beyond it, now heavily shadowed, was the rough edge of exposed rock, running along this scarp, which marked the highest point of the great glacier which had pushed against these mountains.

These traces were still in the earth, but could not all be deciphered. When Idrisil and Tarac had come to these mountains, following their sheep, the flock had found its own way to the best grass, a broad strip halfway between the heavily wooded valleys and the highest ridges, where the ice sheet had reached, twelve thousand years before. When it finally melted it left till and drift gravel along its upper edges, and in the rain of the west winds this was where the best grass grew. The shepherds settled and built their huts at the upper edge of the forest.

In the end it was hard to say whether the people followed the sheep, or the sheep the people. The sheep themselves, valued for their milk and skins and meat, were not European animals but had made their way, with these peoples, from west Asia, grazing at the edges of forests. The dogs, like Tarac's, were to guard them from wolves rather than herd them, for the sheep were fast, lively animals, unafraid of dogs and difficult to fence, since they could jump considerable heights. In the mountains, their life became mutually dependent: the shepherds lived where the sheep found good grass, and the sheep stayed around the settlements in winter, because the people cut grass and made hay for fodder.

Thus the flock and the place of the flock defined the living of the shepherds. It was no longer the life of the seasonal movement of hunters, though the shepherds still hunted and gathered shoots and nuts and berries alongside the hunting families with whom they intermarried.

They brought pots and stone axes and some limited cultivation to these mountains and their valleys, but they also brought a new sense of settlement. The hunters knew their country closely, but along their own bearings of the seasons and the range of the animals. Now there came a different sense of the land itself.

In the first four hundred years from the coming of the shepherds the flocks and families multiplied until small communities sprang up all along the northern and western flanks of the mountains. Although these were always in sight of each other, interrelated by family and marriage, each had its own grazing area. On the slopes above what they called, in their language, Curve River – which a later people called Guuy or Wye – there was a string of settlements:

one above the valley where Incar had set his fire, near the source of the Little Mountain River; two close on the wide grass plateau beneath the bluff which the hunters called High Buck, looking down to two small rounded hills which the shepherds called the Breasts; three again on the wider plateau to the south, where they looked down as the river entered its broad curve; two above the lake, including the first, Dereu, where Idrisil had settled; three more beyond a saddle of the mountains, looking down to the other valley of Salmon River, which a later people named Uisc or Usk. Thus the success of the shepherds, following their flocks, began to be marked in the earth.

For they began to mark their places of settlement and grazing with structures of stones and mounds of earth, which were later seen only as tombs. These were centuries in the making, beginning in the most prosperous communities and dependent, throughout, on a sharing of labour between neighbouring families. They needed the manpower of many settlements to move some of the great stones of the inner chambers. The stones themselves were of their own mountains; some found loose in rockfalls, others dug out from the grass, others, especially the fine flat sandstone slabs, quarried where the ice had ripped into the northern scarp, or wedged and split away from the natural layers on the eroded ridges. Each structure was called the Long House of a place: a Long House in which only the dead might rest but still a building of identity and continuity, in which the fact of a family lived.

The beliefs of the shepherds, in their first centuries in the mountains, remained those they brought with them from across the sea: the changing and recurrent cycle of the Mother, called Danu in these mountains, gave birth to and nourished all creatures, was marked especially by the sacred days of midsummer and midwinter, when she received or pushed away the heavy warmth of the sun. Thus the celebration of midsummer was in the charge of the men, when the sun was pressing warm on the earth. The ceremony of midwinter was in the charge of women: in a withdrawn and darkened time life was secretly nursed for renewal. All over the world of the shepherds, Danu was honoured and worshipped.

Slowly other beliefs developed. The rhythm of the sheep flocks, also the children of Danu, followed a different annual course. The significant times, the putting of rams to ewes, and the birth of lambs, were, in this latitude, quite distinct from the old midsummer and midwinter marks. The moon of leaf-fall and the moon of leaf-bud were now the actual seasons of this central cycle, marked by special fires, on the sixth night of each moon. At these times, although Danu was still honoured, it was as if the flock itself were the real object of worship.

As the Long Houses, in their first stages, were completed, the general climate was changing again. The winters became drier and colder, the summers warmer. In the clearer skies, the shepherds began to look differently at the whole world around them, and especially at the moon. For ordinary midwinter and midsummer an everyday observation of sunrise and sunset, on certain marking hills, had sufficed. Yet now not only the seasons but the nights of the moon became more important. What they observed turned out to be very strange. The waxing and waning of each moon was easily reckoned. But now they noticed the way it rose and set in so many different parts of the sky. Against the recurrent certainties of Danu and the seasons of the earth this uncertain and fascinating movement, which still defied predictions, led to new kinds of thought.

Meanwhile the different beliefs of the hunters persisted and often, in neighbourly tolerance, merged with those of the shepherds. For the hunters all spirit was in the living animals, and the spirit of each animal was closely interwoven with the spirits of those who hunted them. (Thus the hunters understood more clearly the shepherds' reverence for the flock than what seemed to them the mere name of Danu.) There were many distinct spirits: of boar and deer, bear and wolf, aurochs and hare. There were also the lively spirits of birds: the waterfowl at the lake, the hawks, the songbirds. The shepherd families never adopted the beliefs in animal spirits, but they did take over the idea of the spirits of the birds, and even wove them into the ceremonies of Danu. Danu herself, in some minds, was no longer the Mother of the earlier beliefs, around which the traditional hymns had been made. She was not, it was sometimes thought, a mother at all, for a mother must be human or animal, but the world they were now observing was neither human nor animal; it was earth and stone and sky: a place; a settled if intricate place, within which life happened but which was not itself alive.

This change, which at first hardly touched the simple tradition of

Danu, was in a way a convergence of the old beliefs of the hunters and the new observations of the shepherds. The hunters lived by the seasons and by the phases of the moon; they were close observers of weather and of winds. From these movements they learned change and diversity: a flow of life to which they must adapt, but with no single meaning. Meanwhile the shepherds saw what appeared, in the moon especially, to be independent movements which could not be explained or made subject to some single law and origin of the world.

In the long and now prosperous life of these families, for sixteen hundred years, there was a steady growth of knowledge and a strongly developing sense of settled society and law. As the centuries passed these became embedded, and growth came from inside the settlements, rather than without. Much later they were to hear, in their mountains, of extraordinary developments elsewhere: of new kinds of law and of settlement; of new systems of knowledge and belief: growing, as it seemed, from their own but reaching new and surprising ends. Still, however, at the edges of the oakforests, and with good grass for the flocks, their own shapes of life were formed.

The Long House at Midsummer

For many days there had been work at the Long House because the sunrise was approaching the shoulder of Bol Lug. The horned feastyard was swept and trampled. Idris and Gizon, whose hands loved stone, were repairing the low walls of the feastyard, where the winter frosts had loosened them. They were also extending the walls, reshaping their horned ends, glancing back for shape to the ox-horn set above the great stone, where the fire of the people would be lit.

Gorda and Tara, the two oldest women, were working in the earth at the western side of the Long House, by the entrance through which the bones of three of the family had been taken at spring sunstand. When the women had taken the bones there, and Idris and Gizon had reset the entrance stone, plants of thyme and trefoil had been set in the covering earth. But then the entrance was disturbed by animals, probably outlying wolves which had been heard close in that moon. Gorda and Tara were now resetting thyme, though in this dry moon it could not be certain that the young plants would live to sweeten the bones.

There was an excitement everywhere, as the sunrise moved towards Bol Lug. The other families would be coming, for it was the year of Lanoluc. Some might come from as far as the seariver, for there were stories that their ewes again needed the strong seed of the mountain rams. Thus the Long House of Lanoluc must look well. Some of the other families had much older Long Houses, larger and honoured by more feasts. Over seven generations this house had been raised, below High Buck. It had begun as a small mound over the ash house of the beloved Namil, daughter of Orda daughter of Lirisa. Then the mound was hollowed and stones raised and capped in a wedge around it. A new and larger mound was raised, and then again hollowed, for a new and larger stone chamber. Men from all around the mountains had come to handle these great stones. When they had been ropedragged and treerolled to the site, the holes for the standers were dug. Layers and then frames of cut trees and smaller stones were built under the narrow ends. It had taken a moon, at leaf-fall, to get the standers in position, for there was also work on the flocks. There was then an early hard winter, and the stones were left to be covered by deep snows.

Some of the younger men would have left the house at that, once the standers were capped, but the mothers were insistent that their place of living must be properly marked.

'We are marked by High Buck,' the young men argued. Or: 'We are here, our flock is here, there is no need to mark us.'

But the mothers replied: 'It is not you or us we are marking, it is our place of living.'

'Where we already are,' the young men laughed.

'Not only where we are but where we have been and shall be,' the mothers answered, 'for that is the meaning of the Long House.'

But it was many years before the men came again from around the mountains and a new and larger capstone was brought down from the landslip. It took a great force of hauling, on the knotted hide ropes. A ramp was built for it, and the spaces between the standers were filled with earth and tightly wedged with timbers before they could bear the crushing weight. It was finally levered and dragged into place. There was then a fear of going inside, to scrape and pass out the earth and at last remove the wedges. Indeed the capstone moved, as a stander resettled, while the boy Racat was inside. But at last the house stood firm. Several unburned bones were at once set inside, before the snows again covered it.

In the next generations a rising mound of earth and turves was slowly built over the house, with its two chambers. New smaller stones were set for a passage entrance through the mound. But as time passed the mound had to be made still larger, to mark the lasting goodness of this long place of living. In its first enlargements it was still rough and poor, but in the fourth generation a new honour stone was set, at the northern end of the mound. On each side of it stones were raised in the manner of an entrance, though there was only packed earth behind them. It was the feastyard at the honour stone which was now most important, for the midsummer and midwinter fires must be set at it. What then passed between feastyard and mound, when the fires were burning, was a long life through death: the strength of stone and earth as the enduring life of the gathered bones of the family.

The entrance to the first small house, above the ash house of Namil, was on the eastern side of the mound, towards High Buck. In the sixth generation a third small house was built, tunnelled in from the western side. Its stones were smaller but there was a fine oval capstone, brought from a hollow where Alder Brook turned along the edge of the oakwood. New bones were set there and the mound was remade.

The Long House was now a place of knowledge, and of the honouring of knowledge, of 'where we have been and shall be'. It was regularly tended and enhanced. The fine sandstone slabs of the chambers were common under the grass of these mountains. Some projected from the grass on which the flock fed. On the surfaces of the stones there were shapes that the hand could trace, swirls and mounds that repeated, in stone, the movements of water in the peatbrown brooks: eddies and windings of their flow. There were colours among them, crusted grey and orange lichens, where the stones had been in the air, and shadings from reddish to dark brown where dry or wet soil had lain on them. In some stones there were interlinings of pink and green. There was an especially sharp green in Little Stone Valley, beyond High Buck under Horn Point.

All these finer stones could be split, as they had seen already in the layering of the larger stones and in the embedded rocks on the exposed ridges. Small stones from the size of a hand to an arm could be found or hammered free. Shapes made where frost had bitten a layered rock could be repeated as strong dry walls. The men handled and turned and tested each stone, imagining its lie, until they were at last offered to fit together and endure. The fine marker walls of the feastyard were slowly built and improved in this long handling of the stones. For they were the bones of the grassy earth: 'where we have been and shall be'.

The grassy Long House, inset with small chambers and marked by the honour stone, was in Lanoluc the length of thirty paces of a man and the width of seventeen paces. It was not the largest even in these mountains. But it was a good house for a family of fifty-eight people, living between Curve River and the slopes of High Buck.

They had a flock of sixty-three sheep on the grass of the slopes and among the thin oakwood clearings. They had also hunting in the oakwoods down to the river. Their neighbours to the south, between Hawkstone and Glaura, had an older and larger house, for they had been first in these mountains, in the time of Idrisil and Tarc. The people of Lanoluc had followed the flock away from them, as the ewes increased, in the time of Namil, daughter of Orda daughter of Lirisa. The families would be together again now, with other neighbouring families, in this year of Lanoluc.

Idris and Gizon left the walls of the feastyard and went to talk to Gorda and Tara, who were still working at the earth on the western bank. Idris squatted and lowered his head to the sharp scent of the thyme. The bones of his brother-by-blood Suyak, who had died three years ago in fever in the moon of the last snows, were among those which the women had placed in the house. His body, like all others, had been laid in the clearing below High Buck that was marked by a circle of gorse. The flesh had decayed there, in the storm and sun, until the bones were left clear. Then the skull had been removed, and the bones broken, at this year's sunstand, just before the new spring of the grass.

Idris looked down at his hands, which cradled but did not touch the newly set thyme. He could see within the fine lines of his palms the dried earth and stonedust of the work of his hands on the walls. The lines were clear in the brown skin. There were small bones lined in his fingers and thumbs. He would be glad now to dip his hands in the peatbrown brook and to feel the cold of water from the rushing mountain spring. He would find thyme and rub his fingers through it, enjoying its sharp odour over the close sour scent of the earth.

While the old men and women crouched silently at the Long House, on the slopes above them there was running and shouting. The young men had been up to the fireset on High Buck. Through the last moon, cut ash trunks, still green, had been dragged for the sign of the midsummer fire. The young men and boys were now always up there, playing. When it was time to come down they would run headlong down the slope, daring each other, and some of them would fall, into the dark gorse. Two had now fallen together, grabbing at each other, and their shouts echoed in the still air below the mountain.

'Mad as ever,' Idris said.

'Men herd, boys hunt,' Gizon said, standing.

The old women finished their work at the entrance, and began to move away. Idris and Gizon stood watching the young men. The bracken stalks were curving chin-high, on the lower slopes, among the pale brown litter of last year's stalks. On the higher slopes, where their running started, the wide clumps of whinberry, which had been pink in young leaf, were now a shining light green, which made the whole spur brilliant, like the fur of some marvellous animal. In the short grass the yellow birds' eyes of tormentil and the white eyes of heath bedstraw were wide open. The sheep were scattering as the headlong run continued. The young men raced past them, shouting. They swerved round the Long House, pushing out their legs in the dropping run. Then they raced in among the trees to the huts. The dogs barked around them as they ran.

Through the next days the other families arrived. There were formal exchanges of gifts. One large family had come from the seariver, with shell necklaces and fish and salt and black seaweed laver. From the mountain families there were fleeces and hides; from the second icelake family, willow baskets woven with bright feathers; from the Hawkstone family, flints, which they had received for antlers in a journey to the east. There was much news and talk and there was a long gathering and standing to look over the sheep. Soon the men would pick out young wethers to exchange, for breeding into the other flocks. They stood in groups, examining and handling the sheep, while the women were at the huts sorting and preparing the shared food.

There was always argument among the families about the true night of midsummer. There were different ways of counting among the more distant peoples, although the timing was certain within two nights. The argument now centred on what had happened three midsummers earlier, in the year of Hawkstone, when the fireset was prepared and the men of Hawkstone had waited for the fire to spring on the Broken Mountain. For they had heard that Broken Mountain took its sign from the Bald Hills, and beyond them from the Yellow Hills, which in turn received the sign, through other fires, from the distant and honoured White Land. In the White Land, it was said, there were men who knew sun, moon and stars as if they were flocks, and who were certain of midsummer. Here there was still doubt and argument, though with their different reckonings it had come to seem gentler to wait for the fire from Broken Mountain. Yet with sunrise already near their own marker, the distant shoulder of Bol Lug, they had to watch each night on High Buck. When the first fires sprang the beginnings of the feast must be ready. It was for this that the women worked in the warmth of the sun. The sweet scent of the whitehorn, now at full at this height, hung strongly in the air as they sat together on their fleeces.

At the fourth dusk after the other families had arrived, with many already gathered near the Long House, there was a loud cry, pitched to carry along the mountain, from the young men at the High Buck fireset. Everyone turned and watched the point at the end of the long black ridge, dark and solid now under the pale night sky. The flames leaped suddenly into the air: a fierce burning of dried bracken under the ashpile. It was then as if everyone breathed out with the rising flames: a long low breathed sound from hundreds of watchers. But as the flames reached the ashpile and shot higher there was a sudden silence. People turned to look north and west for the fires at Matunoc and Brigan, and further west to Bear Mountain. These should now be springing. Brigan was the first, a growing point of fire on the sharp peak. There was nothing from Matunoc. Then far to the northwest, not a point of fire but a glow on the distant horizon, there was the sign of Bear Mountain. This was good to see, for it did not always come from that hard country. At last, when almost everyone had given up Matunoc and they were moving across to the grass around the feastyard, a small lick of fire appeared on its lookhill: much smaller than it should have been at two mandays' walk. There was a derisive shout. Many laughed. Their own fire, on High Buck, was now streaming into the sky.

Gizon wore a red-ochred fleece as he walked to the feastfire. He carried a blazing pinetorch in his stretched-out right hand. A young ram, hung around with twigs of heavy-scented whitethorn, was led up beside him. Idris lifted a long knife and passed it through the flame of the pinetorch. Then the tup was on its back and its throat was quickly cut. Gizon lit the feastfire, and there was a deep long shout from all the people who were watching, squatting up the slope to High Buck. Then the feasthorn sounded. The families found their places and squatted as close as they could to the feastyard. The goodness of midsummer had come.

The deep goodness of midsummer was that when the feastfire was burning, there was no more counting of time. In the warm dry night, with the families close and touching, there was no care or urgency. All the work of the year was gathered and composed into certainty, by the settled peace of the Long House. Men and women and children looked at the comfort of the mound, and at the great honour stone lit by the feastfire. Most of the work of the feast had already been done, and there was now only the sharing, the close passing from hand to hand. There were pieces of meat and fish. There were scraps of stonebaked cake. There were wooden cups of the foaming berrydrink. Later, dimly later, there would be dancing and loving, but the awaited rhythms of midsummer were always slow and unhurried. It was the midsummer of shepherds, with lambs born and growing, grass springing and abundant, skies clear and warm.

The horn sounded again. Idris, wearing an antler mask on his head and shoulders, walked to the centre of the feastyard. The talking eased away. Idris pitched the first long call. It came back not in hundreds of voices but in one great deep voice. It was then the naming, in the most ancient cry.

'Danu,' Idris called.

'Danu,' the common voice answered.

'For Danu is the mother.'

'Danu.'

'Danu is the mother of men and animals, of birds and fishes, of grass and trees.'

'Danu.'

'We are all her children.'

'Danu.'

'Danu our mother is with us. In all grass and trees, in all birds and fishes, in all animals and men.'

'Danu.'

'Danu our mother is now in our house.'

Idris turned and bowed to the mound. He laid down the antler mask. There was a long silence, and then slowly, in scattered groups, the quiet general talking resumed.

The fire was still burning on High Buck. Far across the great valley the fire on Brigan was bright, but there was now nothing to be seen from the distant Bear Mountain. At Matunoc the fire was still small.

There was louder talk and laughing as the berrydrink passed. It would soon be time for the dance. The young men who had been on High Buck had come down and made ready. The horn sounded again.

Gizon, still in his red fleece, climbed and stood on top of the mound, above the honour stone and the feastfire. The flames of the fire threw shadows over his body. A slow silence settled.

The young men, naked and ochred, sprang into the feastyard. They danced with bowed heads and with their arms wrapped close around their shoulders. Gizon sang.

'Hear the song of the children of Danu.
Hear the song of their journey.'

The dancers halted and squatted, shivering, close to the ground.

'For Danu was cold
The white Danu was cold
All her children were cold
But there was then the first of the great ones.
The first of the great ones of the children of Danu.'

One of the dancers stood. He stretched his arms.

'Talam was the first of the great ones.
Talam the sharpeyed, who saw the golden stones.
Cleareyed he struck the stone with his flint.
He struck the spark and made fire.'

The dancer struck repeatedly, then snatched a burning branch from the fire. He danced with it, alone, whirling it around his body. Then he danced in a circle, around the others who were shivering. One by one they stood up and took burning wood from the fire. Then they all danced with high steps, waving the torches above them.

'Thus the children of Danu could begin their journey.
They could journey in the cold, not waiting for the fire from the sky.'

The dancers threw back their burning branches, then pulled others from the feastfire. They repeated this several times, running and leaping with their torches. Then they turned and stood in a circle, looking up at Gizon in his red fleece.

'There was then Mar, the second of the great ones.
Mar fashioned sticks into spears.
He fashioned stones into axes.
He made snares with strips of hide.
He lengthened the snare to the bow.
He feathered sticks to arrows.
Mar hunted the wild herds.'

The dancers leaped and hunted, taking spears and axes and bows from the horned walls.

'Mar and the children of Danu hunted the herds.
But the greatest of the hunters was Mar.
His bright eyes saw the herds.
His broad shoulders carried the prey.
His long arms plucked the beast from the cave.
Its pelt became his cloak.'

A young man stood out as Mar. He had a spear and a torch from the fire. Two dancers, one sitting on the other's shoulders, had a bearskin hung over them. The bear swung wide arms against the torch thrust at his face and the spear thrust at his body. His claws reached for the young man who was Mar, and the fight jumped and circled. Then at last the bear was killed and Mar snatched its skin. He hung it loosely on his shoulders. There was a long deep shout from all the watchers.

When the shout ended there was a long silence. Then Gizon sang again, in a higher voice.

'There was then the woman Sila,
The third of the great ones.
The woman Sila who looked close and who taught the children.
And the children of Danu made needles
To fashion clothes from the skins of the animals.
The children of Danu made weirs of stone,
Made traps of hazel wands, made knotted nets,
Made new lines and hooks for the silvery fish,
Watched the salmon leap to the high pools,

Watched the waterbirds fly to the lakes,
Watched the red deer in the forest, and strung feathered arrows,
Watched the trees fruit, and the bushes,
Watched the plants to eat and the plants to heal,
Watched the dog at the edge of the campfire and tamed him,
Watched and learned all the ways of the mother.'

The dancers now moved out into a wide circle, facing the people in the darkness beyond them.

'The children became many, they spread over the earth.
The children shared the earth as they shared their feast.
All that came from Danu and the people shared,
And all that they learned was again for sharing.
In the feast of midsummer, the feast of the sons of Danu,
In singing and dancing, in food and in wine,
When the families are gathered at Danu's Long House.'

The dancers shouted together, and then moved out, still dancing, among the families crowded on the grass. Wherever they went, people stood up and joined them, until all were dancing, and new wood was piled on the fire until flames leaped to the night sky. The dance continued until the fire began to die down.

In the early dawn after the midsummer night there was a final ceremony. When it was again full day there would be many arrangements, between the different families: marriages to confirm, trading to be decided, breeding animals to be exchanged. But first the dawn must be marked, after the night of feasting and dancing.

The older women watched for first light, on the shoulder of Bol Lug. Then the horn was sounded, three times at intervals, and there was a rapid beating of the large sheepskin drum. Gorda stood ready by the ashes of the fire at the honour stone of the Long House. She sang the Song of the Shepherds, which belonged to these mountains.

'The flock finds the grass.
The people follow.
The flock is wise.
It is wise to follow.

For they were drowning in the sea, the brothers Idrisil and
    Dubanak.

Dubanak threw his white fleece on the sea, but the waves drowned
   it.
Idrisil raised his crook, and the sea obeyed him.
The sea and the flock moved together to the land.
The flock finds the land.
The people follow.

They were few with Idrisil, but they followed the flock.
The flock led them to these mountains.
The flock found sweet grass under the thin oaks.
The flock showed the people that it was a good land.

The flock is wise,
We were wise to follow.

They leap before us to the brooks,
They find the warm slopes.
In the shade of the oaks
They find places for their lambs.

The flock finds the land,
The people follow.

The milk of the ewes feeds the lambs.
The milk of the ewes feeds the people,
It fills the black pot to the brim,
It swells the grain to gruel.
It turns summer plenty into winter cheese,
For the cold of the two hungry moons.

The flock is wise,
We are wise to follow.

Ram-horns for tools, sinews to bind,
Skins for our backs, meat for our mouths.
Bones of sheep and men in the Long House,
New grass springing for the flock.

The flock finds our place
We follow to the Long House
The Long House of the Flock
Where we are and shall be.'

In the silence after the song ended, people stretched and looked around. The sun was rising, in bright rays, above the shoulder of Bol Lug. They looked towards the sun and then began moving away. Already, up the slopes to High Buck, the sheep were scattered, looking for new grass.

With Antlers to the Seariver

G ordin whittled the stout ashpole and tested the curve where it
would rest on his shoulder. He bound soft fawnskin into the
hollow. He moved to the other end and whittled a second curve and
bound it. He skinned marks along the pole. He took red earth
and spat and smeared it on the white flesh of the ash. At the
front end, with the point of his smallest flint knife, he carved the
marker spiral of the Long House. He then gazed at the worked
pole. It must be wholly fitting, for so uncertain a journey.
Grown and cut in his own place, it would see many strange
things before it was carried back, past High Buck, with its new
load.

Tarc came over and looked at the pole. He tested the hollows on
his shoulders. He ran his fingers along the earth marks and around
the spiral. He smiled.

They had been preparing for the journey since midsummer,
through three moons. At the feast of Hawkstone, in the exchange of
rams, Gordin and Tarc had spoken with men from Brigan, who had
made a leaf-fall journey to meet at the seariver, where antlers could
be exchanged for flintcores from the east and where men from along
the coast came with polished axes. At the full moon of leaf-fall these
came each year, to a bend in the seariver where there was a track to
the Yellow Hills.

Gordin and Tarc had collected a full load of antlers: some from
the cast in the second snow-moon, others from their kills in the
summer hunting. Some they had cut and shaped to picks, from top
to tray and the heavier from tray to brow. Others were still
complete, in full growth, one with as many as fourteen points. They
had now to tie the antlers with thongs to the carrying-pole. They
would put knives at their belts and take up their long walking

spears. They would follow their stream to their river and to the distant seariver and the meet.

Only one thing remained before starting the long journey. Next morning, early, they were at the Long House. All the family came and passed in front of them, taking their hands and saying the words for a journey: 'Until you see High Buck.' Then they lifted their load and walked down to the stream, through the grazing flock. It was a still day, with clear sky, but the morning had been cold. On the trees, already, there were the early colours of leaf-fall.

They were young and strong, but the load was heavy. Making their way on known tracks, keeping the mountain river in sight, they made a steady pace but often halted to take the weight from their shoulders. The first people they expected to meet were the big family at Carvon, on the second day, but sometimes hunters camped at Cambo, the second riverjoin, where there was a wide gravel bank. Men of the High Buck had often been so far, in the duty of carrying, stage by stage, which was part of the law.

It was after sunstand when they began to leave their own mountains. They crossed the wide plateau above the curve from first riverjoin, where the ground was more open. There was a herd of horses grazing across the plateau. A red stallion came out and pointed towards them. The mares and the young had moved back. Tarc laughed and they rested, looking back. They could still see High Buck but its shape had changed, at the end of the long ridge. Below them across their river, was the narrow opening under the jagged ridge-end of Horn Point, to Little Stone Valley.

The stallion turned, still pointing them, as they lifted their load and moved on. With the sun on their backs they went down into the trees towards the shine of the river. There was now more hazel among the thin oaks. They followed the bank to the join and the gravel bank, and set down their load. They lay and drank the sweet water from the river looking down at the flat brown pebbles in its bed. Then they moved along the river, one on either side, leaving their load. They soon found a pool with trout and Tarc moved down river and walked slowly back towards Gordin. Tarc stopped and crouched in the water, trailing his fingers in the current. Then he pushed his arms in to the elbows, staring intently down. A quick jerk and the trout was flung to the bank. Gordin took a stone and killed it. Tarc moved deeper into the pool, again crouched and caught a second trout. They walked back to the gravel bank and flintstruck a fire. When the embers were hot they wrapped the trout in butterbur leaves and heaped ash around them. It was getting cold as they ate, but they collected wood and made a larger fire to sleep by.

Moving a small stone as he lay back, Gordin stopped as he was about to throw it away. It was a roughly-chipped flint spearpoint, with the marks of work but of a quite different kind from any he had seen. It was perhaps a stone of the old people, who had lived in this land. Perhaps one had sat here at riverjoin, holding his rough spear. He tossed it in his palm and then laid it beside him. Across the river, on the high plateau, there was the howl of a wolf. Maybe a pack was tracking the horse herd.

They were cold when they woke next morning. They ran along the bank to get warm. Then with a drink from the river they took up their load and moved on, following the bank as it turned towards sunrise. They were moving better now. The weight still bore on their shoulders but their bodies had accepted it. The trees were thicker along the valley: oak and ash and more hazel. Whenever they stopped they gathered nuts and ate them. In one grassy stretch, where the old trees had been felled, they found mushrooms and peeled and ate them. It was as they took up their load again that they heard the drum.

It was a fast beat, in some repeated rhythm. They had heard that there were drums, among the hunting people, but neither had heard the sound before. They could see no sign of people, except for the old felled trees. They were puzzled because they must now be near the big family at Carvon, who were of their own way. They went on, cautiously, but saw no one. They did not again hear the drum.

At sunstand they rounded a curve of the river and there ahead were the huts they expected. They put down the load and watched. A flock of good sheep were grazing among the oaks. Beyond them two black cows were tethered, pulling at a heap of cut hay. Beside the river a stretch of ground had been cleared and there were plants set out in it, in rows. There were fires outside the round huts, which were of the same building as their own. There were women working near the fires, and in the forest beyond two boys were driving young pigs for acorns.

Gordin and Tarc moved forward until they reached a rough

fence, of ashpoles and dead hazel branches, which enclosed this side of the settlement. As they stood looking over the fence two wolfdogs came out at them, barking loudly. They lifted their spears to fend off the dogs. The older, a bitch, drew back, bristling, but the younger dog jumped and snapped at the hanging antlers, trying to pull them down. There were shouts from the huts, and a boy ran over, yelling at the dogs. Behind him, from the nearest hut, came an old man, with white hair and close white beard, pulling his tunic over his shoulders.

'We are from the Black Mountains, of the family of High Buck,' Gordin shouted.

The old man called off the dogs.

'I am Silak. You are welcome,' he shouted, in a deep, harsh voice.

'We heard a drum,' Tarc said.

'It is the hunters of Mamcala. They are in the forest above us.'

He pointed up to the hill on the other side of the river.

'Are they of our law?' Gordin asked.

'They are not of our people. They keep no flock, they do not plant. But they are not enemies to us.'

'We are going with antlers to meet at the seariver. We have no knowledge of our path, except to follow our river.'

'Be at peace, my sons. There is no danger from men.'

He moved an ashpole and led them in among the huts. A small pool, squared with oak logs, had been let in from the river, and skins of red deer and aurochs were lying steeped on its bed. The water was clouded with wood-ash and there was a strong smell of stale urine. Gordin and Tarc stared at the pool, seeing what was being done. In their own family they sweated and washed and then smoked their hides.

They sat with Silak outside his hut. A young woman came with a wooden bowl of nuts and couch roots and sliced crab-apples, with shreds of squirrel meat. She then brought wooden beakers of fermented berry juice, a dark red, almost black. While they were eating Tarc looked across the river and jumped to his feet. A very tall man was standing on the far bank, watching them. His long hair and full beard were red. Over his shoulders and down to his thighs he wore a brown bearskin jerkin. He was carrying a spear and a heavy club, and a short bow and arrows were slung on his shoulders.

'Be still, my son,' Silak said, anxiously.

For Tarc had already picked up his spear, facing the huge man across the river. Silak stood and took the spear from him, and laid it on the ground. Then he opened his arms to the man across the river.

The man smiled. Through his beard the teeth were very large and irregular. He stepped into the river, without hesitation, barely looking for his step. He waded through, vigorously, and came up to their bank. As he passed the steeping pool he stopped, pointed down, and held his nose. Then he laid down his spear and club and pulled the bow and arrows from his shoulders. Gordin saw then the small drum of stretched white skin that he was carrying on his back.

The big man walked forward, looking intently at Gordin and Tarc. He came close up to Tarc, who was standing, and brought his face within a hand's breadth of Tarc's. His breath was strong with some herb which Tarc did not know. Gordin stood, and the big man came and repeated the action with him. Gordin looked up steadily. The top of his head was well below the big man's shoulders. On a level gaze there was only the finely-worked bearskin and the white necklaces of its teeth.

The big man sniffed as Gordin stood his ground. Then he turned to Silak and smiled.

'Sheep,' he said, speaking the word strangely.

'Sheep,' Silak repeated, and then pointed west.

'Horse,' the big man said, again with a strange sound.

'Mountains,' Silak said.

The big man laughed. He waved his hand across his face, the fingers loose, palm outwards.

'Black,' he said, with a smiling contempt.

Then he turned and walked over to where Gordin and Tarc had put down their load. He squatted beside it and touched each of the antlers. He nodded vigorously. As he stood he looked again at Gordin and Tarc, pointed at the antlers, and began to laugh.

'Sheep,' he said, still laughing.

Gordin stared at him, but then also laughed. The big man came across to him and put his hand on his shoulder. They laughed together.

Silak invited the hunter to sit and eat. He took a single nut and then patted his stomach. He went and lay on his back, with his hands joined under his head, several paces away, looking across at them.

'They follow their own ways,' Silak said to Gordin and Tarc. 'They have their own speech, and they do not share it with us. We have only a few words for when we meet and salute each other.'

'But they do not harm you or the flock?'

'Never. They only laugh at us. They call us the little people. They think that all we do is like a children's game.'

The big man was smiling, looking across at them, as the strange words continued.

'They move far through the forests,' Silak continued. 'But in the winters they return to their caves, Mamcala, above the next river-join, Arcala, where your mountain river flows into a greater.'

'We must pass them then?'

'It is nothing. They will not cross your track. They will see you, also, as the little people.'

The big man laughed.

'Caves,' he said, speaking the word strangely.

Silak smiled.

The big man sprang to his feet and ran to the load of antlers. He pointed down at them.

'Seariver,' he said.

Silak smiled.

'Caves. Seariver,' the big man said, pointing again at the antlers and then at Gordin and Tarc.

'He will take you, he is saying,' Silak explained.

'Why should he do that?'

'They exchange their own antlers for flints. He will take you to the meet.'

Gordin looked at Tarc. He could see his own doubts. But as they hesitated the big man was standing over them and smiling. He again pointed to the antlers and repeated: 'Seariver.'

'You would be sure of your way,' Silak said.

Gordin touched his chest.

'Gordin. Gordin.'

The big man smiled.

'Tarc. Tarc,' Gordin said, touching Tarc's chest.

The big man laughed.

'Imar,' he said, touching his wrists alternately. He swung round.

He slung his bow and arrows on his shoulders. He lifted his spear and club.

'Imar,' he shouted.

Gordin and Tarc, still hesitantly, walked to their load. Silak followed and wished them farewell. Imar beckoned them forward and waded into the river. They crossed carefully, looking down for their footing. When they were on the far bank Imar moved to a slow run. They tried to keep up with him but with the load could manage only a fast walk. Imar turned and laughed at them. Then he matched their pace and led them up a track through the forest. Tarc cast a last look back at the quiet settlement by the river.

They moved on by tracks which they could only occasionally make out, through an ever denser and darker forest. Imar did not allow them halts, though once, under a big oak, he stopped and used his drum. The rhythm was different from the one they had heard on their way to Carvon. Again they hurried on. The forest was crowded with birds and animals. They saw few of the larger beasts, though once a great black aurochs, crashing away down a slope. They were tired and sweating under their load. Tarc called that come what may he must soon stop and rest. Imar could not have understood him but soon, in a grove of young oaks where more light was filtering through the branches, he stopped suddenly. He turned and smiled. Gordin and Tarc dropped their load.

'Where?' Gordin asked, but was not understood.

'Imar,' Imar said.

Gordin pointed and held up his fingers, one by one, meaning to ask for Imar's people.

Imar laughed and stretched out his arms. Gordin and Tarc looked round the grove. It was as if their hearts stopped. In a ring around them, standing silently under the trees, were the other hunters. There were men and boys of different ages, all tall and heavily muscled, all carrying spears and clubs and bows. They had appeared so silently and suddenly that the shock was deep. Gordin and Tarc were used to the long open views of the mountains, with other people first seen at a distance. And while Imar was laughing, these others were not.

Imar spoke rapidly to the hunters, gesturing broadly. In the tumbling speech not only the words but most of the sounds were strange. Gordin and Tarc watched their faces and saw some of them begin to smile. Then an older, unsmiling man, whose long hair was red but whose beard was quite white, came over towards them. He put down his spear and touched their wrists with his open palms. Then he crouched beside the antlers, running his fingers along them and bending close to smell them.

'Sheep!' Imar shouted, and there was a roar of laughter from the others.

'Sheep! Sheep!' Imar shouted again. He put his thumbs to his forehead and extended his fingers like antlers. He danced on the spot, laughing, and the others joined in the laughter.

Then the older man spoke some command, and two men came out and took up the carrying-pole and the load. Tarc made to object, but Gordin said to let be. The load was lifted and suddenly they were off again, now at the run with which Imar had started from Carvon. Freed of their load, they could now keep up, though they had to watch their footing along the tangled paths of the forest.

The steady run continued until Gordin and Tarc felt their lungs almost bursting. Then at last they were going down a long slope, with a broad river below them. The hunters waded in, without hesitation, though the water was soon above their waists. Gordin and Tarc pushed through with the water lapping their shoulders. Then the run began again, up the slope from the river and along the edge of a small rounded hill. The track fell again, following a narrow path through a wide marshy area, and then climbed briefly through a steep bank of trees. Suddenly everyone stopped, and the load and the tools were put down.

'Mamcala,' Imar said, turning and smiling to them.

Gordin and Tarc were exhausted by the run. They squatted and then lay on the ground. They were on a wide flattened terrace, with the ash of a great fire at its centre. All around on the terrace there were wooden structures, with hides stretched to dry. There were two large piles of bones, many of them broken and splintered. At the far edge of the platform there was a quartz anvil, with a layer of flint and chert chippings around it.

Gordin made an effort to stand. He then saw the opening of a cave, at the back of the terrace. In the mouth of the cave women and girls were standing, looking at the strangers. Several of the women were holding children and babies in their arms. They were tall heavy women, most of them with the red hair of the men but some with brown and even dark hair. On two of the youngest children the hair was a very pale gold, almost white.

There were more strange words and then a girl brought a leather bag of water and shyly handed it to Tarc. He stood as she held it out to him, and looked into her face. She was half a head taller, but she bowed her head.

Imar came and took Gordin's arm. He led him to the edge of the platform, facing south and pointing down. Far below them a broad river flowed straight as an arrow between heavily wooded steep banks. Imar pointed along it.

'Seariver,' he said.

Gordin shook his head. Imar squatted and held out his arms, bending them at the elbow. He moved them backwards and forwards. Then he ran back across the terrace, to catch the arm of another man. They disappeared beyond the cave but were quickly back carrying a long boat. Gordin and Tarc saw that it was a hollowed oak trunk, finely thinned and shaped. There were ash paddles in it, like those used in the round hide boats of the lake people of Glaura. They did not need Imar's further explanation, but the hunter, excited and laughing, sat in the boat and lifted the paddle and again pointed down the river. Gordin smiled and reached out, touching Imar's wrists as he had been shown.

The women and children had now come out on to the terrace and a new fire was being prepared. Tarc stood, warily, among the curious crowd. Imar took Gordin's arm and led him to the cave. There was a double entrance on each side of a limestone pillar, and then the cave broadened and curved out of sight. Immediately in front of them was a broad ledge, a pace high. Gordin followed Imar on to it and saw an enclosed lower cave beyond it. Back in the outer cave Imar showed a heavy smokestain on the roof near the outer opening, and pointed to the fire. Then they moved along the terrace on a narrow track to the north, until they reached the opening of a second, smaller cave, of only one chamber. An old woman was lying on a pile of hides and leaves. She opened her eyes and looked at them, but at once looked away.

At the fire a young roebuck had been skinned and was roasting on a slung pole.

'Sheep!' Imar said, pointing and looking into Gordin's face.

'Buck,' Gordin said, smiling.

'Sheep! Sheep!' Imar repeated, and laughed. But then he put his face close to Gordin's and tried to say 'buck'. Gordin said the word again and Imar repeated it and laughed. Then he held his nose, turning away, and again said: 'Sheep!'

When the buck was roasted, and the flesh carved with the tiny flint knives which the hunters preferred, they all ate with their fingers; there were no pots or bowls. The taste was fine and the shares large. Resting after the meal, his legs still aching from the run through the forest, Gordin remembered suddenly the huts and the flock, under the wide sky above High Buck. It was only two days since they had left, but it seemed very much longer. There was talking now round the fire, but no singing. The women and children went in early to the caves. The men settled where they were, around the fire, which they piled with cut wood before sleeping.

In the morning there was little movement, as the others woke. The men and women moved slowly and quietly. No food or drink was prepared. But Imar had already been busy. The long boat had been carried to the river far below, and beside it there was a stack of antlers, which the hunters had been collecting. Gordin and Tarc carried their own load down, moving with difficulty on the steep wooded bank. Imar stacked the smaller antlers at intervals in the boat, but the larger he tied with thongs to the stern, to trail in the water. Then without ceremony he showed Gordin and Tarc where to sit. He gave them each a paddle and pushed off into the river. Almost at once they were moving quickly on the steady current. Gordin and Tarc paddled, looking up at the steep wooded banks on each side.

Soon they were at a riverjoin and Imar steered for the far bank. When they were safely past the mixing of waters Imar pointed back to the smaller river and then at each of them.

'Black!' he said, pointing, and then: 'Sheep.'

Gordin and Tarc laughed. They had recognised the soft brown water of their own mountain river. Now the main river was broadening and there were areas of flat grassland and marsh at its banks. But soon the high wooded banks again closed in, and they were moving through high forest on either side. At one place there was firesmoke from a clearing in the trees but they saw no people. They moved on, easily, but then Imar was suddenly alert. He dipped his hand in the water and then held up his fingers. He wriggled the fingers and pretended to eat them. Gordin and Tarc did not understand. 'Elvers,' Imar said, and again wriggled his fingers and pointed down into the water. Gordin and Tarc guessed his meaning, though they did not know the strange word. Now Imar kept dipping his hand in the water and licking his fingers. They rounded a wide curve and then he shouted excitedly: 'Seariver.' The river looked no different though it was broader. But Imar signed to dip and to lick their fingers. The water was no longer sweet but salt. The current had strengthened and they hardly needed to paddle. Imar moved forward and used his paddle to steer.

There were grey cliffs above them now, and rocky outcrops, the trees far up on their heights. Imar steered for the western bank and kept close to it. They rounded another curve, with a small rocky headland, and then suddenly ahead there was no longer a river but a great expanse of water and waves. Imar shouted to paddle and they bore down west, struggling to keep close to the bank. Ahead, on a low ridge, there were huts, and people moving. Imar steered to the bank, where several boats were tied. He jumped out and began pulling them ashore. When the boat was on the bank he waded for the trailing antlers and laid them to dry in the sun.

Gordin was looking up at the huts. They were round like those of his own people, though larger. On a low headland there was the unmistakeable shape of a Long House. Back along the ridge a sheep flock was grazing, but there was also a herd of cows and there were several large areas, in square fields, which had been dug and planted.

They walked along the beach. For the first time Imar let Gordin and Tarc lead. There were many people moving about but nobody seemed to take any notice of the strangers. Even the dogs did not run out at them. The whole feel of the settlement was open, as if used to strangers and travellers. Gordin went to two men who were sitting on a low wall, mending a fish net. They answered in his own language. The meet, they told him, was a long way upriver, where the channel narrowed at a great bend, Begisso, and where there was a gravel crossing from the Yellow Hills. Gordin thanked them and would have turned back towards the boat, but one of the men called to him.

'You must wait for the tide.'

'Tide? What is that?'

'Where are you from, friend?'

'I am from the Black Mountains, in the family of High Buck.'

The men looked at each other, and then one of them stood and looked along the beach at the boat.

'His?' he asked, pointing to Imar.

'Yes. He is one of the hunters of Mamcala.'

'We know them. But you, from the Black Mountains? What have you got, antlers?'

'Yes.'

'It is the moon of the meeting in two nights. The tide is when the seariver moves. In his boat you must wait until it moves upriver. That will be before first light tomorrow.'

Gordin thanked them. He walked back to the boat. Imar had understood 'tide'. He repeated it, licking his fingers, and made a great sweep with his arm. They sat and rested.

Towards evening an old couple, man and woman, walked down from the settlement. The woman gave them a basket of white fish and green herbs: one Gordin recognised as thyme. When Gordin had thanked her the old man squatted and said:

'I am Silu. This place is Iupania.'

Gordin gave his own name, and those of Tarc and Imar.

'I have heard,' Silu said, 'that you are of the Black Mountains.'

'Of the family of High Buck.'

'There are families to the west, along our shore, who go to your mountains at midsummer.'

'Indeed I have met them. They are Pirani.'

'We do not go inland. We go to other families, on the southern shore of our seariver, in the Yellow Hills.'

Gordin looked across the great expanse of water. Over its rough surface he could see hills rising in the distance.

'It is with them we have our midsummer gathering.'

'You have fine cattle,' Gordin said.

Silu smiled.

'But not so fine sheep?'

'They are heavy.'

Imar laughed suddenly. Silu frowned and he looked away.

'There is a very old story,' Silu said, 'of the coming of Drisil, who was wrecked here in the seariver and taken in by our people.'

'Idrisil?' Gordin said. 'That is a very old time.'

'It is old but it is believed to be true. And Drisil stayed with our people, who nourished him and his flock. And after many moons Drisil followed his flock to the Black Mountains which our people had shown him.'

'Idrisil commanded the waves,' Gordin said. 'His flock and his people found the land.'

Silu smiled. He looked out at the rough water. A wind had risen from the west and the waves were larger and topped with white. As he stood the wind blew his thin hair.

'We honour what we know of our beginnings, my son.'

'Indeed, my father.'

Silu looked across at Imar and spoke to him, slowly, in a strange language. Imar stood stiffly and listened, nodding as Silu spoke. When Silu had finished he turned to Gordin and Tarc.

'I have told your friend about the tide, and the course he must follow. I wish you good luck at the meet.'

'Thank you, my father.'

They ate the fish and then slept by the boat. It was cold all night in the wind from the water. They were awake and stamping for warmth long before first light. Imar prepared the boat and they pushed out into the seariver. He pointed to a star and steered by it, across the wide water. Soon a strong current was heaving under them and they were turning upriver towards the far bank. It was now beginning to get light and Imar was looking for a sign on the shore. There was a tall, slender stone, set back from the beach. He pointed and steered to alter their course.

They were running now in a strong deep current, between wide shallows on which some of the waves were breaking. They had to use the paddles for steering, to stay in the narrow channel. Then the seariver changed again, and the banks were much closer. Imar steered towards the south bank. The land to the south was flat and open, but to the north wooded hills were still close. It was now hard work to keep the boat moving and, before noon, Imar steered to the bank and they pulled up the boat and rested. The west wind had brought in dark clouds and the air was much colder. As they pushed off again it began to rain heavily. The wind scudded along the rough water around them. They settled to long steady paddling but their progress was slow. Their bodies were now streaming with rain.

They stopped once to rest again, but for a very short time. Imar kept pointing at the current. The sky lightened a little, and the rain eased. Soaking and handsore, they pulled on up this seemingly endless river. The banks were closer again and they saw a settlement and fires to the north. Yet soon the river broadened, and there was flat land close on both banks. Imar was looking intently ahead, but there were no more signs. Then at last he pointed and they could see a great curve in the river, and red cliffs beyond it. 'Begisso,' Imar shouted, and it seemed, suddenly, that they all had more strength. But it was still slow progress towards the red cliffs, and the sky was darkening again. Finally the shape which they had seen in the distance became crowded with things and with people. There were fires burning, high above the bank, and men moving around them. They steered in and landed. They had reached the meet.

They were too tired to do more that day, and they were very hungry. They found a bush and slept under it. In the morning, still wet and cold, they caught fish and ate them raw. Then they agreed that Gordin and Imar should go up to the meet, while Tarc stayed to guard the antlers. In a big clearing on top of the cliffs there were more fires and more people than Gordin had ever seen. He and Imar wandered among them, not knowing what to do. There were many piles of antlers, and in other places heaps of white flint cores. At one fire were men in black leather tunics with finely polished axes spread on the grass by their feet. Gordin was looking around, bewildered, when he heard a shout behind him.

'Banak!'

Imar heard the shout and moved closer to Gordin. A dark bearded man, with a long white scar on his left cheekbone, was walking towards Gordin, holding out his hand.

'Banak, it's good to see you,' the bearded man said.

'I am Gordin,' Gordin said, but he took the outstretched hand.

'Hah, some joke!' the bearded man said.

'No indeed. I am Gordin. I am from the Black Mountains, from the family of High Buck.'

The bearded man stared at him, shaking his head. Then he looked past Gordin's shoulder, and his mouth hung open.

'Banak!' he shouted.

Gordin turned to see a young man stop and turn. He came over towards them.

'Banak, look at this,' the bearded man cried, pointing at Gordin.

The two young men looked at each other. They were of a similar height and weight, though Gordin was more heavily muscled. They were similarly dressed, in hide tunics, but Banak's boots were finer, of a tightly-laced whiteish skin. They looked at each other warily, so abruptly brought together.

It was not their reactions, but those of others – first the bearded man and Imar, then other men who gathered around – which prevailed. Imar was looking from one to the other and laughing. The others were smiling, open-mouthed.

'What is this?' Gordin asked impatiently.

'You don't know each other?' one of the newcomers asked.

'He is Gordin from the Black Mountains and this is Banak from Vint,' the bearded man explained.

'And what of that?' Banak asked, irritably.

'Why, that you're more alike than brothers! You are like twins from the same womb!'

Gordin and Banak looked at each other. They had no way of confirming this.

'It's unbelievable,' one of the bystanders said. 'They are more alike than many twins.'

'Did your mother come from across the seariver? The mother of either of you?' the bearded man asked.

'No,' Gordin said.

'No,' Banak echoed.

Imar was still laughing. Towering as he was over all the other men, he laughed without anxiety. As the others stared at him he held up his two thumbs, and laughed again.

'We have come to exchange antlers for flints,' Gordin said, carefully.

'Don't worry about that. It will all be arranged. But this, you and Banak, it's more than anything we've seen.'

An old man pushed in from the edge of the group surrounding them, which was all the time getting larger. He looked intently into Gordin's face, and then into Banak's.

'It is of Drisil and Dubanak, the brothers-by-blood,' he said gravely.

'How can that be?' the bearded man objected. 'Only Dubanak escaped from the great wave.'

'We cannot be certain,' the old man said. 'No bodies were found from the other boat.'

'But everyone knows what happened,' a young man insisted.

'I know of the great wave,' Gordin said. 'It is long ago, but it is told that our father Idrisil was put in danger by a wave and that he commanded it to be still.'

Several men laughed.

'When the great rams fight in the seariver,' the old man said, 'no human can command the great rising of the waters.'

'We shall never know the truth of it,' the bearded man said. 'But here you two are, more alike than brothers-by-blood. It is a good sign. It is good for the meet.'

There seemed no more to say, though many still stared, and others kept coming up and staring. Gordin and Banak were increasingly uneasy. At last Banak put out his hand, and Gordin took it. Then Banak turned and hurried away on his own business. Gordin stared after him.

Imar touched his wrist and pointed down to the river. Gordin walked with him, still shaken. They found Tarc at the boat, with the antlers ready to carry. They lifted their loads and walked back up the slope to the clearing. Many groups still stood by the fires, but as they waited they heard the sound of a drumbeat, and everyone turned in its direction. Walking through from the east came a long line of men, with loaded bags slung on their shoulders. Gordin and Tarc stared at them, and Imar laughed. For although they were walking there was a strangeness in the way they moved together, each following the other in line. And what was even more strange was that at a sudden shout they all stopped, still holding their loads. There was another shout and together they put their loads down.

The bearded man with the scar had found Gordin again. He pointed across to the newcomers.

'From the White Land.'

'With the flints?'

'Yes.'

'Why do they move like that?'

'It is the way of the White Land. They are many and powerful. They are a family beyond blood.'

'How can that be?' Tarc asked.

'I do not understand it. It is what they say. They tell us that we live poorly, that we make no great works. They tell us of digging and shaping beyond anything we could imagine, and they speak of these shapes with strange words.'

'And these are forced to carry?'

'They do not say so.'

'We saw how they walked. It is like the training of dogs.'

'Do not say that, my son. They are quick to anger and they fight as they walk, like one man.'

The drum sounded again. The bags of the newcomers were opened and the flintcores spread around them. Unevenly, in straggling groups, the shepherds and hunters, with their antlers and hides, moved across to the line.

'Take your antlers,' the bearded man said.

Gordin and Tarc and Imar walked across. They put down their antlers and waited their turn for exchange. Gordin passed the time looking at the men who had brought the flints. Many of them were familiar to look at, of the same colouring and shape as Tarc and himself. But others were taller and more lightly built, with brown hair. Gordin saw the man who had struck the drum. He was unusually short but had very broad shoulders. His face was hard and set, and his cheeks were blotched and reddened in some curious way.

Their turn came to offer their antlers. The man who had struck the drum walked up as they were being counted. He squatted and turned them over.

'From where?' he asked sharply.

It was in their own language, but Gordin and Tarc at first barely understood the words.

'From the Black Mountains,' Tarc said.

'These,' Gordin said, pointing to where their own had been set apart from Imar's.

'They are good. They are both good. Come again.'

Gordin stared down at him.

'May I ask a question?'

'Ask.'

'Why do you need so many antlers? Is it for the digging and shaping?'

'It is for our shaping. You would not understand it.'

'But will you not tell me?'

The man frowned. He eased himself up.

'We have been given signs,' he said impatiently. 'We are altering the earth.'

Gordin and Tarc stared.

'When it is done you will know of it,' he continued. 'Even in your Black Mountains.'

He spoke quickly to the men with the flintcores, who began counting them out on the grass beside the antlers. Imar, who had been watching closely, squatted and turned over each core. Some he began to hand back, but the men in the line waved him away. Imar jumped back and began picking up his own antlers. There was a sudden silence. Imar glared angrily and lifted his right arm.

The silence lasted for some moments, but then the men in the line took the cores that Imar had rejected, and replaced them with others. Imar put down his antlers, examined the new cores, and then laughed and touched their wrists. Gordin and Tarc gathered their own load and got out of the way as others still pressed behind them. It was difficult for them to keep up with Imar as he walked back, whistling, to the boat.

They had to wait on the bank for an ebb tide. Gordin looked across the seariver, his mind full of the strange encounters of the journey and the meet. When he closed his eyes, to see the shape of High Buck, it was at first hard to find it and when at last it came it seemed altered.

The Coming of the Measurer

———◆———

'**B**oy! Boy!'

Karan started and swung round at the strange, harsh voice. He could not see where it had come from. He was at the source of the south river, at some distance from the settlement. The earth was scored with deep gullies, all but one now dry, leading down to the stream which began the south river. The bracken grew thickly between them, and stretched away up the steep side of the mountain towards Hawkstone. He could see nothing larger than a bird moving. All his own people were behind him, on the wide grassland on the northern side of the pass. Where the south river curved, at the end of Cross Valley, blue smoke arose from the first south neighbours, too far for even that sharp voice to carry.

'Use your eyes, boy! Here!'

It was a strange voice. The words were clear but had a different sound. The pitch was hard, like a command to a dog.

He stared pace by pace over the near ground. On a low knoll above one of the gullies, almost hidden by high bracken, was a patch of a strange colour, neither blue nor red: a colour nearer the light that came sometimes at evenings, when the air thickened and was darker and more dusty than smoke.

Karan raised his stick and walked cautiously towards it. He was within a few paces when a yapping started, and a strange dog burst through the bracken and stood challenging him. Karan laughed. It was so small and silly a dog: the size of a pup of a real dog but looking fully grown. It had very smooth yellow hair and sharply pointed cocked ears.

'What are you frightened about?' the strange, hidden voice asked.

'I am not frightened, I am looking,' Karan replied.

'You look very carelessly,' said the voice, and then the patch of colour moved and Karan could see the head and shoulders of a man who was lying in a couch of the bracken.

'Is that really a dog?' Karan asked.

The man lifted himself on his elbows. Karan could see his head more clearly. He was an old man, with a deeply lined face, but what was most surprising was that his hair was yellow: not the brown hair that some of the people had, though most had deep black, but a sharp yellow, brighter than birchleaf in fall, nearer the colour of very young oak leaves but more even.

'Of course it's a dog. And cleverer, I may say, than most humans one meets in these mountains.'

Karan was still staring at the surprising hair. What was most strange about it, he could now see, was that at its roots, over the scalp, it was not yellow but white, like that of many old men. There was not much hair on the face, but the short bristles were also white.

'Are you intending to do anything useful?' the old man asked, still sharply, but now with the edge of a smile.

'I am waiting to know what would be useful,' Karan replied. He held the old man's look. The eyes were a very pale blue but the look was sharp and intent.

'I have fallen and turned my ankle. The foot is already swollen. I have crawled a few paces, but otherwise I cannot move.'

'I am very sorry,' Karan said, and went nearer. The dog yapped again but then began fawning on his legs.

'It is a plaything,' Karan said, looking down at the dog.

'It is a companion. It can feed itself. It can sometimes even feed me.'

'Our dogs are very different.'

'You have no need to tell me. I have met the savage brutes. They are as dangerous as wolves.'

'They are better than wolves,' Karan said proudly.

'But wild.'

'Not with us.'

Karan turned away and walked down to the stream.

'Where are you going, boy? You cannot leave me.'

'I am not leaving you.'

He walked along the stream until he found a spread of moss. He tore out two handfuls, and soaked them in the stream. Then he walked back up to the man and crouched by his injured leg. He did not speak but looked up for permission.

'Yes. Go on.'

Karan wrapped the dripping moss gently around the swollen foot. The man winced but did not cry out as the cold moss touched his skin. As Karan looked up, shyly, he even smiled.

'I will go to fetch others to carry you.'

'Thank you.'

The old man sat up, pulling the cloak of strange colour around his shoulders. Karan was again staring.

'You have not seen this before?' the man asked, touching the cloak with his long white fingers.

'No.'

'Feel it, boy.'

Karan rubbed the strange material between finger and thumb.

'It is not skin,' he said.

'It is wool. It is the wool of the new sheep.'

'Wool?'

'Your own sheep have hair. But where I come from there is a new sheep, with this softer coat, and we pluck, spin and weave it.'

'They are not of that colour?'

'The colour is from berries. This is from berries of elder.'

'It is very soft. But it will not last like our skins.'

'In my work it lasts.'

'You are a shepherd?'

The man smiled.

'I am a Measurer.'

'Measurer? What is that?'

'I will explain it to you, boy. You are quick to learn. But you should go first to fetch others to carry me.'

'I will.'

'This is the cloak of a Measurer,' the man said smiling. 'And this is his rod.'

He lifted from the bracken a long, straight ash stave, longer by head and shoulders than a tall man, and marked along its length with many regular notches.

'There will be time to tell you of all the things that can be measured. But when you are asking the others to carry me, you can tell them that I am a Measurer.'

'They will not know what that means.'

'One or two may know. And if they know they will come quickly.'

'They will come quickly because you are hurt. And I shall run all the way.'

'Thank you, boy.'

Karan had no difficulty in finding men to come and carry the old man. It was a fine bright afternoon of late summer, very still and warm. Most of the sheep were grazing in the shade of the scattered oakwood, but some had gone higher up the mountain, where there was grass among the patches of bracken where the trees had been cleared. The women were higher on the mountain, gathering berries. Most of the men were sitting outside the huts, making arrowheads from chert and chipping flickstones and counters from layers of sandstone that had been heated in brushwood fires and then split by throwing water. It was an easy time of year; the men were talking and laughing.

He found his mother's brother and told him about the old man.

'He says he is a Measurer.'

'What's that?' Idris laughed.

'He is wearing a strange cloak. He says it is made from the hair of a different sheep.'

'He's been having you on. He must be a wicked old man.'

'His foot is very swollen. He can't walk.'

'All right, we'll carry him.'

'And he has a dog not much bigger than a hare. He says it is a dog.'

'That'll make a meal for him anyway.'

'No, it is what he plays with.'

Then all the men laughed.

They did not hurry, but Idris fetched two strong ashpoles for lifting and four men came with him. Karan was uneasy that they seemed to think the old man was a joke. He wondered what would happen when they had to see him and talk to him. For he seemed very sure in his strangeness.

As he walked, behind the men, he looked over the wide valley with its thick oakwoods. When he looked from the mountain to that vast green roof it was difficult to believe that so many creatures were alive there: red deer, pigs, aurochs, wolves. Someone might look at the vast green wood and say nothing lived there, or just laugh if he was told.

Above the bend in Curve River, on the far bank, he could see smoke rising. His father had been born there, in Abisso, among the river people. Karan had sometimes gone down with him to fish. The river people of Abisso often laughed about the sheep people on the mountain. The boys there had chased him, once, trying to make sheep noises and curving their hands by their heads to make out he had horns.

'Where is this misseler then?' Idris called back, as they reached the pass.

Karan ran ahead. Nothing could be seen of the old man or the dog, but he knew where he had left them. The others strode down through the bracken and suddenly the little yellow dog ran out and challenged them, yapping fiercely. The men roared with laughter.

'Spears up,' Idris shouted, his eyes watering with laughter.

There was a sudden flash of colour as the old man sat up.

'He's put the dog's hair on his head,' Idris said, and laughed so much that he dropped his carrying pole and bent over, resting his hands on his knees.

'I am a Measurer,' said the old man, harshly.

He took his rod and tried to use it to stand up but the ground was too rough and he sank down again. Ordin and old Karan went quickly forward. Old Karan bent over the foot.

'Be welcome, stranger,' he said.

'In peace,' said the old man gravely.

They touched hands and foreheads.

'Is it your wish that we carry you to our place?'

'It would be a kindness.'

'It is the law.'

The men brought the carrying poles and slid them under the old man's arms and buttocks.

'Hold. Lift,' said old Karan.

But as they lifted the old man cried out in pain.

'Gently. Down,' said old Karan.

He took off his light skin tunic. The younger men were wearing only summer breeches. He spread the coat along the pole under the buttocks.

'Gently. Lift.'

Again the burden was raised, though the old man was still uneasy.

'We should have brought a hurdle,' Idris said. 'This is a clumsy man.'

The lifters had ignored the measuring rod. Karan picked it up. He looked intently at the notches cut into the ash. He put his middle finger in the space between two of the closest notches and then moved it to try it on the others. Each was at the same place on his skin. But towards the thicker end of the stave the spaces were much longer, more than from fingertip to elbow. On the very tip of the stave was a piece of carved bone, with one upright line and then loose curves around it: wider than a climber around a sapling in the forest but making the same shape.

The men were back up at the pass. Karan hurried after them. The dog stayed close to him, as if close to the rod.

The bearers walked slowly and easily, making little of the weight. Old Karan walked beside them.

'You have come far, stranger?'

'I have walked eleven days.'

'I am Karan. This is our place of Lanoluc.'

'I am Measurer Dal Mered. My old name was Ranan.'

'Is it from the east you have come?'

'It is from Menvandir in the White Land.'

'I have heard much of the White Land. In the days of our fathers we sent antlers. Antlers were changed for flints at the seariver crossing.'

'Yes, Menvandir was being built then, for the new Company of Measurers.'

Old Karan stared at him. The young men, carrying in a slow easy stride, were beginning to sing quietly, their voices low along their paces.

'You are journeying west?'

'I am old. I am returning to where I was Ranan. For I was born in the Hills of the Bluestones.'

'It is eight days. I have carried my stage and talked to others who were carrying. But you can walk no further until you are healed.'

'I am in your hands.'

'You are welcome.'

'I can show you many things. And I can teach the boy.'

'It is not necessary. To help you is the law.'

They walked in among the first oaks. Dal Mered, though uncomfortable on the lifting poles, his foot throbbing with pain, forced himself to look around, to find new things to help against the shock of the accident. The sheep that were grazing under the trees were the old breed, that he had seen everywhere west of the seariver. They were small, reddish-brown, with black horns curving backwards over the neck and very short legs and tails. Yet they looked healthy eating the sappy bright grass in the shade of these slender western oaks.

The people also looked healthy, but there was variation among them. Most of the men were like himself, fifteen to sixteen hands tall, heavily muscled, with shining black hair. But a few were taller and more slender, with brown hair and more rounded faces. He had not yet seen any women, but there must have been exchange with some of the old hunting people, who had remained more numerous in these wilder parts.

The small round huts that he could see were well-built in the old fashion, with close turf walls and solid ash poles in the curving roofs, interlaced with tightly-woven hazel. He looked down at the hearth outside the first hut. It was clean and well-built with the layered red sandstone of these mountains. The black pots were old and round-based but in good condition.

As he saw further through the trees he realised that this was one of the largest settlements he had found since he had crossed the seariver. There were more than thirty huts and at least double that number of smaller shelters. There was a hurdled enclosure in which a few sheep were penned, for some reason he did not know. There was a long drying-rack on which deer hides were stretched after curing. There was a stream flowing east, along the line where the oaks began to thicken and merge into forest. But there were also pools in hollows towards the rise of the mountain, where the slender durmast oaks thinned.

It was a simple, well-ordered, well-provided settlement, the kind of safe, quiet place he seemed to remember from his boyhood, though he had often suspected that memory had softened and improved it. Yet it was so utterly different from the great Round House of the Company, with its elaborate furniture, its fine flat-base pottery, its woven and brightly-dyed clothes and its prepared and varied food. It was as if he had moved in eleven days' walk from one time, one world, to another. Yet it had been his own decision to leave the Round House and the Company and walk west. There had been a lifetime of interest in Menvandir, at the growing-point of the world. He belonged to its modernity, and his mind could never slip back into these old settled ways. Yet, quite apart from more particular reasons, he had become old and tired in his body, and it was as if his very breathing seemed to crave the softer and sweeter air of that west in which he had been born.

They were setting him down at one of the huts. He gathered that it was the hut of old Karan. Two of the young men lifted him in their arms and took him in and laid him on a bed of soft skin over bracken. Old Karan fetched him water to drink and a small withy basket of young hazelnuts and whinberries.

'Do you want meat?' old Karan asked.

'You eat mutton?'

'Surely.'

'I will wait, thank you. It is many years since I have eaten mutton. At Menvandir we eat mostly pork.'

'Indeed?' said old Karan, and backed away.

While Dal Mered was eating the nuts and berries, the boy came in and carefully laid down the measuring rod. He was obviously shy and uneasy.

'What is your name, boy?'

'It is Karan.'

'The name of the old man?'

'Yes. He is the father of Idris, who is the brother of my mother.'

'When I have rested, Karan, will you come to talk to me?'

'I will come,' the boy said.

When the women came down from the mountain, with their osier baskets filled with berries and the big dogs barking and running around them, Dal Mered was already asleep. The shock of the fall had exhausted him. He looked very aged and weak, lying on the bed in old Karan's hut. Several of the women came and looked in at him. Karan's mother Seril went in and looked at the swollen foot, now purple with bruising. She covered the thin body with another skin.

'He will not walk before the snows,' she said, moving out to the hearth.

'He is old and weak,' she said again. 'But do you see his hands? They are not hands that have worked.'

'He is a Measurer,' Karan said.

'He is still a mouth and a belly.'

'Yet we have enough.'

'It is easy for you, boy, to say we have enough.'

'Did you see his cloak and his hair, mother?'

The other women smiled. They had all seen Seril touching the cloak and the hair between her fingers.

'He is not like a man,' Seril said.

'He is of course a man.'

One of the girls laughed. Karan frowned and wandered away.

Dal Mered slept through the rest of the day and the night. Old Karan slept beside him, and in the morning gave him food and put fresh wet moss on his foot. It was a bad injury; the whole foot was swollen and dark. In the middle of the morning old Karan was sitting in the sun at the entrance and young Karan came and sat beside him.

'He said that he wanted to talk to me.'

'Be patient, boy. He must rest.'

But then the strange, harsh voice came from inside the hut.

'He has the true spirit in him,' Dal Mered said. 'He knows that I am not an injured animal. He knows that I understand what he wishes to learn.'

Karan looked inside the hut. There was a pleasant brown shade where the sunlight was striking the roof. Dal Mered was sitting up on the bed.

'Do you hear me, boy?'

'Yes, Dal Mered, I hear you.'

In the quiet brown shade, through the bright day, Dal Mered told Karan of the life of the Measurers. He had been a boy in a sheep village, in the Hills of the Bluestones, by the shore of the western sea. One day strangers had come from the east to the village. They had come to see the bluestones but also they carried rods and every night they went out to the hills to watch the rise and set of the moon. The boy Ranan had followed them, 'curious like yourself'. They had told him that they were attempting a new way of measuring the movements of the moon. He had asked why and they had laughed. Then one of them had said that they could measure from the moon how the tides would come, and over the next days Ranan had helped them, placing sticks in the sand to measure the tides.

'And is that why you do it,' Ranan had asked, 'for men to know when to fish and to sail in the sea?'

'It is why we began it,' the answer had come, 'But it is now more.'

'Do you understand that, boy?' Dal Mered asked.

'No,' Karan replied.

'I did not understand it either. But I came to understand it.'

Karan frowned.

'It is for the moon itself,' he suggested. 'It is to know more of the moon.'

Dal Mered reached out and touched his hand, smiling.

'No, boy, though that is what I also thought. It is not for the moon, it is for men.'

Dal Mered rested again, but later continued his story. Old Karan came near to listen.

When the strangers had left, to go back to the east, the boy Ranan had decided to follow them.

'To leave your own people?' Karan asked.

'We were many. We were more than enough.'

'But did you not ask?'

'I asked no one. My mother's brother had died in the sea.'

Karan nodded and waited.

Ranan had kept out of sight of the strangers, following only at a distance, until they came at last to the seariver. Then, while they rested, waiting for the tide, he had shown himself at their camp.

'There is a crossing,' said Dal Mered, 'by a great curve in the river, where there is a red cliff and the riverbed is hard.'

'I know it,' said old Karan. 'It is Begisso, where the antlers were taken for the White Land, when they were digging the great ditches.'

'It is where I crossed again,' Dal Mered said, 'five days ago, on my way back to the west.'

The strangers had not been surprised to see the shepherd boy following them. 'It is how we have all come together,' the oldest of them had said.

So Ranan went with them, to their settled place. It was the great Menvandir. It was where he had stayed to live and work for thirty-four years. It was where he had ceased to be Ranan and had become Dal Mered.

Karan's head was full of questions, but he was too shy to put them. He wanted to know more about the measuring and about the moon and the tides. But even more he wanted to know about sun and wind and cloud, the strange everyday forces that he watched in his own mountains. He was sure that there were answers that Dal Mered could give him, and that they would be much more important than the familiar talk about places and names.

Yet he held back, and the questions – if they were that; they were more like suggestions for the next thing to talk about – came from old Karan, and were all about places and names. Dal Mered said little about what old Karan best knew: the power of the White Land and of its Great Order under the rule of Albhundos. Dal Mered said only that Albhundos was now dead. Of the great ditches and of the lines of great stones, Dal Mered said only that they belonged to an earlier time. Even of the great stone circle, which an earlier traveller had reported, Dal Mered said only that its finest stones were from his own native hills. As old Karan dropped his gaze, disappointed, Dal Mered said quickly that there were many orders and forms of order: of power in learning and of learning in power: there were essential differences. Old Karan did not understand, and was silent for some time.

At last, under the pressure of hospitality, he spoke of Menvandir. The change in Dal Mered was immediate. It was as if he came to life with the word. 'Menvandir,' he repeated, lingering on the word. 'Menvandir is within the Great Order but it is not of it.' Then, as old Karan stared at him he added quickly: 'It was not of it.'

'It is a place. A fine place,' old Karan prompted.

'It is a place like others,' Dal Mered replied. 'But its importance is not the place. Its importance is the idea. For we are not the priests of the Great Order. We are the Measurers.'

Old Karan said nothing.

'It is not the place, it is the measuring,' Dal Mered continued.

'But still a fine place,' old Karan said and smiled.

Dal Mered glanced at Karan, and smiled in his turn.

'Yes, a fine place,' he said, nodding, and turned back to old Karan. Among the many flourishing settlements and the many great monuments of the White Land, Menvandir was a large Round House. It was more than forty paces across, with rings of oak posts supporting a great roof. Outside this house, with its entrance posts facing the summer sunrise, was a platform of blocks and gravel, twenty paces by ten. There was a smaller, neighbouring enclosure, which would contain, within it, more than fifty huts of the size in which they were now sitting. There were other, smaller houses, and around the whole company there was a huge ditch and bank, more than thirteen hundred paces to walk around, which had taken a hundred men more than two years to dig and build.

'It was why they needed our antlers,' old Karan said, proudly, but Dal Mered ignored him.

As a place, he explained, Menvandir was only one of the great centres, but it was now the most honoured, the most respected, within the island and beyond.

'Why should it be honoured?' Karan asked.

The question came too abruptly. He felt awkward as soon as he heard it. He was relieved but also resentful when Dal Mered ignored it. Yet the Measurer was helped to ignore it by old Karan, who had a different interest.

'What animals do you keep?' old Karan asked.

'None,' said Dal Mered, proudly.

'None?'

'None of the kind you mean. Though the Dalen have dogs.'

'The little dogs? Like this one you brought with you?'

'The same,' said Dal Mered. 'When a man has become Dal.'

Old Karan was uneasy. It took him some time to speak again.

'Is it grain then you grow and eat?'

'Menvandir keeps no animals and grows no grain,' Dal Mered said, smiling.

'But how can men live without food?'

'Our food is brought to us,' Dal Mered explained. 'The meat is already butchered, the grain is already flour.'

'Why is that done?' old Karan asked, staring.

'Why?' Dal Mered repeated. 'Why, so that we can eat it, of course.'

Karan looked away. The question had been simple, and it had not been answered. It could be put again, but that was not the problem. The problem was this man, with his strange cloak and hair and his still stranger mind. Down the slope he could see Idris and Ordin building an enclosure with hurdles, under the oak with the old hollow. It was the same every year, trying to build that enclosure strong and high enough to contain all the rams they could catch, to hold back the lambing until after the snows. They were working easily but arguing as usual. He could see Idris stretching his arm above his head and jumping. It would be the same story of that one remarkable ram, which had leaped a fence even higher than Idris could show. The joke had been that they had called that ram Idris, but though pleased at first he had stopped them going on with it, for it was not only a joke about the jumping.

'You spoke a word I do not know,' old Karan was saying.

'There are many words,' said Dal Mered.

Karan again looked away. Was this how questions were asked and answered, by men who could measure the moon and the sea?

'You said "Company",' old Karan continued.

And now young Karan smiled, for he saw that the question had been reached in another way, like a path around a scree.

'It is difficult to explain to you,' Dal Mered said. 'But the Company *is* Menvandir. Menvandir is not the place, it is the Company. It is not even the Company, it is the idea. The idea of true measuring: not an order but a measuring.'

'Yet you have told us of the wonderful place and of the great houses.'

'It is the necessary place of the Company,' Dal Mered said. 'It is the place of the Company of Measurers.'

'Who do not herd or grow?'

'Who do not herd or grow, but who measure the whole world.'

Young Karan leaned forward, now intent.

'The whole world?' old Karan asked.

'Not only the sun and the moon,' Dal Mered said, proudly, 'but all the places of the earth and the movements of the sea. Even the movements, now, of certain stars.'

Old Karan said nothing. He was staring, open-mouthed, at this strange figure on his bed, with his injured and blackened foot.

'And the movements of wind and of cloud?' Karan asked.

'Those are simpler,' Dal Mered said, indifferently.

'Yet I would be glad to learn them.'

'It is not just wind and cloud, boy,' Dal Mered said, and now smiled more kindly. 'It is the learning to measure. And that, if you have time from your sheep, I may begin to show you.'

'It is what I want,' Karan said.

But it was already time for eating, and Seril was bringing Dal Mered his food.

'I have a question,' Karan said, when they were able to talk again on the next day.

'Ask it,' said Dal Mered, leaning back.

'I have noticed the shadows of clouds that move along the slopes of our mountains.'

'Because the clouds are between the sun and the mountains,' Dal Mered said, easily.

'That is not the question. I have looked up and seen the clouds which are making the shadows. From where I have been standing I could often see the sun but if I had been standing where the shadows were running I would not have seen it.'

'Of course.'

'And when the great shadows run I have noticed the wind. Often if they are running towards me I feel the wind on my face, and it is the same wind that is moving the clouds. Or if they are running away from me I feel the wind on my back.'

'This is very simple.'

'It is not always simple. For I have stood when the shadows have been running away from me and I have felt the wind on my face. And I have stood when they have been running towards me and felt the wind on my back.'

Dal Mered narrowed his eyes.

'Often?' he asked.

'Not often. But I have seen it several times. And I do not understand it, for then the clouds are moving against the wind. Is it then something else that is moving them?'

Dal Mered smiled and waited.

'There are stories of the clouds,' Karan said. 'They are the children of the winds and the winds are the children of Mother Danu. The clouds are close to us and bring us many words. All children are told of the clouds that speak to us.'

'You have heard the clouds speaking?'

'I have not heard them. I have heard the thundercloud but there are then no shadows for the sky is dark. When the shadows run there is only a great silence, except for the sound of the wind in the leaves.'

'Of course.'

'But then how can it be that clouds can move against the wind?'

Dal Mered smiled, watching him.

'The answer is waiting, Karan.'

'Not for me, Dal Mered.'

'When they move against the wind, are the clouds high?'

'They are then always high.'

'Yet because you cannot measure them you cannot say how high.'

'It is impossible.'

'But what is also impossible is that clouds should move against the wind.'

'I have seen them moving against the wind.'

'Against the wind on your face or on your back?'

'Against whatever wind is on my body.'

Dal Mered held up his hand.

'Then it cannot be the same wind.'

'The wind is the wind.'

'Not always, boy. I will tell you. In the mountains, especially, there can be a wind near the earth, that may be blowing in your face, but there can be also an upper wind, where the clouds are moving, and it can blow in a different direction. When this has happened you have noticed it.'

Karan looked down. Dal Mered watched him, intently.

'That is the answer, boy, isn't it?'

'If you say so, Dal Mered.'

'Not if I say so. It is the answer because it must be the answer.'

'This upper wind . . .' Karan said, and broke off.

'Yes?'

'We cannot feel it on our faces, or see it blowing in the trees?'

'No.'

'Then perhaps it is just a story, like the clouds speaking to us.'

'With one difference. Think.'

'I am thinking.'

'You feel a wind on your face and you see it blowing in the trees.'

'Blowing away from the cloud shadows.'

'But then you have learned that the upper wind is a different wind. For you can see it blowing the clouds, just as you see the ground wind blowing the trees. You believe what you see in the trees because it is also on your face. You must now take the next step, to go out from yourself and learn to measure what is beyond you.'

'How can that be learned?'

'It is only what you learned when you noticed the run of the shadows.'

'I did not learn it. I only saw it.'

'You saw it. You asked questions. It is the way of Menvandir.'

'I know nothing about Menvandir.'

'Except that we keep these silly yapping dogs?'

'To measure them, I suppose. To see how small they are.'

Dal Mered laughed, and Karan, after a while, also began laughing. He then laughed so much that it was a long while before he could stop.

The injured foot took a very long time to heal. In the first days Dal Mered had to be helped everywhere, but after ten days he could move short distances with his rod to help him. He liked walking around the settlement and talking to everyone. Everyone was interested when he told them about the new sheep, and about the wool and the woven cloth that could be made from them. But they were on different grass, out there in the east, on the plain of the White Land. Nobody knew if they could live on this grass of the mountains. Meanwhile the old sheep were good and gave them all they needed from them: milk and cheese, meat and skins.

'It is said that ours are the old sheep,' old Karan said, 'that were brought in ships from the sea.'

'You have that story?' Dal Mered asked. 'It is a story often told in the yellow hills east of the seariver, that the old sheep were brought in ships from the sea.'

'It is told but we do not know. It is told that all but the first of our flock were lost in the sea.'

Dal Mered smiled.

'In the jaws of the great wave which only Dubanak escaped from?'

'In the jaws of the great wave, but it was Idrisil who escaped. He came to these Black Mountains with the first of our flock.'

'It is told differently in the Yellow Hills on the east of the seariver.

It is told that Drisil and all his people were swallowed by the wave, and that Dubanak alone escaped to the Yellow Hills having spread his white cloak on the angry waves, and with a ram and a ewe to found his flock.'

Old Karan rubbed at his face.

'As I have said, we do not know. But the stories are told.'

'Is it told how Drisil escaped the wave?'

'In these mountains it is told that Idrisil commanded the wave to be still, and that the wave obeyed his crook.'

Dal Mered laughed.

'It was all before the time of the Measurers,' he said. 'In the time before the Measurers anything could be believed.'

Preparations were now beginning for the coming of the snows. There were already sharp night frosts, which were touching the high bracken, turning the ends of the fronds brown. As the frosts continued the oak leaves were touched, and on the ridges above them, from Hawkstone to High Buck, there was glistening rime every morning, and soon in the gullies it was lasting all day. Though his foot was slowly healing, it was clear to everyone that Dal Mered could not set out on his long journey west before the snows. He would have to stay with them until melt and the warm days of spring. What puzzled them, however, and made the women complain, was that as this became clear, and as the days passed, he said nothing about the trouble of providing him with food through so many moons. Old Karan recalled that where the Measurer had come from, in Menvandir, they kept no animals and sowed no grain but had their food given to them, pork and fine flour.

'Then they must be fools on that plain,' Seril said. 'Giving pork and flour so that these misselers can sit with their yellow hair and do nothing.'

'They are the Measurers,' Karan said, as if explaining a mystery.

'Measurers, is it? But so are we measurers. The men measure the hay that has been cut at midsummer. They count the young tups and the moons in which they must be killed. We women measure the moons and our stores of nuts and grain and honey. If it is a long deep snow there is never enough.'

'There is still the hunting in the forest.'

'Yes, and the hunting is work. We all work so we can eat. What would happen to us if we made our hair yellow and sat waiting for pork and for flour?'

'He is an old man, mother.'

'He is a lazy man. He is a greedy man.'

'He has said that he will teach me many things.'

'He has taught you nothing. I have heard him. He only sits and talks!'

'He has given me an answer about the shadows of clouds on the mountain.'

'Then let him eat the shadows of clouds.'

Yet though the frosts were early and there were the usual anxieties, it had been a good season. There were heavy crops of acorns in the more open parts of the forest. This would be good because it would bring up the wild pigs to feed. Not only Dal Mered would get his pork. In some years there were only a few acorns and then the pigs were less, not only through the winter but in the following years.

The real difficulty was always the sheep: how to keep enough breeding ewes until the grass was growing again. There were years in which the whole flock could be reduced to almost nothing. Some in any case had to be exchanged for grain from the seariver. In one very bad year only eight breeding ewes had been kept and even then several of their lambs were lost. Until the flock recovered, over the following three years, they had been dependent on hunting and fishing, and there had been quarrels with the river people about where they could hunt and fish. The neighbours in Cross Valley, further into the mountains, had lost all their sheep in that year and had moved away to the lake, where there had even been fighting with the people of Glaura: a terrible wrong, which it had taken many feasts to heal, when the times eased again and lambs were exchanged for venison and pots. Then the Cross Valley people had moved back to the mountains. In that very bad time there had been no marriages between the families and there had been many sick children. Every sign had seemed to fail. They could burn and dance at midwinter but still the feasts were meagre and the signs failed.

Karan spoke of all this to Dal Mered. He could not pass on his mother's complaints but he wanted to hear what the Measurer would say about the times of shortage of food. Dal Mered said very little.

'Men eat what they can get,' he said, casually. 'When there is shortage it is often their faulty reckoning.'

'Of the food?'

'Of the food and of the time.'

'But how can that be? We can all count the moons.'

'In a rough way, of course.'

'In the cold times, one moon of frost, four moons of snow, one moon of frost again.'

'That many?' Dal Mered asked.

'Yes, indeed, in these mountains.'

'Then you are in the wrong place. In the Hills of the Bluestones there are at most three moons of frost.'

'How can that be? Is it not the same winter?'

'It is the warmth of the sea that protects their lands.'

'Can the sea be warm?'

'It is warmer than the land in the cold season. This shortens the frosts.'

'And on the plain, in Menvandir?'

Dal Mered drew himself up. He seemed to change, always, when the name of Menvandir was spoken.

'It cannot be reckoned by your kind of counting on fingers or by bags of pebbles or scratches on stones. But there are never so many as four moons of snow. The snow is less than in your mountains, and the land is easier, with fields for grain and cattle to nourish their soil.'

Karan looked at him, artfully.

'But if we are in the wrong place, you are here also. Until your foot is healed and you can make your long journey.'

'They've been complaining, have they?' Dal Mered said, smiling.

'No,' Karan said. 'No, they wouldn't complain.'

'Why do you lie to me, boy?'

'I am not lying.'

'If the truth is always told all things can be measured. It is the first law of the Company.'

'All our things are measured,' Karan said, looking away. 'We tell the truth but always with kindness.'

'Then we must measure the kindness,' Dal Mered said, and laughed.

It seemed, all the same, that the conversation had had some effect, for in the next days Dal Mered began teaching Karan the beginnings of measuring, and he took care to do this where others could see them. There was still a steady preparation for the coming of the snows. As the bracken dried it was cut and carried to the huts, and the old bracken from the beds was hauled out and burned. The rams were now penned in the enclosure, to delay the mating. The hunting tools were sharpened and some of the younger men were already going down into the forest, watching for the pigs to come for acorns. The women were also collecting acorns, in case young pigs were caught and could be kept. Among all this work of the season Dal Mered found a level area of grass, already bitten short by the sheep. He explained first to Karan the simple uses of his rod. He showed him the full pace, notched on the rod, and had him measure simple but very exact lengths. Karan enjoyed this at first but complained when he was asked to repeat and repeat it.

'You have seen that I can do it.'

'It must become like breathing, until you are never wrong.'

'I have not been wrong.'

'But now it is all you are thinking about. You must do it and do it again until at any time you are exact.'

Karan obeyed and continued, through the length of the day, and in the end Dal Mered rewarded him, for they went together to cut an ash stave and to make Karan's own pace-rod.

'It will do while you are learning. But for a real rod you must cut and season the stave, if you are to be exact.'

Karan did not mind. He was happy to have the small rod. Steadily, through the following days, Dal Mered took him through all the beginnings of measuring. They marked a pace from Dal Mered's rod on a boulder at the edge of the settlement, graving the mark lines deep so that the pace rod could be regularly confirmed. Then Dal Mered showed him the making of an exact circle, with a stave driven into the turf and a hide rope attached to it and to a sharp stone with which the outline was traced. It was necessary to try this again and again. The rope would be left slightly slack at some point, or its turning on the central stave would be uneven, or the graving of the outline would be disturbed in the irregular ground. It took more than two days before Karan could produce a circle with which Dal Mered was satisfied, and by then the others were beginning to laugh at what they were doing, since the people had always built good circular huts which were tidy enough for anybody.

'It is to get beyond the round hut,' Dal Mered said, grandly. 'From the exact circle many things are possible.'

Karan went on with his practising. In the next days Dal Mered showed him how to find exact places in any circle, by stretching hide ropes from points on its outline and marking exactly where they crossed. When this had been learned he showed him how to make a three-pointed shape within the outline of the circle and to connect the three points so carefully that each rope between them was of exactly the same length. For these measurements they went down from the notched pace to its five divisions, and there was a new long time of measuring, again and again, to these different notches.

The frosts were sharper now each night, and in the mornings the grass around the settlement was rimed white. Yet the sun still shone steadily, through the continuing fine days. One morning Dal Mered seemed especially excited, as if he were bringing a gift.

'Do you know, boy, what you call the middle of the day?'

'I know it.'

'In the way you would now know, exactly, the centre of a circle?'

'It is when the sun is highest in the sky.'

'But how do you know when it is highest?'

'We cannot be certain of that. But we do not need to know it. We know the middle of the day for when we are hunting or following the flock.'

'Yet to know the exact middle of the day is life for the Measurers.'

'Perhaps. But we see that the sun is high. To know more is not possible.'

'It is not only possible. It is very simple. Come, I will show you.'

They went to a new stretch of grass, with a wide outlook. They set up a tall straight ash stave, of the length of Dal Mered's rod. Karan fetched pegs of hazel, and Dal Mered told him to place one at the end of the shadow thrown by the stave. They sat together, looking out over the wide valley. The oakforest was now brown, and the leaves were beginning to fall from the other trees.

'Now, where is your shadow?' Dal Mered asked, after they had waited for some time.

Karan put a second peg at the end of the new dark line. He

thought then that he could understand this. As it neared midday he put in more pegs, at the ends of the moving shadow. They went in at shorter and shorter intervals. Dal Mered watched him, smiling. When there were eleven pegs in place he told him to begin measuring from the stave to each peg. Karan was not surprised, after working with him so much, that the tenth peg was the shortest distance from the stave.

'So the tenth,' he said, 'is the centre of the day?'

'Your tenth is your nearest to the centre.'

'Then I should have put in more, to be exact.'

'Yes, but now that you understand it, it will be simple to do.'

'Because the shortest shadow is when the sun is highest?'

'Yes.'

'But then it can be done once and for all. I can set a stave outside my mother's hut and find the shortest shadow and mark it. Then we can always know when it is the centre of the day.'

'No,' Dal Mered said.

He looked very pleased with himself as he said this, but his look changed when he saw Karan's disappointment.

'We might wish that it could be so,' he said, 'but it is not so. For the sun moves, through its seasons, and at different times of the year it throws different lengths of shadow.'

'Yet always with the shortest as the centre?'

'Yes, but then there are different shortest marks, and you would have to measure between them. That is a whole new kind of measuring, not to be done on one day but through days and moons, and in the end through many years.'

'That is Menvandir?'

'It was the beginning of Menvandir. There it is not now a problem. It is as simple as measuring a man's pace to measure a simple year.'

Karan looked up at him.

'Is that why you left, Dal Mered, to go back to where you were born? Because it is all now so simple.'

'No, boy. For even the year is not simple, by the measurements of Menvandir, though for ordinary measuring it is simple enough. For it is then not only the sun. It is also the moon, as with those strangers who came when I was a boy to the Bluestone Hills.'

'It has not all become simple?'

'Certain things are simple. But it is like these mountains of yours. You see a ridge and you climb to it, but when you have reached it there is a further ridge beyond it, and again and again, seeming always beyond. Here you come at last to your real ridges, but the ridges of Menvandir are as many as the waves of the sea, or as the oaks in your woods. There is always a beyond.'

'So that men get tired? You got tired of measuring.'

'No,' Dal Mered said, with a spurt of anger.

'You have finished all your measuring and now you go back to where you were born?'

'No,' Dal Mered shouted, and abruptly stood up. He cried out as in the rapid movement he put too much weight on his bruised foot. He grabbed the stave that had been measuring the sun's shadows and whirled it around his head and threw it far down. It landed near a sheep, which jumped and hurried quickly away. Karan wanted to laugh at the sheep, but there was no mistaking Dal Mered's anger. He said nothing but quietly gathered up the pegs. Dal Mered did not speak again as they walked down to the settlement.

On the next day the snow came. It fell heavily, in small flakes, out of an east wind. For most of the day the family stayed in the huts, though they kept big fires burning on the hearths outside their entrances and there were always two or three men down in the wood, where the sheep had gathered, finding shelter under the bigger oaks. The big dogs were with them, but Dal Mered's little dog stayed inside the hut, at the foot of his bed.

It snowed for four days, lying deep on the open mountain but in more scattered patches under the oaks. Then during the fourth night the snow stopped falling and the next morning was clear, with a fine blue sky and the sun shining. It was wonderful to look at the white mountains, gleaming under the sun. They seemed different, in their presence, from the familiar shapes of summer. Then there were variations of colour and movement in the growth of the different plants, in the scattered boulders, and in the earth-colouring and shadows of the watercourses. Now the shining white had changed them into simpler forms, and their relative distances seemed to have changed.

Karan stood by the big fire, staring up at the white ridges against the blue sky from Hawkstone to High Buck. But there was now a lot to do and soon everyone, except Dal Mered, was out working. The weight of snow had to be brushed from the roofs of the huts. The areas around hearths and entrances had to be cleared. The young men stayed with the sheep, clearing areas in the deeper wood where there was still some long grass. And now the rams were released from the enclosure and went down to eat with the flock. Bundles of hay were carried down to them. Karan helped Seril to clear their entrance and hearth and woodpile. He did not think of Dal Mered.

It was a little different each winter but it often happened that after the first big snow there was a moon of fine bright weather, though with the air cold and the snow still lying, its surface melting a little each day under the sun but then glazing overnight and keeping its shapes. After three bright days, with the settlement again in order, Karan walked to see Dal Mered. He was sitting on his bed, playing with the ears of his dog. He did not look up. He was still wearing his strange coloured cloak, but he had pulled the bed hides over his legs and feet.

'You have no clothes for winter?' Karan asked.

'It is arranged,' Dal Mered said, hoarsely.

'You thought that before the snows you would be back where you were born?'

'Thought? Hoped,' Dal Mered said, staring down at the dog's small pointed ears.

Karan waited but nothing more was said. He went back to his own hut.

On the following morning he went again. Dal Mered was still sitting on his bed but he was now dressed for winter, in a fur cloak over a thick hide tunic and breeches and with new thonged high boots. His yellow hair had now faded to white, with only a streak remaining. Karan stood and waited. He would not risk saying anything.

'Your people are kind,' Dal Mered said, looking at him.

Karan did not answer.

'Did I frighten you, boy, when I took that stave and hurled it?'

'No, I was not frightened. Your anger was not against me.'

'You saw that?'

'I thought that.'

'You did not measure it?'

Karan looked away. He was always being surprised by this

strange old man, who did not speak by custom and whose words could be praise or blame yet there was no sure way of knowing.

'Will you walk with me, boy?'

'Yes.'

Dal Mered took his rod and they followed what had become a cleared track out of the settlement, towards the place where the near stream tumbled in a waterfall over a wide flat rock. Dal Mered stood, looking down at the waterfall.

'I have a story to tell you, boy. It is not, at first, for the others.'

'All our stories belong to us all,' Karan said.

'Do you think I do not know that? I have heard such stories. Of your Drisil who commanded the wave to be still with his crook. Of Dubanak who was saved by his cloak. Of the clouds who speak. Of the great boar of the forest, who is hunted under the moon. Of how the dead rise and race through the sky on the storm.'

'It is told,' Karan said.

'It is not what I am telling. I am telling you of Menvandir.'

'You have shown me how to measure and that is Menvandir.'

'It is and it is not, boy. That is my story.'

He turned and looked out to the west. Into the far distance there was ridge after ridge of snow-covered hills, shining under the sun but at the greatest distance seeming to fade into mist.

'I was Ranan in that distance,' Dal Mered said, 'among my own people who herded sheep in the Hills of the Bluestones. I have told you how I went with the strangers to Menvandir. At first all I could see was the marvel of what they had made in the White Land. The many hundreds of people, and the great buildings of earth and of stone, wonderful buildings and monuments that were as if they had made their own world, on that great plain, and would endlessly make and remake it. Then I was shown how to measure. Through moons and years I was shown the measuring that I have begun to show you. For there were always new things to know. It was seven years before I was admitted to the Company and then four years again before I was made Dal.'

'What is Dal?'

'The Dalen are the great Measurers. They are the keepers of Menvandir.'

'And you are one of them?'

'I became Dal, and at the same time, for it is the law, I took my new name Mered. For the boy Ranan was now in another life. He did not belong in the life of a measurer.'

'You put away your own name?'

'It is nothing, boy, the name. When you are made Dal there is a wonderful new life. It is the life of the great Round House, eating together, and there is always new measuring and there are many trials of shapes. At times for a whole moon there is the hardest measuring, in which we use no pegs or ropes but try shapes and movements which are not seen in earth or sky but which may be made to tie and to weave, this way and that, all the figures we have actually measured. There are shapes we seem to find, deep within ourselves, that are the underlying shapes of the world. We call these shapes golden, but it is not to be explained, it must be done. And while it is being done, there is no other world, no other life. The hand reaches for food, or stops in the act of reaching as a new shape comes, and there is nothing beyond the shapes, in the minds of the whole company, under the great roof of the Round House.'

'Do the shapes have names?'

Dal Mered smiled.

'It is not a world of names. While we measure in these ways we are Dalen. There are no names in us or in what we are trying and weaving.'

'It is of the moon?'

'You remember well. It was of the moon, through all my first years as Dal. For there was then a new tying of the life of the moon. There had been the waxing and waning that all can see, as we see the life of animals. Season after season, moon after moon, each different but following the same run of shapes, as you might watch it yourself above your mountains. That was how we saw the life of the moon, moon after moon as lamb after lamb in their seasons. But there was then a new tying. For it was found in Menvandir that there is another life of the moon, another shape of its life. Beyond the new moons, which all men can see, there is a strange season, in some other life. It begins and ends through nearly nineteen years, as these are measured by the sun.'

'That is the different measuring?'

'It is very strange. For when we had made the new tying, after the measuring of the Dalen that were before us, it was like a new world. When our food was brought to us we told the people. We were very excited. We also told them that they must build another Round House to continue the new measuring. For it had not escaped us that this new season of the moon is the time of growing from a child to a man.'

'And there would then be new signs?'

Dal Mered pressed his fingers against his eyes, which were watering slightly in the cold mountain air.

'We measure, boy, to find signs, but are all measurements signs?'

'I do not understand.'

'You are not alone. It is the storm of Menvandir.'

'The storm?'

Dal Mered turned and paced around, leaning on his rod.

'What did your mother say about giving me food?'

'She said nothing.'

'It is your kindness to say so, but it is not necessary. It has been said, many times, to Menvandir.'

'About the food?'

'In Menvandir, as I told you, we do not keep animals, we do not grow grain. The people of the plain bring us meat and flour. They butcher the meat, they grind the flour. We have little to do but to eat.'

'And to measure.'

Dal Mered lifted his rod.

'Yet why, boy, do the people bring us food?'

'Because of the signs?'

'Yes, but even you have signs, here in your mountains. You have signs to measure midsummer and midwinter. You have signs of snow and of growth. You have signs of putting the bones of your dead in the chambers of the Long House. You have all these signs, and they are surely enough for you. They are all that you need for your life in these mountains. And you live good lives. Your people are healthy and you are at peace and fed.'

'And the people of the plain?'

'It is the same with them. The priests of the Great Order give the signs of the years.'

'Yet still they come for new signs?'

Dal Mered leaned on his rod. He again looked far out, at the distant hills.

'Is that why they come? This is the story I am telling you. It took a hundred men more than two years to dig and build the great ditch and bank from Menvandir. It was the same men, gathered from the plain, who built our great houses, and their women brought us food that had been butchered and prepared. When they came they were shown signs, and at each new tying there would be a new house, and more in the company, although in some bad years there was neither strength nor food to spare.'

'They could not build and bring you food?'

'They came,' Dal Mered said, and pressed his fingers against his eyes.

'I do not understand.'

Dal Mered lifted his rod. He held it in both hands, high above his head.

'You have seen the wonder of measuring. You know, in yourself, the wonder that moved in me as a boy, that took me from being Ranan to Menvandir and Dal. It is still a wonder. It has never ceased to move in me. You asked if I was tired when I left Menvandir. I was an old man, but I was not tired of measuring. When I get back to where I was born I shall go on measuring. It is a good place, from the mountains, with the long levels of the sea. But I shall measure as I have always measured, for the measuring itself and because it delights me. I will not give signs, for I am not a priest but a Measurer.'

'But you ought to give signs, when there is a new tying.'

'Signs of what, boy? Tell me. To measure the year, to measure the tides, to know when to plant and to breed? The priests have these signs already, and they have helped the people. What new signs should I give?'

'There are the signs of the world.'

'It is said.'

'Are they not the signs of the world?'

'You rebuke me, boy. But you do not understand. While there are signs for living and growing, it is right for us to measure and for others to build and grow food. But it is no longer only so. The best of us measure because we love measuring. The worst of us give signs because it is a way of getting food. I have measured it, through the years, and it is now exact. It will be the end of Menvandir, as of the Great Order itself.'

'How can so great a thing end?'

'In greed, Karan. In greed and in anger, the two working together. Across the plain, while I have lived there, the people have multiplied. They grow and breed well but there are now so many that the land is crowded and trampled. In the bad years the food is not enough even to feed themselves. Then pigs suddenly sicken and die. We cannot measure the sickness, though many have tried, but still the Dalen give signs and ask for pork. The grain blights and we cannot measure it, but again the signs are given and the Dalen get flour. While the people work hard and need rest, Menvandir asks yet again for a new house, a new bank, to be built. Among the eldest Dalen, of whom I became one, there is no measuring of this. The food must be brought, the houses must be built. It must all continue as it has been. But then, Karan, there was the storm.'

'A storm of the great winds?'

'Winds blow themselves out. This was a different storm. After a bad year, in which many pigs and cattle had died, and in which the Dalen asked yet again for another house to be built, the people refused us both food and work.'

'But that would be the end of the measuring.'

'No, Karan. Not the end. We could hunt, like others, and then measure again. It is what a few of us proposed, but we were not listened to. There was then a sign of the sun going dark, that all Measurers knew must happen, whether we measured it or not. But the Company decided to punish the people for refusing us food. The Dalen warned that the sun would go dark if they disobeyed us. They spoke in strange, heavy words, as the priests speak, the priests of the Great Order. And when indeed it went dark, at the time we had measured, it was a sign for fear, and the people cried and bowed down. Within a few days the food was brought to us, pitiful food from the hunting, and men came from across the plain to build the new house.'

'It was not a sign?'

'It was the sun going dark. It would have gone dark whatever we did on our plain. For it was the path of the moon that crossed the path of the sun. It was not our doing. It was not a sign of our power. That is what is known from real measuring.'

'Then it was wrong to threaten the people?'

'It was wrong but there was then a greater wrong. For many generations, under the Great Order, the men of the plain had been formed into packs, for digging and carrying. The old law of portage between families was made into a new law, of packs of men with their leaders, and these were trained as if they were dogs, to make their movements together. All this was already established in the Order of the White Land, which had made it so powerful. But there was now a new step. First the Great Order and then the Company, Menvandir itself, selected young men and called them its guards. They were strong and they carried fine spears. In Menvandir we had no need for a guard. We had never been threatened. But like the sign of darkening the sun the guard would overawe and frighten the people. If the food was not brought they would go out and take it.'

'Did the young men do this?'

'It has not yet been needed. But they are there, in Menvandir, in a cloth dyed red. Guards and signs! That is not measuring. And so, although I had thought that I would die in Menvandir, I took my rod and my dog and I struck out west, for what had once been my home when I was Ranan.'

Karan looked away. In the forest below them there was a sudden barking of dogs and a noise of men shouting. The young men who had gone hunting had started a chase. It would be a big chase, from the noise, which was getting louder and more excited.

He glanced back at Dal Mered. Then his heart seemed to stop as he saw the old man crying in silence, the tears rolling down his cheeks.

'Do not cry, Dal Mered. It is only the hunt.'

'A hunt for an animal.'

'Yes, a deer or a boar or even an aurochs.'

'You do not see the sign, boy?'

'It is not a sign, it is the hunt.'

'I do not mean the hunt. I left Menvandir to be free of depending on others. Then I came to your place and my foot turned under me. Now again I am dependent, asking others for food.'

'It has been a good year. There is food enough.'

'That is not what I mean. I saw Menvandir change, and I spoke against it. But what I must now measure is that I too am of that company. I am too old to hunt, too weak to herd or to build. I am against those Dalen, but I am still Dal.'

'And so you can teach measuring.'

'I can teach simple measuring. But I must tell you, boy, where my whole strength has gone. I have sought a new tying, over eighteen years. It is of the red star, and its path through the sky, that I have measured again and again. I try to think of other things, but I know I deceive myself. My whole mind is filled with that star.'

Karan stared into his face. Below them the hunt was continuing. The pitch of the dogs' barking was higher.

'It means nothing to others,' Dal Mered said. 'They owe me nothing.'

Karan looked away. He wanted to say again that it was a sign of the world, but the old man's sorrow seemed to warn him to keep silent. And now below them were the unmistakeable sounds of a kill, the screams of the wounded animal, the shouting voices of the men. While he looked down at the wood, Dal Mered walked away, down the slope to the settlement. Karan waited and then hurried after him. Dal Mered was forcing his pace, overbearing his bad foot. As Karan came alongside him he looked down and smiled. He put his hand on the boy's shoulder.

'We'll see what they've got,' he said, briskly, in his old harsh voice.

It was approaching midwinter. Since that day by the waterfall Karan had avoided Dal Mered, though he went on thinking about him. It was all happening too quickly: to be shown the skills of measuring, to hear the wonder of Menvandir, and then to be told, almost brutally, that it was wrong or was becoming wrong. The old man was to be trusted when he showed how to measure but he was not steady in himself. It was always uncertain what he would do or say.

The women were preparing the midwinter ceremony, which was in their charge. One day Karan was surprised, coming back with firewood, to see Dal Mered at their hut, talking earnestly with his mother Seril. They hardly noticed as he crouched by the fire and listened.

'The third peak?' he heard Dal Mered ask.

'It is so.'

'You do not wait for the fires of others?'

'No, they wait for us, at the river and in Cross Valley.'

'Who measured the third peak?'

'There is no need for measuring. It is known'.

Dal Mered walked away, hardly noticing Karan.

On the next day, after a further light snowfall, Karan saw Dal Mered walking with difficulty to a high place, towards Hawkstone. He followed him and stood at a distance, watching. Dal Mered had placed two staves, in line to the third peak of Brigan. He was moving around them with a hide rope and pegs.

'You can come, boy,' he shouted suddenly, without seeming to look up. Karan went slowly up to him.

'Your women think they know midwinter,' he said, with the old proud harshness.

'We all know midwinter. It is the setting of the sun over the third peak.'

'We shall see,' Dal Mered said.

He went on measuring, but explained nothing to Karan. It was very cold, but they waited until sunset. The sun was setting between the second and third peaks. Dal Mered set a new stave, and again measured. They walked back together in the darkness.

On the next morning Dal Mered came again to talk to Seril.

'It is a real sign, midwinter,' Karan heard him say. 'It deserves to be measured exactly.'

'I keep telling you we know it,' Seril said, irritably. She was plump in her heavy fur coat. Her dark hair was shining with oil and her cheeks were bright.

'Then I will ask the young men to help me to measure it,' said Dal Mered.

'You will not,' Seril answered. 'After we have kept and fed you, would you do anything so wicked? Would you dare to break the law of midwinter?'

'I am talking only of the measuring. And the time of your holy ceremony would then be exact.'

'Do not ask the young men,' Seril said, angrily. 'Midwinter is the time that only women must guard. It is all for us as women, from the black pots in the ash of the hearth where we prepare the blood drink to the watching of the peak and then the setting of the fire.'

'I know,' Dal Mered replied. 'But because it is so the young men are free for other work.'

'They still have their duty. They must catch the wrens for the message of the Mother.'

'Indeed!' Dal Mered said, with more interest. 'You still do that here?'

'It is the law of midwinter,' Seril said, proudly. 'We prepare the wrens for the Mother. The wrens are her rising from the Long House. They are her messengers to her son in the sky, for the new young sun to be born.'

Dal Mered shaded his eyes.

'That was done,' he said, 'in my childhood, when I was Ranan. It is not done in Menvandir.'

Seril looked at the old man. When she spoke again her voice was edged with pity.

'You are stuck in your Menvandir, Dal Mered. It is a heathen place.'

He moved his hand and turned away.

On a bright cold morning, two days later, Karan went out with all the other young men to catch the wrens for midwinter. They had long ash poles and knotted birdnets. They had woven withy baskets to hold their captives. It was known where the wrens were most likely to be found: on the berrying ivy which was thick on the northern edge of the oakwood. They were small and shy, always darting into cover, but the skills of the hunt were well known. Spreading the nets, a circle of young men surrounded the stands of ivy and then beat the shining leaves with their long poles. As the birds flew out they raised and threw the nets. They had eleven to catch this year: Seril had given them the number. By midday they had succeeded and the tiny live birds were in the baskets. They carried them back, laughing. They put the baskets down at the entrance to Seril's hut. She said nothing to them.

Later that afternoon Karan was astonished to see his mother and the other older women with Dal Mered at the high place where he had set his staves. He walked up and stood at a little distance. Dal Mered was talking and gesturing and the group of women were listening. As sunset approached the women spread out in a line, each holding a light stave. There was a long quiet wait as they all watched the last of the sun. Then one of the women called out. Dal Mered went across and her stave was fixed in the earth. Then they all went back down, the women hurrying ahead.

On the next morning Karan went early to Dal Mered.

'I watched the measuring,' he said, 'but my mother tells me I should have kept away.'

'Midwinter is under the order of the women.'

'I know, but this is measuring. What the women arrange is the ceremony itself.'

'It is right that they should.'

'But then why are you measuring? Is it not midwinter over the third peak?'

'We shall see.'

Karan walked away, but Dal Mered called him back.

'You can come and I will show you. But at sunset you must leave it to the women.'

Karan followed him up. As they made their way along the track through the snow Karan saw the women piling logs of green ash in the feastyard of the Long House. The pile was already high, for it was almost midwinter. The men had dragged the heavier wood to a place thirty paces from the mound, but by the law could take it no closer.

When they reached the high place, Dal Mered pointed with his rod at the line of peaks of Brigan.

'North by west from the second, where the ridge appears to cut the ridge from the third. You see the notch, boy?'

'I see it.'

'The way to measure sunset at midwinter is to look, each night, for the last of the sun in that notch. The women spread in a line and who sees it, exactly, calls out, and her stave is set. On the next night the same, but it will then be found that a new stave must be set. So the next and the next night, and the staves will form a line.'

'You will still not know which is exact.'

'You will learn which is exact, for the line will run towards Hawkstone and then it will begin to run back. At the farthest point towards Hawkstone it will be exact midwinter.'

Karan closed his eyes.

'What is it, boy?'

'You will not know the farthest till the next has been set. And then the midwinter will have passed.'

Dal Mered smiled.

'I was right,' he said. 'You should be in Menvandir.'

'Taking pork and flour,' Karan said, 'and the guards with spears?'

'Or herding sheep, boy, and not measuring. You must not think of that.'

Karan walked away.

Again that evening he watched, from a distance, as the line of women held staves and there was again one cry as the sun set in the distant notch. As soon as he heard it Karan raced down the slope to the settlement, sliding and falling on the patches of slippery snow. He stood by the old oak from which midwinter was regularly signed. The sun had already long set, from this lower ground, but he could see where it had set from its remaining light, and he knew from other years that midwinter would be tomorrow. When his mother came down, and they were eating by the hearth, he did not mention the measuring. He did not know what she and the other women would do, between the old and new ways. Yet next morning he was not surprised to hear the women passing the word that tonight was midwinter. One of the oldest women had been watching each evening from the oak. The old sign had prevailed.

There was busy work all day, preparing the ceremony. By midday, which Karan measured, in the place where Dal Mered had taught him, the fire pile was completed in the feastyard of the Long House, and the best of the young rams had been caught and tethered near the pile. Bunches of heather, with the tiny bells of flowers still holding much of their colour, were hung and strewn at the portal. The space between the firepile and the honour stone was swept clean for the dancing. All day around the huts there was the pungent smell of the grinding of dried thyme, for dressing the ram.

By the cold mid-afternoon a group of the older women, Mother Seril among them, were already assembled at the oak. They stood quietly and talked among themselves. Lirisa the sister of old Karan was wearing the feathered hat and carrying the ceremonial horn. Up at the firepile another group of women stood ready, and the men and children were already gathered and waiting, at some distance from the Long House.

Karan went to Dal Mered, who was lying on his bed with his dog beside him.

'They will not help you to measure tonight. It is the fire and the feast.'

'I know. They have told me.'

'Yet it may not be an exact midwinter.'

'It will not. It is yet at least two sunsets.'

'You have told them this?'

'Yes. They do not believe me.'

'So you will leave the measuring?'

'Do you want me to, boy?'

'No,' Karan said.

Dal Mered smiled, playing with the ears of his dog.

'It will not be easy,' he said, 'but if you wish you and I can set tonight's stave.'

'I would then be missing from the firebirth.'

'For a short time only.'

'It is that short time which matters, in the birth of the sun.'

'Then you must choose, boy. Is your name Ranan?'

'It is Karan, as you know.'

'I am old and a stranger. I shall be at the measuring. If you want to measure you will know where to find me.'

Karan walked away. He found a place by himself between the Long House and the measuring place. He watched Dal Mered walking up there, with old slow steps. He kept his eyes on the women by the oak. He did not know which way he would run.

The sun was now very low, red and large in the pale winter sky. He turned his eyes from watching it. He had already looked too long and was dazzled. Then as he was rubbing his eyes the long shout of the sun's death went up from the women by the oak, and as the shout ended there was the wail of the death-horn. Karan jumped to his feet.

All eyes were now fixed on the body of a woman, which lay in a death fold on top of the honour stone. The body was dark and still. A torch was lit, by a girl wearing a birdnet over her head and face. She held the torch above the dark body. Slowly a hand rose and its fingers extended. A second hand rose, and the fingers of the two hands were joined. Then first the right leg, then the left, were extended and straightened. The body twisted where it lay and then the head was suddenly raised, its long hair hanging loose. Slowly, moving to a knee with a fist on the ground, then to both knees and with joined arms above the head, the body unwound and rose and stood above the honour stone. There was a long silence and then from around the feet, seeming to escape from the Long House itself, birds were flying: a darting flutter of wrens in the fading light. Every eye watched to follow them into the night sky. A high screaming began, first from the group by the firepile, then from all the women and girls. As the birds disappeared there was a sudden plunge of the torch and flames leaped through the firepile. The high screams ended. The men and boys shouted, forcing their voices deep. Karan shouted with the others but he did not move.

He stood looking down. The whole family closed on the Long House. He saw the shape of the ox-horn as it was lifted to be placed on the honour stone as the ram was killed. He turned and ran to Dal Mered at the measuring place. The old man was walking up and down, not watching the fire but the sun, which was still just to be seen in its shining upper edge. Dal Mered held out a stave to him. They had both to move their positions, watching for the last flash of sun in the notch. It was Karan who found the place, and he shouted with excitement. Dal Mered helped him to fix the stave in the earth.

Then they walked down together to the Long House and the fire. They joined the crowd of men and boys. The ram had been skinned and butchered, and thyme was rubbed into the pieces. The fresh meat was laid on the hearth at the back of the firepile. Everyone moved even closer. There was now the smell of feast and the warmth of fire. The ridges of the mountains were very dark above them. They moved closer again, ready for the midwinter drink and then the feast and the dance.

It was on the third night after the fire of midwinter that Karan, setting the stave with Dal Mered, saw the line of staves begin to move back on itself. It was a greater wonder than he had yet known. He went with Dal Mered for two more sunsets, following the return movement. For now the last stave towards Hawkstone was an exact point, and Dal Mered told him to set a stone there, with its flattened side facing the distant notch, so that the exact midwinter could always be observed.

None of the others took notice of what they were doing. After the excitement of midwinter, of the fire and the feast and the dancing and of the answering fires springing from the families along Curve River and in Cross Valley, there were still the coldest and hardest, the least provided days and moons, to live through.

O n the rough track to the road through the pass Glyn stumbled
and almost fell. The full moon was high to the south, above
the peak of the Skirrid which could now be seen above the long
valley of the Honddu. But though the light was clear, the immediate
ground was so broken that on the steep descent it was difficult
walking. This was the area of Cnapiau, the humps that spread from
the pass, but there were also old streambreaks across the track itself
and towards the road the cluster of hollows of the huts of the old
shepherds.

The stumble had shaken him but it cleared his mind. To have seen
no sign of Elis was not deeply worrying, and the previous assump-
tion, that he had been in some normal way delayed, had to be set
aside. Glyn scrambled to the road where he could look both ways
from the pass. If Elis had reached this road, late, he would not have
gone over the mountain in the darkness. He would have followed
the road past Twyn y Beddau and then turned for the road to Croes
Hywel. Up to this hour, even on so remote a road, he might well
have got a lift from someone returning late to one of the farms. Yet,
on the schedule he had written, he should have been here by late
afternoon. If he had been delayed, and then walked the road, he
would of course be safe even if he had arrived while Glyn was
crossing the mountain to the pass. But the greater probability, Glyn
at last admitted, was that he was lying hurt somewhere on the long
track ahead, over Twmpa to Rhos Dirion and down the long ridge
to Bal Mawr and the Gaer.

He squatted and looked south to the long dark ridge. All western
heights were cut off by the rise of Darren Llwyd, with its tumbled
boulders black in the moonlight. He turned his eyes again to the
Skirrid: Ysgyryd Fawr, the Holy Mountain. It was strange how

many legends had converged on that broken peak, significant only in its isolation. Unlike these complex ridges and valleys it declared itself clearly and simply: a condition perhaps of belief.

Yes, he was going – had told himself he had been going – simply to meet his grandfather, to see him over the last of his walk. But it could no longer be thought of only as that. Elis was too experienced to be as late as this, in any ordinary circumstances. Every year, it seemed, someone died on these mountains, but almost always in bad weather, when low cloud and mist came down suddenly and the long ridges showed few landmarks. Or again, there were deaths from exposure when the military drove young men to the extremes of training, disregarding the knowledge of all those who lived in the mountains. In this clear, still weather Elis would never lose his way or be trapped, but a stumble would be easy, was always easy: the turning of an ankle on a trailing heather root or in a rut overgrown with the long tussock grass. When he had first taken Glyn up, as a boy of four, and shown him these shapes and these hazards, these long ways of the mountains, it was the risk of turning an ankle he had most emphasised, after the permanent warning against low cloud and mist. If this had happened to him, anywhere along that eight miles of rough walking from Twmpa to the Gaer, he would be lying in the emptiness, dependent on somebody coming to find him. This was why he had always insisted on leaving a note of his route.

Glyn got up impatiently. To the north, far below him, there were still lights in Hay. There were far lights down the cross valley towards Capelyffin but even as he watched one went out. He crossed the road and went up by the stream which flowed to join the spread fingers of watercourses that gathered as the Honddu. His pass was on a watershed: Digedi flowing north to the Wye, Honddu and Mynwy rising close to each other under Twyn Llech and flowing down their separate steep valleys until they joined at Alltyrynys. Far back, before the last ice, Honddu had flowed to Crucornau and turned south; the moraine had blocked it and turned it north through Pandy. The watercourses of each source were now deeply graved in the slopes. On his right, dark in shadow, there was a landslip above the deep gravings of Digedi. Behind him, in the Cnapiau, the long deep courses were thick lines scored on the pale slope.

The Cnapiau: not really the humps – the knobs. And this broad shoulder of Twmpa, looming above him, was often now called, inexplicably, Lord Hereford's Knob, just as Penybeacon had become, on the tourist postcards, first Pennybeacon and then Hay Bluff. It was like that lane in Madley, once Pey-y-plwyf, end of the parish, now engraved as Pennypluck. Yet the shift of name was much older and more uncertain than these recent and perhaps reversible changes. The pass itself, for example: now the Gospel Pass, the old Bwlch yr Efengyl, and there were stories written to justify the name. But in the earliest records it had been Vyncyl or Fincul, even when copied by priests. The earliest records were, perhaps, twelve hundred years old. But how comparatively recent, here on the mountain, that now seemed.

'Taid! Taid!'

He must shout now every couple of minutes. He was not looking any more for a man walking but for a man lying somewhere, in pain and unable to move.

'Taid!'

'Boy! Boy!'

Glyn stopped and looked around. He called again but there was no answering voice. The harsh shout had been in his mind.

'Boy!': that shout of the Measurer to Karan. The earliest records. But it had been four thousand years since that watchstone, facing southwest to the rough skyline of Bychan and Troed, had been found and set in the earth. Beyond that it had been more than fourteen hundred years from the coming of Idrisil, with the first sheep, to the time of Dal Mered, with his stories of the power of Menvandir.

Menvandir was imagined on the great plain of the White Land, where the great henges and stone circles were built and rebuilt. It was a long way from these mountains, where the life of those years had been the steady clearing of forests, especially on the warm soil near the lake and in the flat fertile valley, Bodosa, beyond Boar's Hill, where the soft wheat for porridge was mainly grown. As the old trees were cleared there was a rapid spread of crowded ash saplings which needed the open light. More pigs were kept, bred from the wild pigs in the deeper forest. The people cleared rough ground for planting, and cleaned it after harvest.

They also brought in a few of the cattle: the smaller breed from over the sea, more manageable than the big wild cattle still hunted, but declining, in the forests. The cattle would be used for draft and for ploughing, down there in the fields of the lower foothills above the floodlands. The stone ards were drawn and redrawn, criss-crossing in shallow furrows to make seedbeds. Around the huts of the lower settlements were plots of pulses and vetches, and in Bodosa the beginnings of flax for oil and fibre. Better stone axes came by gift and by trade, some from the far western coasts. The valued tunics and cloaks of the mountains passed along the same routes. The obligation of carrying, for all able men of the settle-ments, kept the wide network open and brought news.

For Dal Mered's story, though exceptional, was not the only one. More steadily, confirmed through the generations, came tales of a people with a new breed of sheep, who also, it was reported, had knives and even axes of a strange kind: not stone but an earth ore that was burned to what they called metal. None had as yet been seen in or near these mountains, but they were known from the White Land across the Yellow Hills to the seariver. Their words were also reported as strange.

'Taid! Taid!'

The track was broadening but still empty. Glyn climbed, steadily, towards the ridge.

Seril and the New People

◆

S eril climbed, half running, to High Buck, and stumbled, through
sweat and stitch, to a hollow in the heather. She lay face down,
gasping for breath, against the sharp hard twigs. She was now
beyond crying, though she could still feel the weeping in the salt on
her cheeks and the sour wrench in her stomach. None of those
feelings now mattered. This was the end of her world. She would lie
day and night without food and drink. She would let herself die.

For so long there had been the daily cruelty of Laran, but she had
hardened to bear that. Laran had hit and beaten her since she had
first taken her in, just able to walk, when Seril's mother had died in
that winter of the great rains, when so many of the family and of the
flock had died. Life had been slowly getting better again, for the
family and for the flock, but still the hitting and beating happened
every night, after Laran came into the hut and put down her tools and
then crouched in the corner in pain. Laran would never say what the
pain was, never even admit that there was any pain. But Seril knew
the signs, in the sweat at the temples, the tightly pressed eyes, the
bared teeth. As a small child she had tried to stroke and comfort her,
then as a girl to offer drinks and herbs to relieve the pain. But Laran
only hit her and pushed her away. Now Seril would not approach
her, but would watch and wait while the tense crouching lasted.
Then Laran would at last straighten up, and go for the stick. Seril
ran often, but the other women told her that she must go back to
Laran who had taken her in and kept her alive.

That had been her life, with her work, through ten and four
winters and summers. In the last two years she had borne it only by
dreaming of midsummer, when the families met for the feast, at
cross river or Broken Mountain and sheep were exchanged and
marriages made. But each year she had been put in last of the girls,

held back by Laran who needed her. Yet even the first year she had been bigger than most of the girls who had already found boys. That too had been a fault, that her tallness was ugly and clumsy.

What mattered more, she found by listening, was that there were no sheep to give with her. Laran and Kevil had none to spare, to give beyond their blood. Yet other girls with no share of sheep had been taken towards the end. If Laran so hated her that she must always hit and beat her, why could she not let her go, even with the last of the young men, the weakest and poorest, even into the Bear Mountains with the hunters who had only a few sheep between them? In the second year, at Broken Mountain, sure of what would happen, she had thought of this last chance, and was glad of it. She would go away and sleep rough with these hard hunters, ungainly, overgrown like herself, coarse in skin and hair and with big irregular teeth. It was not her earlier dream but she had grown to it. She had been disappointed even in that. Neither to stay without being beaten, nor allowed to go with the very last of the boys: what cruelty was that, breaking all the laws of the people?

It was Laran herself who was wrong, not the family, though since the winter of many deaths their feelings were harsher. The old ones said so and complained of their own treatment. But Laran was beyond this. With her pain she beat pain into a child and then a girl. Yet even now that seemed bearable after today and Kevil.

In the early morning when the sun was striking in small beams through the roof branches, and Seril was just waking in her corner of the hut, Laran had come and stood over her and smiled. Seril rubbing sleep from her eyes, had not understood this unexpected smile, but she had moved and tried to smile back. Then Laran had gone out and Seril had thought the hut was empty. Kevil was always first out and up with the sheep.

When she heard the first movement she thought it was the dog. She turned over, still half sleeping. But suddenly Kevil was on top of her and his hand was over her mouth. She barely knew what was happening, but as his weight pressed down until she was choking she kicked out and tried to hit him. He was much too strong. He slapped the side of her head as he pushed his knee to open her legs. Though she bit his hand he got into her, driving roughly and very hard. His hand slipped from her mouth and she got out a scream, for the pain was terrible. But he hit her again and there were noises in her head like the falling of great stones. He pressed his hands over her mouth and shouted down at her: strange words that she could barely make out through the echoing noises in her ears. He was still shouting when she felt him spurt. She thought he would get off as the rams got off. Yet now he hit her the hardest blow of all, across her nose and cheek. As he got up, suddenly silent, she was sobbing. But even that stopped when she looked across at the doorway and there was Laran, watching. She saw Kevil push past and then everything went black, beyond the tearing pain and echoing noise in her head.

It was mid-morning when she again opened her eyes. She looked round at the empty hut. After a long gathering of her strength she got up and went to the doorway. Women were working at the nearest hut through the trees, and as she watched she saw Laran among them. She crept round to the back of the hut and looked up at the mountain. The flock were grazing along the slopes to the west. The track to High Buck was empty.

She found the waterbag and drank and washed herself. The familiar sounds of the day were coming through, though her head still ached. All the everyday work was being done in the ordinary life of late summer. But could she now be expected to go over and join in; carrying hay, going for berries, crushing the seeds? That must be done to live but how could she live now, with such people? Live and wake any morning to that animal coming and hurting her? For this was how it would now be. It was why she had been kept. At night there would be the hitting and beating from Laran, and in the mornings Kevil attacking and taking her. Moon after moon, year after year. Her only midsummer. She would not stay for that. She would sooner die.

But not die with them, not in their cruel hut. She would get up and beyond them, up to High Buck and find a hollow in the heather, to lie and rest without eating until the mountain took her. The sharp twigs of the heather pushed into her swollen face, but she was glad of their small pains, glad of the sweetness of their growing and of the sour smell of the earth, glad of the silence and the distance and the great sky all around her; glad to have gone from the people she would never have to see again.

There was a voice, suddenly, some distance away, and the sound of a foot on a stone. Seril lay very still. The voice came again, a deep rumbling voice, deeper than any she had heard. There were words but she did not understand them: strange quiet words. Then there was a movement close to her head, but still she lay without moving.

There was then another voice, a woman's, though it also was deep and resonant. A hand touched her shoulder. She swung around and looked up. She was ready to run again but found that she was looking into the face of a girl not much older than herself: a broad face with light brown hair and surprisingly blue eyes. The girl was frowning but as she met Seril's eyes she smiled. She turned and spoke over her shoulder to her companion. He moved forward and Seril saw him clearly. He was a tall, broad-shouldered young man, with the same light brown hair and blue eyes. They looked like brother and sister-by-blood; their strange broad faces were very alike. They were wearing light tunics of some soft material, coloured a dark red. Each spoke, in the strange deep voices, and many words passed between them but not one that Seril understood. Yet the girl was now holding and pressing her hand. She was saying things to her which she could hear as comforting.

The young man went away. The girl still held Seril's hand. Slowly, looking down at her, she reached out to stroke the black hair. Seril found it hard to believe what was happening. Who could these strangers be, with their unknown words, on High Buck, within sight of the family and the flock?

The young man came back and crouched beside the girl. His hands were full of sphagnum moss, which he was wringing between his fingers. The girl took some of the moss and laid it over Seril's cut cheek and nose. She lay very still staring up. As their hands touched again, passing more moss, she saw that the girl was wearing a bracelet of some strange shining material of the colour of oak leaves in spring. The youth was wearing a thick bone guard on his left wrist. His right arm and shoulder were heavily muscled. They were not speaking now, but the girl, with gentle fingers, was touching the cuts and bruises on Seril's arms and legs and laying cold moss over them. Where Seril's short hide tunic had fallen back from her thighs the girl hesitated and spoke to her, again with strange words. When Seril did not answer she wiped between the legs with moss. It came away with blood on it and the girl laid a pad of new moss.

It was very warm and still on the mountain. Seril could hear a lark singing, quite near. She wanted to move to look for the bird but the girl held her shoulders, gently and firmly, and kept her lying still. The young man spoke and got up. He lifted a bow and strange arrows and moved away towards the scarp.

'Netta,' the girl said in a warm friendly voice. As she spoke she smiled and touched her breasts.

'Netta. Netta.'

Seril stared into the face. The cheekbones were prominent and the lower jaw was heavy. The teeth were small.

Netta touched Seril's chest, with one finger pointing. Seril understood.

'Seril,' she whispered.

The young man had come back, and there were many strange words. Then he stood over her, pointing in the direction of the family and the flock. He pointed to Seril and made the movements of lifting, before pointing again beyond the scarp.

'No,' Seril shouted, and with sudden strength broke loose from Netta's hands. She crouched ready to run.

The young man frowned and repeated the pointings. Seril, now terrified, moved her hand, palm inwards, to and fro across her face. Netta came and put her arm across her shoulders. She spoke to her brother. He listened without speaking but at last nodded. Netta pointed to Seril and spoke her name clearly. Then she pointed to her brother and said: 'Anailos. Anailos.' Seril waited. She did not dare to speak.

Anailos was pointing again, away from High Buck along the rising ridge to the east. Seril knew that Stone Valley lay beyond the ridge and that there had been talk of a new people seen there.

But she had never been that far herself. She looked into Netta's face and put her hands together, palm to palm, placing them between Netta's hands. It was a movement of young girls at midsummer to the oldest woman, after the Song of the Shepherds. Netta did not know the sign but she took the small hands and enclosed them. Seril smiled.

They supported her between them, walking east along the ridge. As she walked she began to feel stronger. She thought she could easily walk on her own. But she kept close to them, glad of their touch on her. It was now past midday. The sky was high and pale blue. Away to the south were the many ridges of the mountains, and a blue distance beyond them. Netta and Anailos talked as they walked. The words were still strange but Seril was beginning to hear their sounds: especially the beat of the sounds, in the deep resonant voices.

At the high point on the eastern end of the main ridge Anailos stopped and looked back, shading his eyes. Netta also looked but Seril would not turn. They branched down, half-turning to the sun. The slope was gentle at first but then the land fell away suddenly below Horn Point, and they were into Stone Valley. It was heavily wooded with oaks and some ash. Anailos led the way along the steep northern slope just above the treeline. It was difficult walking and Seril again felt tired. Netta stayed close to her. At last they saw blue smoke rising ahead of them, and under an outcrop of rock stood two large round huts.

A child was running near one of them. Anailos quickened his pace and left them. When Netta and Seril arrived a much older woman had come out of the nearest hut and was waiting. She spoke for a long time to Netta but then they went together into the hut, leading Seril. They laid her down on a bed of heather by a pit. Netta brought water to drink, in a strange small pot which Seril could hold in her hands. There was then fresh moss and her cuts were tended again. As she lay looking around, Seril saw that the hut itself, though larger, was much like the huts of her own family. But there were some very strange objects in it. Three of the small flat-based drinking pots stood on a stone bench. Beyond them lay a knife of the same shining material as Netta's bracelet. There was a length of the soft red material that Netta and Anailos wore as their tunics. The older woman Subra wore a longer dress of this stuff, in a yellowish brown, fastened at the shoulder with two strange black stones, shining and pierced. At her neck she wore a pendant of the shining oakleaf colour.

Anailos had gone but Netta and Subra took turns to sit with Seril, and brought her food: whinberries with grain seeds, but the seeds were odd, with a smoky taste. They brought flat cakes of the same strange grain, sweetened with honey, and a new drink, from the small pot, which was not water or the midsummer berry wine. It was sharp and foaming, with a taste like that of the grain. After the drink she slept.

When Seril looked back to this time many moons later, she could hardly believe that it had been only a day: the attack by Kevil, the run to High Buck, the discovery by Netta and Anailos, the coming into this new family. It had been like one whole life ending and another beginning, in a single arc of the sun. There had been no more talk of taking her back to her family, and she was so absorbed by this new life that she never considered it herself. As she recovered quickly, with her natural strength, she shared all the work of the Stone Valley family. Much of it was the work she had done all her life, but there were differences. There were only seven huts of this family, spread along the dry sunny slopes of the spur below Horn Point. All the people were large like Netta and Anailos, but some had darker brown hair and a few of the men had heavy brows and steeply sloping foreheads. Seril, herself bigger than most of her own people, was now the smallest full-grown among them. The life of the family was the life of the flock, but the sheep themselves were not the same. They were fawn-red like the sheep of Seril's family, but their coats felt quite different, softer and less hairy. This was the stuff the new family wore. Seril watched Subra and the other women preparing it, combing it into long threads and twisting and spinning it on sticks. In two of the huts were wooden frames on which the threads were tightly woven. The horns of the rams were also different: white and curling forward over the sides of the face. The horns of the ewes were short and upright. Both had long legs and long tails. They seemed more docile than the sheep she was used to.

The knives for killing and skinning and cutting were different too: all a hard, shining oakleaf colour: copper, Anailos told her. The work of the men was familiar, except that they had cleared ground under the spur, on a south slope, and dug a square they called a field to plant the strange grain called barley, digging with long-handled axes, which they called hoes. All the men worked on the field but in their work with the sheep they seemed to separate. They knew of the Earth Mother and of the feast of midsummer, but they had not heard of Drisil saving the people and the flock from the seariver, in the beginning of this land. She listened eagerly to their stories and songs, and already before the first snows she could say many things and understand more. Through the long cold winter she learned their language until at times it seemed she could hardly remember her own. The memory of the old words was also the memory of Laran and Kevil and their cruelty. But Anailos, who came often to talk to her, told her that she must keep her own language. He made her speak it to him, and asked questions about it. One day, he said, they must go back to her family, and she could help the speaking between them. Seril did not want this – she never wanted to see them again – but she did what Anailos asked. Anailos, as she had first thought, was blood-brother of Netta, and their mother was Subra. Their father Carvetior had died while they were still at the seariver, before they moved to these mountains.

The deep snows melted, followed by an early spring. The ewes, which had turned greyish-brown during the winter, had their lambs along the spur, not far from the huts. The ewes of Seril's old flock had always moved away from men for their lambing. It was a good birth, though the flock was still small. The grass grew strongly through the warm spring moons.

In the moon before midsummer Netta and Anailos came to talk seriously to Seril. Through the long winter Netta had come to know everything about Seril's life with Laran as well as about Kevil's rape. She had told her brother, but he never spoke of it to Seril. Now, however, he had a proposal to make. He wanted to marry Seril, but it was necessary first that they should visit her family. He would take a gift of a ewe and a young ram, and get their agreement.

Although Seril wanted to marry Anailos, she did not want to go back to her family, even for a day, with Anailos and Netta beside her.

'But they are good people,' Anailos said. 'And besides, it is the law. I cannot keep you here, making myself a thief.'

Seril looked at Netta.

'Tell him, Netta. You know what I have told you. They are not good people.'

Netta touched her arm.

'Laran and Kevil were very cruel. But they are not your whole family. We have met your people, we call you the dark ones, all along our journeying. We have talked to others who have lived close beside them. They are good people. They live by the law.'

'They have taught us many things,' Anailos said, 'as we have taught them many things.'

Seril stared hopelessly at them. She was ready to cry.

'I don't know about peoples,' she said, lowering her head. 'I know only about Laran and Kevil.'

Anailos stood up.

'I have watched for many days from what you call High Buck. They are people I understand, and it is necessary to meet them. If you will help us we can talk to them. We can make an agreement.'

'But Kevil and Laran will grab me,' Seril cried.

Anailos squatted and held her shoulders.

'We shall not go alone. Our men will be with us. But it is necessary to go.'

He turned and walked away. It was left to Netta to talk to Seril and at last to get her agreement.

'But I am only doing it,' she said, 'for you and Anailos, because you have cared for me.'

The day for the visit was settled, and they left at dawn. Seril was surprised that Netta came with her old hide tunic, which had been cleaned and mended. She had not worn it since she arrived.

'You must go,' Netta said, 'as one of your own family.'

They walked west along the steep track above the oaks and up to the ridge. Five men came with them. Anailos drove one of his best ewes and a young ram. Seril walked among them, pale and silent. After the long walk they stopped and squatted on High Buck. She saw at once a whole familiar world again: the many huts among the thin oakwoods, with the blue smoke rising; the flock along the edges of the trees beside the spring; two dogs running and barking.

'Where do you meet?' Anailos asked. 'At your Long House or at your midwinter watchstone?'

Seril was not sure.

'We will go to the stone,' Anailos said. 'The Long House is more sacred.'

They began the descent, the men walking in front. Netta and Seril walked together holding hands. For some time it seemed that nobody had noticed them, but then several men came quickly out of the trees. There was shouting and women came out of the huts. Anailos had roped the ewe and the young ram and he now walked ahead of the others, towards the old midwinter watchstone. The rest followed and stood behind him.

There was a long pause. The men of Lanoluc were talking at the edge of the wood. At last they moved up together, walking close. They were carrying axes and bows. Seril looked anxiously among them when she could see their faces. Kevil was with them carrying his heavy polished stone axe. When they stopped, at twenty paces, in a close group, it was white-haired Idris who came forward. He shouted up. Anailos turned and called to Seril.

'What did he say?'

'He asked what is your people.'

But while the words were being exchanged the men of Lanoluc were talking, for they had seen and recognised Seril.

'Tell them we come in peace and by the law,' Anailos said.

Seril called the words, though she could hardly get her voice.

'Are you Seril who was lost?' Idris called.

'I am Seril. These people have been kind to me.'

While she spoke she was watching Kevil, who had turned away and was now at the back of the group. There were women now coming together, between the huts and the stone. She saw Laran among them.

'Say these are gifts to your people,' Anailos ordered, and as she called he walked forward alone, with the roped ewe and young ram. As he approached the old shepherd there was a sudden excited talking. They were all looking at the sheep. Extending his arm, Anailos gave the end of the rope to Idris. Idris bowed ceremonially, but the others were now crowding around, bending over the sheep, running their fingers over the fleece and the tail, and feeling the bones of the legs. Seril, watching closely, saw Kevil walk away. He went down to the women and she could see him talking with his head close to Laran. The other women began moving up to join the men and the children ran in front of them. Seril looked beyond them to where Kevil and Laran were disappearing into the woods.

All the men from both families, and many of the women, were now gathered around the sheep. Netta and Seril were left together by the watchstone. Then old Gerda and her daughter Tara came smiling towards Seril. Gerda took her hands and kissed her. Tara, two years younger than Seril, embraced and hugged her.

'We thought you were lost,' Gerda said.

'I was never lost, but I ran from cruelty.'

The old woman looked long into her face.

'But have you come far?'

'From Stone Valley.'

'You have lived with these people all winter?'

'They took me in and cared for me and now Anailos will marry me. It is Anailos who brought the sheep.'

Gerda looked away. Her eyes were troubled.

'I will not go to Laran and Kevil,' Seril cried.

Gerda took her hand.

'They took you in as a child, Seril. Whatever they did, it is their word for you to marry.'

'No, I will run again. I will not stay with them, for they broke the law. I will run from the woman who beat me and from the man who abused me.'

Gerda searched Seril's face. Netta moved forward and stood close to Seril, supporting her.

'This is Netta, sister of Anailos,' Seril said. 'She found me when it had been done.'

Gerda looked carefully at them both, and then stood away.

'It will be arranged, child. You will marry your man at mid-summer.'

She walked to join the other women, but Tara stayed and talked excitedly to Seril.

'We were sure you were lost. We all hunted for you for days, beyond Curve River and as far as the lake. But the men said you had probably gone to the forest and been killed by some animal.'

'I didn't think, Tara. I just ran for High Buck.'

Tara smiled.

'It was Laran who cried most for you. She took all the blame. She said nothing against Kevil.'

'Did they believe her?'

'They weren't sure. But the girls believed it was Kevil. We were all afraid of him.'

'It's Laran's sickness.'

'It isn't only Laran's sickness. He has always been cruel to women. You were lucky to get away and find people like these.'

'They're good people, Tara.'

'Not only that. They're good-looking people. Especially the young men.'

'Is that what you're thinking about?' Seril laughed.

'It's what you've been doing,' Tara said, laughing with her.

The men of Lanoluc were now showing the visitors their flock. They were all pointing as they talked. Anailos tried out his new words. Seril kept away, with Netta and Tara, but joined the general gathering when the visitors were taken down for food and drink.

Kevil did not appear, and Laran was late and did not come near her. Seril saw how changed she looked: her body was bowed and her hair was grey, as if many years had passed. Netta said, quietly: 'She is very ill, your place-mother.' Seril did not answer. After the meal two lambs were selected for the visitors to take as their exchange gift. Several men walked with them, on their return journey, along the ridge beyond High Buck.

At midsummer Seril went with her new family to the feast in Cross Valley, and among the other marriages was given to Anailos. Kevil and Laran were in the great company, but Kevil did not come near her and Laran gave her only the brief formal kiss when the hands had been joined. There were the familiar songs and ceremonies at the Long House but the real excitements of the festival were the sheep of the new people and the copper of their knives and bracelets. As she walked back to Stone Valley, with Anailos, Seril was boundlessly happy.

In the two moons after midsummer they spent almost all their time on the high ridges and the plateau. The old flocks had kept to the middle slopes and to the clearings among the thin oaks, but the new sheep were taken to the highest ground, which was now dry and open. Plenty of grass grew in patches among the heather and whinberry. The whole family lived on the mountain, moving from spring to spring. At nights they lay in the open under the stars.

By the end of the second moon they had moved across the plateau and down the ridge to the great rise that was the highest part of the mountains. There they met two other families, of the same people, who had come to these western ridges. The largest, of more than sixty, lived below the peak that was called White Cap. There were many old shepherd families beyond them, on the lower slopes above the valley of Salmon River. Anailos told Seril that the new and old families were all on friendly terms. He meant to reassure her but she followed only her own memory and wanted to hear no more of it. He took her to the very highest point and they looked far around. It was extraordinary to Seril to be able to look in any direction and see only the far distance. In the east was the long line of the Yellow Hills and then, running north, the Bald Hills and the gap to Bol Lug. Other heights were distant and blue in the north, but it was to the west that the hills seemed endless. At the farthest reach of their eyes there were heights so indistinct that they might be mistaken for clouds. Seril made out the Bear Hills, where she had once imagined being taken, in the last of the choices. Above them, to the south, the line of sharp peaks from the Brigan ran into the far distance. But what interested her most was what Anailos said was the line of the seariver, of which she had always heard so much. Anailos told her how many families now lived in the good lands along it. So very many people, he said, now enjoyed the blessings of the great island.

Seril did not need to be told of their happiness. Her own life was more than enough. With the other women she gathered great quantities of whinberries, which grew very thickly down the slopes. The men were bringing in grouse, which were abundant in the long stretches of heather which now flowered all along the higher southern slopes. The men were very skilful with their bows, which were longer than those of her old family. The arrows also were very different, with finely-cut tanged heads instead of the old leaf shapes. Whenever they were together Anailos showed her the many birds of the mountain. She knew the buzzards which wheeled so often above the old settlement, with their sharp high cries, and the larks which were everywhere in the summer but especially common on the tops, rising and singing above them. But she knew less of the busy wheatears which were so many among the rock outcrops, with their calls that Anailos imitated: *whip cluck cluck*. Red kites were hunting the slopes below them. It was strange to look down on their backs, from the ridge, as they circled above the thick oakwoods of the valley. On a rockfall to the north was a colony of ravens, and they often watched them as they rose and soared and darted, making different and surprising cries from the croaking call by which they were ordinarily known. Anailos showed her also the mountain blackbirds, with half-collars of white at their throats. She learned the loud *tew tew* song of the perching male. On the mountain Anailos and the others hunted only the red grouse. When he walked with Seril he always carried his bow and she would shout as a cock rose suddenly, calling *go back, go back*, and skimming the heather in fast beats followed by glides. Then even as she shouted his arrow was in the air towards it and she would run to pick up the fine bird.

It was time to think of moving back, after the long summer, but first, Anailos said, they would go down to the lake for the ducks. Half the family stayed, to begin moving the sheep back across to Stone Valley, but Seril stayed with Anailos. They crossed the next ridge and valley to the spur above the lake. Anailos looked along its shores. There was a big settlement at the northern end, where the river ran out, and another smaller settlement on higher ground to the west.

'We shall not interfere,' he said, 'if we go to the reedbeds in the south.'

They went down early next morning. There were great numbers of mallard on the shining water, and a smaller number of shovelers. Anailos showed her the yellow beak of the mallard male, which made it different from the shoveler though both heads were a lovely bright green. Along the banks were many teal, feeding at the edge of the water. As the hunters came out of the trees the teal were alarmed and sprang into the air. Anailos imitated for Seril the loud *ssrit ssrit* call of the drakes. Then they sat and prepared for the hunt. Three of the youngest men were to go round the south of the lake and get into the reedbeds, which were taller than the height of a man and extended some distance into the water. The rest of the party would take cover in the trees and then Anailos would signal to the reedbeds by raising his arms.

Seril watched the mallard, amused when they upended to feed in the deeper water. The teal had settled again, but on the far side. The beaters were in the reedbeds and Anailos stepped out and raised his arms. Almost at once the mallard took off, rising at first straight up and then stretching their necks to fly from the shouting. The hunters were all out from the trees shooting as fast as they could fit their arrows. Eleven mallard fell, some in deep water where the men had to swim for them. The shovelers had gone also, both north along the middle of the lake. The beaters came back and they rested. Next morning, early, they repeated the operation, and then for two more days. Men had come down, from the big settlement, to see who they were, and Seril had to do the talking. They were friendly enough. Part of their family, they explained, lived on an island they had made in the lake by dropping large rocks in the shallow water and building a base of oak piles and brushwood. Anailos and Seril walked to see the surprising island. There were several huts, and even bushes growing on it. It was hard to believe that men had made it, but they were taken out, in a hide boat, and shown the piles in the clear green water.

At last it was time to go back over the mountains. They cut carrying-poles for their loads of duck. They climbed to the plateau and slept overnight above the pass; the air was now colder. Next day they walked to the rest of the family, who were still with the sheep above Stone Valley. They hunted again for grouse. Anailos said that he would go ahead next morning, to look over the huts and the barley. Seril asked to go with him and he at once agreed. They set off very early and were soon running and laughing down the steep slope. They crossed the little river and walked up towards the huts. Anailos left her and walked up to the field where the barley was ripening. Seril walked alone towards their hut but before she reached it she heard movement inside. Thinking it was some animal, she called up to Anailos. He walked back, smiling, and went ahead into the doorway. As she lost sight of him she heard a loud cry and then Kevil appeared in the doorway. He was holding a heavy axe.

Seril ran forward but then stopped, terrified of Kevil.

'Seril,' he shouted.

She could say nothing.

'Come and see your fine man.'

She pushed herself forward.

'What have you done to him?'

'I have killed him, I think.'

'Why, Kevil? Why?'

Kevil looked down at his axe.

'Seril, he stole you from us. I came to get something back. If he hadn't come in I wouldn't have killed him.'

Seril felt a scream in her body but she could make no sound. She could think only of going to Anailos. She hurried forward and Kevil stood aside and let her bend over her fallen husband. There was a terrible wound from his right eye along the side of his head. There was blood all over his hair and face. But he was still alive, his mouth open and gasping in short harsh breaths. Seril fetched water and began bathing the wound.

'It's no use,' Kevil said, 'he's finished.'

'No,' Seril cried.

Anailos opened his eyes at the sound of her voice, but in the same movement his head rolled and there was a loud choking noise in his throat.

'He's gone,' Kevil said.

He was pale and set, looking down at the man he had killed. Seril could only lean closer, kissing Anailos' bloodied face. She kissed and cried and spoke to him long after she knew that he was dead.

Kevil was standing outside the hut.

'Don't worry, Seril, I'll help you.'

She stared at him, bewildered.

'I'll help you. I'll take you back to the family. I won't hurt you again.'

Seril stared into his face. She brushed and straightened her tunic.

'Yes, I'll come with you Kevil.'

He seemed not to hear her.

'I'll come with you now,' she said clearly. 'Let me just get my things.'

He still looked dazed but he stood back from the hut as she went inside. He could hear her moving around. The valley was very quiet, in the rising heat of the morning. Seril came to the doorway of the hut.

'Here I am,' she said.

He made to move forward, but then saw the flint knife in her hand.

'You wanted me, Kevil. Come and take me.'

Kevil stared open-mouthed, but at last he found his voice.

'Seril, I promised I would never hurt you again.'

Seril looked up at the high ridge, where the rest of her new family were sitting in the sun with their flock. She seemed to smile for a moment. Kevil watched her eyes and the knife.

'There,' she said suddenly, 'you have killed us both.'

She drove the knife into her heart. She seemed to stand, unchanged, for a moment, and then she fell across Anailos. As Kevil leaped forward she was already dead.

He looked frantically around. There was nobody in sight, but they might come at any moment. He picked up his heavy axe. Its grey green was stained with blood. He turned and ran from the hut, north across the spur, towards the next valley. He ran until he dropped out of breath.

It was towards evening when Netta came down to look for

Anailos and Seril. She found them lying dead in the doorway of their hut. She kneeled and examined the bodies. She moved warily around the settlement, her knife drawn. Then she hurried back up to the mountain. Her first fear had been that they had quarrelled and that Seril had killed Anailos before killing herself. It was only when she had looked carefully for the axe that had killed her brother, and failed to find it, that she knew it must have been some attack from a stranger.

The whole family came down at once. Subra led the mourning over the bodies, as they were washed and laid with flowers, naked beside each other. On the next day the men went to cut sandstone slabs for the burial cists. They dug to knee-depth on a dry slope on the opposite side of the valley. Then they cut and overlapped the thick slabs until they were tight stone boxes that would keep out water.

When the stiffness had gone from the bodies they curved them to crouching positions and laid each in its stone cist, turned to its left side. Each face was turned to the east. Behind Anailos' thighs they placed a fine tanged arrowhead of flint. At Seril's groin they placed the knife that had killed her. They laid flowers on the bodies and heaped live green oak branches in an open pyramid above them. They crouched close around the dead through the fading light. When at last the sun was setting and darkness was dropping from the hills the men removed the branches. Subra and Netta lifted a jar of the dark red berry wine which was always stored for a death. Two beakers were filled and placed in offering beside the bodies of Anailos and Seril. Then the family took their own beakers of wine and standing, looking down at the bodies, spoke the familiar words,

> 'Blood to blood
> In blood of our blood.'

They drank the bitter wine slowly, staring down at Anailos and Seril.

Now the men lifted the capstones and closed the cists. They sat close again in vigil. It was some time before Netta looked up to Horn Point and saw a small fire burning there. With three men carrying spears she went up the track to the rocks. Idris and Gerda were standing by the fire, and there were many others beyond them.

'We have come to mourn your child and our own,' Idris said.

'What do you know of it?' Netta asked sharply.

'It was Kevil who killed them. He has been taken and has confessed.'

Netta turned away.

'You should leave us alone,' she called back.

'We are of the same mountains,' Idris replied.

Netta and the spearmen returned to their vigil. They must sit, facing east, until the sun rose. All night, through the heavy darkness, the fire burned on Horn Point. Netta tried not to look at it but Subra stayed close and reassured her. When first light came the family stood at the cists. They raised their hands in the song of otherlife:

> 'Wake with the sun
> In the far pasture
> When the sky is clear
> And the breeze gentle.
>
> Wake by the pool
> When the fish are shadows
> In the clear water.
>
> Wake by the forest
> Where the trees are shadows
> In the green light.
>
> Wake as a darting shadow among fish and trees,
> Wake as a dark shadow that moves on the pasture.
> Wake, wake, with the sun.'

They held their hands raised to the dawn. The valley was silent. Then from far above them came a new and different singing: a long slow chant as of a single deep voice. As they looked up to Horn Point they saw the whole family of the old shepherds standing and singing at their fire. They waited, looking up, and then Subra took Netta's hand and walked up to the other family.

The Earthstorm

◆

Carvor closed his eyes and covered them with both hands, palms inward, fingers touching at the bridge of the nose. He counted to ten and then opened his eyes. He could see the light bloodlines along the edge of his fingers, with the sunlight beyond them. Slowly he spread his fingers until he was again looking out at the sky: the pale cloudless blue above the ridge from White Cap.

The strange bright light was still there. It was to the west of White Cap, and above the ridge. He lowered his hands and looked back towards the sun, which was high and dazzling southwest above Broken Mountain. He looked back deliberately at the strange bright light.

It did not dazzle like the sun. It was a little larger than full moon. This was the fifth day of the new moon. The light was very different from any pale moon of a daylight sky. He looked down at the two dogs. They were staring up at him, puzzled that he had stopped. The sheep, without drive, had spread and settled in a dip of sweet grass.

He looked again at the bright light. He felt a prickling of his skin like sensing an animal in the forest. The light hung in the sky but as he watched there was movement inside it, like the ripple of light on the lake. Then, while he watched, it moved at great speed to the west. It curved and dipped beyond the ridge and was gone.

He sat on the edge of a jutting stone, where the sheep had been rubbing and had worn away the grass. He picked a tuft of wool which had dropped there, and stroked it between his fingers. The breath in his chest was tight, as if he had run to exhaustion. He began breathing deeply, to ease himself back.

He looked up from time to time at the distant ridge and at the pale sky above it. It was the familiar look of summer, as if nothing strange had happened. He could not understand why he still felt out of himself, as if all the ties had suddenly changed. The strange light had gone but if he closed his eyes he could see it again clearly, its brightness still in his head.

The younger dog barked. The sheep were moving away up the slope, working towards the better grass where he had found them. He snapped his fingers and both dogs were away at once, racing round to cut them off. He forced himself up and walked to the head of the track. The dogs brought the sheep streaming down towards it. He left the guiding to them.

It was still as if he were out of himself, taken away by the strange light. He walked the track behind the sheep and the dogs. His feet seemed to know every step. He looked down at the huts, wondering if anything had changed there. But it was all as he had left it at sunrise: the scatter of huts across the plateau, at the edge of the oakwood; the hurdled squares of penned sheep; the women and girls in their bright summer clothes, sitting along the line of the stream: some washing and combing the newly plucked wool, others spinning the earlier gatherings, their arms moving in the spin of the whorls. Part of the movement of their arms reminded him of the dip of the light beyond the ridge. It was the same smooth fast curve. But the speed of the light was beyond anything he had seen, in human or animal, or in cloud or spark from the fire. Perhaps the women would have seen it as they sat along the stream, their faces to the sun. He knew that he wanted them to have seen it. He could not be alone with what had happened.

He penned his sheep but instead of going to the other men, who were resting in the sun between plucking, he walked to the stream and crouched beside Tara. She was sitting cross-legged, with her fringed honey-coloured dress pulled back to her thighs. She looked up as he came, her arm still smoothly spinning her stick. Beyond her Netta and old Samela had watched Carvor come. It always happened like this; the mother watched any man's approach. But it was not often that a girl was watched both by her mother and the mother of her mother. Old Samela was the oldest woman that any of the family or neighbours had known, though there were stories of others of great age from the past, all very hard to believe. Old Samela was small and bent but she still did her spinning, talking through it while the others listened or pretended to listen.

Carvor smiled at Tara. She had dressed her black hair high on her head, over a new brown hairpad which he could see through the shining strands. It was her first summer of wearing the pad and she was making the most of it, but her face was still very young.

'You have fetched your tally of sheep, Carvor,' old Samela called.

'Yes, they are penned.'

'But how come you to sit with the women? You have not finished your work.'

'I have a question,' Carvor said.

The older women looked at each other surprised.

'You cannot see White Cap,' Carvor said, 'but you can see the ridge that runs from it, towards the river and the lake.'

'We know what we can see,' old Samela said.

'You are sitting facing that way,' Carvor said. 'You can see the sky above the ridge.'

'We are spinning,' she said, 'but we can see the sky.'

'When I was bringing the sheep,' Carvor said, 'I looked above White Cap and I saw a bright light in the sky.'

The spinning arms still moved.

'I have a question,' Carvor repeated. 'I have never before seen this light. I am asking if others have seen it.'

Old Samela stopped spinning. She laid her stick and thread on a stone.

'It has come again,' she said very quietly.

'I did not hear you.'

'It has come again,' the old woman said to herself. She was now struggling to stand up.

'You know of such a light?' Carvor asked.

'It is Danu telling us.'

'It is not Danu. It is a light in the sky.'

'It is from Danu. She is telling us.'

Carvor stood and faced her. 'I did not see it rise. I looked over White Cap and it was there in the sky. It was so bright I cannot tell you, though it did not dazzle like the sun. Then it moved and went down beyond the ridge. It moved like I have seen nothing move.'

'It is Danu telling us. It is the tears of Danu. Her tears and her grief.'

The old woman was now distressed. Netta put her arm round her, supporting her.

'No more,' she said sharply to Carvor. 'I will take her to her bed.'

The other women watched them go. Matela, first blood-sister of
Carvor, who had been sitting with her feet in the stream washing the
new wool, got up and walked across.

'What's wrong with the old woman?'

'Carvor saw a light in the sky.'

'Trust him! And trust her to tell some old tale about it!'

'I saw the light,' Carvor said.

'Well what if you did? We all see lights in the sky.'

'This was different, Matela. It was frightening. It was like a fierce
bright eye staring down at us.'

'I can believe that. You look like some tup that has had his tail
pulled.'

'And then I felt a tingling along my head and back.'

'There's plenty could do that for you.'

'Old Samela said it was from Danu,' Tara said reverently.

Matela paused swinging her dripping wool. She watched the
drops falling on her bare feet and on the stone.

'Then we shall all soon get it,' she said laughing. She walked away
swinging the wool in its osier basket high over her head.

The work of the day went on, but that evening, at the fire, Carvor
told again the strange story of the light. Gord listened carefully for
he had heard that a man from the Lanoluc family below High Buck
had seen three small bright lights, just at dusk, on the fifth day of the
last moon. They had hung in the sky southwest, in the direction of
the lake, and had suddenly disappeared. Then Macar, just back
from trading their first wool, said that the new family beyond White
Cap, the tall people with bronze axes, had settled on level grass
above the Stream of Birds, where the old ones had built a long house
and then left it. They had been sleeping by their sheep when they had
felt the ground tremble and they had heard strange sounds from
deep in the earth. New to this land, they were terrified, and had
moved south beyond Curve River.

Old Samela was not at the fire. She lay trembling in her hut,
though there was no fever in her skin. But her first son Idris now told
the story which she had given when he was a child. It was from the
old time of the murder of Anailos when the new sheep had come to
the mountains, and the people of Anailos had the new tools of
copper. All the families had wanted the tools, but it was not then
known that to get the metal the new men were ripping the skin of

Mother Earth. They were breaking the bones of Danu and burning them. When the mothers said that Danu would punish them the men laughed and took no notice. But on a hill above the seariver, where they were ripping for these metals, bright lights were seen in the sky, in midwinter, and at one dawn the whole earth shook and there were heavy rockfalls. Men and women and children were crushed and destroyed. For this was the anger of Danu, that she had been torn and burned.

The story was heard in silence. There were many such stories from the mothers. The nearest to them, by place, was of the lake below their mountains. A young shepherd seeking a lost ewe had come to the lake edge in moonlight and from the water of the lake a maiden had risen in the image of Danu, and spoken lovingly to him. She would live with him, she said, and bear him children, but if he was ever angry with her, and hit her with metal, she and their children would disappear into the lake. The young shepherd loved her for her beauty, and agreed in all things. But after many years, when she had born him three fine sons, he was one morning suddenly angry, for the gate of the ramfold was left open, and though she spoke to comfort him he took his metal dagger and struck her. As the blow fell a sudden mist rose from the lake, and there were loud anguished cries from its deeps. When at last the mist cleared she and his sons had vanished, and his hair had turned white and his hands would not stop trembling. For by the sin of the metal he had betrayed Danu.

Yet in the five generations from the murder of Anailos the old families had lived peacefully and intermarried with the newcomers. In their work they had used all the tools they could get. Most of their tools were still stone but the new copper and especially the new harder bronze were highly valued. They often met and spoke with the travellers who made and traded metals. Yet the earth had not moved.

It was then said by the elders that since the Earth Mother Danu gave all things, she gave copper and tin as she gave stones and grass. She gave signs with pink flowering thrift where copper could be found. She taught her children to dig metals as she had taught them to dig and break soil to plant grain and herbs. All women and ewes felt pain, in the labour of birth, but Danu contained all things and was beyond pain and anger.

Carvor knew these words of the elders. They lay close in his mind with the stories of the mothers. He could not find his way between them. Yet he had seen the strange light, and other lights had been seen from High Buck. The new family beyond White Cap had felt the earth tremble. There could be no tie between this and the story of old Samela. Many such fears came and went, in stories round the fire or at the edge of darkness, but the life of the families was still good and secure. Families and children, grass and flocks, trees and beasts for the hunt, abounded in these good mountains and valleys, under the kind skies. Nothing anyone could touch could really disturb this.

The gathering of the new wool continued. Every day there were drives along the ridges to collect the sheep and bring them down for plucking. The women were kept busy washing and combing and spinning the wool, and soon they would be weaving again. They would especially weave the fine winter cloaks of these mountains, in which deer hair was added to the wool to keep out the rain. These cloaks were always good trade, though the usual honey-coloured cloth, dyed from heather, also traded easily. With the flocks so abundant, on the spring grass, there would be more than enough to exchange for the tools and emmer grain, for the barley and salt and smoked fish that the seariver families had in such plenty.

Carvor stood on the high ridge of the middle finger of the hand of the mountains. He drank at the spring before going on with the flock. There were eighteen ewes and lambs, with the dogs guarding them. Macar was beyond them looking south.

The first strangeness Carvor noticed was that the dogs began howling. It was a wild noise, like the howling of wolves. He heard Macar shout at them, but they took no notice. Carvor ran forward. Other things were happening, but he could not be sure of their sequence. It had begun with the howling of dogs. Or perhaps he had only noticed it first. For now the ewes were restless and were running this way and that. Their lambs ran after them but the ewes seemed hardly to notice, turning suddenly and often knocking them over. At the same time the whole ridge was full of rising birds. All those that had been resting in the heat of midday were now rising and darting through the sky. He ran towards the sheep but there was now again a tingling on his scalp and on his neck, as when he had seen the strange light. He stopped and looked into the sky. It was a calm bright blue, unbroken and undisturbed. He searched the whole horizon but it was all familiar sky, away to the distant low bank of white cloud above the Bear Mountains.

The sheep still ran frantically, this way and that, as if wolves were among them. The birds still darted through the air. The dogs, huddled close, continued to howl.

He reached the dogs at the same time as Macar. Macar lifted his curvehead staff and struck at the nearest dog. It bellied to the grass and evaded him. As he reached down one of the other dogs snapped at him. Then as Carvor went forward the oldest dog, Tip, that he had had since a puppy, rushed and bit at his leg. He kicked him away, shouting. Macar pulled at his arm. Carvor looked where he was pointing. There was an area of grass, much like that all around, into which some of the ewes and their lambs had run. At once it seemed, they were calm again. Some were already settling to graze. The rest of the flock were still running wildly, this way and that. But they soon became aware of the others and began moving towards them. As they reached that grass it was like the end of a summer storm. They were immediately quiet and settled to graze.

Carvor and Macar looked at each other. They were breathless.

'What was that?' Macar asked.

Carvor shook his head. The dogs had moved away, but were still restless and whining.

'Look,' Carvor said.

Several birds, mainly larks and wheatears, had settled on the grass among the sheep. All were now quite calm, though beyond them, along the ridge, many others were still in the air and were flying this way and that, disturbed.

'I see no marks,' Macar said.

'I see none. But let us look closer.'

They walked to the grass where the sheep were grazing. They looked carefully around, to see if there was anything different about it. They could see nothing. Carvor looked both ways along the ridge, to see if some shapes of the land, or perhaps some alignment marked out this place. Again there was nothing unusual. Yet it obviously had some effect. As he watched, a ewe and a lamb went beyond it, if that could be said when there was no mark of a boundary. They were at once agitated, jumping in the air, until they ran back to the flock and again settled to graze. The contrasting behaviour of the birds within and beyond this strange place was equally clear to see. Yet the men felt no difference in themselves.

'We must mark it,' Macar said.

They looked around for small stones and began marking what they took to be the boundary. The only line they could follow was from the sheep, but as they looked back at their stones they found they had been marking a rough circle. While they worked the dogs came back to them. They were still restless and frightened. They stayed out of reach and whenever they were looked at dropped their heads.

Carvor and Macar rested, sitting inside the circle of stones.

Slowly everything became normal again. They noticed this first in the birds along the ridge, which one by one stopped flying and settled on the ground, wherever it pleased them to land. Then the sheep, again gradually, began moving to new grass beyond the stones. The dogs were now watching the men, looking for any signal. When none came they began moving around the flock as the men had trained them.

All around above the ridges, the sky was clear. The farthest hills were blue in the distance. There was a great silence everywhere.

'It is difficult now to believe,' Macar said. 'It was like a summer storm, but a storm we could not see.'

'We must ask questions,' Carvor said.

They whistled the dogs and got ready to drive.

'Do we leave the stones?' Carvor asked.

'Yes, of course, to be sure of the place.'

They drove along the ridge and down to the settlement. They penned the sheep. Before they had finished men and women were coming to tell them how the animals and birds had been disturbed, and how one lot of sheep had broken down their hurdled pen and run up towards the mountain. The unusual happenings were exchanged and talked about, but nobody knew what to make of them. There was hardly any more work to be done, as they talked about the strangeness.

Nobody knew or remembered any story which could explain what had happened, though old Samela said again that Danu was angry. Over the next few days, when they met other families in the mountains, there were similar reports, but nobody had an explanation. Then when Carvor was at High Buck, looking for a ewe that

had strayed, he got talking to a man whose mother knew a story of
Karan the Measurer, in the very old times. It was said that this
Karan had spoken of the strange flight and rushing of animals and
birds, and of these as signs of storms in the earth.

Carvor at once went down to see her. She was old and blind. She
would not speak of anything until Carvor had told his own parent-
age and descent. She then held his wrists tightly, close to her waist.

'You have spoken of Karan the Measurer,' Carvor said at last.

'He was Karan. He was one of the good old people.'

'What does it mean? Measurer?'

'He was a boy in Lanoluc. He went away to the High Folk in the
White Land.'

'Did he tell of storms in the earth?'

'There is a stone of Karan, that we call the Midwinter Stone.'

'I have seen it.'

'There was anger in the White Land. The High Folk were false
children. They lived only for themselves.'

'And did Karan return?'

'When he returned the people were angry.'

'Why were they angry?'

'They were angry at the way he now spoke of Danu.'

Carvor looked around. She still held him close by the wrists. Her
breath was sour.

'How did he speak of her, Mother?'

'It is terrible to say. It is what he said, not what I say.'

'I understand, Mother.'

'He said that the earth was different from its people. It had no
mother and no children. It had only its powers, that we must learn
to measure.'

'And did he measure for storms in the earth?'

'Soon after he returned there was a storm in the earth. Many were
killed above Alaron. It was a sign from Danu, of her anger with
Karan.'

'Yet he stayed?'

'He stayed. He asked the people to go with him, to measure the
storm. He said that when he had measured he could find shelters for
the people. He said that he had watched the flock and the birds of
the air and that some had found shelters from the storm.'

Carvor held his breath.

'Did they go with him to measure?'

'No, for the storm had happened and he had not measured it.'

'What did Karan do then?'

'He walked the mountains, always measuring, looking for shelters from the storm. But Danu was kind. No storm came again.'

'Did he find any shelters?'

'It is not told. He was old and alone. He died above Alaron, where the earthstorm had broken.'

Carvor closed his eyes. He bent his head and kissed the hands that still gripped his wrists.

'Thank you in honour, Mother.'

'Go with Danu, my son.'

She released his wrists. He made his way back across the pass. For several days, though he worked and talked normally with others, his mind was centred on the story of Karan. He was increasingly certain of what he and Macar had found: one of Karan's shelters from an earthstorm. There was nothing to show on the surface because the shelter was from powers in the earth. When he had a chance he went back up. He told only Macar. The stones they had set were in place but there was otherwise nothing unusual. He sat inside the circle but there was only familiar grass under him and sweet mountain air on his face.

'Yet here on that day the sheep and the birds found shelter.'

'There is no tie,' Macar said.' When you saw the strange light the flock was not frightened. When the sheep and birds were disturbed there was no light in the sky. And in living memory there has been no earthstorm in this place.'

'There was a storm below White Cap. And in Karan's time there was a storm at Alaron.'

They went down again, uncertain. On the next day Carvor asked old Gord, who had many stories, whether he knew anything of Karan.

'Of Karan,' Gord said. 'He was one of three wise men, Karan and Mered and Idrisil. They set stones for midwinter and midsummer. With their rods they found new springs and places of water under the earth.'

'Did they seek shelters from earthstorms?'

'There are no shelters from earthstorms. But Karan, it is said, looked for rare sacred places in the mountains, where there is cure for the sickness of aches and fevers and where there is always fertility for woman and for cwc and for seed.'

'Is it told that he found them?'

'There was anger against him because it was said that he had found them and was keeping them secret. But it is known that he found nothing, though he walked searching till he died.'

Carvor thanked him and walked away. He could get nothing clear.

Through the fall and midwinter he thought continually, but had to agree with Macar that there was as yet no tie. Then, in the last moon of winter, on a clear cold night above the snows of the great ridges, a strange light was seen again. It was not like the light which he had seen in the summer. It was more like a streak of high cloud, but it shone brightly and twisted and turned in the sky. It was not as bright as lightning but it lasted much longer, and before it faded it changed colour to yellow. Two days later there was a single hanging light in the south. Tara, who saw it first, said that it had lifted from Wolf Point, moving fast, and then stopped. Many who looked at it now saw it as an object in the sky. A strange darkness pulsed and deepened in wide bands across its centre. Yet others saw only a hanging light. It disappeared suddenly, with no sign of movement away.

There was anxious talk again about the meaning of the lights. A few were frightened, but most were only curious and puzzled. Carvor walked again to the circle on the ridge. The stones they had set were almost covered by deep snow. There was nothing to be seen but the long, bare winter ridge. No birds or animals were around.

It was at the full of the same moon that the sudden earthstorm came. It was just before sunrise. The family was still sleeping in the huts. Then the dogs began howling and as the family woke they felt the earth shaking under them. Carvor, jumping from his bed, was thrown to the ground. There was shouting all around, and the noise of things falling. Clinging to the floor of his hut, he saw the upright stones of the doorway thrown to the ground, and then the timbers of the roof were slipping and falling in. He shouted to get out and grabbed two of the children. He could not stand but he crawled and kneed himself over the debris. As suddenly as it had come, the shaking stopped.

He stood and looked around. Most of the huts had collapsed.

Large boulders had shaken free from the scarp above them and had rolled through the settlement, some as far as the stream. Most of the family had got out but from two huts there were cries. Old Samela was discovered lying under a roof truss. She was still breathing faintly, but she died as they lifted her out. The worst suffering was in the hut of Seril mother of Macar, where a boulder from the scarp had crashed among the sleeping family. There were four dead, two of them children, and Seril's leg was broken. The young men lit the big fires and the survivors huddled around them. The trembling of the earth passed into the trembling of their bodies. Many were silently crying. Then, as the fires began leaping, and the warmth began to reach them, the earth shook again. The children screamed and others shouted. There were loud calls to Danu. The earth shook longer than the first time but in the open no one was hurt.

When the storm at last stopped they looked round at their wrecked settlement. It was then that they noticed that all the sheep had gone. They saw them in the distance, north towards the pass, moving up the long slope. The dogs were still close. While the women heated food the men called the dogs and went after the sheep. It was something familiar to do after the shocks of the storm. Carvor, running with the others, noticed a strange effect: that after the trembling of the earth, when they had been helplessly thrown and moved around, it was difficult to run normally now that the ground was firm again. It was as if the body was expecting a movement in the earth which did not come. Several times, along paths he had followed all his life, he stumbled or missed his footing.

The earth shocks did not come again but the damage to the family was heavy. They had lost five dead, after three deaths in the previous long winter. All their huts would have to be rebuilt. There were heavy losses among the sheep. Many ewes had aborted and several had died. There would be a shortage of new lambs and it would take many summers to remake the flock. For several seasons they would have to depend more on hunting. Some of the men wanted to move the whole family away, to leave this place of the earthstorms. But though many were still frightened, most of the family argued that they knew nothing of other places. From the time of the old sheep they had lived in these mountains and they had never before known an earthstorm. As the days passed the argument died down, for they were too busy to do more than their immediate work. It was a moon

before they had time to go around the neighbouring families and see
how far the storm had struck.

By midsummer, when they had had time to move across the
mountains, it was clear that they had been only on the edge of the
storm. The worst damage was to the south, from White Cap
towards the valley of Salmon River. There many people and sheep
had died and there had been heavy rockfalls. But the most frightening sight was a great fissure in the earth within the dense oakwood
that ran down to the bend of the river. Hundreds of trees had been
uprooted and lay around the line of the fissure. Others had tumbled
in chaos into the broken red earth. The whole oakwood was silent.
All the animals and birds had abandoned it. The men stared in
silence, but next day they went back and began examining the trees
for timber. Several of the older men worked in the forest all summer.
They cut new roof timbers and made stools and bowls and tool
handles and staves. Men from other families also worked there.
There was endless talk about the earthstorm, through the long
summer days, but already as a thing of the past.

It was after the midsummer feast that Carvor made his proposal.
He was certain, he explained, that he had found the special place for
which, long ago, Karan the Measurer had searched. He did not call
it the sacred place, but most of the family when they heard him, gave
it that name. The place was marked by the circle of stones which he
and Macar had set, but Carvor now proposed that they should set
larger stones. They would then touch the stones with water and
make it a place of safety and fertility. Macar supported him, and it
was quickly agreed. Talking about it to other families, Carvor heard
that such circles had already been marked in the mountains to the
west. But with the extra work caused by the storm it was the
following spring, when the young men took the smaller flock back
to the ridges, before new stones were set. Carvor set a peg with a hide
rope and made the circle as smooth as he could measure. By
midsummer the larger stones were in place. Water was carried to
honour them, by the unmarried girls. After this ceremony the circle
was clear as a holy place, though the sheep grazed through it, as if
not noticing it was there.

In the fall it was arranged that the breeding ewes would be
tethered there through the first days of the ram moon. After the
losses in the flock the fertility of the ewes was especially important,

and indeed in the following spring there was an exceptional number of healthy lambs. Yet what most commended the place to the family, and brought members of other families to come and observe it, was that in that same spring the infant son of Carvor and Tara was brought to the circle suffering from the red fever from which infants often died. They sat three days and nights within the circle, nursing the infant at the foot of the largest stone. They rested and waited in the clear mountain air. The fever subsided and the child was well again. They carried him happily down to the family and Tara named him Kargen: Kargen meaning in the language of the people the child of the stone.

The Black Stranger and the Golden Ram

———————◆———————

From the eastern spur of the main body of the mountains there is a sudden scarp to a broad valley. The two rivers that rise within an arrow's distance of each other, between High Buck and Hawkstone, and then flow in opposite directions, at last curve below the spur and run north as a single river. At the very edge of this scarp, commanding a wide view to the east with the earth dropping precipitously below it, the Boat Grave of Telemon the Finder had been sited, nine generations ago. The skills and voyages of Telemon were legendary. He had sailed the great sea, west and north, to find new veins of lead, copper and tin. There were many such journeyings, and many with such skills, but among his own people, around the Bay of the Islands, Telemon was honoured above all others as a navigator and a finder. He had used rods of hazel to find blind springs and buried metals. He could feel with his long fingers the points of life in certain stones, so strongly that as he touched them he would often be thrown to the ground. He lived, it was said, for fifty-eight summers, and in this extremity of age his powers were still active. Yet he had grown beyond the long journeys and now looked only for a place to rest. Seeing this high blue scarp, from a hill above the seariver, he had asked to be taken to it and there, among his people, he had died. He had been buried with his rods and with the small cup he had carried everywhere: a black cup, with holes for a thong, and with his own secret markings incised in the clay.

The long boat of his memorial was in the shape of a crescent, exactly divided by the rising sun at midsummer. It measured twenty paces across its arc, and ten paces from its leading edge at the scarp (where a trench divided it from a low drystone wall) to the centre of the incurve of the low western retaining wall. His family had settled around it, and the bones of eight generations were now added to his own. Looking east, as had been their habit, and trading along the joined river, they were still relatively separate from the shepherd families on the northern and western slopes of the mountains. In a clearing of the valley at the foot of the scarp they kept pigs and grew barley in the fertile red earth. But in the generations since Telemon they had begun also to keep sheep on their spur, and their huts were in both places: at the end of the spur, near the long boat, and far below in the valley clearing, at the edge of the oak forest. The huts on the spur were used only in spring and summer, when the sheep were driven up for grazing. It was only in summer, following the sheep along the high ridges, that they met the shepherd families of the northern slopes. The shepherds still called them the metal people, though since the time of Telemon they had given up prospecting. But they had retained, in each generation, skill of casting and repairing metal tools. They traded some of these to the west, but most of their trading, and nearly all their marriages, were with the families further east, in the low hills between the two wide rivers that flowed south to the sea.

It was to the huts on the spur, in the moon after midsummer, that the stranger came. He was leading a fawn-brown ram that was finer and heavier than any that had been seen in these mountains. He was a tall, powerful man, carrying a heavy axe and with a long wedge dagger at his belt. When he had been seen he stopped and let the men of Telemon's family approach him. They stood ten paces away, keeping an eye on him but looking mainly at the ram. Only the young Telim looked closely into his face and at his arms, which were bare from the elbows. There were strange, dark, nearly black lumps at several places on his skin.

Slowly and cautiously they gathered around the ram. The stranger explained himself. He had been cheated and driven out by his family, beyond the seariver. All he now had in the world was this ram, which he had reared in crossbreeding. He could never return to his old family, but he would offer the ram for breeding to any new family that would shelter and feed him.

It took many days to decide. The young men went down to report to the elders in the valley. The stranger tethered his ram near the Boat Grave and was given food and drink. Two of the elders came to look at him. The young women of the summer huts were kept carefully away. It is still probable that on his own the stranger would not have been accepted, beyond the minimum hospitality of the law. The elders especially were suspicious of him, with his story of a quarrel with his family: a story they believed they could interpret as they looked into his eyes, which were hard and cold. Moreover they had questions about the many disfigurements on his skin, which were of a kind they had not seen. He replied, frankly, that he had indeed been afflicted by a passing disease but had been cured without aid. What they saw was a mere residue, which stained but did not affect his now obvious health. This explanation was hardly enough, but there was still the ram. It was magnificent beyond the finest rams of these mountains: powerful, heavily woolled, yet also unusually docile for a beast of its size. The docility was as important as the strength, for it was a constant problem of these mountains to keep the flocks close to the settlements and to control them in their movements between winter and summer. After further argument it was finally decided to accept the stranger's offer, to breed this fine blood into their flock, but for one season only.

When the stranger was told this he bowed his head and burst into tears.

'Is there no place in the world where a man can rest?' he cried. 'Is it life for a man to wander always among strangers and be known only as a stranger? Is it some new way among men to look harshly at their brothers and close their hearts against them? Is this not the end of the law?'

The elders stared at the ground. They were shocked to see so hard a man crying, but they were also shocked by his words. Could what he said be true, that their way of life was changing and that they had changed with it? Was the old law now only a word, to be forgotten when a stranger surprised them?

'You accept my ram,' the stranger continued, 'but you do not accept me, except as the bringer of the ram. I then see that I am nothing to you, and when you have used my ram you will send me out again as a stranger.'

The elder Malan raised his hand and answered.

'We are grieved by your words. We may indeed be at fault. Yet more and more strangers are coming to this island, as we ourselves came. Our minds are unsettled, for we cannot truly know each other. Thus we beg you not to take it as harshness when we say the one season. After one season there is always another, and we shall talk again.'

The stranger hesitated, then wiped his face and came forward and gripped Malan's hand. They walked together and put their hands on the beautiful ram.

That summer was hot and very dry. The flock had to move over a wider area to find good grass, in the watercourse hollows of springs and above the blind springs which, taught by Telemon, the family knew how to find. But the flock itself knew its own best ways. The stranger's wonderful ram moved with them, its size conspicuous among the rest. To save driving each evening the young men followed the flock and slept wherever they were, through the warm clear nights.

They were on the ridge above Stone Valley, still remembered by the shepherds as the place of the murder of Anailos, when they woke one morning and looked out at the grazing flock. Lying at some distance from the others was the stranger's ram. They rushed over but could see at once that it was dead. They squatted and examined it. There was no mark of wound or injury. They left it and walked the rest of the flock. They were all as normal. Two of them ran to bring the stranger. The others watched to keep the flock away from the corpse.

The stranger came running. He squatted by the corpse and took the head between his hands. He looked carefully into the nostrils, the mouth and the eyes. They watched anxiously. When at last he looked round at them they could see sorrow in his face, but there was also something else: an edge of fear. They questioned him closely but he would say only that these sudden deaths sometimes happened. They all knew that this was true but it did not reassure them.

He then surprised them by saying that he would burn the corpse where it lay. They were against this because of the risk of fire spreading along the dry ridges. But he was determined. He gathered stones and built them around the corpse. It was like the preparation for a sacrifice. Then he started a fire and fed it until it was burning fiercely. They watched for some time but then moved away from the stench to stand among their own flock. The stranger stood close to the thick smoke, and his face and arms were darkened by it. But still he stoked it to keep a fierce blaze. There were tears running down his face among the grime of the fire. As the shape of the ram disappeared he went on his knees and bowed his head to the ground. He beat at the ground with his fists. The other sheep, meanwhile, grazed on, taking no notice of the fire. The men looked from their flock to the column of dark smoke that rose high in the clear air.

The sheep still grazed slowly west, and the men of Telemon's family followed them. There was a wide area of good grass above the spring which flowed to the river of Stone Valley. Two other flocks were grazing there, from the families at High Buck and Hawkstone. During the long day the shepherds of the families met and spoke to each other. The young men of Telemon's family told the story of the dead ram. It was not unusual to find a sheep dead from no apparent cause, though their more regular losses were from wolves. What concerned them, in this case, was that the ram had come from elsewhere. Then one of the young shepherds from Hawkstone had a story of a new flock, beyond White Cap, which had been wiped out that spring by some unexplained sickness. A new family had settled in the place where long ago, during the earthstorm, there had been great damage and the old family and flock had left. But that damage of the earthstorm could not be the cause, although the place was still regarded as unlucky. What connected in the mind of the young shepherd from Hawkstone was that there, also, all the corpses had been immediately burned. This had never, they knew, been the custom of the mountains. Perhaps the strangers knew something about the deaths which the mountain people did not. Yet also, by the rite which they had brought with them, the strangers burned rather than buried their own natural dead.

Towards sunset the flocks separated. The men from High Buck and Hawkstone were driving back towards their families, and the young men of Telemon's family decided also to drive back, to tell the elders about the death of the ram. It was in any case almost time for the wool plucking, and this had to be done near their own settlement. When they got back they found that the young women on the spur knew nothing of the death of the ram. The men had passed the place of the burning on their long way back. The fire had been stamped out and the stranger had gone. Now they found that nobody had seen him along the spur.

Telim hurried down to the valley huts. Nobody there had seen the stranger. The elders were not worried, but Telim was now very anxious. He went up to sleep but was out early next morning, walking carefully round the flock. There were signs of the usual minor sicknesses, but nothing out of the way. Some of the others now said that the death of the ram was what often happened with the wrong crossbreeding. You went for a heavier body or a thicker wool, but if you went too far you got a weak beast, without the hardiness of the rest of the flock. Telim knew that this could be true, but it did not ease his anxiety. It was the immediate burning of the ram that stuck in his mind, and this was strengthened by the story of the burning of the dead flock beyond White Cap. Moreover, it was now clear that the stranger had gone away, had disappeared. What did he know that had made him run like that? The others argued that without the ram he knew that he would not be welcome. But his grief and apparent fear as he had burned the corpse, and then his sudden disappearance without a word, made Telim think that it was worse than that.

Yet what could be done, except to watch the flock? To make sure of watching them continuously he persuaded the others to keep the sheep around the huts, near the Boat Grave, though the grass was not good there. It then seemed reasonable, as the flock continued to look well, to go ahead with plucking the wool. They settled to the job, through two long hot days. The young men plucked and the young women collected the wool for washing.

On the day after the plucking they let the flock graze west again, towards the better grass around the first springs. It was late that same day when they noticed the first trouble. One of the ewes was trembling, as if in drought. As they watched it got rapidly worse. Its breathing was noisy and difficult and then its whole body convulsed. It died that evening.

At first light next morning eight of the flock lay dead. There were no marks on them. Worse still, three of the young men, among the fastest of the wool pluckers, were struck by severe pains in their chests and in their breathing. When they got back to the huts they found that four of the young women had the same sickness.

Word was sent at once to the elders in the valley. The older women came up with their medicines, to treat and nurse the sick. But all the time the strange sickness was spreading to others, with the same harsh and difficult breathing, the same pains and spasms in the chest. It was in the lungs, the old women said, bending over their patients and trying to ease their suffering with infusions of herbs. None of the remedies arrested the disease. Its course was rapid, and soon the first death came, one of the youngest girls. Other deaths followed rapidly, and all the afflicted were in the extremes of pain.

Before noon next day all the young men and women who had been with the flock were dead or dying. Telim, in great pain, passed a message for his father to come. The old women objected, saying that everyone untouched by the disease must be kept away. But Telim insisted, taking his knife and putting the point to his throat. His father at last came. His legs were weak from a chronic illness and it was hard for him to climb to the spur. He came with a white sadness in his face to sit beside his son, in the shade of the doorway of the hut.

'My father,' Telim said, speaking with great difficulty.

'My son.'

'My father, I do not know this disease which has come to us. But it is in the wool of the flock.'

'There is nothing sick in the wool.'

'Yes, indeed it must be so. For the young women are struck also and they have not handled the sheep. But they took the wool that we had plucked, and they carried it for washing. To be safe, my father, the wool must be burned.'

'What are you saying, my son? We cannot burn all our wool.'

'My father, listen. All the wool must be burned. All the dead of the flock must be burned. For the sickness has come from that ram of the stranger, and when he saw that it was dead he immediately burned it. In his land he knew of this sickness.'

'Do not worry, Telim. Save your own strength. We shall see to everything.'

'No,' Telim cried, hoarsely. 'No.'

His voice rose to a shout of pain and a terrible spasm of coughing shook his whole body. He shot out his arm and gripped his father's wrist.

'My father,' he said, his face streaming with tears.

'Rest peacefully, my son.'

'All must be burned. All wool and all corpses. And you must burn also the bodies of those of us who die.'

There was great shock in his father's face.

'Burn our dead sons and daughters! It is not to be thought of.'

'Burn all who die,' Telim shouted, gasping for breath.

'My son, the Long Boat is the home of our family, of all our sons and daughters.'

'It has been and will be so again. But we who die of this sickness must be kept away from it. Our bodies must be burned or all the family will die.'

'We will burn the dead of the flock.'

'And the wool.'

'The wool will be washed.'

'Burn the wool!'

In the frenzy of his effort to persuade his father Telim drew on his last strength. The spasms of coughing became continuous, and he could no longer speak. He rolled in agony on the grass. His fingers still gripped his father's wrist as he died.

The strange deaths became so many that the family of Telemon was reduced to a few old men and women and to the youngest children. The whole flock of sheep was destroyed. The dogs, in spite of attempts to stop them, ate from the carcases of the sheep and died in uncontrollable vomit.

Meanwhile the disease was spreading all over the mountains. Nearly all the sheep, on which the very livelihood of the old families depended, died within weeks. Almost all the young men and women, and even many of the children, who had been handling the sheep and the wool, died in an agony of the lungs. Only some of the families burned the dead sheep. Even fewer burned the plucked wool, which they needed for their clothes and for trading. Yet in the dry summer the few fires that were started, with less people to guard them, raged out of control, across the tinder-dry grass and heather, and spread into the woods on the slopes. By midwinter the whole way of life of the mountains had been almost destroyed. The few survivors went down to the lower valleys, where they lived, still reducing in numbers, by hunting deer and pig. Through the winter reports came that the disease was not confined to these mountains. It had ravaged vast areas all around. Only a very few sheep in isolated valleys had escaped.

It was a disaster beyond anything which the shepherds could have imagined. For several generations, slowly remaking their lives as the surviving children matured, there was a loss of spirit and of belief, and this in its own way was as damaging as the direct destruction from the disease.

It was difficult, any longer, to trust anyone or anything, since what had happened had come so directly from the flocks that were the centre of their lives. All that was sure, and was to last, was a fear of strangers. The story of the stranger and of his magnificent ram – of the Black Stranger, as he was now always called, with his disfigurements exaggerated, and of his Golden Ram, as it had passed into story, the lovely but deadly beast – was repeated everywhere, told and retold in awe and fear.

The scattered and shocked survivors stayed close to their familiar hunting forests and to such animals of their own as they had saved. After several generations they tried at last to breed new sheep, from the few flocks that had survived. But when these were driven up to the now-deserted mountains, where fine grass had grown again, the disease struck once more, as if the very ground contained it.

One story especially was told, as a memory of this time. The families below High Buck and Hawkstone had been struck early and devastatingly by the disease. It was remembered that their flocks had grazed, above Stone Valley, with the flock of the family of Telemon and with the Golden Ram itself. When the agony came among these old shepherd families there were many who blamed it on what they still called the metal people, from the family of Telemon. They linked their suffering with what was often said by the older women, about the tearing of the Mother by the metal-makers. Yet a neighbouring family, in Cross Valley, had their own sacred place, discovered in the old times by Carvor and marked by a circle of stones. In the generations since Carvor and his son Kargen they had come to trust its powers of healing and fertility. Their sick were carried there and many had been cured. The ceremonies of the circle were regularly and devoutly observed.

In the first onset of the disease, among the young shepherds, everything happened too quickly for the sacred place to be visited. It was beyond the carrying powers of the women, and the deaths came too quickly. It was then some time, by their own measuring of the tasks of the year, before the women began working on the wool, which had been set aside while the young men were dying. When they at last began washing and combing it, along their home stream, the disease broke out again, among the young women and children.

In an extraordinary effort the whole family then left their valley and climbed to the ridge and to the circle of stones. With many already sick they reached the sacred circle with relief and joy in their hearts, trusting wholly in its protection. They crowded inside the circle, sitting and lying closely-packed, none daring to move beyond its protecting influence. The ceremonies of the circle were performed, and the whole family sang its songs. Yet then every day more and more were struck down. Those who died first were placed reverently just outside the circle, which it was said, in the beginning, they had reached just too late.

Through the long hot days and the warm clear nights, looking out over their mountains and at the stars of a flake moon, the survivors of the family clung to their place and to their lives, in the love and trust which was strong among them. But still the sickness raged.

For days nobody left the circle, though food and water became desperately short and the children passed beyond crying to a weak silence. In the end, more like animals than people, though trust had been strong until that final morning, the last survivors – an old woman and three children – left what was now a stinking huddle of death. The old woman died on the way back down to Cross Valley. The children were found wandering, days later, by one of the hunting and fishing families of the lake, which had not been touched by the disease.

Through a full moon the sheep children were kept at a distance. Food was put out for them to collect at the edge of the forest. It was past midwinter, with no signs of illness, before they were at last taken in and set to work in the family.

As the children grew in this new place, fishing and hunting, the lake people often saw a strange look in their eyes: what they came to call the blind look, the eyes open but staring into some unreachable distance. They noticed also how often they washed their bodies, standing knee-deep in the lake and cupping their palms to bring water to their faces and arms. It was as if the water had become sacred, though the children gave no reasons and would not answer the lake family's questions. Much later, after many seasons of fishing and hunting, there was a morning when two of them, now a young man and a young woman, were seen holding hands and staring up, in their blind look, at the great dark wall of the mountains, where the life of their families – the life of the wise flocks and of the Long Houšes – had ended as if for all time.

G lyn stood on Twmpath resting his hands on the pillar of the spot height. He looked west down the long track to Rhos Dirion. In the pale spread of the moonlight he could see that it was empty, though at its edges, and among the denser growth, there were dark humps of gorse and heather and any of these might be a man.

'Taid! Taid!'

The wind was stronger now from the west, but not cold. Far below him was the curve of the Wye, with its broad flat fields towards Llyswen, and its upper valley running north towards Builth: that road beside the river which he and his mother had driven, long ago it now seemed. Away to the west the course of the Llynfi led back to the lake, where he could stand and look up at the wall of these mountains, as if at a black stranger.

He must take this short break and settle his breath. This was what Elis had taught him: whatever the urgency there must be regular rest.

He moved his fingers slowly over the brass plate set in the pillar, tracing its letters and numbers. He looked down at the metal. What could any stranger say, finding this pillar and its markings without knowing its system and codes, or any of the beliefs or purposes of the men who had set it in place? No one could doubt that it was a marker of some measurement. From this single trace the mind that designed it would be inaccessible, yet to look at and touch it compelled some reach to understand it.

'From the time of their coming into the island they all fell under the spell of the stones.' That isolated, baffling, early report, offering what seemed a continuity of belief through what, in most other ways, were different kinds and orders of life, had stuck in his mind. It was a quality which he had recognised in Elis: an attentive respect which could drift into superstition but which on these mountains, where the old stones were still undisturbed, sustained touch and question and beyond these wonder. It was still hard, in some parts of the mind, to accept that men moving like oneself, but with quite other ways of seeing, had walked these tracks and stared at these dark ridges and had then set these stones as their own kind of marker. Yet sometimes, as tonight, the physical sense of their long presence became overwhelming. The mind of day, of the lowland, of a life of movement always between buildings, slipped back like the metalled roads and the cultivated fields that had fallen away in the climb.

At rest a questioning mind returned. With his hands still touching the pillar, Glyn remembered the excitement, after prolonged reading, of glimpsing a shape, a connection, within the strong yet uncertain evidence of those distant times. He had described it to Elis, who had listened, as always, with respect.

The early observations and calculations of the Measurers had grown from the customs of the herding and farming peoples. The shepherds, especially, had an interest born of their open life by day and by night with their flocks. Even the simplest shepherds made calendars with rings of posts, and counted the moons and their phases for the setting of the rams, and for the birth of lambs in the changing lands and climates through which, on their long journeys with the sheep, they had moved. More generally there was always a practical interest in the seasonal course of the sun, by which so many tasks were regulated. And for the many who arrived in the island by boats, across a difficult sea, the relations between tides and the intricate movements of moons had been of intense concern.

The problems were not in that phase but in what probably succeeded it. It was here that the reach was most difficult. The everyday habits of reckoning had developed into more organised, more systematic, and then more separate ways. Groups would have formed around fixed places of observation and developed their own forms of exchange and calculation. They noted, and perhaps even predicted the times of eclipses and observed the long and intricate pattern of the rising and setting of the moon, which moved on the wide horizon in cycles of nearly nineteen years. Thus what had been an embedded practice, within the life of the crops and herds, would have been raised simultaneously both to a higher power and to a separation.

Menvandir. The White Land. The Company of Measurers. It was a possible construction, from the many traces. But to live for the new knowledge, to spend each day and night in the long search for its complexities, still depended, physically, on the common life of labour. The nourishment that sustained it would at first have been willingly given, because the observations still connected with everyday practice. Giving would become, within a faith, a reverent custom. Yet the ever larger monuments, the extending systems in stone, developed beyond the powers of simple communities or even of neighbouring groups. At some point, through the generations, what had once been community became order and what had once been gift, tribute.

The next phase could not be known, but it might have been this. The great fixed monuments, at once of belief and observation, were being built and yet almost continuously altered and rebuilt. The increasing exaction of food and labour must have pressed hard on the surplus of the farmers and shepherds, whose own numbers were increasing. The organisation of mass labour would need new structures of control and command. But then the knowledge itself, and the beliefs within which it was organised, could have become inseparable from these shapes of requisition and command. While any such system flourished, this link would appear natural. There would be, at most, complaint or sporadic opposition and revolt. Yet what had now to be traced back, into the heart of such a system, was its eventual and relatively sudden collapse. At a traceable time (but then why?) the monuments and the systems of more than a thousand years had been abandoned.

The broad dates were not in doubt. The collapse came two thousand years after Idrisil followed his flock to these mountains, six hundred years after Dal Mered, three hundred years after Anailos and Netta brought the first metal tools to these mountains, when the power of the White Land was reaching its height. A hundred years later the young Carvor set the circle of Garn Wen. One hundred and fifty years later again, the Black Stranger brought his Golden Ram and with it a plague of anthrax – the disease of the wool sorters. In that same time, as it happened, the monuments of the White Land were being abandoned.

Glyn felt the cold of the pillar under his pressing hands. He looked again along the track. The moonlight was diffused over the wide rough ground ahead of him: a clear but negative light, with indecipherable dark shadows. A hunting owl cried far below. It was strange, always, to be looking down at flying birds. He had sat often with Elis, watching a flock of white pigeons below them, following the line of the valley. Or they had looked down on the slow circling of a buzzard, searching woods and fields far below. At such moments a perspective was altered; an angle of vision was doubled. The mind continually reached and searched.

He pushed his body into a walk, along the pale track where the short grass shone from trampling. Could it really have been like this: that the highest knowledge of its time had become so closely connected with power and exploitation that it would at last be rejected, walked away from, by people whose suffering, both habitual and sudden, had bred new kinds of fear and belief? Could there have been a generation which learned to see these lords of the sun and moon as evil, turned wilfully away from the common life of water and earth? Turned away also from the old human law, in which all were of a family and all families of a family, linked by willing and customary gifts and exchange? And what new belief might then have emerged: a reverence differently embedded from the high system of Menvandir?

On these western mountains, at the edge of that high system, the changes were simpler. Within five generations after the earthquake the number of families increased sevenfold. As more newcomers came, with goats and sheep and with a few cattle, many moved on to the hills further west. The years before the coming of the Black Stranger were a high moment in the life of this whole land. Every ridge, every plateau and every foothill, every clearing valley and cross valley, was busily and peacefully occupied. People and their animals lived more closely together, and until the plague their flocks and crops flourished. The anthrax devastated the mountain economy: for two centuries after the first outbreak the old pastures remained infected or feared. Settlements were slowly re-established in the valleys and in new clearings in the woods. The general climate began to deteriorate once more, with cooler summers and wetter winters.

After the plague all the familiar types of pottery stopped being traded or made. Around the Black Mountains, and in the mountains and valleys to the west, pottery disappeared altogether, for some hundreds of years. The old axes, spears and knives were replaced by new designs. Customs and burial rituals changed. Rivers and streams and other wet places became more central, more defining, more sacred. The communities themselves became more local and isolated, more resistant to innovations and to strangers. What faith, what reverence could there be in these altered conditions?

Glyn was crossing the old track from Nant y Bwch to Rhiw Wen. There were ponies ahead of him, beyond the line of the track. As they sensed his coming they began moving away, but as he continued to walk towards them a white stallion turned and stood in front of the others, facing and watching the stranger.

Tami in Telim and Grain Valley

◆ ───────

Tami was born to the simple woman Calina, whose solitary hut was in an ashgrove on the bank of the mountain stream above the northern riverjoin. The winter settlement of Telim spread in a large clearing in the oakforest, from the riverjoin itself towards the steep scarp below the Old Boat Stones. The woven hazel huts were set close together, within a rough palisade of hurdles, and on the east of the enclosure there was a further fenced area, of hurdles and dead hawthorn branches, for the pigs. From fall to spring the sheep grazed in the big clearing and were kept close with stored hay. Their lambs were born in the clearing but in the second leafmoon the young men took the flock up the scarp to the near uplands, where they stayed until fall. The flock grazed for some distance along the westward ridge, but they were kept away from the heart of the mountains, which was a place of legends and of fear.

Telim kept to its own ways. The settlement was healthy and there was always enough food. As well as sheep and pigs and goats they kept a few cattle, in the lush grass along the riverbanks. Beside the huts in summer the women grew fat-hen and vetch. There was good milk and cheese from the sheep and goats, and apples, pears, nuts, fungi and wild honey from the forest around them. The wool of the mountain flock was plucked after midsummer and carried down in batches to be washed and spun and woven. The fleeces of a few of the larger sheep were cut with shears, to get a mixture of wool and kemp-hair from which weatherproof cloaks were woven. Some of the lighter plucked wool was double-combed and then dyed in hollow trunks by the river. The cold brown water was steeped with lichen for gold, with heather root for yellow and with bracken for beige. But most of the wool was left in its natural colour, for the knee-length tunics and knitted caps of the men, for the short summer and long winter tunics of the women, and for their close short-sleeved jackets. The cloth was woven on upright wooden looms, with big sandstone weights. The women also made narrow braid, on the separate pierced square stones they called tablets. The braid was used for the ends of tunics and in the finer dyed wools, for coloured belts. Leather was cured in urine for shoes, for bags and bottles, and for winter hut-door curtains. It was carefully stitched with the fine bone needles.

Telim was very sure of its own ways. It was on marrying terms with only four other settlements around the great mass of the Black Mountains. Each lived in what were seen as correct ways, with an established winter settlement and summer grazing on the near uplands. There was the close neighbouring Alaron, on the riverjoin below Horn Point, and at greater distances Abisso, on Curve River, Crucio, above Salmon River, and still the big settlement of Glara on the Lake. Journeys between these settlements were along forest tracks in the outer valleys, the longest way round. For the highest land of the mountains, along the dark central ridges and the plateau, was entirely avoided. It was believed, from father to son, in all the winter-and-summer settlements, that these high places were the land of the Black Stranger and of the Strange Death.

The young men of Telim lived all summer in rough dugouts and heather shelters on the near upland. As they looked out at the higher ridges when they were guarding the flock, they could see that there were people living in the forested cross valleys, and that their smaller sheep went up in the dry months and grazed the highest ground. But they kept well away from them, for these were the strange, Old People. The men and women were short and very dark, with black hair. They spoke some incomprehensible language. They lit midwinter and midsummer fires at the places they called their Long Houses – earth mounds set with stones. They lived in poor huts at the edges of the oakforest, which they did not cut and clear. Their fires could often be seen, but they stayed away from the people of Telim and the other winter-and-summer settlements.

Telim, indeed, had turned its back on the mountains. It wanted as few contacts as possible, beyond the people like themselves who could be trusted; people of the same kind of settlement: of Alaron and Abisso, of Crucio and Glara on the Lake. They had only one other regular contact, not for marriage but for trade, with a large settlement in Grain Valley, to the north, where there was cleared flat land, over gravel, along a slow river. There the red earth was cross-ploughed and hoed to grow good barley. There was a regular trade for this barley with their own woven woollens. The women used the barley to bake flat bread on hot stones, and at the end of the season some was used for beer, though the most favoured drinks were berry wines.

Grain Valley itself was more open to the world. It traded regularly north and east for more varied goods. Once, at the autumn trade of wool and barley, a Grain Valley man had shown the men of Telim what he called a pot: a large black bowl hardened from clay, which had been made somewhere in the east. For Telim it was an object of curiosity, of no serious interest compared with their own wooden bowls and cups, though it was noticed that it resembled broken pieces that had sometimes been found around the Old Boat Stones: useless shards to be thrown away or flicked at a bird hanging in the wind above the scarp.

There were other things and other ways, reported back through Grain Valley. But with one exception – the highly valued bronze sickles and axes, so difficult to get, so high to trade for, in the years of the travelling smith – the very unfamiliarity of what was reported was enough, in Telim, for rejection and even contempt. Apart from the bronze tools, nothing good had ever come from beyond the true people, whose settled winter-and-summer life gave them everything any reasonable being could want: good food, good water, good shelter, and above all these the deep assurance and security of their own kind.

Certainly stories were told from the past, of other ways and other beliefs. There were very old and curious stories of the earth as a woman, giving birth to all life. There were other fanciful stories of the magic of set stones and of measuring the movements not only of sun and moon but of the very stars. The stories were laughable: not even children believed them for long. Some idle people had invented them, as they had invented goddesses and magic: words now known only in these stories. There was a more local story about what everyone in Telim called the Old Boat Stones – though the name made no sense, perched there on the very edge of the scarp. In the story this was a tomb of the ancestors, although anyone could see that it was only a poor broken wall of a fold or a summer hut, with nothing in it of any interest to practical people. Indeed the only thing they needed to take seriously, beyond the regular movements of their livelihood in winter and summer, was the certainty of danger in anything that came from outside.

For this was the one true story, that in the time of the Black Stranger, many generations ago, a filthy choking death had come to the people and to the sheep. And this was a disaster that would never have happened if the people had kept to themselves, in their own place and ways. The choking death had been driven back into the heart of the mountains, and the people and the flocks could be safe if they stayed in the foothills and in the near valleys. But something very like it, or something new and equally dangerous, could come again at any time, unless all strangers were kept away. Perhaps, in their inner valleys, and on their dark central ridges, the Old People could live with such danger. For were they not, as some said, black strangers themselves? But it was in any case a duty – the central duty of Telim – to keep these and all others away from the settlement, for life itself to be preserved.

Tami was raised by Calina, alone in her hut with the pigs and goats she also raised. Calina was of Telim, by birth, but from her birth there had been something badly wrong with her. She could understand nothing of the ways of her settlement. Much of her speech was disordered. She could not even dress decently, wearing her short summer tunic loose and broken at the underarm seams. Many of the women said, among themselves, that her natural father, in some chance, was one of the Old Ones from the inner mountains, and that this was her corruption. But in her body she was like most of the women of Telim: tall with brown wavy hair and brown eyes. Simple and very slow as a child, she had become uncontrollable as a girl. When her mother died, at that time, she was not, like other orphans, taken in to the kin of her mother, though this had been offered because it was the law. Instead she had gone away on her own and built her poor hut and found goats and pigs and raised them; at first stolen them, everyone believed. She was left to herself, as a way of least trouble. But the other women were careful to keep her at a distance from their men, for she was without decency and would lie with any man like an animal.

Kept at her distance, in the hut in the ashgrove, she had made her own dirty life. Yet it was said, in quarrels, that even some men of

Telim, and certainly men from Alaron or Abisso or Crucio or Glara, visiting on the business of the settlements, or bringing fish and waterfowl to trade for the fine Telim cloaks, found their way at night to her hut. There was then no surprise when it was heard that a son had been born to her, and that she had called him Tami, which was not a name of the people. As the boy grew, and was seen along the river, it was quickly noticed that he was unusually big. He had broad shoulders and his hair was black as a raven.

Yet Tami's size did not really impress Telim, in the steady life of its winters and summers, until he was twelve years old and his real growth began. Seeing him infrequently, for his mother kept him close to her hut, people were surprised and then astonished by his phenomenal growth. At fourteen he was already taller than any man in the settlement, and still he went on growing, not in a boy's thin body but with a strength that supported his height. At sixteen he was more than a head taller than the tallest man in Telim, and still he grew taller and bigger. Nobody had ever seen or heard of such a giant. 'It is the seed of many men in that simple Calina,' was one opinion, for his great body seemed beyond any natural explanation. When the huge young man, with his slow walk, later began wandering, apparently aimlessly, into the fenced winter settlement, they were all ready to be afraid of him and to take action together against him.

Yet it became clear, in the course of time, that his great size and strength were not really a problem. In his manner and behaviour he was as simple as his mother, but without any of her unruliness. He would stand for long periods, looking at the flow of water in the river, or into the trees and bushes at birds. Often, when he had stood for some time, he would imitate the whistling of some bird, or at other times sing, standing alone, in a deep wordless voice. He always carried a huge bow across his chest, but he had never been seen to use it, and he had only a few long, brightly-feathered arrows. If there were men working, on the jobs of the settlement, he would often stand watching them, at a cautious distance, smiling if he was looked at but showing no sign of wanting to come closer.

As they gradually got used to him, some of the youths and boys began taunting him, but he made no move to respond. One day when a stick was thrown at him, hitting his leg, he only bent down and picked it up, and after a while carried it away. Nobody quite dared to go close to him and provoke him, but it was at last obvious that he was shy and good-natured and in his own distant way friendly. He began coming regularly to watch the men working, and seeing his great strength they would invite him to join in. But still he only smiled and kept his distance.

One winter afternoon, when they were felling trees to enlarge the clearing, Tami stood, as so often, watching the work, and old Nemat thought of a joke. They had felled and trimmed a big cherry tree, and the heavy trunk was taking three men to carry. Walking under its weight, they turned aside to where Tami was standing.

'Here, Tami,' Nemat said.

Tami smiled. They did not know if he could understand their words.

'For you, Tami,' Nemat said, and at a signal the three men shifted the trunk from their shoulders and put it on Tami's left shoulder.

He took the weight, smiling. They stared up at him. Then he turned, slowly, and walked away carrying the trunk, up the river-bank towards his mother's hut. They were at first amazed but then could only laugh.

From that day on, Nemat, the most respected man of Telim, began watching Tami more carefully. Since there was clearly no harm in him, it was a pity that so much strength should simply go to waste. Nemat found himself thinking of the packhorses, of which they had two, for the loads of Grain Valley. The work of training these horses was never easy. It was done by capturing a foal from the herd that grazed in summer along the westward ridge. The foal must then be roped and beaten and at last tamed with food. Nemat's father had been skilled at this work, and he had passed on his secrets: especially one that was still astonishing. He would set aside one bag of the drink that was steeped, each fall, from the berries of elder. He would let it go bitter – as often happened accidentally. He would then take a handful of dried grass and soak it in the sour liquid. Moving close to the frightened foal, he would hold the soaked grass to its nostrils. Always, as if by the power of the man, the creature would become quiet and calm. If the soaked grass was given regularly it would at last learn to carry loads: baskets of woven rush and tied grass, slung over its back on each side.

Nemat knew, thinking it over, that he could not use this method with Tami, who though so large and strange was a man. But there must be some way. The problem was not getting him to accept a load: that had been done with the cherry trunk, and Nemat had successfully repeated it. The real problem was getting him to carry it somewhere useful, rather than straight back up the river to his mother's hut.

Nemat settled to find a way. He noticed that while Tami would come and stand to watch any work being done, he was especially interested when they were working with animals. He had once laughed and begun singing when a calf was born, and he had come unusually close in that season's lambing. Against the protests of the others, Nemat took a good lamb and put it into Tami's arms. Tami smiled and bent his face to it. When Nemat went to him again he closed his arms more tightly around it, but still he did not turn and carry it away. Through the long hours of the lambing he stood, watching, and then as the sun was setting he squatted and released the lamb, which stumbled and then scampered to rejoin the flock and its mother. Tami, still squatting, clapped his hands and laughed, and when Nemat came over to him he got up slowly but did not move away. Nemat, cautiously, put his hand on Tami's right wrist. Tami stood very still, smiling at him.

From that day Nemat was always able to get close to Tami. When the young men took the flock up the scarp to the upland grazing, Tami stayed at the winter settlement and at times followed Nemat around. When the first wool began to come down he watched the women washing and spinning it, and he did not go away but stood, smiling, when the girls began teasing him. One day Nemat gave him an old brown tunic, the largest he could find, to replace the matted and broken tunic he was wearing. Tami came back later, wearing it, but it was much too small for him, and all the women and girls laughed. Nemat's wife, Nema, then unseamed two old tunics – they were of different colours, brown and gold, but were all that could be spared – and stitched one to his size: awkwardly seamed and shapeless, but adequate. He did not reappear for some days, but when he came it was in the new tunic. Mena, encouraged, gave him an old winter tunic and a belt for Calina, and he carried them away. But although her son now came regularly to the settlement, Calina still kept her distance and was only occasionally seen through the trees along the river.

Then, in high summer, Tami stopped coming. After missing him for several days, Nemat went looking for him, but though he watched the whole area around Calina's hut there was no sign of him. It was only when the last wool was being brought down from the upland that there was news of him. He had been seen by the young men who were with the flock, walking out along the westward ridge towards the central mountains. One of them said how huge he had looked, when they had seen him suddenly against the skyline. He had gone on, it appeared, into the inner valleys, in the place of the Old Ones. Nemat was afraid for him, but there was nothing that could be done.

It was in the next moon, with the whole settlement busy with the weaving for the autumn trade in Grain Valley, that Tami reappeared. Nemat looked up one morning and the huge young man was standing under a tree, watching him. He was smiling. His skin was heavily sunburned. His black hair and beard had grown out loose. He was still wearing the brown-and-gold tunic, but there was now a curiously knotted leather thong around his neck, with a polished green stone at his throat. In his left hand he held an ash wand, as tall as himself, and Nemat saw that the wand was cut with regular markings, very close together at the top. Tami lifted the wand above his head and then squatted and laid it on the ground. Nemat stared down at it. The markings were quite unfamiliar. Tami spread his large fingers and moved them slowly along the markings. Nemat waited and then squatted beside him and smiled.

'Kena,' Tami said.

It was the first word that Nemat had heard him speak, but he did not understand it.

'Kena,' Tami repeated.

'Good,' Nemat said reassuringly.

'Kena good,' Tami said.

Nemat waited, thinking hard. If Tami had been, as seemed likely, among the Old People, the risks might be great.

'Kena,' he said at last, touching the wand.

Tami grinned.

'Kena cara, kena bucat,' he said excitedly.

'The black ones,' Nemat said sternly.

'Black vincara good,' Tami said.

'Not good,' Nemat said.

Tami's mouth hung open. He raised his big hand and touched the green stone at his neck.

'Strangers not good,' Nemat said, hardly. Tami frowned. His fingers moved to the cord of his big bow.

'Kill wolves vincara,' he said earnestly.

'Tami kill wolves?'

'With old,' Tami said, smiling broadly.

'In the high mountains?'

'Vincara,' Tami said. 'Vincara serelit Tami lon.'

Nemat got up impatiently. Tami also, slowly, got up. Nemat looked carefully over him, as if examining an animal for disease. He looked all right, though there were several healing scratches on his legs. Nemat turned, impatiently, and left him standing there, waiting, his mouth hanging open.

He did not see him again for some days. The work of the settlement was now at its peak, with weaving and dyeing through all the daylight hours. In this year the autumn trade would be special, for it was the year in which the travelling smith was expected to come. While the women weaved and dyed, the older men collected and examined the few bronze tools of the settlement: sickles, three palstaves and a flanged axe. Most were badly worn and must be taken to the smith, who would either repair them or take them for scrap and give some exchange. To please the smith it had been decided to weave one of the finest Telim cloaks, which were always highly valued. It was a weaving of plucked white breastwool and some kemp, with special seams of yellow-dyed braid and elaborate fastenings of twisted thongs and polished cherrywood. The more regular cloaks and tunics were also prepared, to trade as usual for the barley.

It would be a heavy load to carry along the forest track to Grain Valley, and one of the packhorses was lame. Moreover, since the smith was coming, Telim must give labour time to Grain Valley in the preparation of charcoal. With the young men still on the spur with the flock, Tami must, if possible, be used. Nemat waited for him to reappear and then, after a careful look over his body, which still showed no signs of disease, greeted him warily and smiled and touched the green stone at his throat, saying 'Good. Tami good.' Tami looked happy but did not speak.

Nemat took his arm and led him to the huts where the baskets of

woven tunics were being packed. He made a show of trying to lift
them and then smiled and pointed at Tami. Tami touched his green
stone, and crouched and lifted the heavy baskets across his arms.
'Good,' Nemat said, and touched the carrying straps that had been
made for the packhorse. He showed Tami how to brace them over
his shoulders. Tami was pleased and would have set off walking at
once, but Nemat caught his arm and pointed at the ground. After
some time, puzzled, Tami put his load down.

From then the plan was straightforward. A day was agreed and
Nemat and two other men, with the packhorse, waited for Tami.
When he came Nemat helped him to take up the load. The packhorse was already loaded, and Nemat himself was carrying the fine
cloak for the smith, while the other men carried the tools for repair
and exchange. They set off, with Tami walking among them, and
entered the track through the forest.

It was a hard day's walk, with the loads. At their rests, by brooks,
Tami remained standing with his burden. When they moved again
he walked easily, looking among the trees and watching every
movement of the birds and animals. At the edge of the clearing of
the first Grain Valley settlement they stopped and called. Two
young men, with unslung bows, came out and looked them over.
They listened to Nemat's greetings, but their whole attention was
on Tami. They looked at each other nervously, and then spoke and
pointed. Nemat moved across and patted Tami's arm. Tami smiled.

They went into the heart of the big settlement, and were given
food. The people from all around came and stared at Tami, who had
now, with Nemat's encouragement, put down his load but still
stood, huge, among them. Many of the women smiled but the young
men were obviously nervous and still carried their bows. One, more
finely dressed than the others, kept his hand on a bronze dagger in
his belt.

Next morning, while the other men began the slow business of
trading their woollens for barley, Nemat took Tami to a clearing by
the river where the charcoal mound was to be built. The two
burners were already making their preparations. A low circle of
stones had been laid on the trampled earth, and outside it they were
making another circle of picket stakes, leaving a single entrance. A
hole had been dug in the centre of the circle and now Tami and
Nemat helped raise a smooth trunk upright in it. Earth and stones

were packed to hold it. Then the making of the pile was begun. At the edge of the forest there were cross-stacks of trimmed and barked poles, of varying thickness but each about the height of an ordinary man. They had been cut a year earlier, to season. The burners began on the nearest stack, which was of oak. Nemat led Tami across and showed him how to carry with the others. Tami would now do whatever Nemat suggested. When the first oak had been stacked, radially and cross-laid to the central pole, Tami turned to Nemat and spoke suddenly.

'Vincara resa,' he said, smiling.

Nemat shook his head. Tami frowned and then nodded vigorously.

'Vincara resa,' he repeated, lifting his hands to cover his face.

Nemat turned away.

'Vincara dead,' Tami said, loudly.

The others laughed, and the work was begun again.

It was a slow business, stacking the big pile. Though the Grain Valley burners were glad of Tami for the carrying, they would not let him step onto the pile. They would take each load and spend a long time arranging the heavy pieces, in concentric circles. Sometimes Tami had to wait so long that he wandered away into the forest. Nemat did not follow him. There was plenty of time.

Slowly, over three days, the pile was completed. It was as high as Nemat's head, and five manlengths across. The next work was covering the whole pile with cut turves. A large pile was already cut, but before they had finished they had to cut more, and this Tami could not be encouraged to do, though he would carry them when cut. The two burners were now intent on the covering, going to every join between the turves and filling and packing it. At last they stood back and were satisfied.

On the following morning they told Nemat they wanted Tami on the pile, to lift out the centre trunk. At first the three of them stood and tried to lift it, but there was no room for them all to grip. Tami, seeing what had to be done, moved close to it, holding it tight against his chest, and heaved. It came out smoothly and the others smiled and said 'Good' to him.

'Vincara resa,' he said, nodding.

Then he and Nemat were motioned away, and the burners lit a small fire outside the fence of stakes. When it was burning fiercely they carried sticks of fire up the pile and lowered them into the central hole. Then they packed in other sticks and brushwood until the hole was filled. Finally they sealed the central hole with turves.

There was already some white smoke rising, but soon it was blue and spreading, coming from every gap and join in the turf-covered pile. The last stakes were put in, to complete the fence. The burners spoke words Nemat could not catch, and then withdrew to watch, squatting. Nemat and Tami squatted beside them.

On the next days there was no need to go to the pile. Nemat joined in the long trading of woollens for barley. It seemed to get worse every year, with familiar stories that the harvest had been poor and that Grain Valley already had all the tunics it needed. But while this was to be expected, there was no disguising the others' interest in the finest cloak. The young man with the elaborate bronze dagger, Mafurn, offered five bags of barley for it. But it could not be traded: the fine cloak was for the smith.

After six days Nemat went back to the charcoal pile. The burners were already cooling it with bags of water from the river. The white smoke was acrid. On the following day the pile began to be opened, and the debris was cleared from the charcoal. Everything was now ready for the smith, and they settled to wait.

He arrived late one evening from the east: a dark, short, heavily bearded man, with a tall fair boy and two laden packhorses. He was ceremoniously greeted and given food and drink and a cleared hut. He was tired and spoke little and went early to bed.

On the following morning everyone was assembled to watch the smith's mysteries. He inspected the charcoal, rubbing it between his fingers. Then, under his direction, the boy stacked and lit a fierce brushwood fire. The smith placed a sickle in the flames and watched the fire burn down to hot white ash. He then lifted the sickle, with a forked stick, and held it out at arm's length over the edge of the river. With a sudden shout he let the sickle fall. It hissed in the water. He cried in a high voice. His word was strange but it was like their own word for snake. They shouted their approval.

The smith turned and held up his arms. It was time for the people to go, out of sight of the mystery. Some had seen, from a distance, the next stage of his craft, when he laid and trampled a bed of sand and built an enclosed stone hearth. He then unloaded his sacred stone moulds from the packhorse. But before his next mystery he walked to the edge of the clearing, to receive tools for repair and to settle trading for new ones. When this was completed he stood until everyone, except his own boy, had gone right out of sight.

Nemat had waited his turn in the trading. The smith was obviously impressed by the fine cloak, but at first had offered only repair of their tools in exchange. Nemat refused, but in the end had to add three woven tunic lengths for the repairs and one new socketed bronze sickle. He was not too dissatisfied, but he noticed how carefully the smith took his white-and-yellow cloak and stroked it like an animal as he folded it over his arm.

It was known that the smith would stay for three days. There would then be a wayfeast, and Nemat was invited to stay. Mafurn gave him the invitation and asked that for the next trade Nemat would bring a fine cloak like the one which had been made for the smith.

Since the completion of the charcoal burning, Nemat had not seen Tami. When he eventually asked for him, he was told that the giant – as the Grain Valley people called him – had been seen wandering back towards the mountains. Nemat no longer felt concerned. All his attention was on the tools and the wayfeast.

It was already dusk, with big fires, when the wayfeast began. The men tried to get as near as they could to the smith, for though he ordinarily said little he might be expected to speak more freely, giving them news of his travels, when he had drunk and eaten. Nemat, sitting close to the fire, waited with great attention, his head thrust forward.

At last the smith began to speak. He gave at first only local news, which some of his listeners already knew: of a flood and the loss of cattle beyond Curve River; of the murder of an old man in Brigan; of a strangely deformed lamb born in an isolated settlement in the Bear Mountains, which some had taken as a sign of the return of the Choking Death, though this was not believed elsewhere. Then, speaking slowly and emphatically, he had a new theme.

'These are days of change, little brothers. In your places you are peaceful, and may it long remain so. I come among you and you bring me your broken sickles and your axes. I make you new sickles and axes. But already beyond the Great River they bring sickles and axes and ask for spears and swords. One of my brothers in fire has explained this to me. They do not fight among themselves, but there are strangers come among them. And these strangers are wolves who attack peaceful settlements and flocks. Against the fierceness of these strangers the tools of the harvest and of the forest are useless. At whatever cost men must now have weapons, to defend their flocks and their women and to kill these strange wolves.'

He paused. There was a long silence.

'You have seen these strangers yourself?' Mafurn asked.

'I have not seen them. That is not my country. But I believe the word of my brother in fire.'

'If they come we shall be ready for them,' Mafurn said, touching his dagger.

The smith smiled.

'You will not be ready for them. You have never seen such men.'

Nemat leaned forward.

'Do they come in great numbers?'

'They are not in great numbers. But they have fierce weapons. And there is more than that. It is said that they ride on horses at great speed, so that they are into a settlement before men can gather against them.'

There was a long silence.

'That cannot be true. It is a story from the outland,' Mafurn finally objected.

'It is said,' the smith repeated. 'But in all honour that is no outland, beyond the Great River. You live well, little brothers, in your places under the mountains. But beyond the Great River it is another world, rich in ways that you cannot imagine.'

'What richness could that be?' Nemat asked.

The smith paused before replying. He was staring into the fire.

'I am a smith of your own country,' he said at last. 'I have seen nothing of this richness with my own eyes. But east and north my brothers have told me, and I cannot doubt them. There is a making of gold rings and of fine gold armlets and collars. Certain high men and women wear and display them. They are men and women like our own, but they do not work and wear only fine clothes and gold. One of my brothers, it is said, has made a cape of gold, and it is worn by a woman who is kept pale and out of the sun. It is even said . . .'

Here the smith dropped his voice and looked anxiously around.

'It is even said,' he began, but again broke off. The crowded men waited.

'My mystery is strange to you, little brothers. It is so and must always be so. I carry the mystery of sickles and axes, and I make them well with my helpers of water and fire. In my eyes I can just see the making of swords and of spears. But a brother from the north told me something so strange that if he had not been a brother I would not have believed him. On an island far to the north a brother in fire has learned to beat metal as you would beat a hide: to beat it thin and then to shape it, as you would shape leather to a bag. It is hard to believe, but it is said that on that island there has been made what is said to be a cauldron: an object of great mystery: a beaten metal bowl that is hammered to great size so that an infant might be hidden in it.'

Nobody spoke. The surprise that had come over them when the smith had told of the fierce strangers and of the riding of horses still held their minds. But what they now noticed was the smith's own awe as he spoke of the strange cauldron on the far northern island. They did not know how to ask questions about it, but the sense of a strange and stronger world beyond them was coming through all his words and they were silent and anxious. It was at last the smith himself who broke this mood. He called for more drink and was soon laughing and joking again. Indeed some in the crowd, seeing him so relaxed, supposed that what he had been telling them had been only a tale for the fire.

Nemat was not among these. On the morning after the feast he walked back with one companion, carrying the tools. Along the forest track he thought only of the strangers who were living like wolves. Yet he could not see, if the smith's story were true, what Telim could do about it. There was nothing to spare from their own regular work. If the wolf men came Telim would simply be destroyed.

When he got back, tired, to the settlement, men and women came running with quite different news. He had to make them slow down and speak quietly before he could gather what had happened, though it was obvious from the beginning that it was about Tami.

Tami had come back alone from Grain Valley. He had been seen though he had not come into the settlement. Then on the morning after his return there was a big fire up the riverbank, by his mother Calina's hut. Hurrying to see what was happening, they had found a wood stack burning fiercely, and on top of it, already beginning to burn, the dead body of Calina. Tami had said nothing, but had gestured to keep them away. They were outraged that the burning was being done without ceremony. None of them had even known that Calina had died. The wood was stacked under her body like a fire for charcoal. Tami had walked continually around it, repairing the fire. It had taken a very long time to burn.

They had stayed, watching at the distance that Tami enforced. The fire burned into the night, and they went back to their huts. Next morning the men tried again to get near the burned body, but Tami drew his long bow and kept them away. It was now another day and the ashes of Calina still lay on the pile.

Nemat listened and then rested. He slowly got back his strength, but there was a heavy weight in his mind: the story of the danger from the men like wolves, and with it this new story of Tami. He waited until evening, and then walked alone by the river, head bowed. At last he walked up the bank until he came to Calina's hut. He saw immediately what he had not been told, that most of the wood of Calina's hut had gone into the fire. Also the fence around the pigs had been trampled, and the pigs had gone.

He did not at first see Tami, but a fish jumped in the river and beyond it he caught sight of him, sitting at the bank with his feet in the water. Nemat approached him cautiously.

'Tami,' he called softly.

Tami jumped up. His face and arms were blackened with smoke.

'Tami,' Nemat said again.

Tami looked hard into his face. Then he went beyond the hut to a thick stand of hazel. He squatted and then got up, carrying an old black leather bag. He walked across to Nemat, holding the bag in front of him.

'Calina,' Tami said. 'Calina resa.'

Nemat took the bag, reverently, and pulled back the cord. On the grey ash there were a few small charred bones.

'Calina,' Nemat said, and closed the bag.

He put his hand on Tami's arm and it was at once gripped fiercely, by the fingers. Nemat waited and then turned to walk back to the settlement. Tami followed him quietly, still holding the tight grip on his hand.

Tami and the Devils

◆

Tami was sitting astride the narrow bridge which led to the track running east. He had helped Nemat make the bridge, many years before: he could not remember how many. They had felled a young oak near the bank, so that it crossed the river some distance up from the ford. Nemat had worked to flatten and smooth the top, so that it could be walked over in winter when the river was high. They could go out to find cattle which had strayed into the forest, or go hunting or gathering acorns for the pigs. Tami spent many of his days astride the bridge, looking up through the trees at the sky or down at the moving lights on the water and the fish in the deep pool.

All morning the rooks had been noisy, repairing their nests and fighting over sticks which some had flown out to find. Tami smiled at them as if they were children playing. He liked the noise and the movement and sometimes, swinging his legs above the water, he would cup his hand and echo their cries.

Tami still lived very much to himself, though since his mother died he had been given a rough hut in the settlement, close behind Nemat's and next to the packhorses, which he liked to hear and sometimes go over and touch in the nights. Nemat, it was said, had lived more than fifty winters. He now did very little work in the settlement, though his advice was regularly sought. There was still good living in Telim, with the sheep flock larger in numbers and now five cows. Tami helped to feed the pigs, but when the young men took the flock to the mountain for the summer he stayed in the settlement with the women and children and the older men.

There was a new fight among the rooks. Tami shaded his eyes and looked up at them. It was then strange because they all went suddenly silent, letting in the spring singing of the smaller birds.

Then these too went silent. Tami stared around. Back in the clearing the men had gathered around the ewes that were lambing. Women were moving around the huts, and the thin blue smoke of fires was rising almost straight into the air. Tami looked at the scarp of the mountain beyond them. There was some early green among the faded brown of the fallen bracken, and a faint pinkish colour on the big spreads of whinberry.

He swung his legs, looking down at the water. The silence disturbed him and he wanted to call again to the birds. At first afraid to move, he at last forced himself to turn and straddle back towards the near bank. But as he turned he saw movements downriver at the ford. Stepping into the brown water was a small white pony, with a long mane and tail the colour of charcoal. Sitting astride the pony was a man with long fair hair, wearing a red cloak pinned at his neck. The pony stepped quietly through the shallow water, along the line of flat stones. Another pony, this time brown, with another fair-haired man also wearing a red cloak, followed him in. Tami stared at the strangers. The men with the first ponies stopped in the shadow of the trees on the near bank. One of them turned and waved and slowly, stepping delicately through the water, five more ponies, each with a rider wearing a dark red cloak, followed through and joined them.

Tami shook his head. Everything went quiet again. Even the rooks were silent. Bending low to the oak he eased himself back to the near bank and into the shelter of a big bole of alder. He lay watching the ponies and their riders. They were very strange to him. Although their scalp hair was long there was no hair on their faces, which were pink and smooth, with fat cheeks. The cloaks, he now saw, reached only to their thighs, and were pinned with bright metal at their throats. Under the cloaks they were not wearing tunics but leather divided at the crotch and wrapped around each leg to just below the knee. They held thongs which were looped around the necks of the ponies. Three of them had coils of hide rope slung across their shoulders. Then, as Tami watched, each of the men drew a very long knife, the shape of a long willow leaf, almost the length of an arm and with a cross-handle. Tami saw each man raise the long knife and then suddenly the ponies were moving and were spreading out across the clearing in a broad line. Still the pace was only of walking. Nobody in the settlement, where they were busy with the lambing and with preparing food, had yet seen the riders coming.

Then there was a sudden shout from the men around the ewes. As it came there was a long high scream from the men on the ponies, and suddenly they were galloping forward, holding their bronze swords above their shoulders. Tami stood to watch them more closely. Four of the men rode straight at the flock. Three others turned aside and made for the cattle which were grazing along the riverbank. As the four got in among the flock they were slashing down at the men of Telim, and there were loud cries and shouts. Tami stood, wondering, and then ran towards them. Above the cries at the flock there was a very loud noise in his head.

Many of the ewes had scattered. The new lambs were moving around, bewildered. Several of the Telim men were lying on the grass, bleeding from deep wounds on their heads and shoulders. Others, who were running, were being chased by the men on the ponies, who rode close and slashed down at them. Two of the strangers got off their ponies. Tami saw them kill two ewes and a lamb. One of them got back on his pony with a ewe slung in front of him. Across the clearing the children and most of the women had disappeared, but two girls were running towards their own men, one with an axe and one carrying two bows. Tami saw the girl with the axe, Cali, struck on the arm and falling. He stood, staring around. Down by the river the other strangers had roped the cattle, with the coils they had been carrying, and were driving them back towards the ford. There was a shout from one of the strangers. The killed ewe and lamb were picked up. They began turning to ride back to the river.

Tami had not yet seen Nemat. If he had seen him he would have known what to do. But then one of the strangers – the first man Tami had seen, on the white pony – rode closer to the huts and Nemat came out. His hair was white and he was limping. He had been sleeping in his hut and was rubbing his eyes. The stranger shouted down at him. Lifting his arm, Nemat threw himself at the stranger's leg, trying to pull him off the pony. The stranger lifted his sword and brought its edge down, hard, on Nemat's skull. He fell without a sound.

Tami again heard the loud noise in his head. Then he was running towards the stranger, who had turned away. Throwing himself at the stranger's back, and pulling at the thong, Tami brought pony and rider hard to the ground. The pony kicked and struggled. The stranger reached for his sword. Tami shouted and lifted him up and off his feet, digging his joined hands into the small of the back. There was a break and the stranger went limp. The pale grey eyes stared up from the smooth pink face. Tami dropped him and went to Nemat, who lay lifeless. He put his head on Nemat's chest and sobbed like a child.

The other strangers were already back across the river, driving the cattle and carrying the sheep they had killed. The women were running now from the huts. They bent anxiously over the fallen men and the girl. Three of the men, apart from Nemat, had been killed. Seven others and the girl were bleeding from deep wounds. The women gathered round, tending them. Anail, the tall son of the dead brother of Nemat, walked to look at Nemat's body. He put his hand, gently, on Tami's shoulder. Tami looked up, his broad face distorted with crying. Anail examined Nemat and then shouted back.

'We'll get after them at once. They can't go fast, with the cattle.'

The men ran to the huts for their bows. Tami stayed, bent over Nemat. As the men came back past him, Anail again touched his shoulder.

'Tami, come,' he said quietly.

Tami got slowly up.

'Bring the sword,' Anail said.

Tami stared. The dead stranger lay sprawled on the grass, with his sword just beyond his clenched hand. The pony had moved away and was grazing near the packhorses. Anail swore and picked up the sword and gave it to Tami. Tami lifted it and slashed.

'Good Tami,' Anail said.

They moved to a slow run and went through the river at the ford. The forest track ran east for some distance until the land rose steeply and it veered away to the south.

Anail stopped and examined the earth. The killers had not followed the track but had moved uphill through the forest. There were many marks of their passage in the broken undergrowth and the wet mossy ground. Anail hesitated. Though they had sometimes hunted in this part of the forest they did not know it well. It was the track to the south, to their neighbours of Crucio above Salmon

River, that they regularly followed. He had been certain this was the
way the killers would go.

There was a long argument. Little was known, except in rumour,
of the land to the east. It was an area to keep clear of, in the settled
suspicion of strangers. Some of the men seemed unwilling to break
into it, the strange forest beyond the boundaries of their settlement.
But Anail's anger decided them. If the killers had gone through the
forest, he argued, they would be slowed down, even riding their
ponies. If they followed their tracks, they would be bound to come
up on them, and then with bows in the forest they would have an
advantage against the swords.

They made their way up through the trees. It was slow going, but
it was easy to follow the trail. Tami stayed close to Anail, holding
the sword across his chest. When the others were breathing hard,
after the long climb, he was still easy and fresh.

The trail turned along a ridge and then struck down through a
narrow valley and up the other side, still dense with trees. As the
pursuit tired them, the full shock of the raid began to come through.

'What people can they be?' one man, Metan, asked hopelessly.

Another said, 'Perhaps they are not really men.'

'They are strangers,' Anail said, trying to keep control, 'the wolf
strangers we were told of by Nemat.'

They came out on higher, flatter ground. There were less oaks and
more thorn and rowan. The trail lay directly across it, to the east of
north. They lost it for a while, in a drier area, but Tami, walking
ahead, found it again and they hurried to catch him up. They came
out above a steep valley, with a clearing by the river. They went
cautiously down towards it, their bows ready. Tami walked in
front, holding the bronze sword. They were almost in the clearing
when there was a shout ahead of them. A line of men rose from the
riverbank, their bows drawn on them. Anail and the others stopped
but Tami went on walking towards them. Anail saw the danger and
shouted.

'We are in peace. We are of Telim.'

Tami stopped and looked round when Anail shouted. Three of
the new men kept their bows trained on him. Anail hurried forward.
There were huts in the clearing which were much like their own, and
sheep were fenced beyond them.

'What is he with the sword?' an old man called.

'He is of us. We were attacked. He killed one of the red cloaks and now has his sword.'

The old man came forward. He looked up at Tami.

'He is a giant.'

'He is of us.'

The old man walked on and looked closely at Anail.

'You are of where?'

'Of Telim.'

Anail turned and pointed.

'Of under the mountain,' he added, as the old man hesitated.

'Of the Black Mountain?'

'Of under the Black Mountains.'

'Yet you speak our language. The Black Mountain is of strangers.'

'Deep in the mountains there are strangers, the Old Ones. But we are of winter and summer, and of kin with Alaron and Crucio.'

The old man smiled. He signalled back to his own people. Several of them came forward, though the three with their bows drawn on Tami stayed where they were. Tami bent and squatted, resting the sword on the grass.

'You were attacked by devils in red cloaks?' the old man asked Anail.

'Devils I do not know. Is it the name of the strangers?'

'It is not their name. I do not know their name. But they have twice attacked us. All our cattle have gone and they have killed men and sheep.'

'Today they attacked us. They have taken our cattle. We have followed their trail. It has led us to you.'

The old man stepped back. He looked round at his own people.

'They did not come this way,' he said fearfully.

'We followed their trail here.'

'But there is nothing. You can see.'

'To the ridge there were signs,' Anail said.

'To the ridge, yes. Then you saw our clearing and came down to us.'

'It may be so,' Anail said.

He was looking around. There was no sign of ponies or of cattle.

'Why did you follow them?' the old man asked.

'To get back our cattle.'

'You cannot get them back. You cannot fight against devils.'

'They are men, aren't they? Men who have turned to killing.'

'You say that they are men. But there is no hair on their faces. They sit on horses and ride them. They know no law but just steal and kill.'

Anail pointed at Tami.

'He killed a devil,' he said.

Tami saw that he was being looked at. He got up. The bowmen stiffened but the old man signalled and they relaxed.

'I can tell you the way they went,' the old man said, 'but you will not find them.'

'Tell me.'

'On the ridge, to which you followed them, they turn and ride east. At some distance there is a track to a ford and they cross this. They climb again to high bare land, and then again ride east. To that point we followed them, after their second attack. But we could then see a great distance, and they were not in sight. We came back, sorrowing.'

Anail thanked the old man, and asked if they might drink at the river. The old man led them down.

Anail looked closely at the flow of water.

'It is difficult to be sure,' he said, slowly, 'but I think this is our own river, which rises in the mountain beyond Alaron and flows beside our settlement. It then turns to the north, through the darkest forest.'

'It may indeed be so,' the old man replied.

'It is very strange,' Anail said. 'We live by the same river, we build the same huts, we herd the same sheep. Yet we have not touched each other.'

'It is a fear of strangers,' the old man replied.

'Yet we have no reason to fear ourselves. The strangers we fear are of another kind.'

'It may be so, my son.'

Anail spread his arms.

'We must learn to touch each other. When there are evil strangers we must pass warning to each other. We will bring gifts and speak and arrange this.'

'We will welcome you from Telim,' the old man replied. 'And we in turn have our four kin settlements, along the river to the east. It is said that our river, beyond these settlements, flows south to a great water that is called the seariver.'

'We will begin to learn from each other,' Anail said, and took the old man's hand.

Tami was standing, watching them. When he saw their hands join he laughed. He put down the sword and walked into the middle of the river. He bent and scooped and drank, then splashed water all over his shoulders and arms. The men watching him laughed and he got very excited and splashed himself again. Then he cupped his big hands and brought water in them to Anail.

'Good,' he said. 'Telim.'

Anail sucked at the water.

'Your giant really killed a devil?' the old man asked.

'He has great strength though he is simple,' Anail replied.

'To kill a devil is not simple.'

'He pulled down both devil and pony. He crushed the devil in his arms.'

The other men, listening, gazed at Tami. He smiled and picked up the sword. They at once moved their bows.

'Yet though there is a giant among us,' Anail said, 'you will not join us to follow the devils?'

The old man looked around, and then shook his head.

'We do not believe you can find them. We are not afraid. If they come again we shall be ready. But they ride like the wind and go into the clouds. We have seen this.'

'That's right,' Metan said. 'We shall never find them. We should go back to our women.'

Anail hesitated, looking at Tami with the sword.

'I will go and Tami with me, for the cattle,' he said. The others talked among themselves.

'We will come,' they said at last.

They quickly took leave of the men of the settlement, which was called Carfan. They climbed back up the track to the ridge and soon again found the trail running east. It was then as the old man had said: along the ridge to a track to a ford, then across the river and up through thinning trees to bare high land. They turned east along this, but almost at once Tami stopped, pointing. Moving higher, the others saw a group of four or five ponies grazing in the distance.

'We have found them.'

'It may be,' Anail said. 'But I have heard that at this season a herd of ponies moves from the east. They pass above Grain Valley to the high ground west of Telim and so into the mountains for their summer grazing.'

'That is not a herd. That is five.'

As they walked on, keeping just below the highest ground, they saw more and more ponies, spread out grazing across the open grassland. They now lost all marks of the trail, but still walked east. The pony herd, as they approached it, moved away and formed up, with the mares and foals in the rear and the stallions nearest to the men, pointing at them.

'They have been disturbed,' Anail said.

'Yes. When the devils passed.'

They altered their direction to pass south of the herd, but Tami kept straight on. One of the stallions, yellow with a black mane and tail, moved towards him and pawed the ground. They heard Tami's voice, high-pitched, as he passed close to the stallion. The stallion watched but did not move.

Beyond the herd there was a brook running down to the river, with rushes thick along its banks. They spread out along the brook, looking for signs of a crossing, and these were soon found: not only the hoofs of ponies but of cattle. Their spirits rose and they pushed on. But now the open grassland seemed endless. The river, heavily wooded, was still below them, and twice they saw clearings and the fires of settlements. Clouds were now banking from the west and the air was colder.

They reached a high point and stopped and looked back west. They were amazed by the sight. The long black ridges of their mountains were spread out under the clouds, in shapes they had never before seen. They made out the first ridge above Telim, by the Old Boat Stones, but it was low and small compared with the ridges rising beyond it, and in the distance there was much higher land, with a strange round hump at its centre. Far to the south, in a succession of peaks and ridges beyond the peak of Broken Mountain, there was an unknown country. They could see how they lived at an edge of it. Looking more closely they followed their own river back to where it turned from north to east. They stared at each other. It was a new power in the eyes to see these wide shapes of the land.

Yet now the daylight was going. The sun was soon covered by the high bank of clouds, and there were long rays down from it, through some invisible gap. A golden light touched one of the far dark ridges.

'We shall not find them,' Metan said, 'before night.'

'But they too will stop for the night. We will start early and come up on them.'

They walked on, eastward, but turned often to look back at the spread of the mountains, now deep black before sunset. They watched for a night place, and settled at a narrow brook, moving down to the edge of the forest. They did not make a fire but slept close together. Tami slept beyond them, with his arm stretched over the sword.

Before it was fully light they were up again and moving quickly, to get the cold from their bones. They were hard now with effort, wanting their cattle. The grassland still stretched ahead with patches of bracken and heather and gorse. There was then a deep cross valley, and the river was turning away south. They stopped, baffled. There were no signs of the trail.

Then, beyond the shoulder of a hill on the far side of the valley, they saw smoke rising. They pushed down through the under-growth and into the trees. They crossed a stream and were climbing again, to the shoulder of the hill, where they stopped and looked out. Between the hill and a further rise of ground was a stretch of mossy bog. Above it, among trees, the thin trail of smoke was rising.

They went cautiously down to the edge of the bog. They walked north along it, looking for tracks, and at last, by an outcrop of stone, found what they had been following from Telim: the mixed hoofmarks of ponies and cattle. They moved along this trail, looking nervously up to the smoke. Anail led, with Tami close beside him.

Moving very quietly now, Anail worked his way up a rough path until he could see the base of the smoke. There was a wide earth terrace, above banks which fell away steeply on three sides. The low fire was burning at the mouth of a cave, which seemed to have two entrances in the grey rock. Climbing plants trailed above them. No man or animal was in sight, though there was dung in several places on the flat, trampled ground.

Anail signalled to the others. They moved quietly and spread in a line, their bows ready. They advanced on the cave. Tami stayed close to Anail.

There was then a gasp from one of the men. Beyond the fire, under a rock at the larger entrance to the cave, was a roughly-butchered sheep. It had been hacked to pieces. Much of the meat was pulled about and the blood was staining the dusty ground. Two legbones were charred in the fire. There was wool scattered everywhere, as if a wolf had attacked it.

Beyond the remains of the sheep a rough hide curtain covered the main entrance to the cave. Anail stood, listening. Tami looked into his face. Then Tami pushed aside the curtain and went into the darkness beyond it. There were no sounds. Tami came back and pulled the curtain to the ground. He went into the cave again. Anail waited and then followed him.

Beyond the narrow entrance the cave forked. Anail stared in the dim light. On the fork to the left there was a shelf of rock. Tami climbed on to it and pointed to a lower cave level that lay beyond. Anail went back to the fire. He pushed a half-burned pine branch into the hot white ash and stirred it to flame. Carrying it as a torch, he returned to Tami. The inner cave was dry and compact, with a smooth floor. There were the marks of boots in its light dust. Anail went back and explored the right fork. It broadened into an irregular shape, with a staining of damp and moss on its sides. There were again bootmarks in the light dust. Tami, following him, whistled suddenly. Anail turned and saw him squat in the dust, his big fingers gently brushing it aside. Under his hand was a bronze pin. It was the kind the strangers used to fasten their short red cloaks. Tami laid it on his palm and blew the dust from it. At one end it was flattened to a disc, with markings like the rays of the sun. Tami smiled and stuck the pin in the neck of his tunic, under the knotted thong and greenstone which he had brought from the inner mountains.

'Good. Tami good,' he said and laughed.

Anail went back outside the cave. The morning sun glared through the trees. He walked past the dying fire and the slaughtered sheep to the edge of the terrace. Below him, suddenly, was a precipitous drop, as deep as fifty men, and at its base a broad shining river. It was not the light brown water of the river of Alaron and Telim, but grey and glittering under the sun. It ran south in a line as

straight as if it had been drawn by a man. Its steep banks were
covered with trees: oak and ash and cherry, with different fresh
greens in their leaves. Anail held his breath. He could feel his heart
beating faster. The strange river seemed to point and open to a
shining new world.

'They've gone then,' Metan said, coming close behind him.

'Into a world beyond us,' Anail said.

'We can look again for their tracks.'

'It is late,' Anail said. 'Too late. Our cattle have gone.'

They walked back to the hearth. The others were still discussing
the crude butchering of the sheep. What men could these strangers
be, first to steal and then to waste? This was the savagery of animals,
to kill and to tear. All that had been reared and tended by others
they had slashed and scattered. Meat for a family now lay torn in the
dirt. Skin and stomach-bag and wool were ripped and discarded. To
be hungry was to rear or to hunt, but the stealing and slashing of
these smooth-faced savages, unnaturally striding their ponies, was
beyond men: beyond the ways and laws of men.

They stooped over the carcase with their knives and began cutting
and gathering the meat and fleece that could be saved. The staring
head, with the lips drawn back over the teeth, was lifted clear and
placed by a stone. Tami had come from the cave and was standing
watching them work. When they picked up to leave he began
following the next trail. There was fresh pony and cattle dung along
a path running north. Tami squatted and pointed to it when the
others did not follow him. Anail had to go and take his arm to lead
him slowly back the way they had come.

On the long sad journey home they began discussing the attack in
practical ways. It was hard to know what could be done against
such sudden savagery. Men could not be spared from the work of
the settlement to stand ready and armed through all the moons of
waiting. Yet still something might be done. They could talk to their
new neighbours, in Carfan and the other settlements along the river.
In every settlement some older man or boy could look out, and they
could find ways of passing warnings. It was when they were walking
again on the flat upland, looking west at their mountains, now like
blue smoke under the sun, that one idea came. On the upland
pasture of each settlement a fire could be made ready, and the
watcher could light it if the devils came again. Smoke by day or

flame by night would carry a warning across the land, faster than even the devils could move. The flock could then be gathered and fenced. Men could stand ready in cover with their bows.

As their minds came to this plan other ideas followed quickly. They could weave small hurdles to hold between their bodies and the slashing swords. When the smith next came, they could put more of their weaving to exchange for a copy of the bronze sword which Tami was carrying. They could lengthen their hunting spears, to thrust up at the riders. To get better spearheads they could hold back some of the weaving that they exchanged for barley and offer that also to the smith. It would be a hard shift of custom, but if so much of what they had reared and tended could be slashed and ripped away from them, there would in any case be shortage and hunger.

Anail joined in the talk. He could see that speaking of how to fight back was easing the sorrow of their loss. Yet his mind was heavy as he thought of it. He looked often at Tami, walking as always without words, without any obvious intention, but now with the killing sword in his hand. He would learn to carry a sword as he had learned to carry wood, not because he knew why but because a man he trusted had asked him to. Already Anail realised the others were seeing Tami differently: as the strong man, the giant who had killed a devil and now carried his sword. But all Anail could see was a shift to waste: a simple strength that would now turn beyond the proper uses of men.

'What we could do then . . .' Metan was saying, excitedly.

Anail listened as he walked, watching Tami striding in front. Metan's eager voice continued.

'For if the devils had come when we had taken the flock to summer pasture, so that instead of bursting from the forest they had to climb the steep scarp . . .'

'The women and children would still be open to their swords,' Anail said, sadly.

There was a silence again. They walked steadily, watching for the ford. Ahead of them, as they moved, the colour of the mountains was changing. The blue of smoke had gone, and there were the first browns and greens of their familiar place.

Telim and the Lord Epodorix

◆

Cargen narrowed his eyes against the driving rain. From his watchstone on Bentelim he had seen the storm hurrying from the south, along the wooded valley of Salmon River and over the long back of Broken Mountain, which was now covered with low cloud. He had pulled on his leather tunic and taken shelter at the stone against the wind that ran ahead of the rain. But he must still keep his watch. Two mornings before, there had been the firesign from Alcarfan, and Satelim had made ready to move. But that had come to nothing. The strangers must have ridden elsewhere. Yet they would still be in the district, and he must watch for every sign.

Shielding his face with his arm, he looked down into Satelim. The children had run into the huts, from the rain, but some of the women were still at their fires. A dog was hurrying, nose down, just beyond the hurdle fence of the enclosure, towards the ford and the bridge. The pack-ponies stood patiently in the rain, their hind-quarters turned against it. The sheep, strung out on the slope between Satelim and the spur, had also turned from the rain but were still busily grazing, on short grass among the patches of bracken.

It was a familiar sight, without disturbance. But through the last three years there had been increasing danger. The regular watches had been resumed after many years of peace. Cargen looked back up the spur at the cattle. They also were turned from the driving rain, along the stretch of good grass between the palisade of Bentelim and the big pool and the source.

In this last period of danger, the palisade had been entirely rebuilt, with new ashpoles and birch cut from beyond Satelim and carried up the steep zig-zag track that reached the ridge at the Boat.

The old fence had been good enough for rounding up the cattle, but against the strangers it had to be stronger. It was still not much of a defence. Bentelim relied more on its position, with the steep scarp on three sides and only the long spur open to the west. No danger had ever come from that direction, where there were only the old sheep people, driven down now from the wet tops and hunting and herding along the steep slopes of the cross valleys. They were quiet, secretive neighbours, relying on hiding in their valleys to save them from any enemies.

The rain was easing a little. Cargen pushed his hand back over his long wet hair, which was dripping into his face and neck. His palm was still wet as he grasped the signal horn at his belt. He dried its mouthpiece on his sleeve. The cloud was clearing now from Broken Mountain, and there was a patch of sunlight, far out in the distance, beyond the heavy woods of Salmon River. In the clearer air he looked south to Cornio. Its spur was at the same height as Bentelim, or perhaps Cornio was a little higher; it was often argued about. A thin drift to white smoke was hanging there and was now caught by the wind.

Cargen stared at the smoke. It was so thin that it was almost certainly an ordinary fire. But as he watched it billowed out into a grey cloud, and rose more thickly from its base. There was some blue now in the smoke. The fire had been suddenly intensified. Cargen stared but was taking no chances. He raised his signal horn and blew the four-note alarm. There were immediate shouts from the men who had been sheltering under the palisade against the rain. Several ran at once along the spur to fetch in the cattle. Others ran down towards Satelim to help to bring up the sheep. Their yellow dogs ran barking ahead of them.

He blew the alarm again. There was still little sign of movement around the huts in Satelim, although one woman had stood from her fire and was looking up towards him. Then she saw the men and dogs running, and he heard her shout, in a high carrying voice. At once the other women and the children came running from the huts, and the older men were already collecting the ponies. The dogs had begun to drive the sheep up the scarp, though they had to keep running at them and the sheep kept turning aside. A long procession of women and children began moving towards the track, and the older men were following with the ponies. Some of the younger men went downhill past them, with their bows, to cover the river crossing.

The fire at Cornio was now sending up low, heavy smoke which the wind was scattering. Yet it must, surely, be the firesign. Cargen remembered when he had sounded the alarm on what he had thought was a firesign from Alcarfan, and nothing had happened; they had learned later that the fire was accidental. Most people had blamed him, for disturbing them for nothing, but Namat had reassured him. The disturbance of moving up was very little, when compared with being caught by a raid.

Yet he could wish, even now, that the alarm was false, or that the strangers, whoever they were, would ride in some other direction. In the one bad raid he had known, two summers back, he had been wounded by a sword between his shoulder and neck, while he was one of the bowmen guarding the ford. At that he had been lucky, for two others had been killed, caught in a manoeuvre which they had not expected. The first group of the raiders had ridden fast across them, following the line of the riverbank and drawing their fire. The raiders were bent forward, low, along the backs of their ponies, pushing down and partly sheltered by them. Then, from another direction, more raiders had ridden in, with spears and swords, catching the bowmen from the side. Still, the rest of the family and the animals had been saved. The surviving bowmen had fallen back, and from the shelter of boulders had shot the first riders who were trying to make their way up the steep narrow track. The rest halted. They found pigs in Satelim, and killed what they wanted. Then they set fire to all the huts and rode away.

There was anxious shouting now as the women and children reached the palisade. There was crowding everywhere, as people and cattle and sheep were pushed in. The older men were still only halfway up, with the ponies and the dogs. The line of bowmen was spread out, guarding the ford. Namat came close behind Cargen, looking out at the smoke from Cornio.

'It is a poor firesign, Cargen.'

'Was I wrong then to sound the alarm?'

'No. You were right to sound it.'

Cargen smiled. He looked away from the settlement, over the fall of ground to the south, which was the least steep of the sides of the spur. The cattle often grazed down it, towards the thinned wood, where when he was a boy there had been a raging summer fire. There were dense woods in the cross valley beyond it, and a few hunting trails.

Cargen was not sure why he was suddenly looking so intently. It had never been a side from which danger had come. But something, it seemed, had caught his attention, and now, as he watched, he began to make it out. Riding slowly out into the thinned wood, where there was not much more than shrubby hazel and thorn, was a group of ten, twelve, fifteen horsemen, wearing yellow and brown cloaks and carrying spears upright at their shoulders. The sight was so unexpected that at first Cargen could not shout. Then he reached out to Namat's arm and pointed. He saw the sudden fear in Namat's eyes. The skin above the ragged grey beard went white.

The riders were still at some distance below them. Namat, recovering, ran back to gather the other men. Observing closely, Cargen saw that these horsemen were very different from the raiders of two years ago. To begin with, they were riding not ponies but larger, heavier horses. Then their manner of riding was different. There was more leatherwork, and there was shining metal around the horses' heads. The upright spears fitted with this slower, more controlled riding, but there were also swords at their belts. As they rode closer, still slowly and quietly, Cargen could see that their faces were hairless and that the hair of their scalps was gathered inside tight-fitting black caps. Their breeches were not the leather Cargen had seen on the last raiders. They were woven from brown wool, like the bands of their cloaks. Yet what was most striking was not these details of their appearance, but their whole manner of approach. They were quiet, peaceful and unhurried, like neighbours coming to trade.

Namat took the horn from Cargen and again sounded the alarm. He blew repeatedly, until the bowmen at the ford turned and looked back up at him. He stood on a mound and tried to wave them up, but they did not understand. Meanwhile, within the palisade, the other men had lined up, facing down towards the horsemen, with their bows and axes ready.

It would be a hard fight, Cargen thought. There was something unexpected and disturbing about this controlled, silent troop, with their raised spears. Then, as he watched, they halted, just beyond arrowshot. There was a call and all but two of them dismounted.

They stood beside their horses and then, together, laid down their spears. One of the men still mounted was at the front of the troop, the other back in its centre. Cargen found himself looking at this second man. He could see that unlike the others he was wearing a white cloak and a shining gold cap. He carried no spear although there was a sword at his belt. A twisted belt of gold pulled in his cloak at the waist.

The first man, still on his horse, reversed his spear and drove it down into the grass. Then he unpinned his cloak and let it fall to the ground. He took his sword from his belt and held it up, then slowly, leaning over, let it fall to the grass. He cupped his hand to his mouth and called. The words were indistinct. The men at the palisade waited, bows drawn. The call came again. They all listened intently.

'He is calling Peace,' Namat said. 'But as a stranger would call it.'

'It cannot be peace from a stranger,' Cargen said.

The call came again, and Namat nodded.

'He is from another people, but it is Peace for certain.'

Before the others could speak he stood and called back: 'Peace.'

There was a pause. The first man turned and called to the man in the white cloak. Then, in a quick movement, he dismounted. He spread his arms wide and began walking slowly up the slope, towards the palisade. The rain, which had been easing, thickened again. The bowmen, staring down, kept their arrows trained on him. He walked steadily forward.

At thirty paces from the palisade he stopped, his arms still spread. They could all see that he was carrying no weapon but now, to their surprise, he moved his arms and pulled his tunic over his head, letting it hang loosely in his hand. He was bare to the waist in front of them. They could see no hair on his chest or arms.

'I bring you greetings from the Lord Epodorix,' he called in a high voice.

It was their own language, though obviously spoken by a stranger. They understood it except the name.

'Who are you?' Namat shouted.

'I am Leiron. We are of the Lord Epodorix.'

Namat frowned.

'I will go to him,' he said suddenly.

Cargen tried to hold him back but he pushed through the palisade and walked slowly towards the stranger. The stranger smiled as he saw him approach.

'You have come in peace?' Namat asked, halting a few paces away.

'In peace, brother, as you see.'

'Yet you have come without warning, and carrying spears and swords.'

'We come armed, brother, because this is dangerous country. There are bands of wild raiders who attack settlements and travellers, and who kill without mercy. Against them, but only against them, we carry our spears and our swords.'

Namat stared into the stranger's face. The bare and hairless skin was of a dark, reddish colour. The eyes were dark brown. The hair above the ears, under the tight-fitting cap, was shining black and curled. The voice was deep and resonant, the manner of speaking polite. Namat heard the sense of the words, but still he could not trust them.

'Why do you come at all to our place?' he asked, staring into the stranger's eyes.

'We come in peace and with a gift,' Leiron answered, smoothly. 'The Lord Epodorix wishes peace.'

'Yet we have our peace,' Namat said.

'It is an uneasy peace. An uncertain peace. On any day, while you are working, a band of thieves may come and attack you, stealing your beasts and killing your people.'

'That is true,' Namat said. 'That is why we defend ourselves.'

He pointed back, proudly, to the line of bowmen along the palisade. Leiron, looking up at them, smiled.

'You are shepherds and herdsmen,' he said. 'You have no knowledge of battle. Against men whose whole life is fighting you are weak and defenceless.'

Namat stepped back angrily.

'Yes, we are shepherds and herdsmen. But we are also hunters, and we know how to kill. Since the days of our ancestors we have been renowned for fighting through all this land you see around us.'

Leiron did not answer. He stared, uncertainly, at this proud old man. The rain was wet and cold on his shoulders, and he seemed to be tiring of the exchange. He glanced back at his troop, standing beside their horses.

'From father to son, through the time of twenty fathers,' Namat said proudly, 'the men of Telim have been known for their fighting. It is known in all this land that when the raiding devils came it was a man of our blood, the giant Tamal, who could alone stand against them. He broke their backs with his great arms. He cut them to pieces with his long sword. He showed the men of Telim how to fight against devils and how to defeat them.'

The stranger was interested again.

'A giant?'

'The giant Tamal.'

'Through the time of twenty fathers?'

'It is so. It is well remembered.'

'It is a very long time.'

'It is indeed a long time.'

'Yet the savage raiders still come. Indeed we heard from your neighbours that just two years ago they came and killed your men and your beasts.'

'Two of our men were killed. And the devils slaughtered our pigs. But they were driven off. They will not dare to come again.'

Leiron smiled.

'Yet still you have made this . . . this . . .' He pointed up at the palisade.

'It is our stronghold, it is Bentelim,' Namat said, proudly. 'At the alarm we gather within it, and no stranger can harm us.'

Leiron shook his head. He pulled his tunic back over his shoulders.

'It would be the time of cutting wool from a sheep,' he said, contemptuously.

Namat stared at him.

'In the time of cutting wool from a sheep,' Leiron said, 'men who understand battle would break your stronghold and trample it.'

Namat lifted his arm.

'You dare to threaten us,' he shouted, angrily.

'It is no threat,' Leiron said, 'it is the simple truth. Do you not see that ridge running westward, where your cattle were grazing? It is without defences, except your few stakes.'

Namat hesitated.

'It is not your fault,' Leiron said, quickly. 'You are shepherds and you are brave, but to fight is a craft, which takes long to learn. A fighter now is as a smith, a man with his mystery.'

Namat looked away.

'The Lord Epodorix knows this,' Leiron continued. 'He is angry that peaceful shepherds and herdsmen are attacked and killed and their animals stolen. He has vowed to end this, by restoring peace in the land.'

Namat frowned.

'Of what place is this man Lordepodorix you speak of?'

'He wishes to meet you and to offer you a gift,' Leiron said, smiling.

Namat hesitated.

'I must ask our people.'

'Better than that,' Leiron said. 'The Lord Epodorix will come to your people and will offer his gift.'

Namat looked round at the men on the palisade. He saw that Cargen especially had his long bow trained on the stranger.

'He comes in peace?' Namat asked.

'In peace.'

Namat walked back to the palisade. Behind him the man in the white cloak and the gold cap rode slowly forward, to where Leiron was waiting. One of the other horsemen was leading a bullock on a rope. Namat stood with the others and looked down. The bullock was very dark, almost black, with a white patch between its slightly out-turned horns. Although looking no more than a yearling, it was more heavily built than their own cattle. When they reached Leiron, they stopped.

'My friends,' the new stranger called loudly, 'put down your bows. I come in peace and with this gift.'

The voice of this stranger in the white cloak and gold cap was as deep as that of Leiron, but his words were not easy to understand. The men of Telim stared at him and at the bullock.

'Do not trust him,' Cargen said.

But the others were watching and waiting.

'I am the Lord Epodorix,' the stranger called.

'We are of Telim,' Namat called back.

Epodorix bent from horseback and took the rope of the bullock.

'This beast is now yours,' he called loudly.

'Do not take it,' Cargen said, anxiously.

'Do you want it?' Epodorix called.

There was a long silence. The men were staring at the fine bullock.

'I will go,' Namat said.

He again walked down from the palisade. He stood below the stranger on horseback. Epodorix gave him the end of the bullock's rope. Namat pulled and slowly led the bullock back to the palisade. His eyes were shining with excitement. Some of the men cheered.

While the bullock was being looked at, Epodorix rode up to the palisade. Leiron waited for the other horsemen to remount and ride up. They carried their spears reversed but looked carefully around. They spread out behind Leiron as he mounted and rode up to the palisade.

'The peace of Epodorix,' Leiron called.

The bows of Telim were set aside. All the men except Cargen crowded round the bullock.

'There are more to come,' Leiron explained to Namat. 'The Lord Epodorix will bring his fine heifers and they will graze with your own.'

'But the bullock is ours?'

'It is yours. It is for breeding. It will improve your herd. And when the Lord Epodorix brings his own heifers, every tenth calf will be your own.'

'Why should he do this?' Namat asked, looking across at Epodorix who, in his white cloak, was now riding slowly around the palisade.

'Your grass is good,' Leiron said. 'You will have more and finer cattle. And with the Lord Epodorix to help you, you need never again fear these raiders who attack you. He will protect you from them, for he has men trained to fight.'

Namat looked at the troop of horsemen, who were still mounted with raised spears.

'These are the men who fight?'

'None can stand against them,' Leiron said.

'Then should *we* not fear them?' Cargen asked, roughly.

Leiron looked across at him.

'There will be no fear. This is the new order. Do you see that older man, on the big grey? His name is Voratin. He has been a great fighter. But he is getting old now, and he wishes to settle among good people. If you will let him settle among you, he will teach your own young men how to fight, and he will show you how to build strong defences against the raiders. When he has seen your young men he will choose two or three of the bravest, and if they wish they may then come to the Lord Epodorix.'

Cargen turned away.

'They will be brave and strong, I am certain,' Leiron continued, raising his voice so that the others could hear. 'For it is known in the whole land that you are strong men in Telim. You are the seed of the great fighter, the giant Tamal.'

Cargen continued to walk away, but the others crowded round, hearing the great name of Tamal. It pleased and surprised them that his fame had reached the ears of this stranger.

Namat clapped his hands. The enclosure within the palisade was crowded. Epodorix, in his white cloak, was still riding and surveying it. With the danger passed, the cattle were driven out, along the good grass to the west. The sheep were released and the dogs drove them down the track towards Satelim. The women got together, and it was agreed that this night there would be a feast in Satelim, for Lordepodorix and his horsemen.

As the enclosure cleared, Epodorix turned his horse and rode through the palisade where it had been opened for the cattle. The rain had stopped and there was sunlight on Broken Mountain and on the wide valley of Salmon River to the south. Epodorix sat, turning his horse so that he could look in every direction. Namat and Leiron walked across to him.

'You have chosen a good place,' Epodorix said.

Namat did not understand until Leiron had repeated the words.

'Bentelim is indeed very strong,' he said, proudly. 'It cannot be taken.'

There was a fleeting smile on Leiron's lips.

'Under the orders of my deputy Voratin,' Epodorix said, 'it will now be made secure, to protect the herd.'

Namat caught only a few of these words, but did not wish to give offence.

'You have only a few and inferior cattle,' Epodorix continued. 'But your grass can support a good herd. And you will yourselves become richer, with one in ten of the better calves, with dung for your ploughing, and with your share of the cheese and the hides.'

'The meat,' Leiron added, 'the Lord Epodorix will take for his fighters.'

Namat was puzzled.

'The meat of his own herd,' Leiron said.

'I understand. Of course.'

Epodorix swung his big horse, making it rear. Namat, though he stepped back quickly, was fascinated by the arrangement of the bit and bridle, and by the fine bronzework rings which joined the leathers. He admired also, looking up at the tall rider, the intricate workmanship of the twisted gold belt around the cloak, and the softness of the decorated hide of the boots.

'What peoples lie west?' Epodorix asked, looking out along the spur.

Leiron had to repeat the question.

'There are good winter-and-summer people at Alaron and Abisso,' Namat hurried to explain. 'Their sheep graze to fine uplands.'

'They are your kin?'

'They are kin.'

'We shall have to go and see them. We may help them also. At what distance are they?'

The question had again to be repeated.

'Alaron is close,' Namat said, pointing. 'Abisso lies west at a winter manday.'

Epodorix looked to Leiron, who then spoke in strange words. Epodorix nodded.

'But within these mountains?' he continued. 'Are there no other people?'

'There are the old shepherds.'

'Within the higher mountains?'

'And in the cross valleys.'

'Yet the rainfall is too great for sheep on those heights. Is there not grazing for cattle on some of those ridges?'

The question had again to be repeated.

'We do not go to their places,' Namat said. 'They are another people, though they give us no trouble.'

'Of what descent are they?'

'We know them only as the Old Ones, or as the Stone People. But it is said that their name for themselves is Sons of the Mother.'

Epodorix spoke again to Leiron, who answered in strange words. Epodorix looked around, his eyes following the line of the westward ridge.

'This little fence you have made,' Epodorix said, pointing down at the palisade.

Namat nodded.

'It is to collect your cattle and sheep?'

'Indeed,' Namat replied, 'but it is also our stronghold.'

Epodorix smiled. Namat saw now that some of his teeth were black. He was surprised by the contrast with the hairless face, which though dark in complexion was smooth and looked younger.

Epodorix drew his sword. He held it out, pointing along the ridge.

'If I were attacking,' he said, smiling, 'I would first gain that ridge, at a distance from your arrows. I would then have the speed of my horses to sweep through your fence.'

Namat caught only some of these words.

'And because this is so,' Epodorix said harshly, 'there can be no strangers allowed to the west. Those Old Ones must be moved.'

Namat heard these words, but could not understand them. He stood anxiously waiting for the idea to be explained. But Epodorix had lowered his sword and said no more. Leiron spoke to him, and Epodorix nodded. Namat caught the name of Voratin.

Epodorix reared his horse and galloped away, beyond the fence to the westward ridge. Leiron took Namat's arm. The men who had come back from driving the cattle were now standing, watching them. In the south corner of the enclosure, behind the watchstone to which Cargen had returned, the horsemen of the troop were dismounted and talking busily among themselves. Their spears were stacked in an open pyramid, like charcoal wood for drying.

Leiron led Namat across to them. The horsemen watched him come. Leiron called for Voratin and a man of forty winters, his hair white under his close black cap, came to Namat and gripped his arm.

'It is good of you to receive me.'

'You are very welcome,' Namat replied.

'I am as yet a stranger,' Voratin said warmly. 'But I will learn all your ways. You must teach me.'

'We have a good life, brother, we have much to teach.'

Voratin smiled and put his arm across Namat's shoulders.

'You take in a stranger, an old man,' he said. 'But he with his poor skills will try to repay you. You will learn to guard your herd, and your women. We shall bring you peace from the men who are like wolves.'

Namat smiled. Beyond the stacked spears he saw Cargen listening intently. His face was flushed and angry.

'It is so, and it is good,' Namat said with formality. 'And now you and your kin must come down with us to Satelim. We will make ready for the feast. We have much to show you.'

Voratin patted his back. Leiron spoke sharply to the horsemen, who retrieved their spears and walked across to their horses. When they were formed up, they rode slowly down into the heart of the settlement.

'Taid!' 'Taid!'

On the high, bleak top of Rhos Dirion there was no single track to follow but only an intricate network of sheep paths. The main tracks run through the mountains: from Nant y Bwch to Rhiw Wen, from Bwch Bach to Rhiw Cwnstable. Like the modern roads of Wales, it is often said: not for internal use but for conquerors and traders passing through.

In the wide, desolate stretch, Glyn knew he must move slowly and call more often. He had left the main track to keep clear of the white stallion guarding his herd, and it had been difficult finding his way again. The only advantage was that the moon was now high in the sky and seemed much brighter, clear of haze. Over the whole sky, a full high dome above him, the stars were bright in ways never seen from the valleys, let alone from gardens and streets. In the lower parts of the sky, away from the immediate spread of the moon, their infinite numbers were astonishing.

At the division of a sheeptrack he came to a boundary stone: one of the line which ran from the track above Rhiw Wen towards Tal y Cefn. He knew it as the old boundary that divided the lordships of the eastern and southern foothills from those other lordships of the valleys of Wye and Llynfi, their centres now far below him at Bronllys and Llyswen. The stones were almost overgrown with heather, but they were markers which Elis had often shown him and explained.

He thought of the many lords who had marked these mountains. It had been in a way the greatest of all changes, beyond the natural variations of climate and livelihood. The old life of the families and local communities became part of a network: not the old social networks of beliefs and gifts and trade, but a new formal network of

property. Land and families became property within a system quite
beyond them.

In Telim, and in the valleys, in the lifetime of Tami, they had
traded locally for grain and relied on a travelling smith for their
tools, but they were still self-subsistent and self-reliant, the old
island-wide trade and beliefs largely gone. They burned rather than
buried their dead. The travelling smith, like all his brothers, had
beliefs about the spirits of fire and water, and these were made
formal in some of his rituals. But it was never easy to distinguish
these rituals from the secret methods of his craft, and they were in
any case not understood by the herdsmen and farmers who came to
trade with him.

It was different in the land of the mountains: on the high ridges,
on the great plateau and in the high, steep cross valleys under High
Buck and Hawkstone and Wolf Head. Here it had taken longer for
the scattered survivors of the old shepherds to move back up to the
land which had been their sweet place – the home of the wise flocks
– for more than two thousand years. When at last, in small groups,
they moved back to the old grazing, the high confidence of their past
was never recovered. They lived less well and grew in numbers only
slowly. Yet at midwinter and midsummer they still met at the
nearest Long House and lit their fires and sang their old songs. All
the stones of their ancestors were profoundly respected, and in even
the poorest family someone knew what the stones marked and the
ways in which they must be honoured.

But on this higher land the steady worsening of the weather
brought inevitable changes. The old hot dry summers and cold
winters had gone, replaced by a wetter climate, with lower summer
temperatures. The heaviest rainfall was now on the northern and
western slopes, where most of the early families had settled. On
the southern and especially the eastern slopes the rainfall was less,
in the lee of the mountains, and those areas were now more
developed.

The useful land now lay between the oakforests on the lower
slopes and the boggy peat of the uplands where there was good
grazing when the bracken was cleared. But in the inner mountains
and cross valleys, land at this height was on much steeper slopes.
Here, where the old families were trying to re-establish themselves,
the area of grazing was narrow. This kept their flocks small, and

their stock deteriorated. Hunting became more important and they developed an especially effective form of bow.

Another effect of the changing climate was that the outer grazing, with longer grasses, was often better for cattle than for sheep: and the raiders were, from the beginning, more interested in cattle. Little was known of them. They were a fierce, fast-moving people, their lives centred on their horses and their leaf-shaped swords. Some believed that they had settled far to the east, beyond the Great River. Others said they were a travelling people, moving across the whole island, raiding and fighting but also prospecting and trading in metals.

In the first generation after Tami the story of settled and savage strangers was more widely believed. But the raids, though still cruel, became less frequent, and there were reliable reports from the smiths that the strangers had established defended villages, on hilltops and spurs, from which they fought and raided. In these remote Black Mountains there were times when a father and son, and even the son's son, might live their whole lives without seeing an attack. The system of warning weakened and was almost forgotten. Yet the beacons, hastily arranged to the east, from whence the raiders came, led to closer contacts and new marriage arrangements. Telim came to have less contact with the far western settlements of the lake, for now the forest trails were difficult to follow. Telim and Alaron were still closely linked to Crucio in the south, above Salmon River, but their main orientation was now east, towards Alcarfan and the other settlements along their own Mountain River.

If some fortunate lifetimes passed without raid, others were overwhelmed by them, until life settled again. In these contrasting ways, about four hundred years passed from the lifetime of Tami to that of Nemat and the Lord Epodorix.

Through these centuries, Telim did not greatly change. More forest was cleared between the scarp and the riverjoin. The cleared land of the time of Nemat was ten times larger than in the time of Anail and Tami. The lush grass of the flat lands along the rivers made good hay for winter fodder. They still lived mainly by sheep but were able to keep more cattle. The grass grew in the valley from March to November, while on the summer spur it grew only from May till early October. For most of its corn Telim still traded with

Grain Valley, where the alluvial drift and gravels made ploughing easier. The simple plough, without a mould board, could not turn the deeper soils of Telim, but the earth was dug in plots for pulses and vetch. In Grain Valley itself there was a change from spring-sown naked barley to autumn-sown hulled barley, and spelt-wheat. In one season of heavy surplus Telim exchanged extra woollens for seed of the hulled barley, and began to grow grain of its own, south of the clearing where the soil was lighter. This made it easier to stand equal in the autumn exchange.

Thus Telim established a steady pattern of life. But in the generations before Nemat different forces were moving in the east. The smiths brought tales of a new people as savage as the old raiders but more numerous, settling over a wide area. Others told of forays up the seariver and attacks on settlements in the prosperous coastal lands. The name of this people was said to be Pretani, but there were many names. Their speech was strange, though some said it resembled the speech of the earlier raiders. The only certainty was that they lived by fighting.

Through two generations these reports continued, though the people of the Black Mountains did not see the new raiders. Instead, people of their own kind, not far to the east, began to follow the new ways. Living close to the dangerous strangers they defended themselves, by building new high-ground strongholds, trading for more weapons and even fighting and raiding, not only against the strangers but against the weaker settlements of the west.

Telim came to fear and curse the name of the Pretani, although the smiths described them as an extraordinary people, with fine feasts and songs, gold ornaments and brilliant enamels, and colourful clothes and dances. What mattered more in Telim was that the Pretani counted their wealth and status in cattle. The old raiders had stolen beasts for meat, but the Pretani raided to increase their own herds. They were not themselves herding people. The ruling warriors and their women (who were said also to be skilled in fighting), attacked existing settlements and herds. After the first killing they forced the people they conquered to work the animals and the land. Their whole life was fighting and the celebration of fighting. It was even said that their honours were the severed heads of all the men they called enemies.

As the people of Telim heard of the strongholds in the east, they thought again of their own defence. In the winter settlement they had always fenced their cattle, driving in ash stakes and laying dead brushwood, blackthorn and hawthorn between them. On the spur they built light fences and dead hedges, to collect the cattle and sheep overnight. Now they made these fences stronger, but in one devastating raid the new fences proved useless: the horses jumped over or broke them, and fire was set to them, to drive off the cattle.

The raids were always in the summer, after haycutting, when the cattle were on the spur. The steep scarp slowed the raiders' horses, and a heavier fence was built, beyond the Old Boat. Stout ash poles were driven deep into the rocky soil, and more closely set. At the second building, after new raiders had partly broken in, the fence became a palisade: that pride of Namat behind which Cargen had stood guard.

Yet the men of Telim were still only lightly armed. What others called weapons were for them the tools of clearing and hunting: axes and bows and hunting spears. They were learning to fight to defend themselves, but they understood little of the new order coming to their country, which had already been bloodily established elsewhere. It was from this order that Epodorix, a lord of the long-feared Pretani, rode with gifts and talk into their defended spur of Bentelim and then rode down with his warriors into the heart of their settlement. The great change transforming the whole island came to these mountains without fighting and without excitement. Indeed to most of the people it seemed a kind of common sense.

The Lords of Banavint

S lowly, against their own customs, the people of Telim learned the actual meaning of lord, which they had at first taken simply as a name. It was now, they learned, a condition. What they had considered their own settlement was now a part, a resource, of their lord.

Yet they still knew very little of Epodorix himself. All their direct transactions were with the deputy, Voratin, for whom they built a new large hut in Altelim. He then showed his friendship by marrying Netta, the young grand-daughter of Namat. He now began teaching the young men the true practice of weapons, especially the slashing swords which could be used from horseback. An ever larger part of their trade went for the new swords, which more smiths from the south and east were supplying. The swords were of bronze, long and narrow below the hilt before broadening to the shape of a willow leaf.

Voratin himself had a similar sword in iron, which he wore in a decorated bronze scabbard. The name of this sword was Talon. It was greatly admired by the young men he was training. As the months passed, he selected six of them for further special drills, and when these were completed they had the honour of carrying Talon, as each rode in turn and shouted as they slashed at straw figures set out on poles from the palisade.

Voratin now told them that they would form part, when needed, of the troop of the Lord Epodorix himself. The Lord Epodorix, he explained, had come from a rich country along the seariver, where he had been the youngest son of a still greater lord. His skill in fighting had been part always of his love of honourable peace. His most hated enemies were those bandits who lived by raiding and stealing, and he had devoted his life to training warriors who could outfight them and defend all peaceful settlements.

As the years passed, the full lordship of Epodorix became known. His main stronghold was to the west, on a spur above the upper valley of Salmon River. He had a large cattle herd there, and subsidiary herds in eight other settlements. There was a deputy like Voratin in each of the settlements. His troop of trained warriors moved between the settlements, protecting them, and in each place were lodged and given their meat. When they left they took meat and hides and selected young beasts for the winter of the Lord Epodorix, whose generosity in feasting and in rewarding the bravest of his warriors was celebrated in the songs of his bards.

Voratin died in the great fever which carried away so many of the people of Telim after the winter of the Great Floods. The storms of that winter had been more violent than any in living memory. But even while Voratin and the others were being mourned there came news of a great battle in the east, beyond Broken Mountain, in which the Lord Epodorix himself had been killed. What struck home more closely in Telim was that one of their own young men, Mat, had been killed in the same battle. His body was not, as they had expected, brought home to Telim. It was reported later that his head had been savagely struck off by the strange fighters from the east who had killed him.

There was then, Telim learned, a new lord, whose name was Maranoc, from a stronghold named Caeriddon beyond Curve River to the east. Maranoc was not seen for many years but a man who was said to be his brother's son Magulan, came and took the place of Voratin. Magulan's manner was very different. He assured the people of Telim that while they tended the lord's herd they would be kept in peace and safety. At the same time he informed them that by the order of Maranoc what they had known as Bentelim, the stronghold on the spur, would now be known by all as Banavint, which he said meant 'the hill lookout', and that Satelim, along the river, would now be known to all as Masona, 'the pasture by the river'.

There was now anxiety in Telim. The life of the spur, with its cattle and palisade, became more and more separate. They still took their few cattle to the upland for summer grazing, but in return for this right, Magulan ordered, they must provide all the winter fodder for the lord's herd, when it was brought down to the valley in the fall. As the lord's herd steadily increased this became a much heavier provision. For their own livelihood they continued to rely on sheep, and on pigs and goats with which they could clear new areas of forest along the two rivers.

Magulan did not, like Voratin, marry into their people. He brought a woman from a distant place, the daughter of a neighbouring great lord. He still trained the young men in fighting but he selected them more quickly and after a short period sent the most skilful away to the main force in Caeriddon. Increasingly, also, he made all general decisions about cattle and trade. In Masona, as they had now to call it, the most active men turned away, as they could, to extending their own clearings and making new and better-protected minor settlements. They still worked as a community on the major tasks of hay harvest and shearing, but the huts were no longer so close together. A man and his sons who had cleared a new area of forest would build new huts and pens inside it and then fence an enclosure. Some of these new places became the most prosperous in Masona.

Magulan was only the forerunner of a long succession of rulers in old Telim. They varied, individually, as did the name of the lord above them. But steadily, through the generations, the new order established itself, though the place of the High Lord still varied between Caeriddon in the east, on Curve River, and Madrun in the west, above Salmon River. The names of these rivers, they now learned, were Guuy and Uisc. All through this period the weather was worsening, with years of heavy storms, including many at harvest, and flooding along the rivers. In the depth of the mountains, the small group of old shepherds lost more of their grazing and came to rely mainly on hunting, with their skilful bows. In bad years they hunted down the long forested valleys towards the clearings and grasslands of the settlements.

One late spring in the time of Carvelan in Banavint, when the lord was Decanix, a large force of horsemen arrived on the eastern spurs, between Banavint and Crucio. They were divided into troops, each to ride out westward on the long ridges. The people of Masona, looking up at them, were astonished by their numbers. Even the troop that rode west from Banavint was larger than they had supposed the whole force of the lord to be.

The cattle had been brought up from the clearings, and the sheep were spread out along the lower slopes. On each of the spurs to the south the long line of horsemen stood ready, their swords raised. Then signals were passed and each line rode steadily to the west. They could be seen, clearly, on each successive skyline. The selected young fighters from Telim rode among them.

It was three days before they reappeared. Watching from the herd, the men of Banavint saw that some of the horsemen had been wounded, and that several empty horses were being led. At the front of the troop was Carvelan. Hanging by the hair from his bridle were two severed heads, each with matted black hair. Then over the near skyline came more than thirty men and women, walking unsteadily, with four horsemen spread out behind them. As they came nearer it could be seen that the wrists of the men were tied behind their backs with thongs. The women walked in a stumbling group, several of them holding the hands of children. They were driven together to a hollow below the palisade, and were made to sit down. Then they were left in the hollow, and the people of Banavint were ordered to keep away from them. They were the old ones, Carvelan explained, the thieves of the inner valleys. But they had been defeated and now at last there would be peace.

In the months that followed, the people of old Telim learned a new word from Carvelan. It was the name of these old ones, which was slaves. As ordered, they kept well away from the strangers, though they often saw them being whipped.

Carvelan went away and was replaced by his son Carnad. Carnad ordered the people of Masona to keep away at all times from the spur. The summer herding, he explained, would in future be managed by the slaves. To the surprise of the men of Masona, who had discounted this idea as that of a young man of no experience, this actually happened, though in the early years there was always a group of armed horsemen to watch over the slave herdsmen. There were stories that some of them had escaped back to the forested inner valleys where a few of their families survived. But slowly the new ways settled. There were now, it was confirmed, three kinds of people in the settlement: the lord's deputy and his horsemen and their families; the old families of Masona in their enlarged clearings with limited rights of grazing on the spur in exchange for the winter fodder; and finally the slaves, now a settled group, who were the summer herdsmen, and who lived with their women outside the enclosure of Banavint.

Generations came and went, in the new order. But in the country beyond them many other things were changing. There were alarming stories of new warlords in the east, and of much bigger and more dangerous raids. What had once been occasional conflict and raiding passed to a state of almost continuous attack and defence: a state which the lords of Banavint, in another new word which they taught Masona, called war.

It was now that the stronghold of Banavint was completed. The old palisade of Altelim had long been replaced by a double ring of heavy posts, with cross timbers and stone walling between them. A deep ditch and bank were dug outside it. After further fighting, a second ditch was dug, and a system of offset banks covered the track from the valley. Through several changes of lord – for the Pretani, it was learned, fought fiercely among themselves, and under many names – the defences were strengthened and repaired. In the time of Velanoc there was an attack which few understood, from the lord himself, with horsemen from the old Salmon River, the Uisc. Velanoc and many others were killed, and a new high bank to the west, filled with rubble, was quickly thrown up. But in the following year there was fighting all over the northern and eastern spurs. Banavint was captured and Masona burned. The deputy and his warriors were killed and their heads severed, but the people of Masona and the slaves of the spurs were not harmed. Rule had passed finally, they were told, from the cruel Lord of Uisc to the great and wise Lord of Caeriddon.

In fact, through the next generation their trading improved. They began to get good clay pots from the east, and supplies of grain were more abundant. Banavint was again fortified, with a new defended gateway and watchtowers on the south. More huts were built inside the protective wall, and the stores of the whole settlement came to be gathered there, around the larger huts where the deputy and his family now lived. The big clearing along the river was still intensively used, for winter pasture and for the pigs fed from the forest. But it was now regularly patrolled by armed horsemen, against enemies from the south, and the people were under orders to go up to Banavint whenever they were told that there was a danger of attack.

Slowly through the generations of danger, Banavint became the main settlement, with isolated homesteads below it. It was now an impressive place, with its strong wall and gateway, its larger huts and stone-laid paths, and its outer enclosure, beyond the slave huts, for herding the cattle. The outer wall, where the cross-timbers often decayed, was faced with drystone to shoulder height and topped with a high façade of birch trunks. The ground beyond the surrounding ditches was dug to a new steep bank. A second gateway was made on the eastern side: without guard towers but with a long curving entrance, overlooked from the projecting wall. One of the banks of this long entrance cut through a corner of the Old Boat Stones. The walling they found there, now covered with turf, was used for infilling.

There were now new beliefs in the settlement. At the riverjoin where the first valley clearing had been made there was a place where young oaks had been spared from cutting. These oaks, beside the river, where the two fast streams of brown water – Myngui and Hodeni – met and flowed on together, were now known as Nemeton. All the people gathered there, kin and farmers and slaves, when the Wise One, the Druida of Banavint, had mysteries to show them, at the seasons of fertility and harvest, Beltan and Samain.

It was now six hundred years after the life of Tami. It was a thousand years after the burial of Telemon in the Boat Grave, where his sons and daughters had settled and where the now-forgotten anthrax had ravaged them. It was almost three thousand years since the fathers and mothers of the slaves had followed the wise flocks to these mountains.

The Wise One and the Slave

———◆———

From the hill above Alcarfan, where they had rested their horses, the birch trunks of the palisade above the rampart of distant Banavint shone white in the sun.

'It is the sign of your welcome,' Clutacos said to Mation, anxiously watching the young lord's face.

Mation smiled. Since he had left Caeriddon, where he had been fostered and trained by the High Lord Buelac, his temper had swung between pride in returning to his father as a man and a warrior, and shame in the smallness of Banavint after the greatness of Caeriddon. For Buelac was High Lord of all lands between Hsabren and Guuy, and of the Black Mountains beyond Guuy. Sent to Buelac when he was seven, with his companion Clutacos son of Magios parasite of Eliudon, Mation had grown for ten years in a rich and powerful household, from which his native Banavint seemed an outlying hut. Yet Banavint would be his inheritance, on the death of his father Eliudon, whom he had not seen face to face since he was first sent to Buelac. For when Eliudon had visited Caeriddon, in councils of war or for trading, Mation had by custom been kept away from him. A son in fosterage, learning to become a warrior and a ruler, must not look upon his father until he was grown and trained. He must become horseman and swimmer, skilled in sword and broadspear and slingshot, word perfect in challenge and display.

Now that the day had at last come when Mation could ride back to his father in his warrior's red tunic and gilded helmet, with his own long sword at his waist, the pride was as he had expected, but Banavint, it was certain, would be too small to contain it. Before he had set out, Buelac had taken formal leave of him. He had promised that among all his foster-sons Mation had the highest chance of renown.

'For it is not the smallness of Banavint that will be your life, Mation. To the south, beyond you, are the Fisher Kings of the seariver, the Siluri, and they reach and press into your mountains. There will be wars beyond Banavint, and you can attack as well as defend.'

As Mation smiled at this, Buelac hesitated and then added:

'Your father Eliudon does not agree. He believes that there need not be war between us and the Siluri.'

'Does my father take their fish?' Mation asked arrogantly.

'We all trade for their sea fish,' Buelac replied, 'but the Siluri are always greedy for the pastures of your mountains, and the day will come when we must put our hooks through their noses.'

'It will be my life, my lord,' Mation swore.

'Never alone,' Buelac said, frowning. 'For they are many and powerful, those proud Fisher Kings.'

Since they had descended to the track through the oakwoods Mation and Clutacos had lost sight of Banavint, but after the long dry summer they found the rides easy. By mid-afternoon they saw again, through gaps in the forest, the dark wall of the mountains, now close in the west. After resting their horses for the final approach, they galloped through Hodoni, the brown river which was the frontier of Banavint. They saw the valley farms of Masona spreading to the riverjoin and along the banks of the mountain river Myngui. Peasants, men and women, were moving in the fields; a large group in the distance were cutting the yellow barley. Clutacos stopped to watch, but Mation was already looking beyond them, to the ramparts of Banavint on the edge of the high spur, where the white birch trunks gleamed.

It was a steep track, and stony, to the east gate. Mation now rode in front, with Clutacos following in his place. Clutacos had reversed his broad spear, pointing its blade to the ground as a sign to the watchman. But Mation, lifting his face, had his hand on the decorated hilt of his sword. He was not coming as a stranger but as the inheritor: the young Lord of Banavint.

There was the sound of a horn from above, on the rampart beyond the intricate banks of the first defences.

'I am Mation, son of your lord,' Mation shouted.

He heard echoing shouts beyond the ramparts, and rode slowly forward.

On the bank above him, as the track narrowed, was a line of slaves. They were climbing the steep slope by the zig-zag track from Masona. They were girls and young men of his own age: short and black-haired, as slaves commonly were: sweating heavily, on their dark skins, as they carried firewood for Banavint from the forest below. Several of them looked across at him but he took no notice. They had heard his name, and that was enough.

Clutacos observed them more closely. One girl in the line standing on the bank above Mation was looking intently down at him, her eyes shining, her lips parted. Then as the line moved behind her she stepped to go forward, but her foot slipped on the short grass and thyme. With the load on her shoulders she fell heavily from the bank. Her tied bundle of wood swung into the flank of Mation's white horse. Putting out her arms to stop herself, she grabbed Mation's boot.

Mation, surprised, drew his sword, but when he saw the girl he reached quickly down with his left hand, and caught hold of her black hair, which was long and braided. Pulling on the hair, he twisted her face up towards him.

'She meant no harm,' Clutacos called, anxiously.

'She is a careless bitch,' Mation shouted, tightening his grip on her hair.

The other slaves had now halted and were looking down at them.

'Shall I cut her hair to teach her manners?' Mation said, lifting his sword.

A young slave on the bank above them shouted words that Clutacos did not understand. On guard, his spear raised, he looked up at the slave. He was, like the others, short in stature, and his shoulders were broad and heavily muscled. Yet his eyes were most striking. Clutacos saw them at first as like the eyes of an animal. They were a strange yellowish green, and their shape, seen closer, seemed quite artificial, like eyes in a painting or as if they were not eyes but shining leaves. And it was now as if the whole face spoke through these eyes.

The young slave had put down his load. Others in the line spoke anxiously to him, and one older man held his arm. Mation, who had been glaring down at the girl, now looked up.

'Did you raise your voice to the son of your lord?'

The young man swallowed. He had difficulty with words. But then he said slowly and distinctly:

'You are hurting my blood-sister.'

'Your blood-sister? This bitch?'

'You are hurting her, lord. Let her go.'

Mation stared up at him, amazed by his insolence. From the bank the older man spoke.

'My honoured young lord, you will have seen what happened, and that the girl fell by accident. She meant no offence to you.'

'Yet she committed an offence,' Mation answered, and tightened his grip on the hair.

There was silence for some moments. Mation, sitting tall on his horse, with the bluebar of his rank freshly painted on his forehead, and with his long reddish hair sweeping down from his gilded helmet to the bright red shoulders of his cloak, looked up at the sweating slaves, with the dirt of the firewood over their bare dark shoulders and their thick black hair. Then he fixed again on the slave with the strange eyes, which were not like those of the rest of his people.

'Take your loads, the rest of you,' he ordered, 'but leave this bitch and her blood-brother to me.'

The slaves, except the older man, picked up their loads of wood. Mation lifted his sword.

'Hurt her no more,' shouted the young slave.

His voice was deep, and his words, in the language of the lord's, had a strange sound.

'Do you want my sword in your guts, slave?'

The young slave hesitated. The older man spoke quickly.

'Derco, come away. We will explain and all will be well.'

Mation rose from his saddle.

'Are you hungry for my sword in your guts?' he shouted. His pink cheeks were now flushed with excitement, and his voice had risen to the pitch of formal challenge, though to a slave this should not have been his choice.

'Lord, I will take your sword from you before you can hurt either her or me,' the young slave replied quietly.

The fixed glare of his eyes now seemed, to Clutacos, inhuman: the eyes of an animal or of a god.

There was a hurrying of people from the gate. There were guards in leather tunics, and among them, white-haired, the Druida Lugon, brother of Eliudon father of Mation.

'My young lord,' Lugon was calling, smiling his welcome.

'Peace, my uncle,' Mation replied formally.

As Lugon came stumbling down the stony track, through the banks of the outer defences, he was still spreading his arms and smiling. Then, as he came close, he stopped suddenly, with what seemed an exaggerated surprise. He had seen Mation holding the girl's braided hair, twisting her head into the flank of his horse.

'Is this a captive you have brought us?' he asked.

'It is a slave bitch of Banavint,' Mation replied. 'She threw her filthy body at my horse.'

'One of our own slaves?' Lugon said, raising his hands. 'It is not possible.'

'And now her dog of a blood-brother has threatened me.'

Lugon stared anxiously around. His eyes settled on the young slave, who stood poised on the bank looking down at his sister.

'Is it you, Derco?' he asked.

Derco did not reply. Lugon moved forward.

'And is this Gorda?' he said, trying to see the girl's face.

The older slave who had tried to restrain Derco now hurried down the bank and dropped to his knees before Lugon. Lugon reached down and touched his hand.

'May I speak, wise one?' the slave asked.

'I am listening, Karan.'

'Wise one,' Karan said, lifting his wrinkled face, 'this is a misfortune which calls on your wisdom.'

'I am listening.'

'Wise one, the girl Gorda was carrying her wood load with us all. On this bank that you see we all stopped while the brave young lord and his companion rode below us. We stood with respect to see them pass us.'

'That is proper, Karan.'

'It is proper, wise one. But there was then a misfortune. As we moved to go on with our wood for the fires, the girl Gorda slipped and fell. She fell, without intention, against the horse of the young lord. He was perhaps startled but quickly, like any brave warrior, he reached out against attack. Against what he thought was attack.'

'By the girl?'

'The girl had slipped, wise one. But as she fell from the bank . . .'

'Yes, you have told me. You need not repeat yourself. But then what is this about a threat?'

Karan hesitated. He looked round at Derco, who had not moved his eyes from his sister.

'Wise one,' Karan said slowly, 'misfortune and misunderstanding have led to further misunderstanding. But they should not lead, unless we will it, to further misfortune.'

'It is the teaching,' Lugon agreed.

'Derco is young,' Karan said, 'and it has also to be remembered that the face of the young lord is not known to us. He is only now returning in honour to the place of his birth. It is hard to say, wise one, but Derco saw only a danger to his sister, in what he under-stood, wrongly, as the grip of a stranger.'

'If a stranger, yet still a lord.'

'That is true, wise one. That is indeed a misfortune.'

'A threat is not a misfortune, Karan. Did he make any threat?'

Karan hesitated. He looked round at Derco who had still not moved. Mation, who had been listening impatiently, though he knew he must respect the laws of attention to the wise, now shouted angrily:

'The dog said he would disarm me. To free this bitch.'

Lugon looked anxiously around. Then he fixed on Derco.

'Derco, answer me. Did you use those words?'

Derco said nothing.

'It is the language, wise one,' Karan said anxiously. 'He is not skilled in the language of our lords.'

'That is a lie,' Mation shouted. 'He spoke like a dog but it was in the proper language.'

'Then answer me, Derco. Did you threaten the Lord Mation?'

Derco turned his head slowly. The staring eyes fixed on Lugon.

'Yes,' he said clearly. 'While he hurts my sister.'

Lugon threw up his hands. Karan shouted angrily at Derco in their own language. Mation lifted his sword and his horse moved under him, throwing Gorda sideways.

'The law, my lord,' Lugon said sharply.

Mation glared angrily but lowered his sword.

'A misfortune, a misunderstanding . . .' Karan was saying, desperately.

Lugon raised his right arm. He spread his fingers in the sign of authoritative judgement.

'Take the girl from my lord,' he ordered the guards.

The guards moved forward. As Mation hesitated, tightening his grip on the hair, Lugon added:

'She will be whipped with six lashes for her clumsy offence.'

There was silence from the slaves on the bank. Mation released Gorda. The guards led her away. The other guards moved closer to Derco, watching him closely.

'Take the offender Derco,' Lugon ordered.

The guards scrambled up the bank. Derco did not move. He did not resist as they reached out to hold him. He scarcely glanced at them. He had turned his face to look still defiantly at Mation.

'There will be need for mercy,' Karan said anxiously.

Lugon reached out and put a hand on his shoulder. He told him to get up. Then he said, slowly:

'It is a capital offence to threaten a lord. You know this, Karan.'

'I know also, wise one, that wisdom must interpret the law.'

'But Karan, there is nothing to interpret. The threat was admitted and repeated.'

'Within a misunderstanding, wise one. A misunderstanding that followed a mere accident.'

'No, Karan, a deliberate and repeated act of defiance.'

'That could be said, wise one. But consider this day and this place. It is the return of the young lord. It is a day of welcome and happiness. It is not the time or the place for a sacrifice.'

'Sacrifice! But you know it is not that. It is an act of the law.'

'Which wisdom must still interpret, for the sweetness of this place.'

'You are talking in riddles. What sweetness?'

'Of our earth, wise one. Of this place in our earth. To shed blood would sour it.'

Lugon hesitated. He turned, watching the guards leading Derco away. The other slaves were still standing along the bank, looking down and listening.

'I've been delayed long enough,' Mation shouted. 'I am riding in to see my father.'

'Indeed, my lord,' Lugon said.

'These slaves behave like dogs and talk like heathens. At

Caeriddon, I can tell you, there would be a quicker way with them.'

'In Caeriddon or here in Banavint, my lord, there is above everything the law.'

'Then enforce it,' Mation shouted, and kicked his horse forward.

He rode up through the defences, with Clutacos following him closely.

Lugon looked into Karan's eyes.

'What he says is the truth, Karan, though he says it impatiently.'

Karan hesitated.

'It is your truth, wise one.'

'My truth? It is the truth of the law.'

'Of your law, wise one, to which we have bowed our heads.'

'You have bowed your heads, but the law is for all men.'

'We have bowed our heads, wise one, because we are slaves.'

'You have bowed your heads but not your minds. Is that what you are saying?'

'We have only our minds, wise one.'

'What is it, Karan, you are daring to say?'

'What I must say, wise one. In the truths of my people.'

'Be careful, Karan.'

'I am being careful, wise one.'

Lugon hesitated. Above them, inside the ramparts, there was shouting and the sound of horses. Mation was being welcomed and soon the feast would begin.

'You have gods and laws among your own people,' Lugon said, as if ending the argument.

'Not gods, wise one.'

'You live without gods, without laws?'

'We have truths, wise one, those truths are the law.'

'What kind of truth could that be?'

'I have said it, wise one. It is the sweetness of this place.'

'You say those words. They mean nothing. There is this place or another, and in every place there is the law.'

'In every place there are truths, wise one.'

Lugon smiled.

'You use my proper title, but you do not speak as if I were wise.'

'I know that you are wise in the ways of your people.'

'In the ways of your lords, you should say.'

'Indeed, wise one, I say that.'

Lugon smiled again.

'Your tongue is careful, Karan, but also subtle. I cannot change the lawful punishment of Derco, but I will talk with you again.'

'I would be honoured to talk with you, wise one. But if Derco is put to death there will be nothing I can say.'

'You would refuse?'

'The truth would refuse.'

Lugon looked up again at the camp. There were renewed shouts.

'I am needed at the welcome and to begin the feast. If you will not give proper answers I cannot wait for ever.'

'I will give answers, wise one, while Derco lives.'

'You are tempting me, Karan. It is the duty of my order to explore all knowledge, including the knowledge of slaves. Yet if you will not give me proper answers . . .'

Lugon hesitated. He looked up at the line of slaves on the bank. They had again put down their loads and were listening intently.

'Three nights,' Lugon said. 'For three nights we will keep him alive, if you will give me answers.'

'I have promised this, wise one.'

'Then come tomorrow, at dusk. Come alone.'

As he spoke he looked up at the slaves squatting close above them.

'I thank you in honour, wise one,' Karan said, and again went on his knees.

Lugon looked down and held out his hand to be kissed. Karan bowed over it. Lugon turned and hurried up to the gatehouse. The slaves, without speaking, stood and hoisted their loads.

Within the ramparts of Banavint the main living area of the chief Eliudon and his kin was below the high bank to the west. Here there were eight round houses, timber-built and thatched with heather, and ten smaller huts for storage of food, wool and hides. At the east gate of the enclosure there was a large guardhouse and three huts for storage, one for weapons. The huts of the slaves were outside the ramparts, on the spur running west: twenty-eight huts smaller and more roughly built than those of the kin. The feastfire of Eliudon, to mark the return of Mation, was on the flattened earth front of the houses of the kin, where the young men did their military exercises.

That night, as the kin held their feast, and the bard Caradon, son of Lugon, sang, to the lyre, of the lineage of Eliudon and Mation, the slaves beyond the high western rampart also gathered round a fire and those who had been serving at the feast came out to join them. As the kin drifted towards sleep they could hear, beyond the scattered noises of their horses and cattle, the strange deep sound of the singing of the slaves, which was unusual except at their ceremonies of midsummer and midwinter.

Most of the kin were indifferent to the habits and superstitions of the slaves. They knew them only as quiet and tractable people, good herdsmen and builders in earth and stone. But the bard Caradon attended to their singing, which was of a different kind from anything of the kin. They were squatting in two circles round their small fire: women and children in the outer circle, men in the inner. Only the men were singing, though Caradon knew that there were songs for women at the sunset of midwinter and at the dawn of midsummer. The men did not sing individually, as in the music of the kin, but in a deep chorus, the voices pitched in a low breathing sound as if of a single strange voice. The words, Caradon knew, were of their own old language, and he could follow only their rhythms.

There was a high moon above Broken Mountain. The night was still and cold. While the kin slept in their huts, with the big fire dying down, Caradon lay and listened to the strange singing of the slaves. There was a sadness in it but also, in its persistence, a strength of some unusual kind. It was a force different from that of the battles and challenges which were sung by the bards of the kin. Hearing the long rhythms, so often repeated, Caradon tried to set words to them, but found he had lost the facility of his long training. For the rhythms, though compelling, were too unfamiliar for the words of his own people's songs. He stared at the shadowy figures around the lowering fire and watched as they rose quietly and moved away to their huts.

On the following day, at dusk, Karan came to Lugon at his house. Caradon was in the house and stayed to listen.

'I have nothing to say of Derco,' Lugon began. 'The decision is made and the law will take its course.'

'A law of sacrifice, wise one?' Karan asked.

'You refuse to understand,' Lugon answered angrily. 'It is not I and certainly not you who decide the law. The law is above us all, for it is the order of the world.'

'Of your gods, you would say?' Karan asked.

Caradon heard, clearly, the slight shift of tone in his voice. The words were quiet and respectful, though the formal title had been avoided. What had changed was the deep sound. Caradon could hear the emphasis of an older people, who had known and passed through the kinds of wisdom they now encountered.

'Men recognise their kings,' Lugon explained as if to a pupil, 'by the rites which the gods have prescribed. Thus the king and the law are revealed by the gods. All that follows is obedience.'

'You have many gods, wise one?'

'There are more gods, Karan, than your head could contain. There are gods of justice who are represented by the kings and wise ones. There are gods of power who are represented by our warriors. There are also gods and goddesses of fertility, to whom you as herdsmen make sacrifices at festivals.'

'Yes, standing together we attend your sacrifices.'

'You do more than that. Be very careful what you say. I am trying, in peace, to explain the nature of the world.'

'Of your gods.'

'Indeed, of our gods. Of great Math, the Master of Darkness. Of great Lug, the Master of Light. Of Modron the Mother of the Earth. Of great Dana who nurses the dead.'

'Dana, wise one?'

'Dana the Mother of all men.'

'It is a name I have heard.'

'If you were wise in our order you would know all the holy names. You would know Beli the shining one, who protects the whole kin. You would know . . .'

'That is as you say, wise one. The names are too many for my head. I am, as you say, ignorant, but I am eager to learn. I hear you speak of these great gods and goddesses, yet it seems in my ignorance that you are speaking of men and women.'

'Not of men and women. Of great gods.'

'You speak of he and she. Of fathers and mothers. Do these gods then couple and bear children?'

'You understand so little,' Lugon said patiently. 'What I show you now is a world of the spirit. It is not your base coupling on the earth. Yet the world and the lives of all men move through these spirits who form us.'

'As powers of the earth and sky, wise one?'

'Spirits and powers. Of this world and of the other world.'

'There is another world?'

'It is everywhere around us, Karan. We visit it in death and there continue our lives. It is very close to us, always. Some even enter it and return.'

Karan was silent for some time.

'I have heard the name Riganon,' he began again.

'Yes, Riganon is a shape that is taken by Modron, when she welcomes the dead with a flight of birds.'

'That is known also to us, wise one.'

'In your burials?'

'Not burials. But it is a ceremony of the Long House.'

Lugon moved away and took a drink. He did not offer the bowl to Karan.

'I am glad we have taught you a little of this life of the spirit,' he resumed, easily. 'But the purpose of your coming was to give me honest answers. It was not to ply your own questions.'

'I was interested, wise one, in your particular beliefs.'

'It is proper that you should be. You may yet attain the truth. But now you must answer. You have spoken of a Long House. Is that the stones you still worship?'

'We do not worship the stones, wise one, though we keep them in honour. But there are many forms of stones. The Long House is only one.'

'The others are circles and standing stones?'

'Those are old, wise one. They are also of different times.'

'But they are all sacred to you?'

'They all mark places and powers, that some have lived or measured and marked.'

'You believe you can measure such powers?'

'I cannot wise one. Yet at certain times they were measured. For it was learned that there are powers in the earth and in what we see from our earth. There are powers of the sun and moon and powers of the rocks beneath the earth. None of these is shaped like woman or man.'

'By spirits then? Primitive spirits?'

'Not spirits, wise one. They are powers beyond us, but they can be measured and tied.'

'Tied? You think you can control them?'

'It is our word, wise one. It is how we describe an understanding of a relation or a power.'

Lugon looked away. Karan, unobserved, shifted a flake of sandstone from his left hand to his right. He rubbed it, now concealed, with his thumb.

'I will look at what you say are these markers, Karan. With our own more developed ideas, the wise order may interpret them. But it is still very serious that you live in a world without gods. A world without gods is a world without reverence. You have seen where that leads.'

'Are you returning to Derco, wise one?'

'Certainly to Derco. To his criminal insolence.'

'His words were angry, wise one, but they were spoken in reverence.'

'What nonsense is this?'

'You say, wise one, that we have no reverence. It is your chosen word. But what was measured and tied taught our people respect. We respect this place in which we live. We respect all the powers which affect it. This respect is our tie with the place and with each other. Derco spoke within that, to protect his blood-sister.'

'To protect her against a lord?'

'Against anyone, wise one.'

'Be careful, Karan. It is always a duty to protect our own kin, but this must be within the law. And Derco has no right, Gorda has no right, to insult or threaten a lord.'

Karan pushed the flake of sandstone to the tips of his long fingers.

'That is understood as we are, wise one. But it was learned in the measuring that there are sometimes marks which do not agree. When that happens all must be measured again. In the same way, there is a law and then a different law. It is then a time for new tying in which we must think again and interpret.'

'You are saying that slaves, to suit themselves, can interpret the law?'

'For the sweetness of their place, Lugon brother of Eliudon.'

Lugon threw up his hands. Karan watched him carefully.

'Your words are skilful, Karan,' Lugon said with an effort, 'but you are speaking within a wider delusion, indeed an insanity. Can you not see, even now, where your beliefs have led you? They are the beliefs of slaves, and you have become slaves. In excluding the gods from your world you have fallen to fear death, as Derco now fears it. You speak of this place and its sweetness. Yet all you are saying is that you are tied to it. You are tied to clods and stones. You have no freedom of spirit, no movement of the heart. Have you not seen, by contrast, the life of your lords? We are tied by no place. We put little trust in any possessions but ourselves. We move as free men, between this place and another, as between this world and another. We live as our gods have taught us, in movement and change. Even our greatest gods shift and change their shapes, for that is the nature of all life. We do not fear death, for our spirits go beyond it and return to us, through life and death alike. We ride the wind. We make music. We astonish the world with all the moving colours of life. And that is why we are lords, for we have taken life and shaped it, and moved in its shapes. We have made life dance to our songs, while you still creep close to the earth.'

'Then let Derco have life in his own shape.'

'No. He is a slave. He threatened his lord.'

'That is a different argument, wise one. It too has shifted shape.'

'It is the same argument. It is because we move in this spiritual world that we are lords with the powers of lords. It is why the world has been good to us.'

'And why you are good to the world, wise one?'

Lugon raised his right hand. He spread his fingers on the sign of formal judgement.

'The sentence on Derco stands. The sentence on Gorda stands.'

Karan got up slowly. He did not go to kneel at Lugon's feet. As Lugon turned and walked away Caradon came from inside the house. Closing his lips he hummed the rhythm of the slow chorus which he had heard the slaves singing. Karan looked angrily up at him.

'Yes, Karan, I heard your singing.'

'It is of our people, lord.'

'I could not understand the words.'

'They are very old words. Some are of a time before the measuring.'

'Are they the sweetness of the place?'

'They remember its sweetness, my lord.'

The old man turned away, but Caradon caught his arm.

'When a man dies, Karan, tell me what happens.'

'You ask me to tell you.'

'Yes, Karan, it is important.'

'He rots, my lord. He rots down to bones which are broken or burned.'

'And that is all?'

'That is all of the mark that is Derco or Karan.'

'The mark?'

'The mark of a tying. I cannot say the words in your language. But we cherish each mark where we and the powers have joined.'

Caradon stared. Karan freed his arm and left, walking slowly, his head bent to the ground.

On the next day at dusk, Karan came again. He asked only if Derco was to be put to death. Lugon answered, formally, that he was. Karan bowed and turned away. On the third evening he came again, and got the same answer. Gorda would be whipped and Derco ritually strangled, in front of all the slaves at the dawn of the next day.

That night was unusually cold. Mation and a troop of young horsemen had ridden in late, from a reconnaissance to the south. They had reached the bank of Salmon River, which the Siluri called Uisc, and had seen Siluri horsemen in the clearings beyond it. The slave men had waited up for them, to feed and water the horses.

It was much later, after the moon had risen, that a shouting spread through Banavint. A fold of rams had been separated from the ewes, to delay the rut and the lambing. The fold was beside the steep track to Masona. Two slaves came running up to the gate-house, shouting that wolves had got in among the rams. The whole guard was roused, and torches were lit. Guards and slaves took spears and bows and ran down to the ramfold. By the hurdle gate the fence was broken and three rams lay dead, torn at the throat. Following the shouting, men were now coming up from the farm huts in Masona. Their dogs were loose and barking furiously. Under the moon all could see their immediate surroundings but it was difficult to identify particular tracks. There was no sign of the wolves or of the other rams, until it was thought to go to the ewefold. Two of the rams were found in among them. Guards and slaves and farmers searched every track and clearing, shouting to each other to control the hunt.

At the edge of the forest the search had to end. There were several reports that the wolves had been heard, but they had not been seen. At last, tired and dispirited, the guards and slaves from Banavint made their slow way back up the steep track and through the bank-and-rampart defences. They were making for their huts when there was an angry shout from one of the guards. The single guard left at the hut where Derco had been bound to a pole was found lying unconscious in its doorway, his wrists and mouth tied. Derco had disappeared. The guard's spear and bow had been taken.

Eliudon and Mation were roused and took charge. The slaves were closely questioned but had seen nothing. Lugon was fetched and he questioned them again. Then, taking Karan with him, he went down to the ramfold. Torches were held above the killed rams and Lugon put his fingers into the wounds at their throats.

'These were human wolves, Karan,' he said quietly, looking down at the blood on his fingers.

'I do not know, wise one.'

'It was cleverly done. It is like the tearing of teeth. But it was no wolf who cut Derco loose.'

'A god, perhaps,' Karan said and smiled.

Lugon stiffened with anger.

'This will make no difference. With those yellow eyes, like an animal, he will be quickly hunted down. And this new crime will be punished.'

In Banavint, when they returned, guards and horsemen had surrounded the whole body of slaves. Lugon spoke with Eliudon, and they stood together on the fighting ground, waiting for dawn. Then Gorda was led in. Her long hair was cropped with shears. She was stripped and bound to a pole. She was then whipped with a hide thong, six times and then six again. Karan stood with the other slaves, watching. Then at a signal from Lugon two guards moved to seize him. He smiled and stepped forward while they grasped at his arms.

Lugon himself brought the strangling rope. He ordered the guards to bind Karan's wrists but Karan objected.

'There is no need, wise one. I shall not leave this place.'

Lugon handed the rope to a guard.

'Behind your heathen words,' he said loudly to Karan, so that all the slaves could hear him, 'there was only cruel deception and the planning of evil. For this you must die. Your body will be given, under law, to the water.'

Karan lifted his head.

'I tell you of this place,' he called, in a clear high voice. 'I tell you of this place and of wolves who eat wolves. I tell you of your downfall. I tell you of the grass that will cover both master and slave.'

Lugon raised his hand and spread his fingers. A guard put the thick rope over Karan's head and inserted a spindle rod in the knotted loop at the back of the neck. He then turned the rod, sharply. Karan remained standing for some moments, then fell on his face.

'Wise one!' the bard Caradon said clearly, looking deep into his father Lugon's eyes.

The Mirror and the Song

◆

At the Hand Spring, under the ramparts of Dun Riganon, Karin tethered the yearling and drank the cold grey water. Looking up at the ramparts, he scooped the fresh spring water over his shoulders and arms, where the sickness had been spreading. The dogs of Dun Riganon, tethered at the inturned entrance, were barking angrily. His own wolfhound, Fan, was growling towards them. Karin looked ahead, along the old sunken road, to where a mountain brook was spreading a pool. He loosed the yearling and let her along to it. Fan followed, snarling back at the dogs of the fort. The heifer drank deep at the pool and Fan went past her and rolled in the muddy brown water. When he came out he shook himself dry, wetting Karin's bare legs.

The long journey had begun before it was light, on the day before the night of Belitan. But now the sun was warm and the air of the upland was clear and fresh. By noon Karin would, as ordered, arrive with the heifer at the court of Madrun where King Henwin was returning for the feast of Belitan. It was said that he had been in battle, beyond the seariver, and that he had shared in a victory over the Dobuni. But these stories of battles were strange and distant to the herdsmen. In the past, beyond six generations, there had been fighting all over these mountains and valleys, when they had been ruled by the sons of Buelac from Caeriddon beyond Guuy. But there was now the peace of Henwin under Veramos, in the lands of the Fisher Kings, the Siluri.

Karin prodded the heifer along the grass of the sunken road. Above them, rising to the sharp ridge of the Grib, the gorse was in yellow flower and the pink leaves of the whinberry were beginning to unfold. Larks were singing on the higher slopes, where the heather bushes were still black. Following the slow heifer, Karin

had time to look down at the broad green valley of the river which
the lords called the Uisc. As a boy he had once been shown by his
father the old Long Houses of his people: two now in sight, the grass
and scrub still cleared around them though they were not used for
the bones of the dead. They were the Long House of Mecan and the
Long House of Idrisil. In the lost times there had been feasts at these
houses of the earth. The old hymns had been sung.

Karin would not hurry the heifer. It had been difficult enough to
get some weight on her after the shortage of winter, and Caradon
had given him only two moons to prepare her as a gift for Henwin at
Belitan. With his early start he would reach Madrun not long after
noon, in plenty of time for the preparation. Yet he kept wanting to
hurry, for this was at last a chance to see his youngest daughter
again. Seril had been taken by Angarad wife of Henwin when they
were visiting Crucio. 'That one,' she had said, pointing, seeing the
lively girl of thirteen who had been one of the servants at Caradon's
welcoming feast. Karin had not since seen her over nearly five years,
but had heard from others who visited Crucio that she was well and
content.

Fan was circling above the old road: setting up grouse, and
excitedly if hopelessly bounding in chase of them, through the thick
gorse and whinberry. Karin smiled, watching him. The sun was now
warmer and his slow walk behind the heifer came through as an ease
of the place. It was like the honoured walk of the old father Idris,
who had followed the wise flock to these mountains. Round a
shoulder of the ridge which the lords called the Grib he could see
Madrun below him. Blue smoke was rising from many fires. They
were already busy and rushing down there. Fan came back and
brushed his leg before again bounding off among the gorse. The
heifer stopped but Karin prodded her on.

He could hear the sounds of Madrun while still at some distance.
Always, when the lords were at home, there was this lively noise.
Noise and colour: these, his people said, were the special ways of the
lords. They would be fighting, feasting, singing their loud songs,
and today, for a certainty, at Belitan, wearing their finest clothes.
And while they lived like this they seemed to spread their liveliness
to others: even to the servants and slaves, and to the farmers and
herdsmen bringing food for the feast. It was not how everyday
people could live, through slow moons and seasons. It was like the

playing of children, but still it quickened some pulse in the heart, as they shouted and danced and displayed their fine clothes and decorations. It was the vigour of colts on new grass; the bounding – Karin smiled as he thought of it – of wolfhounds.

There was a flock of grey geese outside the ramparts. They flapped and threatened noisily, as they saw the heifer and the dog. Then the dogs of Madrun were rushing out and barking, scattering the geese and ducks and gamefowl around the big gatehouse. The birds were lucky to get no worse at Belitan. Many would already have been plucked to hang for the feast.

There were guards at the gate, but they were relaxed and laughing. A pig was loose, inside the gate, and two slaves were running to catch him. Karin waited behind a shepherd who had four good yearlings: the man was deaf and the guards were waving their arms at him. At last Karin got in. He had slipped a thong lead over the heifer's neck. 'Not much good stuff on that,' one of the guards shouted, and Karin smiled. He looked at her again. She had improved wonderfully since he had picked her out. The black coat was shining, the tail was long and clean, and between her short horns, on the high frontal ridge, the unusual white patch was attractive. Yet now, in the yard, with all the noise around her, she was beginning to slaver. Two of the Madrun dogs had run past her, snapping at Fan. As he drove them off, yelping, the heifer drew back in stubborn fear. Karin pulled on the thong and led her through to the small huts where they were butchering and preparing the food. He left her with the words he had been ordered to repeat: 'To the honour of King Henwin, from Caradon Lord of Crucio.'

'Crucio,' the old headman shouted, brusquely, and turned away.

Karin went back and looked around the court. The big round house of Henwin was on the far side, across an open space. Keeping close to the other houses Karin made his way towards it. He thought to squat near the entrance and watch for Seril to come out. Or if some other slave or servant came out he could send word to her. Above the doorway of Henwin's house there were signs of the battle that had been reported. Three heads were set on the sharpened stakes above the heavy oak lintel. He stared across at them. Two were of young men, both red-haired: they looked like brothers. The other was of a much older man, with white hair and flowing white moustache, on which blood from a gash on his cheek had caked.

There was a cloud of flies around the heads and Karin thought for a moment that he was smelling blood. Then from inside the house there was a high screaming of women's voices, and two girl slaves ran out and crouched close to the wall, out of sight.

The screaming came again, and then running from the doorway was one of the lord's women: not Angarad, whom Karin remembered, but a young woman much like her: very tall, with flowing red hair and brightly reddened cheeks. While he watched her, open-mouthed, he saw Seril beyond her. He recognised her at once, though she had grown and her features had matured. Beside the lord's woman she was small. With her cropped black hair and pale skin and in her simple brown woollen tunic, she was almost inconspicuous. But then as Karin stared and smiled at her, his attention was pulled away by the shouting of the lord's woman, who had turned and called back into the house. He could barely understand her words, though he made out Henwin and Dobuni and saw that she was pointing at the heads on the stakes. Then another of the lord's women appeared in the doorway. Looking closely he recognised Angarad, though she was so remarkably dressed that it took some moments. A long tunic reached to her ankles, fitting closely at her shoulders but very broad and flared at the waist. It was in many colours: bright yellow and green stripes from the waist but over the breasts a checkered pattern of greens and blues. There was a heavy gold collar at her neck and three gold bracelets on each arm. Her fair hair was separated into many strands, standing out from her head. Gold and enamelled beads were strung along the hair. The blue spot of her rank, as large as a man's thumbnail, was clear in the centre of her forehead. Her cheeks were painted bright red.

Karin looked back at the other woman, who had gone silent as Angarad appeared. Her tunic was of the same shape, but in checks and stripes of yellow and red. Hanging at many points on the tunic were small coloured glass beads, with what looked like small bells strung below them. Her red hair was braided and tied with woven yellow strings so that it rose from the crown. There was no spot of rank, but in her hand she was holding a shining bronze disc, with inlaid curves which caught the light.

Angarad walked slowly towards her. At two paces she stopped and spoke.

'It is mine by right. Give it now and stop playing the fool.'

The other woman did not answer. Angarad stepped forward and reached for the disc. She got her hand on it but the other woman would not let go.

'For the last time, Edra,' Angarad said, her voice rising.

With a sudden movement Edra pulled the disc away but in the same moment Angarad jumped and with both hands grabbed Edra's hair. The force of her movement twisted Edra's head towards the ground but then Edra kicked hard at Angarad's stomach, and as Angarad closed they were locked together, pulling and kicking. Each was now shouting again, and as the fight continued people came out of the houses to watch.

Edra was hampered by the disc, which she continued to hold tightly by the handle. Angarad got a hand free and clawed at Edra's red-painted cheeks. Edra screamed but was strong enough – she was many years younger – to swing Angarad round and off her feet. They were down on the ground, grabbing hair and hitting and kicking at each other, rolling to try to get clear and gain an advantage.

Karin watched in astonishment. The fine tunics were being torn and covered with dust. The long hair of each woman was now loose and dishevelled. The small bells on Edra's tunic were ringing whenever she moved. And now the harsh screaming had begun again. Struggling for breath, as they fought with all their strength, they still shouted at each other. Many of the words were incoherent but the name of Henwin was constantly repeated, and there was a strange word, *adaltach*.

The slaves and servants watched quietly, but the men and women of the kin, who had come from their houses, were laughing and shouting, joining in the excitement of the fight. Then there was a movement at the door of the king's house and suddenly Henwin was standing there. He was heavily muscled under his short, fringed gold tunic. His gold dagger was sheathed at his waist. The blue bars of kingship crossed his forehead, above the purple hornmark of his lordship of Madrun.

Everyone but the two women now looked towards Henwin. He was staring across at them as they rolled and scratched on the ground. Then he threw back his head and laughed and laughed. It was a very loud, coarse laugh. The rest of the kin joined his laughing, and soon there was a ring round the two women, looking down at the fierce fight, shouting applause and encouragement.

As the ring formed Karin saw his chance to go to Seril. She had seen where he was sitting, but had been distracted by the fight. She was very pale, as if her own person had been attacked.

'What madness is this?' Karin asked in their own language.

'It is the queen and the adaltach.'

'What is *adaltach*?'

'It is the king's right: his second woman, the adulteress.'

'And the queen has discovered this adulteress?'

'No, the two live together in his house. That is the lords' law. But when Henwin came from his war he gave the queen a gold brooch but gave the adulteress that mirror.'

'What is mirror?'

'It's a looking-glass. It's to see the face and the hair. They say it's the mirror of the queen of the Dobuni, taken when the Lord Henwin defeated them in battle. My lady Angarad believes that since it was the mirror of a queen it is now her right.'

'Though the king had given it to the adulteress?'

'He gave it openly. He said that the gifts were his right.'

There was still shouting from the ring. The fierce fight continued. Then across the open space two figures came hurrying. Seril identified them to Karin as the wise one Assarac and the bard Cangu. Assarac, an old man, with tightly-curled grey hair, and the blue bar of rank on his wrinkled forehead, lifted his staff and shouted 'Peace,' in a loud deep voice. The watchers in the ring went silent and moved back. Henwin continued to look down at the women struggling on the ground. Assarac went forward and put his staff on the shoulders of the women. He again shouted 'Peace.' Slowly dazed and dishevelled, the two women separated. Henwin laughed.

'Adulteress,' Assarac said, 'why do you break the law?'

'I break no law, wise one,' Edra said, gasping for breath. 'I was given the mirror by my lord. The queen used force to take it from me.'

'She is allowed to use force,' Assarac said, sternly. 'Any wife can beat an adulteress, and the adulteress has to endure it.'

'I know this, wise one,' Edra said, getting to her feet. 'But this was to steal my lord's gift. That is not within the law.'

Angarad stood up. She brushed down her fine tunic. As Henwin stood, still smiling, she went across and swung her fist at his face. His hand came up quickly but only half deflected the blow. He was not angry with Angarad, though now he held her right wrist firmly.

Assarac reached out and took the mirror. He turned it over in his hands. He showed it to Cangu beside him and Cangu extended a long finger and traced its intricate engraving. Assarac waited and then held up its polished surface. He stepped forward to Edra and held it in front of her face. She shrieked as she saw her reflection. Then Assarac took the mirror to Angarad. Angarad looked in it calmly. She freed her wrist from Henwin and looked into Assarac's face.

'It is the mirror,' she said, 'of the queen of the Dobuni, whom my lord defeated in battle. It is now properly the mirror of my lord's queen.'

Edra lost her temper again.

'Angarad is of the Dobuni herself,' she shouted. 'It was there my lord found her, when they made an alliance. But now the heads of the Dobuni are on the stakes of my lord's house. They are perhaps her brothers and cousins, the enemies of my lord. It was because my lord knew this that he gave me the mirror.'

'Be quiet,' Henwin said harshly. 'You are beautiful but you are stupid.'

'Not so much stupid as ignorant,' Assarac said firmly. 'It is of no consequence that there was once an alliance and there is now bloody enmity. These are the normal courses of the world.'

'I was given the mirror,' Edra said stubbornly.

Assarac lifted his staff, with his left hand. He raised his right arm and spread his fingers in the sign of judgement. Everyone was silent. Even Henwin listened attentively.

'The judgement is by the law,' Assarac announced. 'The mirror is the gift of Henwin to the adulteress. It will stay in her hands. But she fought with the queen, which is not her right, though it is the queen's right to strike her. For this serious offence, Edra will forfeit two of her own jewelled brooches or bracelets, to be chosen at will by our lady the queen.'

Edra opened her mouth to protest but thought better of it. Angarad turned angrily and walked back into the house. Seril quickly touching her father's hand, jumped up and followed her.

Edra looked down at her ruined tunic, which was badly torn at the shoulders. She hurried away to another house. Henwin stood facing Assarac and Cangu, and again laughed.

'You will make a song of this fierce battle, Cangu?'

'No, my lord.'

'You have better songs?'

'I have a song and a story of war in the east.'

'I will listen. Let them be good.'

All the kin now moved off. Karin, moving quietly, got out of their way. He was still dazed by all he had seen and been told. If he set out now, he could get back to Crucio to sleep, and in a way he wanted this: to get back to a life he knew and could understand. The long walk would settle his mind, in the quiet of the mountains. Yet he still wanted, very much, to see Seril again: to get her news and give news of her family. Calling Fan close and rubbing his rough head, he decided to wait through the feast and return the following morning.

Through the rest of the day the whole court was busy. On the open space, where Angarad and Edra had fought, the slaves of the household were sweeping the ground and setting up hearths with spits. The biggest hearth was in front of the king's house. Then the field slaves carried in firewood: kindling and branches and thick logs. Around the houses the slave girls were busy with preparations for dressing the ladies. Young warriors began to appear, in their brightly-coloured feast cloaks and with their hair carefully dressed. A few of the warriors had straight fair or reddish hair but most, Karan saw, had hair that had been brown and curling before the setting. It was now closely limed, into spikes, and each spike had been bleached and coloured, in yellow or red. All the warriors were clean-shaven except for their heavy moustaches, which came down on each side of the mouth. There were streaks of blue paint from their cheekbones. Decorated swords and daggers hung at their belts.

Karin found the shepherd who had been before him at the gatehouse. They began talking about their own places. The shepherd was from High Buck beyond Hawkstone, where Karin had never been. It was the place, the shepherd said, of the Stone of Karan, but Karin was only puzzled by the echo of the name. They then talked, steadily, about sheep and cattle, and about the different kinds of grazing. The lords, they agreed, smiling, knew nothing of all this, though some were good judges of hides and meat. Yet it was still a fine sight, the shepherd said eagerly, when they dressed for battle, on their horses, and when they talked and sang as if their whole lives were above the earth, and as if their very blood were strong drink.

'You saw those ladies fighting?'

'No,' the shepherd said. 'Do their ladies fight too?'

'Like dogs,' Karin said.

'I wish I had seen it. I could have told the story in High Buck.'

The sun was low now, above the western hills. There was a busy carrying of meat and jars and bowls from where the animals had been butchered and the other food and drink prepared. As the sun was setting a long horn was sounded. Karin and the shepherd got up and moved to where they could see the feastground. The fires were now burning strongly, with the slaves over the spits where the heifers and sheep and pigs were being roasted. Henwin, with Angarad on his arm, came out to the main hearth, where they sat on a spread of hay. Angarad, Karan saw, now wore a long red and blue tunic, with beads and bells strung on it. Her blue spot of rank had been freshly painted on her forehead. Edra the adulteress, in a blue and yellow tunic, her hair shining with beads in the firelight, sat a little way from them.

The horn sounded again. Henwin raised his hand and Edra stood and walked to the hearth. Two young men sounded drums and danced, facing Henwin. He shouted and clapped his hands. The drummers came to the hearth and beat a different rhythm. Edra slipped back to her place and two young warriors ran out, holding their long swords. They danced facing each other, thrusting their swords, at first slowly but then, as the drumming quickened, fast and shouting wildly as the swords darted. The dance ended as their swords clashed, high above their heads.

There were shouts and applause from the whole company, which now covered the feast ground. Beyond the kin at the hearths nearest Henwin there were other large hearths for the freemen and farmers. The slaves, other than those who were attending the hearths, stood in a body beyond them, watching the bright feast.

The bard Cangu now came forward to the king's hearth. The company went silent. Cangu touched his lyre and sang.

'Henwin over Hsabren,
Bright the harness,
Helmet and breastplate,
Henwin in battle.

Briars and brushwood
Brimming the highland,
Hailstorm of bowmen,
Hard the handwar.

Harsh the trumpet,
Horsemen breaking,
Battlecry of Henwin
Brave in his breeding.

Bold the red brothers
Hailing Henwin,
Bitter the battle
Before Henwin breaks them.

Henwin over Hsabren,
Bloody the harness,
Heads on the bridle,
Bright harvest.

Brave from Hsabren,
Bread of Henwin,
Heritage and household,
Harvest of battle.'

There was silence as Cangu bowed to the king. Henwin waited
and then stretched out his arm. Cangu went forward, Henwin rose
and embraced him. The company shouted their approval.

The attendant slaves now began serving the feast. There was ale
and fresh bread. The watching slaves looked at the bread in wonder.
They had never eaten it but could imagine the taste from its smell of
warm harvest. And now the roasted meat was being carved. At the
principal hearth the first and finest joint was carried to Henwin. He
lifted it to his mouth and bit into it, then smiled and raised his hand.
Other joints were now cut and brought in turn to Henwin. As each
was presented he pointed in turn at the warriors sitting nearest to
him, who were watching anxiously. The order in which the joints

were given was the mark of honours in battle. Soon, all over the feastground, the whole company was eating and drinking, and there was loud laughter and shouting. The moon rose, in the clear sky above the Grib and White Cap, which the lords now called Pencalc.

There were outer fires where the meat and other food had been prepared. The slave women were preparing a meal for themselves and their own men, but this must wait for the end of the feast. As the bread was eaten and the joints bitten down, and as the ale went round again, it was the time of the story. Cangu was already preparing himself. It was much harder, this time, to get silence. Finally Henwin himself had to get up and shout. He stumbled as he sat again, close between Angarad and Edra.

Cangu stood at the hearth. He had no lyre. He pitched his voice differently: loud and deep. He raised his right arm.

'There are many wars. This war that I tell of is a war of strangers, against those who are even more strange. It is a war and a victory, of the new Gallish kings of the White Land.'

He paused, compelling attention.

'It is a truth,' he called, as if in a challenge.

Nobody spoke or moved.

'A lie breaks the cauldron. A truth mends it. My story is a truth.'

He waited again.

'I tell the truth of this war. There came a strange people from beyond the waves of the sea. The strangers are small men and dark. They resemble our slaves. They rub their bodies with oil and they scrape dirt and oil from their skins. They do not fight like men, in the challenges of battle. They are herded like animals, into tight companies. They carry spades and axes as well as swords and shields. They dig as much as they fight. Their name is Romani.'

Cangu stopped, his arm raised, and looked eagerly around.

'You have not heard, my lord, of these strangers. It is known that they come from beyond the grey sea. They come also from beyond the high snowy mountains, far in the southlands. They have conquered many weak peoples.'

Cangu stopped again. Henwin, lifting his cup, shouted a question.

'What name did you give them?'

'Romani, my lord.'

Henwin laughed.

'Is it a truth?' Cangu called.

There was no answer.

'It is a truth,' Cangu continued. 'Their name is Romani, and they are as I have told you. Their king is a bald man named Julion, whom they call Caesar. Yet he is less their king than their herdsman, driving them together. He does not fight like a true king or warrior. He commands no chariot. He makes no challenges. He marches like a coward behind his herds.'

'Then it is a lie to call him a king,' Henwin shouted.

'It is a truth,' Cangu answered, pointing at the cauldron beside the king's hearth.

There was a silence while everyone waited and watched.

'It is a truth,' Cangu cried exultantly. 'It is the truth of the king of the Romani.'

Henwin laughed and drank.

'The bald Julion,' Cangu continued, 'was in Gallia, where he had bribed their kings and their warriors with gold. But then men of the Pretani, from the White Land in the east, came among them and said: "Are you slaves, you Galli, to take gold to submit to these animals? If you were of our blood you would put them all to the sword." The bald Julion heard of this, and raged against the Pretani. He swore at once that he would cross the sea, with his herds and his gold, and see what these boasting Pretani were made of.'

Beside Henwin, in the light from the torches, the adulteress Edra, who was not listening to the story, had lifted the bronze mirror and was peering in it at her hair. Angarad, seeing this, reached angrily across to strike her but Henwin intervened, holding Angarad's wrist and with his other hand pushing the mirror away and slapping Edra's face.

'The herds were packed into ships,' Cangu cried. 'In other ships they put their horses, but the wind took these and they were blown back where they came. The herds of footmen landed, sick and trembling, and the king of the Pretani in that part of the island awaited and fell on them. Yet there could be no true war. The kings and warriors in their chariots stood out and challenged the herds, but none was brave enough to answer. The kings returned to their camps but then, without shame, the herds were driven forward, and they killed or burned all that stood in their way. When they heard of these base actions, against all the laws of war, the kings gathered their horsemen and charged the cowardly herds. They bruised and killed many, but still the oily cowards fell back to their ships. The bald Julion, terrified, turned his back and fled over the sea.'

Henwin clapped his hands and shouted.

'What did you call these cowards, Cangu?'

'Romani, my lord.'

'It is a new name for sheep,' Henwin shouted.

The whole company laughed.

Cangu again raised his arm.

'It is not the end of the story, my lord.'

'There is more about these sheep?'

'A year passed,' Cangu continued. 'It came to the year of our last harvest. The bald Julion came again, with many more herds. The sea was dark with eight hundred ships, and the black herds were packed into them. And in treachery. Mandibrac, a son of the Pretani, had fled to Julion. He promised to lead him in the island by secret ways. The Pretani gathered against them, and Casvelaun was elected High King. The herds were driven forward as before killing and burning, until they came to a great river. They could not cross it, but Julion had bribed warriors of the Galli, who swam the river and took Casvelaun by surprise. Then treachery spread. The Trinovanti, the Segonti, the Bibroci, the Cenimani had quarrels with Casvelaun. In return for gold, they promised Julion to betray the stronghold where Casvelaun waited with his warriors. And through the whole land the herds of Romani had been burning the harvest. Casvelaun and his people were without food. Casvelaun sat down with his wise men around him. He decided to send messengers to ask for peace.'

Henwin jumped up.

'He is old, this Casvelaun?'

'He is old my lord, but he is a great king.'

'He is no king to ask animals for peace.'

'He sent the messengers, my lord. The bald Julion came out from his herds and agreed to a peace. The Pretani must pay tribute, of hides and slaves, and give hostages to return with Julion to Gallia.'

'This is a bad story, Cangu.'

'It is a truth,' Cangu cried, and again pointed to the cauldron.

Henwin raised his arm.

'They are weaklings, your Casvelaun and these Gallish kings of the White Land. How could a true king submit to these herds?'

'It was the hunger, my lord.'

'Then why did they not feed on the bodies of their enemies?'

As Henwin shouted he lifted his sword. The painted warriors at their hearths stood and raised their swords and shouted with him. Cangu stood still, with raised arm.

'It is still not the end of the story, my lord. Casvelaun made the peace, but in secret he ordered his warriors to ride and attack the ships of the Romani, where they were beached by the grey sea. When the Romani saw that their ships were being attacked, and that many were being burned, they drew back and hurried to return to Gallia. The bald Julion again turned his back. Casvelaun took command and gave orders that none of the tribute should be paid. Across the rough sea the Romani reached Gallia, where now in turn the Galli rose against them. There were many fierce battles, yet it is now known from Gallia that the coward Julion has taken his herds and marched back to the south far away from our shores. It is believed in Gallia that he will not again dare to challenge the bravery of the Pretani. Even one of his own bards has sung memorably, that he had turned in terror from those he had come to attack.'

Henwin was silent, rubbing his mouth with his hand.

'Eight hundred ships,' he said. 'Is that a lie?'

'It is a truth, my lord.'

'They breed many, these herds.'

'They breed and bribe, my lord, these Romani. But they are now gone away to the southlands.'

'We shall not hear of them again?'

'We shall not hear of them again.'

Henwin was silent for some time. Then he stood and bowed his head to Cangu. Cangu, accepting the sign, bowed low in front of him. The company began to stir around the hearths.

'Is it a truth?' Cangu called, in the last act of the ceremony.

'It is a truth,' came the answer, in hundreds of voices.

Cangu moved away and sat at his hearth.

All around the darkened feastground, with the fires lowering, the company was now dispersing. Karin, standing with the slaves who had been listening to the story, turned and walked to the place where they could now get their food. He got a neck end of sheepmeat, and a legbone for the wolfhound. He found a place below the rampart where he could lie down and sleep. Fan followed and lay by his head.

The moon was now high in the clear sky, and the night air was cold. On the hard ground Karin slept uneasily, often waking. Whenever he woke, with the warmth of Fan at his head, the strange acts and words of the lords turned and sounded in his mind.

———————◆———————

G lyn had reached the high ground of Tal-y-Cefn. To the southeast, with Orion rising beyond it, was the hump and long spine
of the Skirrid, its dark body a sleeping animal. Much closer, to the
south, Waun Fach swelled above the reservoir. Beyond it, seeming
higher but by measurement just lower, was the fine prominence –
the shieldboss of old Bron Cateir, now Pen y Cadair Fawr.

'Taid! Taid!'

The shouting seemed hopeless on this desolate height. He looked
back north. Below the wall of the scarp were the roadlights of
Talgarth. Above them somewhere in shadow lay the earthworks of
an old British camp, perhaps a court. The *llys*, it might be, where
Cangu had sung.

The oldest traces – the arrowheads, the dolmens, the hut circles
and the earthbanks – had been wholly material, in a country open to
the spade. But some traces had now for the first time been written, in
the marks of reed on papyrus and of chisel on stone. After ten
thousand generations of conscious life and memory, these written
traces, by convention, would be called the beginning of history: the
true, because recorded, story of the land.

Actual stories are told by both winners and losers. Yet what
becomes history is a selection by the winners. This is trustingly read
back into earlier times.

Thus when Britons encounter Romans in the history, there
is conquest and then an imperium. The island becomes Roman
Britain. The story told by Cangu, in the Black Mountain court of
Henwin, is seen at best as local bragging, in a parochial rhetoric.
The solid universals of empire, and of imperial history, at once
override it.

Yet what Cangu reported would have been firmly believed, for at least the next eighty years, by his own people. There were many reasons for believing him, and few against. For indeed the Romans had invaded with mixed fortunes, in successive years, and then through a very long lifetime had not repeated the attempt. If this British story differed from that written elsewhere by Caesar, who had commanded the invasions, that could be easily understood. Had not Caesar to explain and excuse his frustration and withdrawal? The loud resonance and authority of Caesar and of empire were a product of much later events.

Certainly the British account would have been wholly believed in the west and north of the island, where there had been no direct contact with these early Roman invaders. In the southeast it could have been different, for before the invasion these later-arrived Britons were already trading with the Romans in Gaul. They were also fighting them, in a complex of tribal alliances and rivalries across the narrow sea channel. After Caesar's invasion, still within their alliances and rivalries, and driven by endless disputes about frontiers and succession, they had come to accept, some willingly, some temporarily – relations of tribute and embassy under a Roman overlordship. Alien as these Gallish kings were to the longer-settled rulers of the west and the north, they could still have seen the Romans as no more than a factor, however powerful, in their own local ambitions and disputes.

Indeed, when the next invasion came, after a gap of eighty-nine years – an invasion that was eventually to settle into occupation and empire – it had been directly provoked by the appeal of one of their number, Verica of the Atrebati, who asked for Roman assistance against the pressure of the neighbouring and expanding Catevallauni, under Cinbelaun and his sons Togodominos and Caradoc. But what could be seen as a temporary intervention by a convenient ally became, on Roman terms, a general occupation and domination. This left the contending kings and lords with only one choice: to submit and serve under a Roman title, or to be hunted down and destroyed.

It was a very strange meeting between these Britons and these Romans. Within the universals of an imperial history it is a relatively simple encounter of victory and defeat between two unequal warlike peoples. Yet war has many meanings, and in no case more clearly than this. For while it is obvious that the Britons were exceptionally warlike, still their understanding of war, of its methods and purposes, was radically different from that of the Romans. A fighting aristocracy, with its own code of combat, found itself opposed by the organised militarism of a quite different social order: warriors against an army. This is why Cangu could speak, fairly, of the cowardice of the Roman commanders. For indeed they refused the ethic of single combat and of the occasional battle or raid, choosing rather the organisation and engineering of a directed and occupying army. Within the same difference of perspective, the Romans could see the Britons as brave and reckless, but also braggart, volatile and unstable: never lacking in courage but always deficient in military stability and persistence. Thus the whole purpose and method of the fighting, in those early years, would have been differently seen on each side. And in the eventual reckoning of the victors this would continue to be misunderstood.

Again, within what was to become the universal account, deeply embedded in any language that can be used to describe it, the diverse and fiercely contending peoples of Britain were generalised as the Britons. Imperial description and allocation overrode more particular and more honoured tribal names. Moreover the majority of the inhabitants of the island were the descendants of much earlier, pre-British peoples, who had been conquered by the contending warlike groups who had given the island a new name. By the nature of the order imposed on them, this majority of the people did not bear arms. War, in the British order, was reserved to the lords: to the kings and their kin; to those who ruled the people. The whole island had the new name of Prydein, replacing the old Albion or White Land. But while the lords in its many regions spoke a more or less common language, the social identities that mattered were still those of their own places and tribes. The people of another lord in another place might be allies or enemies but were in any case other, known by a different and not by a common name. This diversity and mutual rivalry both influenced and directed the outcome of a war against an invading order which had developed a common and even a universal name.

The account of the victors changed this condition, but retrospectively. The divisions and rivalries of what the Romans called the Britons were as carefully recorded as they were practically exploited. But as the imperial order settled the generalisations overrode them. All were now Britons, whether lords or subjects, in this place or in that. A further generalisation later offered to confirm this. What the lords and their kin spoke became known, eventually, as one of the Celtic languages, though this common name of Celt was from a people of the south, on the coast of the Mediterranean. What was more immediately evident was a general community of art and lifestyles: now in scattered material traces and records. And then beyond these indications there could be a larger projection: of peoples related in these ways who had fought and conquered over a large part of what the Romans, extending the name from a region of Greece, were later to call Europe. Thus the Celts, universalised, were known to the Romans as having sacked Rome itself, invaded and colonised the Balkans, commanded Central Europe and Gaul, and settled in Ireland and in Britain. Within this Roman perspective, also within any universal perspective inspired by a Roman version of order, the Celts could be projected as an earlier though inferior kind of Romans, their empire as a sketch for this greater empire, commanding a continent. Yet this was never how they had seen it themselves, as they pursued their separate invasions and enterprises. The ideas of a central identity and of a central order were not theirs but Roman.

Glyn stopped and closed his eyes. It was only long after their defeats and subjections, and within the different forms which they used to survive them, that such a version of their identity and their history could begin to make its way among the British. Not in stories like that of Cangu, celebrating a resistance which had given a lifetime of freedom from Roman invasion, but in legendary reconstructions, which would give what their rulers now craved – a Roman history, a Roman style of a dominant identity which they had never had but which they could now believe they had lost.

Now? Then? In the persistence of these mountains and their families it was difficult to mark periods. It was more than five thousand years back to the first shepherds: an almost inconceivable time. Twenty-five thousand back to the first human hunters. A counting, an accounting: foreshortened now by a modern scheme of dates which neither the British nor their Roman conquerors knew. A failed or aborted Roman invasion in 55 BC or 699 AUC: *anno urbis conditae*; a numbering from the supposed foundation of

Rome. There would be also some unknown date of British reckoning, itself superimposed on the long counting of years and moons by the shepherds. It would be perhaps the fifteenth cycle, each cycle of thirty years, in the sung lineage and inheritance of the western lords of the island. Or again the two hundredth cycle of that long-observed sequence of the shifts of moonrise and moonset, each repeating sequence of about nineteen years: a reckoning and re-reckoning of time within the bearings of changing cultures: all foreshortened until the much later discovery of solid traces in the earth.

'Taid! Taid!'

The Fisher Kings

◆

To Henwin and his neighbouring kings in the mountains the threat always came from the east, and especially from the Dobuni, the powerful people of the Yellow Hills across the seariver, the Hsabren. For they had repeatedly raided west of the great river, and with their allies pushed beyond the Bald Hills to the northern bank of the Guuy. The upper valley of the Guuy then lay open to them, encircling the Black Mountain kingdoms. Facing these pressures, Henwin and his father before him had made alliance with those who had in the past been their enemies: the kingdoms along the estuary of Hsabren, now united for war as the Fisher Kings, the Siluri. Without the Silurian alliance, the Black Mountain peoples were too few and too small to resist the long pressure from the east.

In the late years of Henwin there was a run of decisive victories, soon sealed by new alliances and by marriages. These took the territory of the Silurian federation north of the Guuy and beyond the Bald Hills to the broad Hsabren itself. Under the powerful Fisher Kings this became a defensible frontier.

Henwin died after ruling for seventeen years. His son Peroduron by Angarad succeeded him. Peroduron ruled for only seven years; he was killed in battle with the Dobuni along the Hsabren. He had no sons and was succeeded first by his wife Gueness and on her death by their daughter Cardil, who gained fame as a powerful queen. She strengthened the Silurian alliance by marrying Mereauc, younger son of Redaunos, the most powerful of the Fisher Kings. Madrun, one of the poorest kingdoms of the Silurian federation, especially by comparison with the rich and populous kingdoms of the better lands along the estuary, grew in prosperity under Cardil and gained its long reputation as the Land of the Mountains of the Queens.

Yet Cardil was not immediately succeeded by her own daughter but by her son, another Peroduron, an exceptional warrior, who in a further period of fierce fighting with the Dobuni was for some years War King of the northern Siluri. In his last years as king he gained further influence through the marriage of his daughter Andrecca to Vertougos, King of the Ordovici, a powerful people of the hills north and west of the Silurian federation. His son Berauc succeeded him, and there was then again a succession of queens: Berauc's widow Cera and then their daughter Edra. It was while Edra was queen, in a time remembered as very prosperous, with big herds of cattle in the rich meadows along the Guuy, and good flocks of sheep on the lower hills, that news came that the Romans were again invading the island. They had come in great numbers and had already gained many victories.

The High Council of the Siluri met at Iupania on the seariver. Envoys were sent east to discover the course of the new war. The news brought back was grave. For it was established that Verica, the elderly King of the Atrebati of the plain, had travelled to Rome itself to ask for a Roman army to help him against the Catevallauni. The Prince Togodominos was already killed in battle and the Prince Caradoc had been defeated. A lord of the Atrebati – his name was still uncertain – had made formal peace and was claiming the title of Legate of the Emperor of Rome, offering to negotiate a similar peace with the other peoples of the island. By the end of the summer this traitor, now identified as Cogidon, had persuaded Bodvic, King of the Dobuni, to enter the Roman peace. A great danger was then obvious: that the Roman army, when it had finished its campaigns in the east, would have direct and peaceful passage through the lands of the Atrebati and the Dobuni to the very borders of the Siluri.

It was still not known whether the Romani indeed intended to march west, into difficult mountainous country, but there was immediate organisation for war. In fact nothing happened until the following spring, when an envoy arrived from Cogidon with terms for a peace. By unanimous decision of the council the envoy was killed. His severed head was carried by a raiding party across the river Hsabren and left on a stake on a hill overlooking Magalonium, the court of the traitor Bodvic. His slave was bound to the stake, with a message of defiance.

Through the early summer there was more serious news. A Roman legion, as it was now known the herds were called, had marched west, south of the estuary and was successfully attacking the strongholds of the Dorutrigi. Much more became known of their barbarous methods of fighting, for they refused all challenges and princely combats, demanding only surrender, and fought only as a herd, with powerful machines of assault.

In the late summer, with the Dorutrigi defeated, Caradoc of the Catevallauni made his way west with some of his warriors. He had put on a disguise to pass through the Yellow Hills of the Dobuni, where there had been an unsuccessful revolt by a nephew of Bodvic. The defeated rebels of the Dobuni joined Caradoc and his warriors and came to the Council of the Siluri at Iupania.

Caradoc, with experience of fighting the Romani, now proposed to the Siluri that he should command their army when the legions marched west to the Hsabren. His proposal was rejected. The Siluri would command themselves. But they argued long about how this barbarous herd should be fought and defeated. Never fully re-solved, this uncertainty determined the strategies and fortunes of the next thirty years.

The younger warriors, impressed by what Caradoc had told them and by reports of the defeats of the Dorutrigi, argued strongly for adapting to the new methods of fighting. It was useless to fortify their strongholds and wait for the legions to assault them. It was even more useless, when the herds came, to meet them in the customs of the old wars, with high and jealous warriors facing each other with proud challenges and accounts of lineage and prowess, and with trumpets and plumes and the charges of horsemen and chariots. To fight these legions, so deaf to the laws of military honour, new tactics of battle must be found.

The older kings objected. Victory would be no victory, honour in battle no honour, if the laws and traditions of war were set aside. Yet it was soon clear that the younger men would prevail. The next stage was more difficult: a deep division of opinion about what these new tactics might be.

Caradoc, from the beginning, had a simple proposal. All the warriors of the Siluri should move out from their courts and strongholds and become a large single army. Their commander would then choose his ground, with strong natural defences away from inhabited settlements, and draw the Romani into a killing ground. Only so great a concentration of warriors, taking full advantage of the difficult country, which they knew well and the Romani did not, could defeat and destroy a legion. It was at once objected by the older kings and nobles that this would mean maintaining a large and indiscriminate army, perhaps for many years. This was against all the customs of both peace and war. Moreover the command of such an army, which it was evident Caradoc was proposing for himself, raised difficult political questions.

As the argument continued there was important support for Caradoc from the order of the Druida, who were alarmed by the exceptional hostility of the Romani to their sacred customs and beliefs. In the lands already conquered the order had been ruthlessly suppressed, with unspeakable blasphemies against its religious dignities. A devout people was being trodden and corrupted by foreign heathens and blasphemers. The kingdom of the Romani would be a pit of eternal slavery, heathenism and barbarism. All the free peoples of the west must unite to resist it, under the High Prince Caradoc, who alone had experience of such war.

There was objection to Caradoc's plan by the younger warriors and especially by those from the small mountain kingdoms. It was wrong, they insisted, to fight a herd by becoming a herd. It reduced battle to the driving of cattle between the fires of Belitan. They pointed to the Dorutrigi, where great strongholds were overrun and their inhabitants massacred. Yet always behind that slaughtering herd, over the marches of many days, there were single tracks: the old British routes which the Romani were widening and straightening but which still, along most of their extending length, were in the depths of forest. Clearly they should attack the Romani while they were strung out, two by two, along these dark forest roads. Places of ambush would be chosen, for sudden assault, and the warriors would regroup in the woods to strike at will, again and again.

There was great interest in this plan but also, from the older kings and from Caradoc himself, deeply shocked objection. It was true that the Romani had abandoned the customs of honourable war. But to go even further, to lurk like hunting animals in the forest, to spring out without challenge on an enemy, was to forsake all manly

decency. What would be said or even sung of a warrior who instead
of challenging his enemy to open combat and the trial of arms could
boast only that he had sprung from a tree and stabbed some
sweating legionary in the back? It would be a war of animals or at
best slaves: the low and furtive fighting of thieves and cut-throats. It
was not to be thought of. Even honourable defeat would be
preferable.

Yet while silenced in the council this party held to its opinion. In
Madrun the idea was especially strong, and was encouraged by
Queen Edra. As the months passed, and there was still no Roman
attack – it was reported by messengers that the legions were no
longer advancing west but were fighting north and east – they went
on discussing the new tactic. But as they thought it through something unexpected began to happen. If there was to be fighting of this
kind from the forest they could use men who had never hitherto
been seen as a resource for war. The old wars, before the Romani,
had been the exclusive affair of the nobles and, for supplies, the
freemen. The unfree were directly forbidden to bear arms. Yet look
at these unfree, though it was at first shocking even to think of it.
They had the weapons for such fighting: hunting bows and knives.
From the distant past, before the ancestors of the lords had brought
the honourable new order, the men of these mountains had been
bowmen. Against a barbarian and slaughtering enemy should such
men be left at home with their cattle when they could instead be
killing Romani?

The case was well argued, but the shift of thinking was too great
to come quickly. The Druida of Madrun, after consulting with his
order, directly forebade it. To give arms to the unfree would be an
offence against the gods. Some of the nobles supported him with
their own arguments. To encourage slaves to fight would put the
whole social order in jeopardy. In the end only Edra herself, among
the ruling family, continued to support the idea. She did not doubt,
she asserted, the loyalty of all her people, free and unfree. And was it
not the secret of the Roman victories, and of their empire, that
around a core of their own warriors they enlisted all who could bear
arms? They had taken such men from all the conquered peoples and
marched them on to conquer, in turn, the next and the next. It was
this endless absorption, this steady building of an empire, that had
now to be faced. This was not the temporary ambition of some

proud king. It was the making of whole peoples into armies who would then subdue each other.

'And when this great herd marches westward,' Edra cried, 'into our own dear lands, can it be defeated by men who will not have other men standing beside them, fighting to defend our own place, our own lives, our own children and women?'

Meanwhile the more general debate among the Siluri continued. The Roman army was still conquering and reordering the lowlands to the east and south. They had been seen across the Hsabren, among the collaborating Dobuni, but not in significant numbers. Yet the forts they were building were at only three days' march. In a new council at Iupania, Caradoc, with the support of the Ordovici from the north, now gained the ascendancy. War parties were gathered, under his general command, along the western banks of the Hsabren. At dawn on the sixth day of the moon after Belitan the warriors, led by the cavalry, crossed the river and rode east. A quick, fierce battle followed, of the old kind. They struck deep into the lands of the Dobuni, burning their settlements and killing male kin and Roman detachments among them. They took heads in triumph, sparing only a few older men as prisoners, to be whipped back across the Hsabren and questioned for news. The success of the attack was applauded everywhere, and the prestige of Caradoc was high.

Yet even as they were rejoicing the Romani, who had been taken by surprise, were quickly reorganising under the command of Ostorius Scapula. With the legions still at a distance, he assembled auxiliaries – Gauls and Thracians and Iberians – and marched them west towards the Hsabren.

Now for the first time there was a Roman fort on the east bank of the great river. It was built and reinforced through that summer, and patrols began crossing, not as raiders but to reconnoitre the country of this dangerous enemy. By the end of the summer a legion, the Twentieth, had arrived at the fort and was poised to strike west.

In the following summer detachments of this Twentieth Legion and auxiliary units, mainly cavalry, began crossing the Hsabren, seeking lines of attack. There was again dispute at the Council of Siluri, on ways of responding to this pressure from the legion. Indeed the council was still in session when news came that between the Hsabren and the Guuy west of the Bald Hills there had been heavy Roman attacks which had overrun and burned several strongholds. Warriors were at once sent north, but beyond the Guuy found the Romans already withdrawn. At the resumed council a bitter argument followed, and led to a split in the federation. Caradoc, aware of the great danger if the Romans reached the broad valley of the Guuy, with its route into much of the Silurian heartland, wanted an army assembled to march north, to choose a place for that pitched battle – still his dream – into which the enemy legion could be drawn. Several kings supported him and committed their warriors, but others refused. Caradoc, with several hundred of the Silurian warriors, then marched north to the Ordovici, who had always supported this strategy.

There was then again a pause. The Roman pressure seemed to relax, though there were disturbing reports of a new kind of threat from the south. Across the wide estuary the Romani were building harbours and signal stations, and their ships were now often seen in the channel. As in the attack on the Dorutrigi, a combined invasion, by land and sea, could begin once the harbours were completed. The coastal kingdoms began preparing seaward defences, but still the main thrust of Roman pressure was to the north, beyond the Ordovici to the Deganwi, and there were constant appeals from the Druida for a unified defence against the invading barbarians. Yet those of the Siluri who had not committed their warriors to Caradoc stayed where they were, keeping regular watch along the estuary, and along the Hsabren and Guuy.

In the next summer the heaviest blow fell. Caradoc, faithful to his idea, had assembled a great force on a plateau above a steep scarp, over a tributary of the upper Hsabren. He had spoken movingly of a day of final battle, which would decide forever between freedom and slavery. He recalled the defeat of Caesar, and the many honours of the war kings. His warriors swore by the signs of their own kingdoms to fight to the end. Yet in one single black day the battle was lost. Many Romani were killed, but Caradoc's army was broken and he was a fugitive. The Silurian warriors, returning with many losses to their kingdoms, were shocked and bitter, and those who had always opposed Caradoc considered themselves vindicated. The pitched battle, obviously, was the wrong way to fight.

The bitterness was even greater in the following year, when it was

learned that Caradoc had been betrayed to the Romans by Carti-
mandua, Queen of the Briganti, and was to be taken in triumph to
Rome. Even worse, the Romani were now calling him King of the
Britons, whose defeat meant the end of all effective resistance. Stung
by this lie, the Siluri regrouped and attacked across the Hsabren
well south of the legionary fortress. They destroyed several Roman
outposts and pacified settlements of the Dobuni. They took many
Roman prisoners and made a point of humiliating them, sending
them round the kingdoms to be publicly whipped and abused, as
animals whose boasted powers were a fraud. Invigorated by their
successes, they attacked again to the north of the fortress, from a
base in the Bald Hills. Again they burned many settlements of
the collaborators and overcame small Roman detachments and
working parties.

Among their prisoners, on this raid, they took a rich Gaul who
had become a Roman citizen, Aulicus. He could speak their
language. He was taken to Iupania to face the new High King
of the Siluri, Magimarus, who had led the first attack across the
Hsabren. Offering a large quantity of coins that he was carrying, as
a ransom for his freedom, Aulicus explained that he had been
granted a concession to mine silver and lead in the hills of the
Mendipi, south of the estuary. He had been returning to this
operation, from the site of another possible concession for a silver
mine among the Ordovici, when he had so unexpectedly been
captured.

Magimarus took the bag of coins which Aulicus held out to him.
He reached in for some of the coins, which he examined closely.
They bore both British and Roman names. He then ordered the
guards to bring Aulicus to the small lake which had been enlarged
from the stream that ran beside the court. Drawing his long sword,
with its bright red enamelled hilt, he raised his arm and shouted:
'Death to these animals and honour to the Gods!' He then threw the
coins into the lake and, turning, put the point of his sword to
Aulicus' stomach.

'You are a man of our language,' he said, fiercely, 'yet you have
come with these herds to pillage our lands. You are worse even than
the Romans, who in their own ways know how to fight. You are the
scavenger of carrion, and you now offer me the corruption of silver.
You live as if honourable princes, or any man or woman, might be

bought or sold. But we have no use for your trifling faces, your coins. We do not use them. We live only by the fruits of our land. Thus, for the disgrace you are, and for the disgrace you offer, you have deserved death. Tell me why you should not die.'

Aulicus was pale and sweating.

'Great Prince,' he replied, 'I am a man of peace and of peaceable trade. I am no part of your wars or your enemies. I have no enemies.'

'And that is your disgrace,' Magimarus said, angrily. 'You will not even fight for your wealth. You drag it like a rat from the corpses of brave men.'

Aulicus looked around. He seemed to read his fate in the hard faces of the warriors pressing close to him.

'I have heard of you Siluri,' he said, in a different tone. 'I have heard Commander Ostorius speak of your barbarism and cruelty.'

Magimarus smiled.

'I have heard Ostorius swear,' Aulicus continued, defiantly, 'that for your cruelty and your insolence the very name of the Siluri will be completely wiped out, as happened to the Sugambri, who with the same cruelty and insolence thought they could defy the Roman power.'

'Ostorius said that?' Magimarus asked, smiling.

'Yes, I have given you his actual words.'

Magimarus laughed and turned to his warriors.

'The actual words of Ostorius! The words of that little oyster! Oyster Ostorius! Ostorius Scapula, the Little Bone!'

All the warriors laughed. Magimarus looked around and smiled with them.

'Ostorius Scapula,' he said quietly, 'will die with the name of the Siluri in his heart. For we are the Fisher Kings. We know how to deal with this oyster.'

Aulicus, with the point of the sword at his stomach, took a small step back. At this movement Magimarus, the blood rising in his face, lifted his sword and slashed Aulicus on the neck, below his left ear. Aulicus fell, his blood gushing from his wound.

'As we now deal also with you,' Magimarus shouted, and slashed again. In the second heavy stroke the head was severed from the body. The warriors shouted their approval.

Magimarus lifted his stained sword. There was silence.

'Let the dogs have him,' he shouted. 'We have men's work to do.

After this boast of Ostorius, that he will wipe out our name, there is not a man in our kingdoms who will not fight to death and beyond death. So let it be shouted everywhere, until it breaks Ostorius: *Siluri! Siluri!*'

The warriors of all the kingdoms joined in the shout of the name.

The Battle of Claerion

Taroc woke to the early sun. Pushing back the red fleece which had covered his legs and stomach he rolled from his night shelter under the jutting rock. The flock was already grazing along the ridge. The dogs were still asleep but opened their eyes and watched him as he moved. He stretched and looked out towards the sunrise. It was on the shoulder of Bol Lugu, which the old people said marked the time of the Long House. Yet there would be no gathering today. The great fire of the burning of Caeriddon, by the new enemies that the lords called Romani, had died down only yesterday. Mecan, along the ridge, had seen a troop of the warriors of Caeriddon, some wounded, riding south, defeated. There had been orders from Clutacos that all the shepherds were to look out for the enemies, to see which way they were marching from the embers of Caeriddon.

Taroc had heard of the battles with both fear and doubt. It was said that the lords would defeat the new enemies, but since spring all that had been reported from across the river Guuy was killing and burning. The fall of Caeriddon, the biggest stronghold north of the Guuy, had now brought this much nearer. Yet the new enemies, it was said by his own people escaping from them when their lords had been killed, did not want the mountains and the uplands. They moved only through the forests of the valleys and at certain places built forts of earthbanks and timber. In the mountains, with luck, the flocks and their shepherds would be left undisturbed.

Yet there was still the order from Clutacos. Looking over the flock, letting his eyes rest in turn on each animal until he was sure that all were well, Taroc walked north over the short springy grass until he could look down over the great forested valley of the Guuy. It was peaceful under the sun. It was as if no man had ever entered to disturb it. Yet along the north and east banks there was an old long track, running from the lake and Madrun as far east as Caeriddon and then on to the Bald Hills. There was no sign of it from above, though it was easy to trace the river in its shining straights and in the second great curve where it turned towards Caeriddon. Thinking of the place he seemed still to see the fire: the high rising cloud of smoke that had at first been black, then grey, then on the second day white and at last a thin blue. He looked again in its direction, on its low hill beyond the Guuy. There was nothing, and it was as if there had never been anything.

He squatted, looking down over the near valley. The steers which had been on Claerion, the low hill just over the river which had been cleared as pasture for Clutacos, were not in sight now. They had been there yesterday, for he had stood and tried to count them, though the lively beasts kept moving and made reckoning difficult. They must have been moved overnight, though he could see no reason for that. Still staring at the pasture, for it was wrong to leave good grass with no beasts to graze it, he saw movement at its northern edge, where the trees thickened as the slope dropped away. It was a horseman, riding into the empty pasture, and then another and suddenly, putting their horses to the gallop, many others. In the still air he heard a distant high shout. The horsemen were spreading out over the low hill, gesturing and calling to each other. Taroc, frowning, settled to watch.

They were large horses: much bigger than the Black Mountain ponies. They looked black or dark brown, though there was one big grey. There was a flash of reflected sunlight from the man sitting astride it. It did not look like a troop of the lords, unless perhaps they were strange lords from Caeriddon or the east. Yet who they might be he could not tell. They were not riding beyond the hill but looking around it. Some had already dismounted. As they settled Taroc counted them. He made the number forty and three. He looked back at the flock, still quietly grazing. He whistled up his dogs but did nothing when they came.

Again there were flashes of sunlight on metal. This was an armed troop. But they seemed only to be inspecting the pasture. After some time he saw three of them walking down towards the river skirting the steep forested bank in his direct line of sight. He lost his view of them for a time, but then saw them coming back up. Across the hill two others were walking with steady paces as if measuring. He again heard distant shouts.

Taroc walked back to his flock. He went in among them, with the dogs following, but from time to time looked back to see if the horsemen were still there. He knew the question which he ought to be asking: whether these were what the lords called the new enemies. Yet he did not want to put it, and especially to have to answer it. The world of all those names, of Siluri and Romani and of changing kings and lords, was still strange and distant. Yet there had been the burning of Caeriddon. He looked again where the dark smoke had risen into the sky. He stood for some time facing east, letting the sun warm his face. He closed his eyes against its dazzle, though he still felt strange lights through his eyelids. Old words came back to him: words he had heard as a child at the midsummer Long House; words he no longer understood. *Kena cara, kena bucat.* He found himself saying the words aloud.

He turned and looked down again. All the horsemen had re-mounted and were forming together in a long double row. There was a shout that seemed to echo and then they were moving again, north, back into the forest, along the old track towards Caeriddon. He watched the last riders disappear. At once the forest was green and still as he had first seen it, as if no man had ever entered to disturb it.

Taroc whistled the dogs and walked along the spur to the old thorn and rockfall from where he could see his hut, far below. After noon his son Gared would be coming up with cheese and beer, but Taroc had decided not to wait. He cupped his hand and shouted in a high carrying voice, the old alarm call of the shepherds of these mountains. He waited and then repeated it. The dogs barked with excitement, knowing the alert of the call. There was a sound of chopping beyond the hut. This now stopped. Gared came into view and looked up. Taroc repeated the call and waved him up. Gared ran towards the long climb.

Watching his son race up the steep zig-zag path Taroc wondered again if what he was doing was right. Yet it might be that no one else had seen the strange horsemen; at least the message should be passed. But as Gared scrambled towards him all the doubts returned. He had come as if for danger to the flock, carrying his big axe and hunting spear. Although breathless, he would scarcely now listen to his father. He was looking around for the danger. But still across the spur the flock was grazing quietly.

'Then what is it?' Gared said, turning angrily.

Taroc put his hand on Gared's arm and explained what he had seen. Gared listened carefully.

'You think they were Romani?'

'I do not know Romani.'

'They burned Caeriddon.'

'It is said. But now you must take a message to Clutacos. It is for the lords to know.'

Gared rested for some minutes, getting his father to repeat every detail, and then went down for his pony. Clutacos was most likely to be at Banavint, the main stronghold of eastern Iuas. Three years before, already Lord of Erdyl, which ran east to the long south bank of the Guuy, Clutacos had married Guenedd daughter of Edra, Queen of Madrun, and now ruled both Iuas and Erdyl within her realm. Taroc watched his son ride away, moving up from the valley to the high open ridge that led to Bocalt, which had once been called Buck Height. From there he would ride the long ridge to Banavint, which commanded the rich valley join of the mountain rivers.

Taroc went back to his flock. He lay in the sun and slept. When he woke he was hungry, and Gared would not be bringing food. He walked to the spring and drank deeply. Then, taking the dogs, he walked again to look at Claerion. Nothing was moving there now. He squatted and waited, looking out over the forest.

Then the dogs barked and along the ridge, riding furiously and scattering the sheep, came a troop of horsemen, Gared among them. The leading rider, his long sandy hair blowing back, was the Lord Clutacos himself. Taroc brushed his tunic and hurried to meet them.

It was then questioning and questioning again: a hard questioning, once with a threat of the whip. Taroc told and retold what he had seen, and admitted and readmitted what he had not been able to see.

'These are Romani, little shepherd,' Clutacos shouted down at him. 'They will cut the throats of your sheep and then your own stubborn throat.'

'I understand, my lord.'

'You understand nothing. You should have at once gone down and got near them. You should have looked for the colours of their tunics and the arms they were carrying. You should have listened to their speech.'

Taroc did not answer. He stood by while the Lord Clutacos talked with the other warriors. The only detail he understood was that there had been an order, after the burning of Caeriddon, to drive the cattle up into the hills. That explained the empty pasture at Claerion. The other talk, of Romani at strange places whose names he scarcely knew – Burra, Alabim, Nedon – and of the death in battle of the High King, Magimarus, whose name he had once heard, found no real place in his mind. Yet the sense of great danger was obvious, and he at least understood his son Gared, who had waited to ask a question: whether the Romani would now follow the riverbank of the Guuy.

'Not only follow it, boy,' Clutacos exclaimed. 'What they were doing at Claerion, though your idle father took very little notice, was surveying their next camp, where they will try to build a fort. If we allow that fort to be built it could be the end of Iuas.'

'Can we stop them, my lord?' Gared asked.

'We can stop them,' Clutacos answered, and laughed.

He called to his followers and rode away down towards Claerion. Taroc stood watching them go. Then he told Gared to watch the flock while he went down to the hut for some food. His stomach was aching, after so long and strange a day.

The news of the danger, as the Lord Clutacos had interpreted it, spread quickly through the mountains and as far as Madrun. Two days after he had first seen the horsemen, Taroc was with his flock when Queen Edra herself, with a large troop of painted warriors, arrived to look down at the probable Roman campsite. Taroc kept his distance but was eventually called to her. She looked down at him, not speaking. She was a woman of nearly fifty. Her red hair had been dyed and her face was brightly painted. Two blue bars crossed her forehead and below them, above the bridge of the nose, was the purple hornmark of Madrun. Her cheeks were reddened. She was wearing a tunic of red and blue check, with a blue and yellow cloak loosely folded on her saddle. At her shoulders two gold spiral brooches pinned the tunic, and there was a wide gold belt at her waist. A long sword was attached to the belt by a chain. She wore leather sandals, with fastenings of gold wire.

'You are Taroc,' she said, after a long look into his face.

'I am Taroc.'

She smiled. When she next spoke it was in his own language. He looked up in surprise.

'You did well, Taroc. We thank you. But now you must tell me once again all you saw.'

Taroc repeated his well-trodden account. Edra listened carefully, and waited until he had finished.

'You are sure that they were measuring?'

'It is what we call measuring, my lady.'

'Your people are known as great measurers, Taroc.'

'It was only simple pacing, my lady.'

'But that would be enough.'

She turned and spoke with her warriors. Taroc waited. Then she called him and spoke again in his own language.

'I will explain this to you, Taroc, and I will ask you a question. The Romani are our enemies and they are also your enemies. They kill and seize without distinction. To them we are all Britons.'

Taroc said nothing.

'They have great power, Taroc. In all the lands that they have conquered they have taken men to fight for them. When we meet them in battle we do not know if we are fighting Romani or Galli, Iberians or Thracians; indeed men from any land where they have passed, who will fight for gold or under the whip. You understand this, Taroc?'

'You are telling me in honour, my lady.'

'We believe they will now march to Claerion and build a powerful fort. From this fort they will command and defeat us, for they are very many, with those lands at their backs. Our call to war has gone out. All the warriors of our kingdoms have been called. But to the south and west of our Silurian lands there are other Roman forces. Only a few of our kingdoms can answer our call, for they are themselves under attack or in danger. We shall be as many as we can, and we shall fight to the death. We shall strike while they are building their fort, for there would be no better chance later. And this will be any day now, for you saw them, Taroc, choosing and measuring their ground.'

Taroc waited.

'I explain this to you, Taroc, because I now have a question. Our warriors will come and will fight to the death, but they may be too few. And if that is so, Taroc, would your family fight beside us?'

'My family, lady?'

'Is that not your word? You of the Old People?'

'I do not know that name, my lady. I have heard men like myself called the Old Ones and I know we are now called slaves.'

'Yes, Taroc, that is my question.'

'I do not understand you, my lady.'

'I am asking if men like yourself would fight beside us when we attack the Romani.'

'I am not a warrior, my lady.'

'Yet you have your fine bows and your hunting spears and your axes. Would they not kill Romani?'

'They kill our food, lady.'

'And that is all?'

'It is our way, lady.'

Clutacos, who was listening impatiently, now moved in his saddle and spoke behind his hand to the queen. She shook her head.

'I know your ways Taroc,' she said, smiling. 'I learned your ways and your language from my nurse Cala, one of the wisest of women. You have suffered great change, perhaps more than you know. But now all may be changing again. You will not be left as you are. That is why I have asked you this hardest of questions.'

Taroc stared up at her. He was disturbed by the closeness and kindness of the words, and he could not think how to answer. Then Gared, standing behind him, spoke impulsively.

'If you want fighters, ask the hunters of Menhebog.'

'This is your son, Taroc?'

'Yes, my lady, it is Gared my son.'

'It is a wild place, Menhebog,' Edra said, ignoring Gared. 'Is it what you call in your own language Hawkstone?'

'I have heard both names, my lady.'

'And these hunters of Menhebog, what of them?'

'They are the finest bowmen in these mountains, lady. Not only for hunting, but they shoot also for play.'

'There is one called Derco,' Clutacos said, sharply.

'Derco,' Gared said.

'He has an evil reputation. He is known as wilful and lawless. He has stolen our cattle.'

'You said for fighting,' Gared replied stubbornly.

Edra smiled. When Clutacos began to speak again she lifted her hand.

'We have very little time. Taroc, go now to Menhebog. Say in honour to them what I have said to you. I will send a lord with you. He will bring me his report. Will you do this for me, Taroc?'

'But my flock, lady?'

'Your flock will stay with your son.'

Taroc hesitated.

'I will go, my lady.'

Edra at once kicked her pony, a strong young grey stallion, and the troop moved away at a gallop, down the slope towards Claerion. Taroc waited by the lord who had been left.

Over the next days there was intense preparation. Clutacos set watchers from Erdyl in the woods along the southern bank of the Guuy. Hundreds of warriors had come together in two main groups: one in the steep valley below Uroicaissa, where Taroc had first seen the strangers; the other to the south, in the forest near Madrun. Every day more warriors came in, many from Carvon in the east and beyond. Messages were exchanged with the kingdom of Elfael to the north, in the lower hills across the Guuy, and their warriors also were gathering. But what was most surprising was the coming of the hunters of Menhebog. They stayed close together on Uroicaissa, uncertain of the crowd of warrior horsemen. As the news spread, other hunters from the mountains joined them. Each carried a hunting bow and spear.

Yet the lords still did not know the identity of Derco. Whenever the hunters of Menhebog were asked about him, they replied that he was not with them but would soon be coming. Clutacos, riding up to inspect them, walked his horse through, staring into every face and asking for Derco. He stopped longest above a young, dark man, who was sitting without speaking.

'Where is the bandit Derco? Derco Ladrun?'

The young man looked up. He had strange eyes, of a yellowish green, which shone like painted slits in his dark skin.

'He will soon come,' he replied, in his own language.

The answer was translated for Clutacos. He jumped from his pony and seized the young man's shoulders. He pulled him upright.

'Why are you lying? Your own name is Derco.'

The young man stared back at him. He said nothing. Clutacos waited and then pushed him roughly away.

That afternoon the message came from Erdyl. The Romani were preparing to move. The lords gathered between Madrun and Uroicaissa, and confirmed the plan of attack. Nothing would be done to alert or hinder the Romani on their march through the forest from Caeriddon. Hunters from Erdyl would track their progress and report their numbers, but they would be allowed to reach Claerion and settle to work on their camp. In the late evening of the first day, when the Romani were tired from their digging, the warriors would ride to the attack. The northern wing, under Clutacos, would go through the forest to the ford north of Claerion. They would cross in small numbers and wait for the signal to attack along the old track. The southern wing, under Edra herself, would be hidden overnight in the forest south of Claerion. The warriors of Elfael, now pledged, would wait in their hills and attack later from the west.

The lord who had gone with Taroc to Menhebog, old Elidur of Crucio, had been given orders to speak to the hunters. He began by asking again for Derco, for tomorrow was the day of the fighting. The only answer he got was that Derco was not there but would be coming. There were now many more hunters, from all over the mountains, but they kept together and silent.

Old Elidur tried again. He described the plan of the lords for the attack at evening. It was the wish of Queen Edra that the hunters should move down through the forest until they were near the riverbank. They would be given their own signal, before the signal to the warriors, and would shoot their arrows into the camp, against the tired Romani as they broke from their digging. They would shoot to kill. When they had done this the horns would sound again and the warriors would ride in.

'Drawing the herd on to us?' said the very dark young man.

Old Elidur looked at him.

'You are Derco Ladrun, the chief of the hunters?'

The young man seemed not to hear, but asked his own question.

'When we have shot our arrows, do we stay where we are, for the Romani to come on us?'

'There will be the river between you.'

'We do not cross it, with our spears?'

'You do not cross it. You shoot your arrows as I have said, and you may shoot again if they have horsemen with them. But in that case shoot only for the horses, for the riders have strong tunics that can stop arrows.'

'We then run from the hunt?'

'You withdraw. Your duty is done.'

The young man turned and looked around. The others waited for him to speak.

'Empty-handed from this great hunt,' he said, his eyes fixed on Elidur.

'You will be rewarded in the victory.'

'With the ears of the Romani?'

Elidur gaped. He looked away to Taroc, who was standing ready to help.

'What can he mean, Taroc?'

'It is his way of speaking, my lord.'

'It is a way I do not understand.'

'That is true, my lord.'

The young man moved impatiently.

'You will give the signal for our arrows?' he said to Elidur.

'Yes, for I know the whole plan of attack.'

'Can you move like a hunter through the forest?'

'I am a warrior, Derco.'

The young man smiled. His strange eyes were now lighter, almost a clear yellow.

'We will try to show you our ways, Elidur of Crucio.'

Next morning at first light the Romani marched. The hunters of Erdyl tracking them were awed by their numbers and their weapons. A troop of some forty horsemen, with long fair hair under their leather helmets, and carrying long lances, led the column, galloping ahead and returning to report. Then came the marching Romani, in groups each of nearly one hundred men. Over their ribbed tunics they were heavily equipped. Each man carried a saw, a pickaxe, a hook, a coil of rope, a basket and a cooking pot. They wore iron helmets, with projections covering the back of the neck and the cheeks. Metal plates covered their chests and upper backs. Each man carried two long throwing spears, and a short sword slung at his waist. At the head of each hundred was a commander wearing a short sword and dagger, and carrying a thick stick of some dark wood. This man's helmet was different, with metal plumes like the crest of a bird on its crown. The hunters of Erdyl, moving unseen through the forest, counted seven of these hundreds, all young and vigorous men. Then came another troop of horsemen, more than a hundred and fifty, in grey cloaks, and following them a smaller group of horsemen, in fine armour and with horses decorated along harness and bridle. At the centre of this group was a grey-haired man, older than the others. The hunters marked this man especially, and reported every detail of him. Finally, behind this group, there were three more hundreds each with its commander, and in the rear, a line of loaded ox-carts, piled high with material. The great size, the fine weapons and equipment, the steady step of this army, deeply impressed the watching hunters. They could pass their messages, but they could not imagine how anything so powerful could be stopped.

The news reached Edra in mid-morning. She questioned the messengers and announced that the plan was unchanged. The warriors moved along the tracks to their assemblies in the forest. The hunters made their own way down through the trees, in groups of four or five. They did not wait for Elidur to give them the order to go. Derco, among the first to go down, climbed a great oak above the river and was first to see the head of the column come through on to Claerion. They were the fair-haired horsemen: 'Like these lords of our own place,' Derco said when he came down. It was noon of a hot, clear day, but it was cool in the forest. The hunters settled to watch and wait.

The enemy horsemen spread out over the hill looking outwards. As the columns of marching hundreds followed them in, their chiefs, pointing their dark sticks, directed them to their places to make a long squared enclosure. The Romani sat on the grass in the sun. Many took off their helmets and unstrapped the tools they were carrying. Others lay flat on their backs, looking up at the sky. When the other horsemen rode in, again spreading out to protect the marchers, a group gathered in the centre of the enclosure, around the grey-haired man who had been especially reported. There was talk and pointing, and the men with the dark sticks went back to their marchers. Lines were set out on the grass and then the marchers got slowly up to dig. Derco, again in his tree, saw that each Roman set one of his long spears upright in the ground beside him and hung his helmet on its point before starting. As the last marchers and the ox-carts came in they gathered at the centre, and many of these soldiers began cutting down the smaller trees across the pasture.

It was soon seen that they were digging a long squared bank and ditch. The marchers dug fast and efficiently, using pickaxes much like the people's own mattocks to skim the turves, which they piled carefully. As they dug further into the rich red soil they threw it inwards, to begin the bank. The digging continued, with troops of soldiers working in turn through the hot afternoon, and the bank rose quickly, with the ditch outside it. The horsemen protecting them gradually thinned out as the work continued without disturbance. Small groups began riding down to the riverbank to water their horses: at first with spears raised against attack but later more casually. Many of the marchers, working under the hot sun, had now taken off their metal bodyguards and were digging in short-sleeved tunics or stripped to bare chests. Their periods of work were intense and concentrated. The men with the dark sticks walked up and down the bank inspecting it. And already, stacked in piles inside the bank, there were hundreds of stakes, cut from the trees that had been felled, ready to be set in place when the bank had been built and turfed.

In the forest the hunters rested, taking turns to watch. What was being done to make this defensive bank and ditch was entirely familiar to them. Their brothers had done the same work on the lord's strongholds. The difference was that these fighters were doing the digging themselves. This was very surprising. Derco eventually decided that the horsemen were the lords and the digging soldiers the slaves. When Elidur came again, in the late afternoon, repeating his orders, Derco said sharply:

'It was said that the Romani were short dark men.'

'It is so,' Elidur replied.

'I heard the Lord Clutacos say they were like his slaves.'

'They are indeed short and dark, as you can see.'

'Yet those cannot be the Romani, for they are working. The lords on their horses have hair like yourselves.'

Elidur looked away. He took some time to answer.

'The horsemen are those they call their auxiliaries. They are Gauls or other peoples whom the Romani have conquered and taken into their army. The Romani who are digging are their famous legionaries, who are their best fighting soldiers.'

Derco stared at Elidur, as if he did not believe him. Elidur tried again.

'The grey-haired man in the centre is the Roman lord.'

Derco thought for some time.

'They are different, these Romani,' he said, moving away.

The sun was now lower in the sky. There were spreading shadows on the hills of Elfael beyond the river. In several sections the bank was now completed and turves were being laid on it and stakes driven into its top. Other sections were being worked on, with shouts to hurry the diggers, who were now obviously tired. Elidur called Derco to him. A trumpeter was waiting, holding the long battle-horn with its carved ram's head and clappers between its jaws.

'Get into your positions and shout when you hear the trumpet.'

The hunters spread out through the trees. They moved quietly down to positions above the river. They lifted their bows.

The trumpet sounded suddenly in two long blasts. Almost in the same instant the arrows flew. The hunters chose their targets among those who were still working on the near banks. They saw many legionaries fall and at once shot again. In the centre of the enclosure the horsemen were galloping to the banks and there were shouts everywhere. Derco saw the grey-haired lord, gesturing and shouting from horseback, and tried a shot at him, though the distance seemed too great. The arrow fell short.

But now the horsemen were breaking from the enclosure and galloping down towards the river, while the legionaries settled behind their defensive banks. As the horsemen slowed on the difficult slope, the hunters shot at their horses, and several fell. The others then quickly retreated. There were now other, fainter blasts of trumpets, and in the distance, down from the hills of Elfael, warriors were galloping. Their wild shouts could be heard above the noise from the camp.

The first warriors to reach the enclosure burst from the northern forest track. With the advantage of surprise they got through and over the bank. With their long slashing swords they attacked the legionaries from behind. The auxiliary horsemen regrouped and charged them. There was confused fighting at the northern end.

Then the warriors from the south, with Edra prominent in the leading troop, were galloping up the hill. They rode in, slashing down at the crouching legionaries. Orders were shouted, and many soldiers stood from their banks and formed close groups to face the horsemen. There were wild cries and long high blasts on the trumpets as the battle was at last fully joined.

There was now nothing more for the hunters across the river to do. But Derco, after watching for some time, raised his arm and scrambled down the steep bank to the river. It was not easy to cross, for the central current was swift; the regular crossing was the ford which the northern warriors had used. But, holding his hunting spear high, he waded through and many of the hunters followed him. It was hard going, up the steep farther bank, but the centres of the battle were now well away from the ditch on that side. The hunters reached the ditch which they had seen being dug and took cover in it. The fighting was so confused that there was now little use for arrows, but they had the small wooden and iron-tipped grospi which they used for bringing down birds. As they saw targets among the enemy horsemen they stood and hurled the grospi. This at once drew the legionaries on to them. They advanced in close formation, holding their big shields above their short stabbing swords. Some of the hunters stood and threw their spears, but these were taken easily on the shields. As the legionaries came nearer the hunters prepared to run back down the bank, but then a group of warriors, led by Clutacos, who had blood all over his shoulders and arms, came on the legionaries from behind and slashed down with their swords. Many fell, including one of those with a dark stick, who was standing with sword drawn. Clutacos, shouting wildly, galloped on through, for he had seen the grey-haired man on horseback in a clear space away from the closest fighting. Clutacos rode hard at him and struck him from his horse. Then he jumped down, pulled off his helmet, and slashed repeatedly at his neck. A legionary came at him from behind and they rolled on the ground, reaching for their daggers. One of the hunters from Banavint at once ran foward from the ditch and, lifting his hunting spear, killed the legionary. Clutacos jumped to his horse and rode back into the centre of the fighting.

There were now many dead on both sides, though more among the Romani. It seemed, suddenly, that they were about to withdraw, for a group of some twenty of their horsemen fought their way through to the northern track and galloped away along it. But the legionaries were again reforming, in close order and with their shields raised and almost touching. The warriors of Iuas and Madrun outnumbered the auxiliary horsemen and killed and drove away most of them. But as the legionaries drew together, under the protection of their shields, it was difficult to get at them. Several charges were fatal, as the legionaries threw their long javelins. At last the trumpet sounded and the warriors rode back into the forest. It was now almost dark.

The night was uncertain. Across the river, the hunters found that Elidur had gone to Edra. It was almost dawn before he returned. It had been, he said, a great victory. The Romani were now sur- rounded and none would get out alive. The Lord Clutacos was the hero of the fighting, for he had killed the grey-haired man who was one of the highest officers of the whole legion: what the Romani called the Prefect of Camps. Many auxiliaries and legionaries had been killed, but the auxiliaries – treacherous Gauls – and many of the legionaries themselves had proved cowards. Only the bravest had stood and fought, and especially the commanders with the dark sticks whom the Romani called centurions. Eight of these were now dead. At first light the warriors would attack again and finish off the rest. The hunters were ordered, on pain of death, to keep out of the battle. But they could stay in the woods to help with the work of the dead.

As a first grey light came there were trumpets across the river and then the high cries of the attacking warriors. They rode in from three directions, but the legionaries were now again manning the banks, which had been repaired and strengthened through the night. A troop from the south broke through and took them from behind, but the other defences held firm. Many warriors were killed as they charged repeatedly at the staked banks. There was then a loud shouting along the northern bank. A large force of enemy horsemen, who had ridden through the night after getting messages from the beleaguered camp, were attacking Clutacos' warriors from behind. They killed many of them, and broke through to the camp. Everything then seemed prearranged, for the legionaries reformed, in order, holding the banks to allow columns to assemble in the centre. While the new horsemen guarded a broad way to the track they began marching in close order through the gap. The warriors from the south and the west, seeing their enemies escaping, redoubled their attacks, but a fighting rearguard was formed against them, under the protection of close shields. As one unit after another marched away along the track the rearguard closed and threw their javelins against the charging warriors. It was only on the very last group that the warriors got close enough to kill, and they had then to engage the new horsemen. Fighting went on all over the hill, until slowly, in small groups, the horsemen withdrew to the track. The warriors chased them along it, but as the track narrowed there was little they could do, except in fierce single combats. Beyond this scattered fighting what was left of the Roman force was marching quickly away.

Derco and the other hunters had watched the whole battle from the far bank. The Lord Elidur, once he had made sure they were obeying their orders to keep out of the battle, had left. Derco saw him, eventually, up on the hill of Claerion, in a group around Queen Edra. Many of the warriors had dismounted and were walking round looking at the dead.

'So the boar is wounded but not killed,' Derco said, quietly.

'What boar, brother?'

'Did you not see the sign that the Romani carried: the ones they call the legionaries? It was the sign of a boar.'

Others had seen the sign and agreed.

'The hunt is not finished,' Derco said.

He lifted his bow and the others acknowleged him. They moved quickly, following the river through the trees until they reached the ford. They struck north through the forest, along a hunting trail, until they knew they were near the main track. Spreading out as for a hunt they crept slowly towards the track. The marching soldiers, many wounded and limping, were moving in file through the forest. Derco killed a wounded soldier with his first arrow. Others soon fell, hit by arrows and grospi. Under this new attack they were quick to form and face their enemy, but the hunters were already away, moving back in the forest and circling to come on another part of the long marching column. Wherever they saw horsemen they chose to shoot at the legs of their horses. Several fell. There was shouting from the column and some pursuit among the trees, but the hunters were very fast, in their own woods. Through all that morning, while the long column made its way back, they appeared and reappeared. One of the men killed by Derco was carrying a long pole with many signs, among them the mark of the boar. As he fell another legionary was quick to pick up the pole and raise it again. At last, judging the course of the day, Derco broke off the hunt. So much had changed for the hunters, in so short a time, that as they walked back they were silent, as when a hunt had failed and there was no meat to carry home. Yet there had been, unforgettably, this quite different action, against men, and their minds were full of what it would now mean. They remembered the words that Tarco had spoken, in honour, from Queen Edra.

Four days after the battle of Claerion, when the dead had been buried and there had been victory feasts and songs in Madrun and Banavint, Clutacos rode with a troop of twenty warriors into the steep wooded valley of Menhebog. The hunters had already been visited by the Lord Elidur, who brought the thanks of Queen Edra for their action at the river. Elidur, old and confused, seemed not to know that they had followed and attacked the retreating Roman column, and they said nothing of it. But on each visit, when it was seen that the lords were coming, Derco had gone deep into the woods, taking his bow and spear. Elidur did not ask for him, but it was now the first question from Clutacos. There was an uneasy silence. The men gathered at the group of huts appeared not to understand him. When the question was repeated in their own language by a groom of Banavint, two men answered immediately that he had not been seen.

'Seen since when?' Clutacos asked.

'Since the day of the new enemies, my lord.'

'You are saying he did not return from the battle?'

'It is not known, my lord. He has not been seen.'

'His body was not among the dead.'

'We do not know, my lord. We buried none of our own.'

Clutacos looked into their faces. They were obviously uneasy. Nobody outside the family yet knew that they had buried their own five dead in a bank of the old Long House. They thought this might be betrayed or discovered. Clutacos, also, could not say all he knew. He had heard from his groom in Banavint that the hunters had pursued the retreating Romani. This counted in his mind as the second wilful disobedience by his slaves. He had spoken of it to

Queen Edra, identifying Derco as the source of the disobedience. He was a dangerous man who must be dealt with quickly, before the slaves drew dangerous lessons from their new experience of fighting men. Edra was angry. The Romani would return and they would need the hunters again. No action of any kind must be taken against them. But Clutacos was determined. One way or another he would find this dangerous slave and destroy him.

'This Derco has a wife?' he asked through the groom.

'No, my lord.'

'Has he a brother?'

'No.'

'A father?'

'His father is dead.'

Clutacos rubbed the hilt of his sword in his palm. He could not act openly against Menhebog, because of the queen's clear orders. But he could not afford to leave Derco unpunished.

'You know that you are all my subjects, my slaves,' he said loudly.

'Indeed, my lord.'

'Slaves are weak men unfit for battle.'

'We are just hunters, my lord.'

'When your Derco appears, you are to bring him to me. It will be dangerous for all of you if you try to disobey.'

'We understand you, my lord.'

Clutacos was not deceived by their deference. He kicked his pony angrily. He led his warriors out of the valley towards the high plateau and the long ridges to Banavint. Derco, high in an old oak above the track, watched them riding across the skyline.

Last

◆

G lyn stood, listening, on the silent heights. He had reached Tal y
Cefn and ahead lay the reservoir, gleaming in the moonlight
with the dark ridge of Gofenion rising beyond it. Ahead too, he
thought, in these rising visions of the past, after the battle of
Claerion, lay the long Roman occupation and gradual withdrawal,
the Celtic lordships and the Saxon invasions. His search for Elis on
the high moors was part of a quest for himself, for a history and a
landscape that had shaped his being. His search must go on and he
knew now that this long history, too, would continue to unfold –
the heritage of 'The Eggs of the Eagle', told through the long-
vanished voices of the people of the Black Mountains.

'See this layered sandstone in the short mountain grass. Place your
right hand on it, palm downward. See where the summer sun rises
and where it stands at noon. Direct your index finger midway
between them. Spread your fingers, not widely. You now hold this
place in your hand . . .'

Approximate Dates of the Stories

Place Names

———◆———

Abisso Aberllynfi settlement, Gwernyfed
Alaron Longtown
Arcala settlement near Monmouth
Bald Hills Malverns
Bear Mountain Myndd Eppynt
Bentelim Altelim, Banavint, Pen Twyn hill fort
Bodosa settlement in the Dore Valley
Broken Mountain Isgirit, Skirrid Fawr
Burro Burrium, Usk
Cambo settlement where the Monnow bends to flow east
Caeriddon Credenhill Camp
Carvon Carfan, Alcarfan, Skenfrith
Cicucio Roman fort at Brecon
Claerion Clyro
Cornio Twyn y Gaer hill fort
Cross Valley Vale of Ewyas, Valley of the Honddu
Crucio Crugader, Crug Hywel, Crickhowell hill fort
Curve River River Guuy, River Wye
Dun Rignan Dinas Rhiangoll, Dunon Osniu, Castel Dinas
Elchon Ewyas Harold
Elfael region north of the River Wye
Erdyl Ercing, Erging, Archenfield
Ferdun Ferddin, Mynydd Merddin
Glara settlement by Lake Llangorse
Glevum Gloucester
Gobanio Gofanio, Bergavenny, Abergavenny, Y Fenni
Gofyf iron works at Gwernyfed
Grain Valley Valley of the River Dore

Guenta Gwent
Guerinou River Grwyne Fawr
Hawkstone Maenhebog, Menhebog, Glan Bwch, Twmpath
High Buck Bocalt, ridge from Pen y Beacon to Gospel Pass
Hodoni South River, River Ondi, Honddu
Horn Point Crib y Garth, Cat's Back
Isca Caerleon
Iuas Euas, Ewyas
Iupania settlement on Severn Estuary, near mouth of Wye
Lanoluc settlement under Pen y Beacon
Leucara Lake Locara, Ara, Syfaddon, Llangorse
Little Mountain River Upper Monnow
Little Stone Valley Olchon Valley
Lookhill Little Doward
Madrun settlement near Talgarth
Mamcala Home Cave, King Arthur's Cave (Paviland Cave is also referred to as Mamcala)
Masona Telim, Satelim, Altyrynys
Menvandir Durrington Walls and the round houses on Salisbury Plain
Myngui River Mynwy, Monnow
Riverjoin junction of River Monnow and River Dore
Sacred Circle Garn Wen
Salmon River Uisc, Usk
Satelin Telim, valley settlement at join of River Monno and Honddu
Seariver Hsabren, Severn
South River River Honddu
Stream of Birds River Rhiangol
Telim Altyrynys
Uroicaissa 'place of heather', upland from Cusop Hill to Urishay Common
Venta Silurum Caerwent
White Cap Pen Cerrig Calch
White Land southern England
Wolfhead Mynndd Llangorse
Yellow Hills Cotswolds

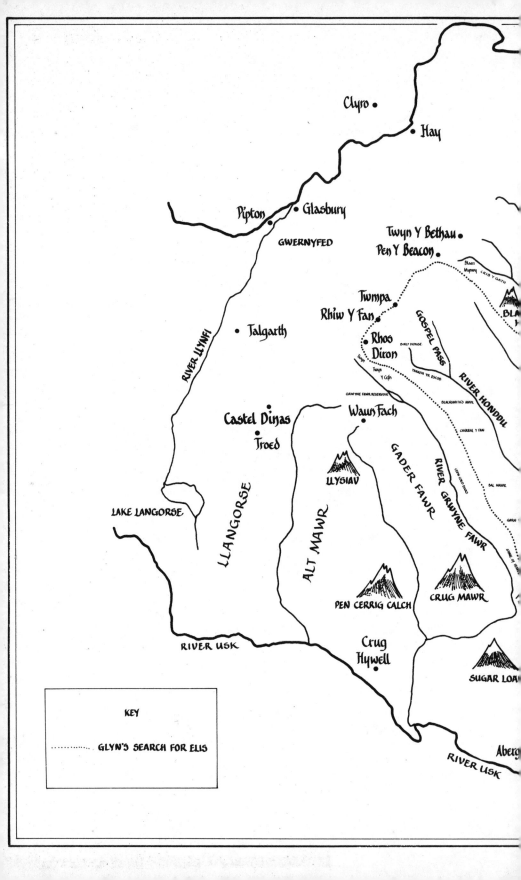